"WAIT
"WAIT! W
I'LL GIVE YO

The crone turned slowly back and fixed him with her red eyes. "Now he pleads with us, he does. Anything, he says, anything!" Her voice became hard and ruthless. "Do you know what *anything* covers, stripling? It covers your mother's soul, your sister's life, your brother's breath, you father's damnation.

"Think, young one, think long and hard before you use the word *anything* again . . ."

Also by Dennis Schmidt and published by Futura

TWILIGHT OF THE GODS: THE FIRST NAME

DENNIS SCHMIDT

Twilight of the Gods: Groa's Other Eye

Futura

An Orbit Book

Copyright © 1986 by Dennis Schmidt

First published by Ace Fantasy Books, New York

This edition published in 1987
by Futura Publications, a Division of
Macdonald & Co (Publishers) Ltd
London & Sydney

ISBN 0 7088 3041 2

Printed and bound in Great Britain by
Collins, Glasgow

Futura Publications
A Division of
Macdonald & Co (Publishers) Ltd
Greater London House
Hampstead Road
London NW1 7QX

A BPCC plc Company

This book is dedicated to
Thor.

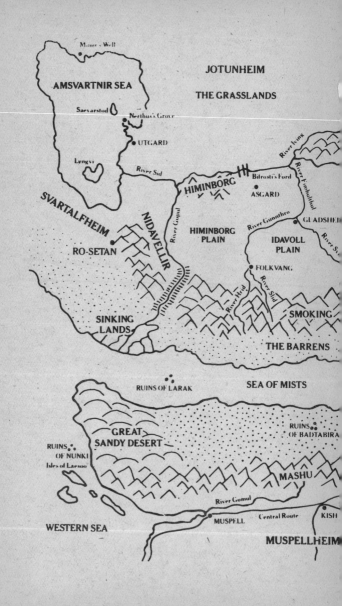

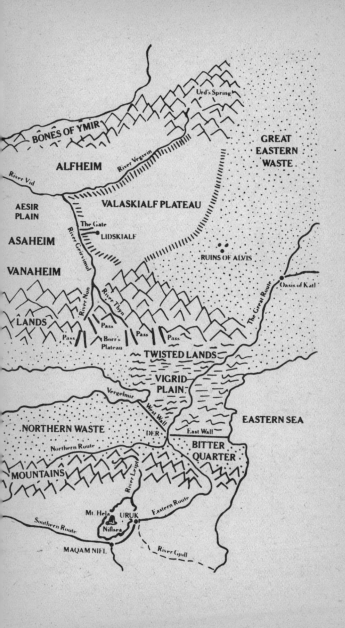

IN THE MOUND

I

SEVEN arrows left. He counted them one more time as he ran, to be sure. Seven. He knew there were at least twenty of them on his trail. That meant all he had to do was kill three with each arrow and everything would be perfect.

A grim smile curved his lips as he nocked an arrow. I'll be lucky if I hit one with every three arrows, he thought. Should have spent more time with Yngvi learning to shoot. Those foresters can hit a wand at fifty paces while running and dodging at full speed.

He threw a quick glance over his shoulder. As always, one or two of the bastards were out front, driving him on, while the rest hung back in a clump, ready to move right or left if he broke in either direction.

As first they'd tried to stay hard on his heels in a bunch, probably assuming he'd wear out quickly and hoping to close for the kill in a pack. He'd disabused them of that idea pretty quickly. Three of his arrows had slashed into them in rapid succession, every one of them finding a target in the closely packed mass. They'd dropped back then for a while, waiting for him to tire. That had been late morning. Now the sun was beginning to set somewhere to the west.

3

One of the close ones was getting a bit careless, gaining a few yards, hoping to get within range so he could throw his short spear. The young man tightened his grip on his bow, slowing his pace ever so slightly. He cast another glance over his shoulder. Just a few more feet, he thought, and you'll be in bow range. He estimated the distance carefully. These creatures were very good with their spears. If anything, they were better than the Valkyrja. Their weapons were fairly short and slender, with long iron heads shaped like leafs. They could be thrown farther than he had originally estimated. And with much greater accuracy than he had thought possible. One graze on his right side and a long, shallow cut on his left leg had taught him important lessons. Both wounds ached dully and still oozed a little blood. He'd been lucky, he realized. Since he didn't expect to be lucky again, he carefully kept his distance from his pursuers.

Ah. The eager one was almost within bow range, but still too far to throw his spear. Another few steps and—

The runner whirled suddenly, planted his feet firmly, and loosed his arrow. The shaft sped true, catching the slender dark man square in the chest. With a scream he flung up his arms and tumbled to the forest floor.

Not waiting to see the results of his shot, the blond runner spun back around and leapt off again. His pursuers gave one howl of fury as their comrade fell, but so intent were they on their prey that no one even stopped to check the fallen man.

Six arrows. The only hope I've got is to find a place to make a stand, he told himself. Someplace where they'll have to come at me one or two at a time and have to use those spears to jab rather than throw. He knew that with his sword and ax he could wreak great havoc among his pursuers if he could find such a place. Maybe then they'd decide to cut their losses and leave him alone. Somehow he doubted they would, but it seemed worth a try. Besides, he realized as he sucked in great gulps of damp, fetid forest air, I'm getting tired. I've lost some blood and I've only got a few hours of running left in me. Worse yet, night's coming. It's hard enough to run in this damn forest in the daylight. In the dark it'll be impossible. I wouldn't be able to take more than a dozen steps before tripping over some vine or root.

A strange sound rose from his pursuers, and he gave a quick glance over his shoulder to see what was going on.

They were calling back and forth in what sounded like warn-
ings. Although he had trouble understanding the strangely in-
flected way they spoke the Common Tongue, he could figure
out that they were telling each other about something up
ahead. Two words were repeated over and over, words that
sent strange shivers up and down the young man's spine. He
couldn't quite make them out, but one sounded like "Niflheim" and the other, odder yet, sounded like "Tuat."

In the Common Tongue *Niflheim* meant "abode of darkness" and referred to the realms where those who led evil lives
were doomed to dwell when they died. *Tuat*, on the other
hand, was a word he'd never heard and which didn't even
sound like it came from the Common Tongue. It echoed with
age. Could it be from the Elder Tongue? Or perhaps even the
Original Tongue? In either case, he didn't know what it meant
and wasn't too sure he wanted to find out.

The noise behind him was becoming more insistent. He
glanced back. His pursuers were shouting now, urging each
other on. He gauged the distance carefully. Yes, they were
gaining, trying in one burst of speed to catch him before . . .

Before what? he wondered as he picked up his own pace to
match theirs. He sucked in great gulps of air, filling his aching
lungs. The shadows that filled the dense forest were rapidly
becoming deeper, flowing into one another to create a seam-
less darkness. Were they trying to catch him before dark?
Were they afraid of losing him? Not likely, he realized.
Woodsmen like the small, black men who pursued him would
be capable of following him by the noise of his flight alone.
He was good in the woods. At an ordinary pace, he could
move as silently as a ghost. But this was no ordinary pace.
And they were better than he was, for they'd obviously been
born to it for many generations. Besides, these were their
forests through which he fled.

Then why were they making such a dash to catch him?
Clearly before something, but before what? He couldn't imagine, but as he picked up his pace once more to stay ahead of
them, he realized he couldn't last long at this speed. Could
they?

Suddenly, unexpectedly, he broke into an open space in
the forest. It wasn't really a clearing because the giant trees
arched over the open area to form a roof as impenetrable as
any in the rest of the forest. Yet for a space of some hundred

yards or more, in an almost perfect circle, no trees grew. Indeed, the only thing that covered the ground was short, soft, dark green grass.

More surprising still, in the exact center of the area stood a mound of grass-covered earth. No, he realized, not just a mound. There, in the side facing southeast, was a shadowed area that might be an opening!

He shifted direction slightly as he ran toward the mound. Yes, it was an opening! Crudely carved stones formed the sides and arch of a doorway. He'd have to stoop to enter, but he could go in. And any creatures that wanted to follow him would have to come one at a time. He'd found a place to make a stand! His pursuers must have known it was here and had been trying to catch him before he reached it.

He turned to see how close they were . . . and saw no one. No, that wasn't quite true. There was one. There, another. And over there, two more. But they were simply standing, just within the cover of the surrounding forest, watching him. He gauged the distance carefully. Within throwing range.

As if in response to his discovery, he heard the slight swish of a spear in flight. Just in time he jumped to the left and avoided the razor-sharp blade. It had come from his right. They were surrounding him!

He turned back to the opening in the mound and started to enter. Suddenly he stopped, his heart beating furiously. A cold sweat broke out all over his body. It was so dark within that opening. Darker than it should be. The hair on the back of his neck rose. "Niflheim," they'd called to each other, abode of darkness. And "Tuat," a word that carried its own freight of dread even if he didn't know its exact meaning. Was Niflheim-Tuat this mound?

He looked over his shoulder again. Another spear came from the forest and slammed into the mound next to where he stood. Too close for comfort. If he stood very long like this they would kill him.

Then another thought hit him. The dark men weren't entering the open space. They were staying within the forest. He couldn't see the other side of the mound, but he was sure they were there, too, waiting, half hidden within the trees.

But they weren't coming into the open space. Why? He remembered the sound of their voices when they'd called back and forth. They'd sounded worried, perhaps even frightened.

He'd thought that was because they were afraid of losing him. Now he wondered. Could it be that they were afraid of this place?

He heard the whistle of another spear and threw himself instinctively to the right. A hot pain seared his shoulder and he cursed. Damn! The thing had slashed him, a deep gash. The next one wouldn't miss. If he waited much longer, he would die.

There wasn't any choice. He turned to the opening in the mound, gritted his teeth, and stepped into the darkness. Behind him the forest men set up an eerie, ululating wail.

Slowly, with infinite care, he felt his way forward, one hand on each wall, his feet probing the ground ahead before he trusted his weight to it. After what he judged was about five feet, the entranceway widened to form a larger chamber. Like the opening, the chamber was made of roughly dressed stone. He felt carefully along the left wall, realizing that it was curving slightly to his right.

About five feet around the wall his hand touched something rough sticking out from the surface of the stone. Cautiously he ran his fingers over it. The shape reminded him of a torch, the material felt like wood. He tugged gently at it and it slid out of what must have been a hole in the wall that served as its mount.

He squatted down and shrugged both his quiver and sword from his back, where he had slung them while fleeing from the forest men. Then he took off his backpack and rummaged in it blindly until he found his flint and steel. He groped around in the dark and found some leaves and litter that had blown into the chamber from the outside. Making a small mound of them, he took his tinder, placed it at the base of the pile, and struck a spark. His fourth try took and a small flame shot up. By its light he saw and gathered more litter. Then he put the end of the torch into the tiny fire he'd built and prayed to Fornjot to let it light.

Surprisingly, it lit almost instantly and burned brightly. Stamping out the fire on the floor of the chamber, he held up his torch and looked around.

What he saw stopped him dead in his tracks and made his breath catch deep in his throat with a small sob of fear. The chamber was circular and much larger than he had imagined, fully twenty feet across. Toward the back wall was a raised area, topped by a large rectangular stone. A dark and sinister stain covered the top of the stone and seemed to dribble part way down its sides. Below the stain a dry, gray-green lichen covered the rest of the surface, muting and partly hiding strange and disturbing carvings. They looked vaguely like writing, but not like any he'd ever seen.

It was an altar, he realized. The stains were blood. Old, old, impossibly old blood. Somewhere, deep in his mind, the altar woke sleeping memories, and dreams stirred once more. He'd seen this thing once before. Somewhere else. Somewhere . . . He shut the thoughts down with a shudder of fear.

Frightening as it was, though, the altar was not the most horrible thing that met his gaze. For around it, scattered all about the floor, were skulls and skeletons. Hundreds of them, piled and tumbled in a horrid sprawl of death.

And they were *wrong*. He knew beyond doubting that human flesh had never covered them. The shape of the skulls was short and wide, the eye holes overly large and oval, the nose opening massive, the teeth in the upper jaw long, yellowed, and bestial, those in the lower jaw identical. The things had had fangs like those of a wolf!

The skeletons were oddly distorted too. The legs were short and bowed, the arms long and powerful. The chests were massive, larger around than even Gagnrad Beargrasp's.

For several moments he stood in silent wonder, staring about him at what he realized was a charnel house, a mass burial barrow for a long-dead race. How many ages had it been since they had walked or shambled the face of the earth? He couldn't even guess. But it had to have been deep, deep in the past, perhaps long before the First Dark Empire, for he'd never heard mention, even in legend, of such beings. This place was ancient. More ancient than anything he'd ever seen or heard of in his life.

It was more than ancient. It was disturbing, even frightening. There seemed to be a sense of dread and evil permeating the very air he breathed. Obviously the forest men felt it, for they'd refused to even enter the open space around the mound.

Yet the evil didn't seem to menace him directly. Perhaps any evil such creatures had created to guard this place was so alien that it wasn't a danger to him. That seemed a thin hope, but for the moment he had no sense of immediate peril.

On the other hand, he thought as he turned back to the

entrance, the danger out there is very immediate and very real. He put the torch back in its niche in the wall and slowly moved to the opening. Night had fallen. He couldn't see the dark men, but he could sense their presence. They would wait for him. Eventually they would kill him.

I should've known better than to enter that place, he scolded himself. But it was so strange and interesting. He sat down, leaned back against the stonework of the passageway, and remembered.

The plains of his own people, the Aesir, were far behind. Even the forests of the Vanir were so distant they were only a dim memory. He'd left both more than a year ago. When he'd reached the River Gopul, he'd almost lost hope. It was a wide, crashing river, swift and dangerous, sharp rocks stabbing its surface like thousands of spears. He'd walked along its banks for days, looking for a calmer place to cross. Finally he'd found what he realized was the best of bad choices. He'd cut saplings and bound them together to make a raft. The thing had been dashed to pieces by the rocks and he'd barely made it to the other side alive.

Then he'd trudged through Nidavellir, the lands of the Dverg. The home of the gray men was a tangled, trackless forest wilderness covered with trees so huge and ancient that the sun never reached the forest floor. It had taken him two full months to cross this forest before he'd struck the spur of the Smoking Lands that thrust its mighty peaks northwestward toward the Amsvartnir Sea. In the entire time, he'd never seen the slightest sign of the Dverg.

When he'd finally passed around the northern tip of the mountains, he'd entered the land of the Svartalfar, the small, dark men of the forest. Once they'd served the lords of the First Dark Empire. But when the world had convulsed with war and the Empire had fallen in fiery, demon-filled ruin, the Svartalfar had left Muspellheim and made the long trek northward to this out-of-the-way corner of Yggdrasil. They'd lived here cloaked in secrecy and silence ever since. No one ever saw them. They never traded, never traveled, never dealt with outsiders. Any who entered their realm simply never came back to speak of it.

On the border between the Dverg and the Svartalfar, at the base of the Smoking Lands, he'd passed his first winter. Game was plentiful, and though he was often bitterly cold, he never went hungry. When spring came, he entered Svartalfheim.

Here the forest was, if anything, even older, denser, darker, and damper than in Nidavellir. It was like a vast maze, cut by small streams filled with black water and dotted with swamps that sucked all life down into their bottomless depths. He'd backed, doubled, and gone around obstacles so long he was no longer sure how far he'd traveled.

Then, just a few days ago, he'd seen a light ahead in the gloom. Like a moth drawn to a candle, he'd moved toward it. Amazingly, it was a genuine clearing. Overhead he'd been able to see a tiny patch of sky and clouds. It had been afternoon, so the sun was too far down in the west to be visible, but the light was the brightest he'd seen since leaving the plains of his childhood behind so long ago. He'd been drawn out of the woods and into the light by a force stronger than he could resist.

When he'd entered the clearing he'd been stunned by the sight that had greeted his eyes. Everywhere he looked there were tall poles, some over twenty feet in height, rising from the ground. Clearly someone had placed them there. At the top of each pole was what he could only describe as some kind of clothing or war gear. A cap or helmet, some with a single horn, some with two or three or even four, some with antlers, others with animal skulls, surmounted the poles. Below the helmets were masks. Though they were hideously contorted, with bulging eyes, distorted, fang-filled mouths, and twisted, bestial noses, they were still human.

If the helmets and masks were strange, the things that hung below them were even more bizarre. Some appeared to be cloaks, others breastplates, a few were large shirts. All were covered, over every square inch, with small bones, colored feathers, beads, claws, teeth, bits of wood and stone, knife blades, and what looked, in a few cases, like mummified human hands!

As he stood gazing in wonder at the unexpected spectacle, a breeze somehow found its way from the sky into the clearing. A rattling, clanking, tinkling murmur rose and filled the air as the wind stirred the things that hung on the poles. The sound seemed querulous, complaining, as if expressing resentment at his intrusion. Then the breeze grew stronger and the noise became louder, more threatening, a warning and an admonition.

For a few moments he'd hesitated, half ready to fly and escape the sound, half wanting to stay because of the feel of the breeze on his skin and the light that poured down from the sky. Then the breeze had died, the murmuring, mumbling threat had become silent, and he'd decided to stay. He would sleep that night among the poles and their weird burdens. He would stay so that he could lie on his back and watch the stars once more.

The next morning he'd gone his way before daybreak. By afternoon the Svartalfar had attacked and started chasing him. It was then he realized he'd transgressed and entered one of their holy places. He hadn't meant to, but that made no difference. They would kill him.

For the moment, though, he knew he was safe. The Svartalfar were out there in the forest with their spears, waiting. He was in here, where they couldn't get at him, waiting. Sleepily he wondered whose patience would give out first.

With a lurch he stumbled through the last underbrush onto the soft grass of the clearing. The sounds of pursuit were louder now and seemed to come from all directions. In panic he glanced around at the dark wall of the forest. With a shudder he moved toward the center of the moonlit openness.

In the middle of the clearing a rock stood. It was strangely shaped, rectangular and flat on the top. It was unnatural. He approached cautiously. The thing was lichen-covered. Beneath the lichen, the side near him seemed to be carved with some sort of design. He leaned over, running his fingers across the surface, trying to make it out in the dim light. It seemed like writing. This line, this shape, seemed full of meaning. If only he could make it out, he might—

Something touched his shoulder. In sudden fear he spun around. And screamed—

He sat bolt upright, his own scream echoing in his ears. The torch was still burning, bathing everything in a dim light.

Slowly, fearfully, he rose and went back into the chamber. Drawn against his will, dreading what he already knew he would find, he approached the altar. He moved carefully, avoiding the skulls and bones, fearing to touch them or disturb them.

Reaching the altar, he knelt and looked at the design on its lichen-covered side. It was identical to the one he had seen in his dream.

He stood up and looked around the charnel house, the mass tomb that held the remains of a people ancient before his race had ever walked the face of Yggdrasil. He did not remember it. Somehow he knew that it had been built later than the altar, that originally there had been nothing here but a clearing and the rectangular stone. He also knew that the stone was the very same altar he'd seen in a dream years before. But that was impossible! He shivered, suddenly cold.

For a few more moments he stared around the chamber. Then, sensing there was nothing he could do standing there, he turned and went back to his place near the entrance of the mound. He sat down and drew his sword from its scabbard. Holding it in his hands, he felt better. His eyes followed the gentle curve of the blade. Once again he marveled at the beauty of the weapon. It was unlike any sword he'd ever seen. Those of both the Aesir and the Vanir were straight and edged on both sides. The swords the Jotun carried were more sharply curved and shorter. This weapon was perhaps forty inches long with a slightly curving blade approximately thirty-four inches in length, sharpened on only one side. He couldn't imagine what sort of metal it was made of. Whatever the material was, it was lighter, harder, and more flexible than that used in Aesir or Vanir blades, and it held an edge incredibly well. Even more amazing, it didn't rust!

He'd found the weapon in Nidavellir, at the base of the mountains that formed its western border. There he'd stumbled over the ancient and mostly rotted remains of what must have been an incredible battle. Bones, flesh, cloth, leather, and even most metal had long since dissolved with age. Here and there, though, he'd found pieces of a shield, a helmet, a dagger, an ax, or a sword that had somehow partially survived the ravages of time. As he came to what must have been the center of the battle, the debris became thicker and thicker. Then he'd seen it, shining in the rays of the sun. The helmet it had cleaved was mostly gone, but the sword itself looked as if it had recently been polished and sharpened. He'd made a scabbard for it out of a piece of deerskin, and he'd carried it with him ever since.

His sword set, he placed his knife and his throwing ax on the floor next to his right hand, ready for instant use. Whatever was happening in that chamber had damn well best stay there, he thought grimly. If it tries to come out here, I'll smash it to pieces.

And if it's not something that can be smashed with cold metal? he asked himself. Then . . . then . . . He was unable to find an answer.

After a long and weary wait his eyes began to droop, despite his best efforts to stay awake. Tired beyond imagining, he let them close.

II

HE spent the rest of the night in fitful sleep punctuated by disturbing dreams. As dawn brought a lighter shade of gray to the gloom of the forest, he peered from the entrance and scanned the line of trees opposite. It took a while, but he finally managed to pick out the hidden shapes of the Svartalfar, lying in wait, watching him as he watched them.

Though he was far from being in high spirits, he waved in a friendly manner to the few he saw. It was a gesture of sheer bravado, but it made him feel better.

He opened his backpack and did an inventory of his food supplies. He still had several strips of smoked and dried venison, a couple of balls of fat, two handfuls of dried berries, a few pieces of edible bark, and several roots he'd dug a few days ago. Ah, and some mushrooms. He heard a noise and looked out the entranceway. Somewhere up above the forest it must have begun to rain. There was a constant drip from the huge trees, but now it was much more rapid than usual. At least he'd have no trouble with thirst. Carefully he pushed a gourd bowl out the entranceway, where it could catch some of the dripping water. He could make the food last a good week if he rationed it. Would the Svartalfar give up that soon? He

14

divided the food into several packets, took one, and placed the other back in his pack.

After eating, he turned his back on the forest and went into the chamber. The torch was still burning, but it was more than half gone. Looking around, he noticed that other torches were placed at regular intervals along the walls of the chamber. Over to the right rear of the altar was what looked like a pile of still more torches. Scattered around the floor of the chamber was plenty of litter to use for starting fires. He gathered as much as he could without going too near the piles of bones and skulls.

Housekeeping chores taken care of, he turned to grimmer matters. He raised the half-burned torch high and inspected the chamber more carefully and thoroughly. As he'd noticed last night, the walls were made of crudely dressed stone and described a circle some thirty feet in diameter. They rose straight from the floor, which appeared to be hard-packed soil, to the height of about six feet, then sloped inward to form a spherical dome. He was surprised by the strange mixture of sophistication and crudeness. The dome was something he'd never seen the likes of. He had difficulty understanding how it worked. Why didn't all the rock come tumbling down? The people who could conceive of and create such a thing must be pretty advanced. Yet the stone itself was rough and poorly fit together. It was almost as if one group had designed the chamber and another, more primitive group had built it.

He approached the altar once again, moving carefully so as not to disturb the skeletons. It was definitely the same as the one he'd seen in his dream. He closed his eyes and conjured up the dream image again. No, there was one difference. The dream altar didn't have that dark stain on its top surface. In addition, it had been out in the open, not in a chamber under a mound. It was almost as if the scene from his dream was from a much earlier time in the history of the altar. Yet clearly this mound and chamber were incredibly ancient. How could he dream of something this old, much less something immeasurably older?

A new thought came to him. Perhaps all these skeletons were the remains of the hapless creatures that had been sacrificed here and had stained the top of the altar with their blood. Even if that was so, he realized, it still didn't solve the mystery of exactly what manner of beings they'd been. Looking once more at the misshapen skulls and bones, he shuddered at their oddity.

Turning his attention back to the altar, he squatted in front of it and tried to trace the carvings with his forefinger. On the conscious level they meant nothing to him. They appeared as meaningless as the tracks worms make in the mud after a rain. When he let his conscious mind relax, however, and allowed the deeper and darker parts of his mind to come closer to the surface, the markings suddenly seemed fraught with significance. He had the distinct feeling that if he could tap the magical Galdar-power that dwelt, still unformed and undisciplined, somewhere within him, he would be able to decipher and understand these carved symbols.

He looked more closely. This one was repeated here and there. And this one appeared several times. All of them consisted of groups of straight and angled lines, meeting and intersecting. One, for example, was an upright stem with two shorter lines angling up from it toward the right. Another was made of two lines angled at forty-five degrees, crossing each other at right angles. A third looked like a spear, a fourth resembled a trident. Others were more complex, with lines crossing and then recrossing. On the other hand, here was one that was a single vertical stroke.

With a start he shook his head and sat back. He'd been drifting, moving slowly but definitely on a current that had been drawing his mind into the inscription on the side of the altar. With a slight shudder, he stood and gazed around again, trying to regain his bearings. His head felt strange, as though full of cobwebs, his eyes seemed slightly out of focus.

After a few moments the feeling passed and he began to look at the sides of the altar. They were plain and uninteresting. The back was about four feet from the wall of the chamber. He moved so he could look behind it. Holding the torch high to give light, he noticed an indentation in the floor between the altar and the wall.

He stepped behind the rectangular stone and began to brush at the indentation. He'd soon uncovered what seemed to be a handhold carved into the face of a stone block, much more smoothly dressed than those that made up the wall. As he cleared more of the area around this block, he realized that possibly the entire floor was actually made of stone paving that had become covered with dirt over the years.

The stone with the handhold was perhaps a foot and a half square. His curiosity aroused, he put his fingers in the recess and tugged at the stone. Surprisingly, it came up quite easily. Beneath it was a cavity, stone lined, slightly smaller than the stone that covered it and no more than twelve inches deep. It contained one item: a pouch that was made of black leather. Carefully, he reached into the cavity and picked out the pouch.

Being in the vicinity of the altar made him increasingly uneasy, so he took the pouch and retreated to the entranceway. He sat just inside where the light was best and began to examine the black leather bag. It was tightly closed by drawstrings made of the same leather as the bag, fastened with an intricate knot.

For a long time he simply turned the bag this way and that, trying to figure out how the knot could be untied. It was incredibly complex and seemed to have no beginning and no end. He drew his knife and was about to cut it when a sudden sense of danger made him halt. He put the ancient iron weapon back in its sheath. He didn't know how he knew it, but the knife didn't want to cut the knot, and the knot would have resisted the cutting. The whole enterprise could have been very dangerous. There was only one way to open the bag—untie the knot.

He stared hard at the knot, letting go of the conscious, willing part of his mind, allowing the problem to sink down into the unconscious, unthinking realm where his undeveloped Galdar-power lurked. He was not sure exactly how long he sat there, looking at that knot, but suddenly his fingers moved as if by themselves, and in a mere matter of seconds the bag was open and he was spilling its contents into his lap.

One by one he picked up each of the twenty-seven disks. They were made of bone and were roughly oval in shape. A symbol was inscribed on each. A brief look through them was enough to excite him. The symbols were identical with those carved on the front of the altar! No, he realized as he inspected them more closely. Not quite identical. These seemed stronger and more powerful. Plus there were three disks that had nothing whatsoever on them. They were clean and smooth, completely blank. Yet they didn't seem any less powerful than the others. If anything, they seemed to emanate an ever greater strength, as well as a sense of profound mystery. What, he wondered, could be so great and awesome, so vast and terrifying that it could not even be symbolized? For he was more convinced than ever that these symbols stood for something.

As he touched and examined the disks, he felt a strange sense of satisfaction anad pleasure suffuse his mind and body. The dry, hard bone felt good in his hands, natural and right.

Eventually he put them back in their pouch. How to fasten them once more? He let his conscious mind go idle once again and almost instantly his fingers knotted the drawstrings into a complex knot. He looked at it critically. Not the same as the one that had originally closed it. But somehow better, less menacing, more inviting and friendly. Good. He reached over to his backpack and fished around until he found a length of rawhide. It was a good three feet long. He pulled out his knife, measured off a length and cut it. Then he looped the piece through the drawstrings of the pouch and placed the whole thing around his neck so that it hung down, hidden, inside his doeskin shirt.

The rest of the day he spent doing what any warrior does when he has idle moments: he patched his gear and catnapped. His naps, however, were never very long, for no sooner did he approach the realm of sleep than a sense of hovering dread welled up and brought him wide awake. The first few times it happened he grabbed his sword and prepared to fight off the Svartalfar, for he was sure he had awakened because he'd sensed their swift attack. But there was never anything there. The forest was quiet and seemingly empty in the gentle drizzle. Only a sharp eye could detect the carefully hidden and waiting forest men.

As night approached he grew more and more restless and nervous. He thought he heard strange stirrings and rustlings both from the woods and from the dark chamber behind him. Long before it became dark, he started a small fire so he could light another torch. Unsure of himself, he carefully examined the chamber again. Nothing that he could see had changed. As near as he could tell, there were no secret doors in the walls. The only way in or out was the stone arch through which he had come.

He was unable to rest comfortably. At first he blamed it on the hard floor and the dampness of the forest. But he'd slept soundly on ground just as hard and damp before. Then he decided he was uncomfortable because of his growing hunger.

Yet he knew he'd been far hungrier in the past and still spent nights deep in sleep.

As the night drew on, though, his eyelids got heavier and heavier. Sooner or later he knew he'd fall asleep. For some reason he dreaded the idea.

At first he fell slowly through the dark, gliding as if he could fly. Gradually, though, he sped up until he was going at a frightening rate. There was no way to tell how far or in what direction he fell. It was the same anywhere he looked—infinite blackness, thick and oppressive.

Then a light, tiny and winking, appeared in the distance, and he sped toward it. Soon he realized it came from a fire that was burning in an open space some distance off, through the forest. Cautiously he moved forward until there were only a few trees between him and the fire.

Carefully he peered around the base of one of the huge trees, hugging the point where the tree met the moldy forest floor so as to make detection harder. Before him was a round clearing in the center of which burned a large bonfire. Strange shadows galloped and leapt around it, jumping and twisting, throwing long hairy arms toward the sky, tilting fanged mouths at the sky to let out bestial howls and wails.

Behind the fire stood a great stone, rectangular in shape and flat on top. Standing behind that was a small figure, hidden in dark, flowing robes and a deep, cavernous cowl. Nothing could be seen except an occasional reddish glimmer of firelight reflecting off eyes deep within the cowl.

Suddenly the creature behind the altar looked up and directly at the spot where he hid. He could see the eyes, burning red deep within the darkness, staring into his own. The thing knew he was there and recognized him in some unknowable way.

His eyes were locked on those of the black-robed figure. He could feel a force pass between them, a power that beckoned to him and urged him to come forward, to show himself, to join in the dance, to come closer and closer and closer. . . .

With a shudder of horror he broke the contact and whirled away, running as fast and as silently as he could. Behind he heard a sudden howl of fury and the sound of many feet in pursuit.

●   ●   ●

With a mighty heave he pulled himself awake. He was trembling, his body soaked with a rancid sweat of fear. His throat was parched and aching, as if he'd been running all day. His head spun in confusion.

His knees watery and weak, he slowly stood and walked back from the entrance into the chamber. He took the torch from its place on the left and held it high. Nothing had changed. It was the same stone, the same altar.

What in the name of Fornjot was going on? That thing in the dream, the one that had stood behind the altar, it had *known* him. Even more frightening, it had been excited at discovering him. He could feel its desire even now. The creature had *wanted* him, needed him in some strange and obscene way.

With a shudder he turned away and went back to his post by the entrance. He kept the torch with him because the light made him feel less alone. Of course, it might also make him an easier target for a spear thrown by one of the Svartalfar, but he doubted the angle was right. His back against the wall, his elbows on his knees, his hands clasped in front of him, he sat and stared into space, trying to make sense of it all.

Eventually, for no reason he could determine, his focus shifted to his hands, and in particular to the left hand, which grasped the right. Something glinted dully in the torchlight. He looked closer. It was the ring Fiorgynn had given him many years ago when he'd first gone to Folkvang as a hostage to secure the peace between his people and the Vanir. She'd gotten it in trade with the Dverg somewhere along the River Gopul, he remembered. It was iron, very ancient, and not of much interest to the gold-hungry little men of Nidavellir.

He'd worn it for years and hadn't really paid it any attention. But there was something. . . . Suddenly excited, he held it close. It was crudely made. Around the band there was little ornamentation, merely a single line of scratches. He looked sharply at the scratches, moving closer to the torch, his excitement growing.

Yes! Yes! The scratches weren't some random design. By Fornjot and the tits of Audhumla! They were similar to the symbols on the altar and those on the bone disks in the pouch around his neck! They were so small and worn that he could barely make them out, but he was positive he was right.

What could it mean? Fiorgynn, he remembered, had said

that the Dverg claimed to have found the ring buried in the forest mold. Neither they nor anyone else recognized the style or workmanship. Yet the markings were similar to those he now found all around him. And what was more, they seemed to raise echoes of recognition deep within him.

Deep within him? Could it have something to do with the Galdar-power, that magical force ruled over by the dark and dread Vilmeid? He'd sensed its fearful growth within him on several occasions. Jalk had hoped to help him learn to control it. But Jalk had died too soon.

He shivered now, suspended between excitement and fear. All this meant something. But what? The questions kept chasing each other around and around in his head. He slept fitfully, if at all, for the rest of the night.

When the morning dawned, he felt exhausted. Slowly, chewing and savoring each and every bite, he ate his small ration of venison, roots, and berries. He allowed himself half a ball of fat, saving the other half for later. Then he took the bone disks from their pouch and studied them for a long time, closing his eyes as he held each one in his hands, trying to feel it and ask it its meaning. The effort made him more tired than ever.

From time to time he checked to see if the Svartalfar were still in their places. He felt a strange sense of reassurance when he determined they were. They weren't giving him up, weren't abandoning him. Or were they just confident that he wouldn't be able to stay in his shelter forever? Did they know something he didn't? Whatever, he shrugged, I feel better just knowing there are human beings just across a short stretch of short grass, even if they do want to kill me.

He tried several times during the day to doze, but every time his eyes closed and he began to slip into sleep, he felt a strong sense of dread, as if someone very powerful and very evil were watching him. Once he even thought he saw a pair of burning red eyes glaring hungrily, invitingly at him. When he shook his head and opened his own eyes, however, the image dissolved.

As evening drew closer, his sense of impending doom grew stronger. It almost seemed as if a tension were growing up within the chamber, a tension that reached out and touched his mind, trying to wrap tendrils around it and draw it closer and closer. By the time he lit his torch for the night, his hands were shaking badly and he had to try several times before he could get the fire started in the tinder.

Can't sleep tonight, he told himself. No matter how tired I am, I can't fall asleep. He sat down, his back against the crudely carved stones of the entranceway. The dim light of the torch crept out of the chamber and crawled along the walls and floor almost to his feet. He looked at it. So dim, so weak, so old . . .

He found himself falling again, falling through that now familiar emptiness of space and time, down and backward to a place and a past unimaginably far away.

It was the forest, as deep and dark as always, the primeval and original forest that had never felt the touch of human foot, never heard the sound of human voice. Somehow he knew it was before the time of the things in the mound, perhaps even before the gods themselves.

Yet there were powers here, nameless, formless, surging back and forth, forces that were destined, in the distant future, to become gods and demons and eventually even men. He was one of those forces, elemental, restless, seeking.

He moved through the forest, a wisp of energy, floating between the twisted branches and gnarled roots, close to the ground, yet of the air. He was searching for something, something that drew him on through the gloom between the towering trees.

Ahead he sensed it, a place of great energy, a welling up of force, a sucking down of power, a flux and flow that linked where he was with somewhere utterly other. Slowing, he approached cautiously. The forest opened to the sky, and there in the middle of a clearing he saw it.

Stopping at the edge of the forest, he gazed in wonder. He knew this thing, knew it down through endless ages. He moved forward until he stood in front of it. Missing nothing, he let his eyes range over its surface. There were no bloodstains on its top, no lichen on its sides. Nor was there any writing on its front. It was smooth and untouched, pure in its power, a junction point between worlds, a passage between this and somewhere utterly other, a link between light and darkness, order and chaos.

He stepped back, dazzled and confused by the energy and force of the stone. This is a place of incredible power, he realized, power that could be shaped to any end. He took another step back, mutely understanding the inherent danger in such a spot. Power like this did strange things to the soul and being.

He felt the presence of another and looked up. There, on the other side of the stone, was a form, amorphous and vague like his own, but utterly different. It was totally alien, the darkness to his light, the negative to his positive.

It was watching him, measuring, judging. He looked back, repelled yet fascinated, for despite its difference, there was something familiar and compelling to it.

Then he felt it reach out, reach out to touch him, to sample him, to taste him. He shuddered. It was hungry, deeply and elementally hungry. The full strength of its need hit him suddenly and unexpectedly.

Shocked, he stepped back several paces. Then, as the demand of the other grew stronger, he turned and fled. He knew fear, deep and instinctual. This utter otherness *on the opposite side of the stone in the clearing wanted to devour him, to make him a part of itself.*

He awoke in cold fear and desperation. There was something far more powerful and vastly more ancient than mere bones in this tomb beneath the mound. It had been here as long as the stone altar. No doubt the creatures who'd left their bones scattered around it had once served its purpose. The hooded form he'd seen in his recent dreams had probably been one of the physical shapes it'd taken.

The thing knew him, had known him forever. He simply couldn't grasp how that could be. Yet he knew, deep, deep inside that it was true. His dreams weren't mere fantasies. They were visions of a truth that went to the very center of things.

The thing that dwelt in the mound wanted him. How long could he hold out? He didn't know, but he was grimly determined to resist as long as he was able. He remembered his fight with Od in the wrestling circles of Folkvang. He hadn't really had much of a chance there either. But he'd made the Vanir youth pay, and pay dearly, for his victory. This was a far more serious battle, with nothing less than his very being at stake. This time if he lost, he lost everything. For that reason he knew he'd have to put up the fight of his life. He smiled grimly. Eventually the thing in the tomb might defeat him, but he was determined to battle it for as long as he could.

The boundary line between dream and waking disappeared entirely. He entered a place where life became an endless dream and the dream itself was of endless lives. He became other than he was, and in ever-new forms battled the power that clung like a thick, evil cloud to the stone altar.

He fought instinctively, reaching within his own mind for things Jalk, his mother, Father Bear, even the demon Despair had taught him. Although he couldn't control his Galdar-power, couldn't even find his way to it, he tried to tap as much of its power and energy as he could reach. At times he improvised, crudely, clumsily, getting results nonetheless.

Every battle drained him. Bit by bit his energy ebbed. And the power he faced seemed to become ever greater.

The time came when he ate the last of the food from his pack. How long can I continue the battle without food? he wondered dully. He knew that he needed physical energy to battle the force that dwelt in the mound. When his physical energy failed, he'd fail. As he swallowed the last fat ball, he knew that the point of failure was only a day or so away. He looked down at his body. So thin, so emaciated so quickly? He was burning himself up, throwing his flesh on the fire that drove his effort. Soon there would be nothing left to fuel the fire. Soon. Too soon. He closed his eyes to rest.

III

HE sensed a tall figure looming over him. Could this be the thing that dwells in the mound, come at last to claim me? he wondered blearily. He opened his sleep-heavy eyes a crack and looked upward. If it's some kind of demon, it's a strange one, he told himself. It looks very human, like a thin old man dressed in a travel-stained yellow robe.

He blinked his eyes and looked more closely. Long, silver hair intricately woven into a pigtail hung down the creature's back, and an equally light, wispy beard reached almost to its chest. The eyes were strange—dark but with a sparkle of light deep within them, and almond shaped, like those of his mother. The nose was somewhat snubbed, the mouth full and ready with smiles. How long the ears were! Gnarled hands, blue with veins, twined around a staff of strange black wood bound with iron strips with iron end caps. Hanging from its left shoulder was a large, flat pouch, decorated with a strange circular design.

"So," the strange apparition said with a slight chuckle, "this is young Voden, the Wanderer of Yggdrasil. Or, shall I say this is what's left of him. Not eating enough young man. Working too hard and not eating enough. Ah, your mother would not be pleased to see the way you're caring for yourself. Hah, I'll just make up a bit of soup to refresh you. Yes, that's what I'll do."

The strange man gathered and piled some leaves in the center of the floor and touched them with the tip of his staff. Instantly they burst into a blaze that sustained itself, even though no more fuel was added. Next he took a bowl from his pouch, then a small tripod. He arranged the tripod over the fire, put the bowl in place, then added water from a skin bag he wore strung over his other shoulder. As the water began to bubble he took several things from his pack and added them to the bowl one at a time, muttering strange words as he did so.

A delicious aroma soon rose from the bowl, and the young man sat up, sniffing hungrily. "Ah," the apparition chortled with glee, "young Voden awakes! Hail Vafudar, Wanderer of Yggdrasil! Welcome back to the world of the hungry. Here now, drink this. It's light, but just what Vestla would have given you if she wasn't off being Mother of Animals right now."

Voden looked up at the thing that appeared to be an old man as he gulped the soup, waiting for it to disappear in a peal of demonic laughter. Or perhaps it would suddenly take on a horrid aspect and fling a spell at him. Or perhaps it would— But nothing happened. The old man stayed an old man, and Voden finished the soup. He felt a strange, delicious power coursing through his body. Perhaps this wasn't the demon of the mound after all. Maybe it was actually what it seemed to be.

The old man laughed at the expression on Voden's face, then leaned forward and gave him a good pinch. Voden yelped at the sudden pain and scowled as he rubbed his arm. The yellow-robed old man laughed again. "There! That proves we're both real! Or at least as real as things that are just partial manifestations of the Tao can be.

"Ha! Wondering who in the world this old man is, aren't you? Well, well, I'm not like the rest that have visited you here in this musty old place. Whew! This place stinks of power!

"To answer your question before you ask it, I'm called Kao-Shir at this particular moment. Yes, ever since I came west out of the Han-Ku pass I've been Kao-Shir. Though at other times and other places, I admit I've used other names."

He winked at Voden in a conspiratorial manner. "Sometimes it's best not to give your real name, eh? Just in case you don't want them to be able to find you later." Then he laughed uproariously at his own sly joke.

"Kao-Shir," Voden mumbled, the name wakening memories from a time that seemed forever ago. "Kao-Shir." He saw his mother, wasted and thin, dying in their hall back in Asgard. He heard her whispery voice. "One comes. One called Kao-Shir. He will be your guide. Trust him."

"That's me," the old man nodded solemnly. Voden realized he'd spoken out loud. "Vestla sent me to you," the old man continued, "in ways you cannot understand. Been a while in coming. I, uh, got sidetracked along the way, I'm afraid. Sorry about that. I meant to be here sooner, but, well, better late than never, eh?" He laughed again, his head tossed back, his thin, white beard pointed at the ceiling.

"Not much of a place you've got yourself here," he said, looking around. "Damp, musty, full of old bones and old spirits. Ugh. Nasty. And," he continued, nodding toward the forest outside, "the neighbors leave a bit to be desired too. Ah, well, I guess it's a case of any port in a storm. Though from the feel of this place, I'd say the worst storm's here and out there's a regular haven of safety by comparison."

Kao-Shir sat down gracefully, crossing his legs and spreading out his robe. "Hmm. How about filling me in on what's going on around here?" he asked once he was settled. "I might be able to offer some advice, or who knows, maybe even a little help."

Almost unable to control his desire to unburden himself, Voden poured out his story, beginning with his discovery of the clearing with the strange things on the poles right down to the current moment.

When he'd finished, Kao-Shir sat and looked at him in thoughtful silence for some time. Finally the old man cleared his throat and nodded. "Hmm, hmmm. Yes. Well, what we have here is something rare but not unheard of. Yes, indeed. Even in the Sunrise Empire, where I come from, by the way, there are such places, places where the worlds touch one another, where power can pour from one to the other. And where creatures from one world can penetrate to reach another.

"In the Common Tongue that other world is called Niflheim. I don't know the language of the Svartalfar, so I'm not exactly sure what the word *Tuat* means. But from the context, I rather imagine it refers to the same thing as Niflheim.

"In the Sunrise Empire we call it Ti-yu and say there are ten levels in it. The first is the domain of Ts'in-Kuan-Wang. He judges the souls of all who die and sends them to the level they have earned in their life. The last of the ten is ruled by Chuan-Lun-Wang. There the souls prepare for their rebirth back into the world. There the Lady Meng-p'o feeds them the Broth of Oblivion so that they may return to life fresh and clean.

"Ah, but there are bad ones in Ti-yu as well. Indeed, the Pi-Li-To, demons that hunger after the souls of men, dwell there. And the gigantic A-Hsiu-Lo, ever warring with the gods, lurk at the roots of a great mountain. The Na-Chia, with their human faces and serpent's bodies, slither there. I've mentioned only a few of the many horrors that Ti-yu holds. To name very many more would be dangerous here.

"You see, this place, this tomb within a mound, is a doorway between the worlds, Voden. It is a portal from here to Niflheim, Tuat, Ti-yu, whatever you wish to call that other world. The thing that calls you is a demon from the other side, one that has managed to slip over the threshold into this world. You say it seems familiar, so perhaps it's one you've battled with down through the ages. . . ."

Kao-Shir paused again and looked curiously at Voden. "Hmm. It appears there is more to Vestla's child than I'd been prepared for. Yes. Let me see the bone pieces and the ring you mentioned." Voden took the bag from around his neck and handed it to the old man. Kao-Shir glanced quickly at the knot and swiftly untied it. Then he took out the twenty-seven pieces, one by one, and examined them. "Old, Voden," he muttered as he turned them this way and that. "Very, very old. You say they match the symbols on the altar and those scratched on the ring? Hmm. Give me the ring."

Voden pulled at the ring to take it off. It wouldn't budge. He looked up and saw Kao-Shir watching him intently. He tugged again. "Odd," he mumbled, holding his hand up to look more closely at the ring. "It's never been hard to get off before." He pulled again, much harder, and was rewarded with a swift, sharp pain that made him gasp and fall back against the wall, his head swimming and his vision blurring.

Kao-Shir nodded solemnly. "Won't come off, eh? Suspected as much. Yes, it all fits. Have you anything else old on you? I mean very, very old?"

Voden nodded and took the iron dagger Buri had gifted him with. The thing was ancient and had passed down through many generations. No one could even remember its origin. Kao-Shir hefted its weight in his hands, tested its edge, and grimly handed it back. "Very good. Ancient and extremely powerful. You'll have need of it, Voden. Keep it ready."

The young man drew his sword from its scabbard and held it out. "I think this is ancient too. At least it feels that way, even though it looks new."

Kao-Shir's eyes lit up with interest as he saw the shining curve of the blade. He examined it carefully, running his hand along the blade, swinging it a few times, and finally pulling a white hair from his head and lowering it slowly to the sharp edge of the sword. It parted neatly.

"Ah," the old man sighed. "I've heard of swords like this. They're said to come from an island far to the east of the Sunrise Empire, many days' sail out into the Sunrise Sea. It's claimed they're made by wizards who quench them in the blood and poison of gigantic serpents. They supposedly test their edge by placing them in a slowly moving stream and floating a lotus down. If the lotus touches the blade and isn't cut, the blade is destroyed. If the lotus is cut in half, the blade is considered adequate but inferior and is sold to ordinary warriors. But if the lotus goes around the blade, ah, then it's considered wonderful and given only to great heroes. It's a pity we don't have any lotuses here to test it." Almost regretfully the old man handed the sword back to Voden.

In thoughtful silence Kao-Shir returned the bone pieces to their bag, reknotted the cord, and handed it back to the young Aesir as well. "These I don't understand. They have power as well, but it seems neutral, sleeping. I think they're a tool, a way to direct greater power, but I'm not sure. Hmm. If they have any value for you, you'll have to find out on your own. I have my suspicions, mind you, but we'll just have to wait and see.

"Right now we have a much greater problem. I fear we're about to receive a visitor from across the threshold, Voden. I'm afraid your demon is coming for you. I'll be what help I can, but, sadly enough, this is your battle."

He could feel it now, a tingling growth of tension that filled the air. It was coming from the chamber. He stood, strangely drawn by it, and walked to the doorway of the round room. A slight shimmering disturbed the air in front of the altar. Something was appearing there, slowly taking shape.

As it began to solidify, Voden found himself surprised and disturbed. The figure was small and slight, hardly larger than a ten-year-old Aesir child. Could such a form be so powerful? The face was thin and charming, with large liquid eyes, small, pointed ears, a button nose, a full, smiling mouth, and a slight chin covered with a stiff, jutting brown beard. The forehead bore two sharp horns. Tiny hands with slim fingers that ended in sharp claws stuck from the full sleeves of a loose-fitting brown robe, the cowl of which was thrown back. Voden heard the sudden sucking intake of breath that Kao-Shir gave as the creature turned its gaze on them.

"So," it lisped lightly, its voice like the sound of wind soughing through pine trees. "Jafanhar. And another. Soft, weak, we find two where one would be enough."

The creature stretched in an almost feline manner. "Umm, yes, so long asleep, so long hungry. And now two!" It trilled an utterly evil laugh, its lips curling back to reveal bright rows of sharp, viciously pointed teeth. A long red tongue licked out, across its lips. "Umm. So nice. So helpless. Now I will take you both." The thing held out its hand to Voden, the claws making a beckoning gesture. "Come to me Jafanhar. You are mine. I will eat you and become you. And then I will consume your friend as well. Come to me. It is useless to resist."

Voden gritted his teeth against the temptation to move forward. "I beat you once," he growled, "and I can do it again."

The eerie trilling laughter echoed in the tomb again. "Yes, Jafanhar, you beat me once. But that was long, long ago, when you were as high as the mightiest. Now you are weak. You do not remember the True Names nor can you even chant the Rune-Ristings. Look, look at the iron band on your finger! You cannot read what is written there! It binds you to me, Jafanhar, binds as strongly as the iron of which it is made. Come to me, for I hunger after my long sleep!"

Voden felt himself take a step forward. With all his might he tried to keep rigid, to keep from moving. He took another step. The creature laughed. "So pathetic! So weak! I could make you run to me, run and throw wide your arms in welcome! I could make you offer your throat to my teeth! But I will have you approach slowly, slowly, dragging it out, Jafanhar, so that you may savor the terror to its fullest. It will make you a better meal! Come, take another step. Yes! And another!"

Voden's vision narrowed until all he saw was the mouth of the creature. The mouth, full of shining, razor-sharp, pointed teeth. The mouth, calling, calling, urging, summoning, demanding. The mouth, waiting to devour his body and his soul. Waiting to devour Jafanhar.

No! he felt something within him cry out. I am not Jafanhar! I am the highest! I am Har!

He looked up into the creature's eyes. "No," he whispered. "I . . . am . . . not . . . Jafanhar. Not Jafanhar." Sweat broke out all over his body. "I will not come to you. I am not Jafanhar!" He stopped moving and stood still. "I am not Jafanhar!"

The smile left the creature's face and a snarl replaced it. "Fool! You resist! There is more power in you than I thought. But you *are* Jafanhar, whatever you say. Yes, a good part of you is Jafanhar, and that is a True Name! You are bound to me by it! I command you to obey!" The thing made strange movements in the air with its hands. "Come. Come."

With his last ounce of strength, Voden tried to resist the thing. As his foot rose to stumble forward, he forced it back down again by sheer willpower. The sweat poured from his body and he gasped for breath as if he'd just run a long way very swiftly. His foot rose once more, as if with a mind of its own. He struggled, feeling his strength waning, feeling the power ooze slowly out of his body. A third time the foot rose, but try as he might, he could not force it down. It took a step. His other foot rose and he fought again, his body trembling with fatigue, a rushing, roaring sound filling his head. Behind the roaring he heard the gentle, insistent calling of the demon. So soft, so smooth, come, come, come, his will was falling away, away. . .

Then he heard another voice, weak and distant, but gradually becoming clear. It was Kao-Shir. "The knife, Voden, the knife. Cut off the finger with the ring. Use the knife to cut off the finger. The knife, Voden, the knife . . ." Over and over the old man repeated the words, in a kind of chant. They began to sink into Voden's foggy, confused mind.

For a moment his eyes cleared and he looked up. He was

only a pace away from the grinning demon. It held out its hand to him. He was reaching out his own, the left one, the one with the ring on his third finger, the ring Fiorgynn had given him, the ring with the strange markings on it. Fascinated, he watched his hand come up to touch that of the demon.

"The knife, Voden, the knife. Cut off the finger with the ring. Use the knife to cut off the finger." Kao-Shir's drone cut through his mind once more. He drained his last reserves to obey. His right hand found the hilt of the ancient iron knife thrust in his belt. Swiftly he pulled it out and slashed forward in a blur of speed. He struck true and the finger was severed, just below the ring. With a shriek and an explosion the demon disappeared. Voden fell forward. The last thing he saw before hitting the ground was Kao-Shir grabbing the cut-off finger, which was trying to wiggle its way across the floor of the tomb and escape.

A delicious aroma filled the air when Voden finally regained consciousness. He looked up and discovered Kao-Shir gazing down at him. Turning his head slightly, he saw a small fire with Kao-Shir's tripod arranged over it. On the tripod was a merrily boiling pot. "So," the old man said gently, "at last the Wanderer returns from his journey through dream. And much better for his long absence, I see." He turned and went to the pot, tilting it to pour part of its contents into a bowl. Voden sat up as he returned. Placing the steaming bowl in his hands, the old man said, "Drink this lad. It's a special mixture of many health-giving things. We call it Aam soup."

Greedily the young Aesir gulped the soup and then another bowlful. Kao-Shir sat across from him, nodding encouragement and smiling in delight at his appetite. "A good appetite is a good sign. Never saw a dying man yet who ate a hearty meal. Yes, yes, get your strength back. I fear we're not out of the woods yet, if you'll pardon the pun."

As Voden finished his second bowlful, he noticed that things were suddenly a bit fuzzy and that he was feeling immensely relaxed and calm. He yawned once, nodded, and tried to tell Kao-Shir he felt sleepy. The old man held up his hand to forestall him. "No need to tell me. I, uh, put a little something extra in the soup. The most sovereign medicine for what you've suffered is sleep. We can discuss our next moves when you wake up."

Voden's sleep was deep and dreamless. He never knew exactly how long he slept, but when he awoke, he was stretched out near the entrance of the mound and it was day outside. He drank two more bowls of Kao-Shir's soup. This one was quite different in taste and texture from the two previous selections. "Meat in this one," the old man explained. But he never bothered to explain what kind of meat or where he'd managed to find it.

When the young Aesir had finally dulled the edge of his hunger, Kao-Shir sat back and stared at him intently for quite a few moments. Voden returned his stare unflinchingly. He liked this old man, even if he was a bit odd.

Finally Kao-Shir nodded and smiled. "Yes, yes, much better, Voden. Not well yet, but much better. Sorry about that finger. Does it hurt much?"

In surprise, Voden looked at his left hand. Where his ring finger should have been was a scarred stump, almost completely healed. "My finger!" he said, remembering what had happened. "I cut off my finger!"

"Yes, indeed. And a very neat job of it, I might add! Made healing easy." Kao-Shir's expression became serious. "Voden, the loss of the finger was necessary. It was the only way to beat that demon. That was one I recognized. I won't name it, that's dangerous to do, especially since it's still with us." He reached into his pouch and pulled out a small bundle wrapped in silk. Slowly he opened it and there lay Voden's finger. It was moving gently.

"The demon's right there, trapped!" Kao-Shir crowed with delight. "The ring drew it. I suspect the ring was made by this particular demon long, long before the San Miao—the first race of men to walk Yggdrasil—were destroyed by Chu Jung for their wickedness. Perhaps it was forged in the very fires that rose from that time of destruction. It lasted eons, you know, and many creatures of chaos existed then.

"In any case, all the others that attacked you were manifestations of the force that exists here. It's hard to know how far back your relationship with this place goes, but it clearly goes back at least as far as this creature." He chuckled as he rewrapped the finger. "It came to possess all of you. But you cut it off before it got past the ring. It had to go in that way. Your timing was excellent. Excellent!"

They sat for a moment in companionable silence. Finally

Voden spoke the question that was on his mind. "Kao-Shir," he began, "you said my mother sent you to me. You also said I wouldn't understand how. I accept that, but where did you come from? How did you know her? What can you—"

The old man held up his hands in mock protest. "Wait! Wait! One question at a time! I'll be happy to answer as many of them as possible. Hmm. Let me see. I know! I'll begin at the beginning. What an original idea!

"I refer, of course, to my individual beginning, not that of the world of differentiated Tao. Let's see. It was the fourteenth day of the ninth month in the village of Ch'u Jen in the district of K'u Ch'u of the Sunrise Empire that my mother was leaning against a plum tree and gave birth to me. It was no real surprise to her for I'd been conceived some sixty-two years before when she had admired a falling star. I looked much then as I do now, white hair, beard, the whole thing. After all, I had sixty-two years to develop! Ah, and I spoke too. Yes, indeed, no sooner had I come out than I pointed to the plum tree and stated, quite clearly I might add, 'I take my surname from this tree.' So I was known as Li. To that I added the name Erh, which means ear." He touched his long ear. "For obvious reasons. In any case, that was the name I had chosen for myself, Li Erh, and that was what I wanted to be called. But," he shrugged, "things being what they are and people being what they are, the fact that I was born with white hair and a long beard was accounted of more interest and importance than my own wishes, and everyone called me Lao Tzu, or Old Boy." He sighed. "Miserable name to live with," he muttered.

"My youth was normal and uneventful. Typical wrestling with tigers, riding dragons, fighting demons, that sort of thing. Eventually, though, I made the serious error of getting involved with the Emperor of the Sunrise Empire. Foolish turtle. I left my wonderful, comfortable, muddy pond and went off to court to find fame and fortune. I had my shell encrusted with diamonds, rubies, sapphires, inlaid with gold and silver, ah, a beautiful, useless sight. Especially for an old turtle!

"Well, after about a hundred and sixty years of that I grew tired of the corruption and wickedness I saw about me and decided to leave. I hitched my black ox to a cart and set out to see more of the world. From Loyang I went westward through the Han-ku pass that leads through the Kunlan Mountains.

"The guard of the pass, an old friend who'd been exiled there for sipping his soup too loudly at court, a fine chap named Yin Hsi, wouldn't let me pass until I agreed to compose a book for him. It took several years, but I finally finished and left the Sunrise Empire forever."

He sat back for a moment, remembering, a slight smile on his face. "Ha! The first three nights after the pass were most curious. I hadn't come to Prin or Kara Khitai yet. I was sleeping beneath a mulberry bush in the midst of a high and wild plateau. There were towering mountains on all sides.

"The first night, the Evil One himself appeared and offered me a kingdom if I would become his helper. Ha! I'd already had enough of that! The second night he offered a huge bag of gold and jewels. The third it was a beautiful woman. Ha! A bag of gold and a bag of blood and bones! No thank you, said I. At over one hundred and sixty years, plus having been born sixty-two years old, I didn't feel a driving need for either of those two bags!

"Knowledge, Voden, knowledge is what I wanted! And knowledge is something no one can give you. You must gain it yourself. There is pain in that. And ecstasy.

"Well. I went first to Kara Khitai and studied with the Yellow Robes." He indicated his staff, leaning against the wall. "I chose the staff as my weapon and became a warrior monk.

"But after a number of years, that paled, too, and I set out again. I went to Prin and helped to train the women of the Floating World. They needed mind training and spirit training as much or more than physical training. I tried to open their minds and their souls to the Tao, that they might live happy and fulfilled lives. Now and then one of them even understood a little of what I was teaching.

"Your mother was such a one! She took to the Tao the way a caterpillar takes to fresh young buds! Devoured what I had to say! A joy for any teacher. Yes, yes a joy.

"And then," he sighed, "one day what we always knew would happen, happened. An, the eldest Son of Muspell, purchased her. She left in the midst of a great caravan, riding a magnificent wagon, destined to be consort to a great and powerful wizard.

"The rest you know. She called to me in a way those who

are deep within the Tao can call to each other. I came. But she was dead, and you had left to wander Yggdrasil. I came after you and found you here.

"That's all there is to tell," he said with a self-deprecatory shrug. "Vestla called me and said her son needed my help. She said you had a great and terrible destiny and needed the teaching of the Tao to ready you for it and help you accept it.

"But, my fine Aesir friend, we are faced with a problem which must supercede any teaching of the Tao or anything else. Yes, indeed. For we are here in this stinking tomb, out of food, low on water, and surrounded by some rather hostile neighbors. It seems to me there's only one way to handle this situation."

"What . . . you mean you have a way out?" Voden asked in wonder.

"Well . . . not exactly a way out. Let's just call it a way to deal with, umm, an awkward situation.

"I propose we surrender to the Svartalfar!"

VANAHEIM

IV

EIR looked at the other two old women and shook her head. "There isn't much more I can do." She frowned at the floor of the hall, then looked back toward the door of the room she'd just left. "It's only a matter of time, and not much of that." Her gaze swung back to meet that of Vor. "Is there anything *you* can do, any sorcery?"

Vor shook her ancient head slowly. "No sorcery can defeat death when she has this strong a grip. No, there's nothing I can do to save her."

"Hmm," Syr began, clearing her throat to gain their attention. "The question is whether either of you should do anything more. Yes, that's the real question."

The other two turned considering glances on her. "If the Vanadis dies, it must be because Audhumla wills it. Perhaps Audhumla's angry with Fiorgynn over this ill-fated treaty with the Aesir. Perhaps it was the presence of those two Aesir brats at some of our sacred festivals that annoyed her. Who knows? But if Audhumla wills the death of the Vanadis, who are we to interfere?"

Vor's dark eyes glittered. "When Syr talks of the will of Audhumla, there is something more than meets the eye behind

39

her words. Speak. We would hear your thoughts."

"Wellll," Syr drawled, assessing them both with her sharp glance, "Fiorgynn has been Vanadis for some time. She hasn't always paid attention to the wishes and advice of the Distingen. In many things she's been very, very independent. Wiser heads have tried to advise her, but she's young and hot and often foolish. She listens too much to people like Syofyn."

Vor nodded slightly. "True, Fiorgynn has been stubborn. And she has a soft heart. But . . ." She let the words trail off.

"A new Vanadis, one chosen because she would be more malleable to the wishes of the wiser heads on the Distingen, might not be a bad idea," Syr continued. "There's a great deal happening in Vanaheim right now, a great deal that takes quick, harsh action, a firm, relentless hand on the reins. Think only of the shattered peace with those cattle-loving barbarians to the north. Or even closer to home, these foresters under Yngvi that helped young Voden. Eh? Yes, yes, there's a great deal going on."

Eir looked concerned. "Are you suggesting we let Fiorgynn die? That we do nothing to save her?"

Syr shrugged. "Save her? You yourself said there's nothing more you can do. And Vor says magic is no use. All I suggest is that we let the will of Audhumla have its way without any further interference. That, and that we begin to organize to chose a new Vanadis . . . one we know we can dominate."

The old healer looked sharply at Syr. "Her sickness was quite sudden and strange. I've never seen its like. I wonder where it came from. No others have caught it, not even those attending her every day. It's strange."

Syr met Eir's gaze, her tiny black eyes unreadable. "Strange indeed. But then, Audhumla works her will in strange and wondrous ways." She kept her gaze steady until Eir dropped her eyes and mumbled something about odd diseases.

Vor, the most ancient of the three, was staring off musingly into space. "The will of Audhumla," she murmured. "Hmm, yes, yes. It must be so. Too many changes. Can't remember a Vanadis who allowed so many changes. We must be ready to pick a new one very soon."

"Syofyn will try for the honor," Syr said.

Vor smiled slightly. "Of course. She must not win."

"No. But how to stop her? She's popular."

"Cancel her out with her opposite."

Eir frowned. "What do you mean, Vor?"

"Syofyn will try. Another must try who is her opposite, someone she will have as much desire to see lose as to see herself win. So . . . Syr will also try for the honor. The vote must be unanimous, so by planning ahead we can be sure that neither one will win. That will throw it to a third. Who?"

"Hlin would make a good Vanadis," Eir suggested.

Syr shook her head. "No. She'd see herself as the protector of all the Vanir. It'd be impossible to control her. The same's true of Syn. What about Gna? She's nothing but a messenger."

"There is a better one," Vor mused, her eyes focused on emptiness. "One who is recently well after a long sickness. Young, weak, malleable . . ."

"Freyja!" hissed Syr. "Yes! Freyja's perfect! She'd be easy to control, especially without her mother to guide her. The death would throw her off balance, she'd turn to the first that showed themselves friendly. Yes."

"I'm not too sure Freyja would be able to handle the strain," Eir commented. "She's been sick for a long time." She hesitated, obviously unsure of whether to speak the words in her mind. Vor impatiently gestured for her to continue. Reluctantly the healer began. "Well, there's something that worries me about her. Her recovery's been long and hard. The mandragora did some strange things to her . . . to her mind . . . I think. I'm really not sure of what I'm saying, mind you, but somehow the girl seems different than she was before the drug. She has dreams, strange ones. At first they frightened her, and she told me about them. Eventually she was able to cope with them . . . or else they stopped. She doesn't confide in me anymore. Freyja's become much more . . . secretive. There's something odd about her now, something I can't quite put my finger on. . . . "

"Bah, you're just imagining things," Syr interrupted. "What could mandragora do to her?"

"I simply don't know. You forget that we're not talking about normal doses for short periods. Freyja had massive doses for many months. No one's ever undergone anything like that." Eir shrugged. "In any case, I wouldn't underestimate Freyja. I've been close to her all during her recovery. There's an iron core in that girl's will."

"Then we'll bend the iron to our design," Syr said scornfully. "You're spooking at shadows. The girl's still weak from the mandragora, her Voden's gone, her mother's dying . . . she's ours to do with as we wish."

Vor grinned. "We have another card to play. Young Od. Don't forget young Od."

Syr cackled gleefully. "Yes, yes! We'll dangle Od in front of her. Perhaps make him her first king. Both are so young and foolish, they think only with their crotches. Od will be easy to control. And through him we can put another rein on Freyja!"

"Is it decided then?" Vor asked. "Fiorgynn will die. When we choose a new Vanadis, I will suggest Syr to offset Syofyn. We will vote for her until you, Eir, suggest Freyja. That will seem natural since you have spent so much time with her. Then we will vote for Freyja."

"Yes," Syr nodded eagerly. "We'll vote for Freyja, and the Distingen will have a Vanadis it can control." She paused for a moment. "Then we'll have to find a way to neutralize both Syofyn and Lofyn. There're hard things to be done, and soft people won't do them well."

"We will talk of this later," Vor said so softly that only Syr caught the words.

"So we have a new Vanadis," Yngvi said thoughtfully.

"Aye," Harbard replied, "and a new king. You remember him. One of the town men. Od his name is."

"Od, you say? Aye, I know him. A good wrestler, but hardly strong enough to become king."

"He's changed, then, since you knew him. He won the southeast quadrant easily. I saw the final match in Sessrymnyr myself. He fought well. Almost unnaturally strong for so slender a lad, I admit, but fast and tricky. Made the other three look slow and stupid, he did."

Yngvi shook his head doubtfully. "It seems strange, too perfect in a way. Fiorgynn suddenly gets sick and dies just before the matches. Freyja's named Vanadis despite her age and her recent illness. Then Od, her lover from a short time ago, suddenly becomes a better wrestler and wins the championship to become her king. I smell an old sow in this."

"Syr?" Harbard asked. "Well, now I think on it, old Syr was always right next to Freyja everywhere the girl went. Aye, right there with her mouth in her ear."

"And Syofyn?"

"Strange you should mention Syofyn. She was sent on a mission to trade with the Dverg just after the election of Freyja, she was. Still gone when I left."

"Yes, Syr's in this. Vor too. We're in for some trouble if those two control the Distingen and the Vanadis." A sudden suspicion crossed Yngvi's mind. "Harbard, did you and the others come back directly to the cave? Did you use the circle route?"

"N-No . . . I mean, we came direct. Figured you'd be wanting the news, so we didn't want to waste time and—"

"Shit! Who's on guard? Get more men out immediately! By the tits of Audhumla, it'd be just like Syr to—"

Yngvi's words were interrupted by a sudden scream and shouts of anger and surprise. Harbard turned to Yngvi, a look of astonishment and fear on his facae. "What—" he began.

The other man cut him off with a chopping motion of his hand. "You were followed. The Valkyrja trailed you! Damn, damn, damn! We're not ready! Arm yourself, Harbard! We've got a fight on our hands!" Without another word, Yngvi, Harbard, and the other men grabbed their weapons and ran from the cave.

Several foresters could be seen behind trees on the slope that led up to the cave. They were shooting arrows at dark brown figures that ran swiftly from cover to cover, rapidly advancing up the slope. Yngvi and the men with him ran to reinforce the others.

Joining a man behind one of the trees, Yngvi asked the situation. "Don't know for certain how many they are," the man said with a growl. "Come on us quiet like. Musta killed the guards. First arrows got Gylfi in the throat, Byggvir in the shoulder. He's over there, 'hind that tree. Still shoots pretty straight."

Yngvi shot at a figure, then stooped low and ran to Byggvir. The wounded man nodded to him and loosed an arrow. There was a yell of pain, and Byggvir laughed. "Still shoot good enough!" he crowed. He turned to Yngvi. "Must be twenty or thirty of 'em. They caught us napping, they did. Lost Gylfi and most likely Ragnar, and Thorir as was on watch. Near as I can figure, odds are two to one against us."

"Most of our men are still in Folkvang at the festival," Yngvi muttered as he shot at and hit one of the Valkyrja.

"Huh, not a bad shot," Byggvir granted. "Aye, most of the lads are gone. I'm thinking we don't stand a chance of holding 'em. Too damn many. Once they get in ax and spear range, we're in deep trouble, if you want my opinion."

"Uh," Yngvi replied as a spear slammed into the tree next to him. "Agreed. We meet at the usual place tomorrow?" Getting a nod in reply, Yngvi gave the call of the forest eagle on hunt, loosed two quick arrows in the direction of the advancing enemy, and turned and ran through the brush, melting instantly into the shadows of the forest.

A few moments later, when the Valkyrja arrived at the spot where the foresters had been, they found nothing but two dead men, one with an arrow in his throat, the other with one in his chest. The second man's throat had been cut so that he wouldn't fall live into the hands of the enemy.

"Four? You only killed four of them?" Syr said in anger. "You outnumbered them and caught them by surprise and you only killed four? How many did you lose?" She glared at the captain of the Valkyrja, who stood before the Distingen giving her report.

"We had three dead, two wounded," the woman replied stiffly.

"And their leader, Yngvi, what of him?" Vor asked.

The woman shrugged. "Gone. A forest eagle cried and they all disappeared like the morning mist. We destroyed all the supplies they'd gathered in the cave. We also placed the curse wands as you directed. It cannot be used again."

Freyja looked confused. "I don't understand. I thought I was in charge of the Valkyrja. I didn't send them out on a raid. What is this all about?"

Syr leaned close to her and said softly, "Ah, Vanadis, it all happened in the middle of the festival. We heard some foresters were planning to attack us, that they wished to overthrow the Distingen and set up their own rule. We had to act, and you were busy. I apologize for failing to tell you, but it slipped my mind. So much to think of, you know, what with Od becoming king and all."

"Yes," Freyja nodded, distracted by the mention of Od. "Yes, of course, I understand."

Syr looked in disgust at the Valkyrja. "You failed miserably. What punishment would you suggest for yourself?"

Before the woman warrior could answer, Freyja leaned forward and said, "She did the best she could. Let's not punish her. After all, it's a holy time, and we have a new king. Everyone should be happy now."

Syr began to object but Vor cut her short. "The Vanadis speaks wisely," the old woman said. "Yield on issues of no importance," she muttered to Syr in a tone so low no other ear could hear. "Cross the girl too often and she'll rebel."

"Very well then," Syr said meekly, looking at Freyja and smiling. "If the Vanadis wishes, the Valkyrja captain will be forgiven her failure." She turned her glare on the warrior. "It is hoped that the graciousness of the Vanadis will be cause for even greater efforts on the part of the captain in the future." The Valkyrja gave Freyja a look of gratitude, bowed, and left the room.

When she had gone, Vor spoke for some time, outlining the problem represented by Yngvi and the rebellious foresters. When she'd finished, the Distingen voted unanimously to take stern measures, including the arrest of several young men in Folkvang at that very minute who might well be part of Yngvi's group.

Lofyn asked when Syofyn would return from her trip to the Dverg. Syn smiled and said she would be back when the mission was completed, probably by fall. With no further business to conduct, and with Freyja obviously anxious to end the meeting and get back to Od, Vor intoned the blessing of Audhumla and they left.

Vor walked with Eir and Syr. "When *will* Syofyn return?" she asked.

Syr chuckled. "I sent a letter with that fool addressed to Durin, king of the Earth Dverg. I begged him, as he valued our trade and friendship, to keep Syofyn going from place to place in Nidavellir for as long as possible. Bah! If I could have arranged it, I would have sent her to seek out Svarin in Joruvellir and let her follow the sunset until the end of time! But she'll be back, perhaps next spring. By then it won't matter any longer. We'll be completely in control. If she objects too strenuously, we'll arrange for an accident or a rare disease." She looked out of the corner of her eye at Eir. "One that can't be cured by medicine or magic, eh?"

"What of the foresters?" Vor asked. "They're warned now. They'll be very wary."

"We'll use the Valkyrja to hunt them like dogs," Syr snarled.

Vor wheezed a laugh. "Ah, ah, I doubt it will be as easy as that. I think Jalk is behind all this. He has plenty of cause to hate us, he does."

"But I thought he died during the rite. . . . " Eir left the statement open.

"I thought so too," Vor responded. "He went off into the forest, leaving a goodly portion of himself behind. We assumed he was eaten by beasts drawn to the blood. But we never found a trace of him. Not even bones. He may have survived. If he did . . ."

Syr nodded thoughtfully. "It would take someone like that to organize the foresters. This Yngvi is a bright lad, but not up to setting something like this in motion, no, not he. But to keep it in motion once going, well, yes, yes, he's brave enough.

"We've got to smash it. It's small yet, and easily wiped out if we get to the leaders. Let it go too long, and only Audhumla knows what might happen."

"Well," Vor mused. "That means we can't send any more of our lads north to fight with the Aesir. We will have to breach the treaty completely. How will Borr respond?"

"Borr has too much to keep him busy with the Jotun to be of any concern to us," Syr snorted. "Damn the treaty! If we'd never sent any of our men north to fight beside those cattle-dung barbarians, they'd never have learned to be warriors! We made a bad mistake there. We created a group of men who're as used to battle as our own Valkyrja. We handed Jalk the core of a trained army! The treaty was a foolish idea from the very beginning. One of Fiorgynn's stupidest moves. We're well rid of it!"

Vor smiled slightly at Syr's vehemence. "Then let it slide. Yngvi is our first concern."

"How many did they catch?"

Bjorn chuckled. "They thinks as they caught five. But none of 'em as was caught was with us. Just poor fool lads as weren't never part of this here group, they wasn't. Clever to send Harbard to warn us, Yngvi. They'd a caught more'n a few with their pants down and in some girl if you hadn't a sent up a scare."

"How many were in Folkvang?"

"No more'n twenty in all, I reckon. I fear as two or three may have got bushwacked by the Valkyrja on the way. Forest is crawlin' with 'em, it is."

"Thick as ticks in hatchin' season," Byggvir growled. "Nearly got ambushed myself the other day. Killed one, wounded another."

"Byggvir, how many men do we have in all right now?" Yngvi asked.

The other forester scratched his head in thought. "Maybe some twenty in this camp. Another fifteen over closer to the gap. 'Bout twenty more in the hill camp. Maybe thirty or so scattered in the swamp. 'Nother forty in small groups here and there. Then there's the lads up north fightin' the Jotun with the Aesir . . . maybe fifty in all. 'Bout a hundred twenty-five we can count as effectives right now. Almost two hundred if we send for them as is north."

"Good. Send our fastest and smartest wood-runner north to bring them back. We'll be needin' them soon. In the meantime, it's time we gave the Valkyrja and the Distingen something to think about. Something to make 'em pull in their claws a bit. We'll need about twenty of the best foresters we can get. Here's my plan."

As the other two heard Yngvi out, their grins grew wider and wider.

Damn, the Valkyrja thought, this is boring duty! While the others are out in the woods chasing down those foresters and earning fat bonuses and promotions, I'm standing guard on the outskirts of Folkvang! She looked over her shoulder through the trees. In the distance she could see the dusk falling over the clearing around the city. It was already dark in the woods at her post, about three hundred yards into the forest beyond the clearing's edge. Her post was one of twelve designed to give early warning of any enemy creeping up to the edge of the forest. No one's attacked the city since those damn Jotun tried years ago, she mused. Who would ever be so stupid as to strike at the strongest city in the—

Her thoughts were cut short by the arrow that flew from the darkness and caught her in the throat. Before she could hit the ground two figures reached her side, each striking twice with their knives to make sure she was dead.

• • •

The guard at the north gate saw a patrol of twelve Valkyrja come out from the dark of the forest into the dusk of the clearing. They were coming swiftly in that mile-eating stride the women warriors prided themselves on. Must be coming back from patrol, the guard thought. Maybe now we'll have some relief here in Folkvang. Getting tired of pulling double watches because they've got most of the others off chasing foresters in the woods. She tried to pick out someone she knew in the group. Leaning forward over the wall, she concentrated hard, looking carefully. The noose was around her neck and tight before she could yell out. Her body landed with a muffled thump and two knives found her heart before she could so much as move.

The twelve Valkyrja passed through the gate and dispersed swiftly. In a few moments they gathered again, turned around and trotted back toward the forest. They'd hardly reached the darkness beneath the trees when the bright glare of leaping flames lit the deepening dusk. Yngvi and the other eleven turned and looked as the fires they'd set in the outer northeast and northwest quadrants of Folkvang grew and spread. They grinned as shouts of alarm filled the night.

The two men who'd killed the guard at the gate joined them. "Fire's took good," one chuckled. "How many'd we get?"

"Thirteen, counting yours," Harbard responded.

"Let's go," Yngvi ordered. "We've made our point. I expect there won't be as many Valkyrja out on patrol anymore. We'll have time to gather our forces and begin hunting them for a change."

"What're you thinking on?" Byggvir asked.

"The woods are ours," Yngvi answered. "I intend to make that clear to the Distingen. Any Valkyrja that leaves the clearing around Folkvang is free game. We'll kill as many as we can. Force them to go around only in large numbers. Harass them when they do. Keep them off balance, strike when and where we please. The more they concentrate, the easier it'll be for us."

"Oh, you're a rare one, Yngvi." Harbard laughed delightedly. "Jalk hisself couldn'ta planned it better!" He shook his fist toward Folkvang. "The city's yours, bitches!" he cried angrily. "But the forest's ours!"

"Aye!" the others took up the cry. "The forest's ours!"

"And someday," Yngvi said softly, "so will Folkvang." He turned back to the darkness of the forest. "Come lads," he called, "we've had our fun for the night. Tomorrow we begin to hunt Valkyrja! And that won't be as easy as setting fire to a few halls in Folkvang!"

They turned as one to follow him. A moment later the clearing was empty of everything but the twisting glare of the flames and the cries of those who fought them.

V

"WHAT do you mean we can't take the wagon around Vana-heim for the fall blessings?" Freyja asked, a tone of petulant anger creeping into her voice. "The Vanadis always does it. My mother always did it. Now I'm the Vanadis. I should do it."

"It just isn't a good idea this fall, dear," Syr said, trying to make her voice as pleasant as possible. "Perhaps next spring."

Cold anger showed in Freyja's eyes. "It's because I want to take Od with me, isn't it?"

"No, no," Vor protested. "It is a bit unusual for the king to go on the blessing journey, but not totally unprecedented. In ancient times, long before I was born, the king went, and then at the very end he was . . . uh . . . well, we stopped that practice eons ago."

"No," Syr sighed, "no, Od has nothing to do with it. Though we must have a little chat soon about him and the way he's been acting lately. No, the real reason is Yngvi and his foresters."

"But I thought the Valkyrja had that under control," Freyja said, her brow knit in a deep frown. "You told me—"

Syr held up her hand in protest. "Well, yes, we told you of

the victories. We didn't want to bother you with the details. You've been so busy with Od that—"

"I am the Vanadis," Freyja said coldly. "Why haven't you kept me informed of the things I need to know to rule? You are my advisers. Why haven't you advised me?"

Anger and the need for control battled for supremacy in Syr's little black eyes. Control won, but the anger was still there, barely below the surface. "We didn't feel it was necessary. Vor and I conferred and felt capable, in our age and wisdom, of handling the situation without disturbing you."

"How much more have you handled without disturbing me, I wonder?" Freyja asked, her voice deceptively sweet.

"Nothing you wouldn't have approved of, my dear," Vor answered stiffly. "Don't you trust us?"

"Of course I trust you. Why shouldn't I trust you? I trust you as my mother trusted you. My poor mother, who died so suddenly, so mysteriously. Now tell me what's going on with my Valkyrja and Yngvi."

"Why certainly, my dear," Syr began. "Vor and I will prepare a report and give it to you tomorrow or the next day."

"Now."

"Now? Why that's . . . that's hardly practical. There's so much to review, so much to remember, so—"

"So age has befuddled your memory and dulled your mind, Syr? You should have warned us of this sooner," Freyja said sarcastically. "If you're unable to give me the report I desire, I'm sure I know who can." She turned to the Valkyrja who stood at the door, and commanded, "Bring me the captain of the group that made the first raid on Yngvi. I believe her name is Rota."

Stunned silence reigned in the room until the captain Freyja had pardoned appeared in the doorway. Freyja motioned her forward. She bowed low to the Vanadis and gave a curt nod to Syr and Vor. "You called, my Vanadis?" she asked.

"Indeed. Tell me of the situation with Yngvi."

"Freyja, I must protest," Syr interrupted. "This is a mere captain of the—"

Freyja's voice was calm, but as hard and cold as the cliffs of the Icerealm. "The Vanadis will hear her. I command you to silence while she speaks."

Turning to the Valkyrja, Freyja nodded. The woman drew herself up and began to speak. "After the raid on Folkvang we made three sweeps into the forest, designed to intercept and destroy as many of the foresters as we could find. We never saw them, but we knew they were there."

"How did you know?" Freyja queried.

"Because they ambushed one of the columns and killed seven of us. They also lurked just out of range of the other two groups, shooting and melting away before we could respond. Three more were wounded that way and one was killed."

"What has happened since then?" the Vanadis asked, turning a cold eye on Syr.

"On two other occasions we have sent parties out to fight them. Both times we came back with heavy loses."

"You've been a leader on all these expeditions?"

"Yes, my Vanadis. Always in the hottest action."

"You're lucky to have survived."

"Yes, my Vanadis."

"Isn't it a bit unusual for one person to be sent out on such dangerous assignments so often?"

"Yes, my Vanadis."

"Ah. Who sent you?"

"The Disir Syr, my Vanadis."

"Ah, yes, of course. I was too busy to be informed. Captain, I'm putting you in charge of my personal guard. See to it that it's made up of only the finest Valkyrja, the most faithful to their Vanadis."

The captain was unable to hide a slight smile. "Yes, my Vanadis. I'll do it immediately!" She bowed again, and at a wave of Freyja's hand, almost ran from the room.

Freyja turned her glance to Syr's scowling face. She smiled innocently and said, "I remember that girl. We studied the Thiodnuma together in the practice yard under Geirahod. Good soldier. Dependable. Utterly loyal. An excellent set of qualities, don't you think?"

Before Syr or Vor could answer, a frown crossed Freyja's face and her voice turned harsh. "We cannot make the fall trip because we no longer control the forests of Vanaheim! My Valkyrja are no longer safe beneath the trees of my own realm! We wage a war against our own people! And this wasn't important enough to tell me of?"

"Freyja—" Vor began.

"Vanadis!" Freyja commanded.

"Yes, my Vanadis, we thought that with Od—"

"Od is my king, my husband. We aren't talking about him. We're talking about Vanaheim, my kingdom, and a war we're fighting that should not be fought. We will send a peace mission to Yngvi immediately, find out what it is he wishes, why he fights. This must end as swiftly as possible. Send Gna and Lofyn. And Hlin. See that it's done." Without another word Freyja rose and left the room.

For several minutes Syr and Vor simply stared at the doorway through which the young woman had disappeared. Vor spoke first. "A peace mission to Yngvi. Could such a thing work?"

Syr frowned thoughtfully. "Who can say? But any peace with Yngvi would be to our detriment. He's a friend of Voden's and totally lacking in respect for the old ways. We can't allow any such peace to take place."

"Well," Vor said, "a peace mission could lead to peace . . . . or it could lead to even greater hostility."

"How is that possible?"

"Ah, if the mission were not received peacefully, if it were attacked before it had a chance to deliver its message . . ."

Syr grinned crookedly. "Yes. Such a thing could be arranged. We control men who could be made to look like Yngvi's foresters."

"Arrange it," Vor said harshly.

"Two parties set out?"

"Aye, Yngvi. One left in the early mornin'. Bunch a town men and some foresters that are partial to Folkvang. Dressed like our lads they was. Then about noon a second party. Looks to be three Disir and fourteen Valkyrja. They be headed our way . . . leastways they're comin' down the Hrid."

"Could you tell which Disir?"

"Wasn't no old sow, dammit. Like to bushwack that un! No, seems to me it was Gna and Lofyn. Maybe Hlin. Best of a bad lot, those three. What could they be wantin', comin' into the forest like that?"

Yngvi grinned. "Gna usually carries messages for the Distingen, so I imagine they want to talk to us. It's about time for the Vanadis's fall blessing trip, and with us controlling the woods, she can't take it. I'd say they're coming to see if they can get us to let the trip take place." He rubbed his hands together delightedly. "We've got them worried, Harbard! They don't have the run of the forest anymore! They're coming to beg us to let them do something!"

Harbard chuckled. "Aye, that's likely the truth of it."

"It's got to be Freyja. Maybe she's come around to what's happening. Maybe we'll actually be able to talk with her."

"Think ya so? Could be. She's a young one. Might be able to talk sense to her. Worth a try, says I. We've hurt the Valkyrja for sure, but they done their share a hurtin' too. Five good lads we've lost. Ahhh, peace might not be such a bad thing if the Vanadis would just listen a little."

"That explains the second group," Yngvi mused. "Wonder what that first group was all about?"

"Strange, that one. What do townmen want with wanderin' around in the forest dressed up like us?"

The blood suddenly drained from Yngvi's face and his eyes went wide. "By Beyla's balls!" he muttered. Harbard looked up in surprise. "By the tits of Audhumla!" the young leader of the foresters cursed. "Dressed like us! Of course! Harbard, call as many men as you can! We've got to get to the Disir before they do!"

"They? They who? What are ya talkin' on?"

Yngvi's voice was a low growl. "That peace mission is coming from Freyja, I'll bet my life on it. The other group, dressed like us, is from Syr and Vor. Dammit! They're going to ambush the peace mission and make it look like we did it!" He grabbed his bow and quiver and ran, calling for Harbard and the others to follow.

Syr stood in front of the Distingen, quivering with rage. She held an arrow in her hand and shook it at Freyja. "This," she hissed in fury, "this is the answer to your offer of peace to Yngvi and his forest vipers! This arrow through the heart of Lofyn! They kill our Valkyrja. And now they kill one of us! Lofyn is dead! Murdered from ambush by the foresters! Sacrilege!"

She turned to the rest of the Distingen, her face twisted. "This can only mean one thing! War! Total war! We must annihilate these blasphemers! All must die! All!"

Hlin looked dazed. There was a bandage around her shoulder and a large bruise on her forehead. "I . . . I was there Vanadis." She shuddered. "It was . . . the arrows came from nowhere. They came and hit us and there was screaming and crying and Lofyn was bleeding and it hurt so horribly . . . I . . ."

Freyja nodded compassionately. "Yes, Hlin. It must have been terrible." She turned to Syr. "Were any of the foresters cap*ured?"

"No. The attack was too sudden. They struck and fled, cowards that they are. The Valkyrja that survived were too busy caring for the wounded to give chase."

"I wish we had one of them to question."

"I wish we had one, too, Vanadis," Vor said, "but not to question. There is a rite of atonement, a bloody rite, one to assuage the fury of Audhumla. I fear that fury if we do not act swiftly against the foresters. Lofyn must be avenged. We must appease Audhumla for this blasphemy against her chosen Disir."

"Strike immediately, I say," Syn added, her voice shaking with anger. "Strike harder than we have ever struck before. Hound them from the face of Vanaheim."

Freyja leaned back and carefully watched each of them as the discussion continued. Syn, Hlin, and Gna were honestly aghast and infuriated by what had happened. Eir looked confused, as if uncertain how this horrible thing could come to pass. Vor was as ancient and impassive as ever. Syr boiled with rage, but just beneath the surface Freyja detected a cold, controlled joy. The meeting of the Distingen could only have one outcome. The council would declare war against the foresters. Valkyrja from all across Vanaheim would return to Folkvang to sweep the forest to the south and west of the city bush by bush. Yngvi and his men were somewhere between the Himinborg Plain to the north, the Smoking Lands to the south, the Gunnthro and Hrid to the east, and the River Gopul to the west. It wouldn't be an easy hunt. Many Valkyrja would die. But they would find the rebels and kill them all.

Where would that leave her . . . and Od? Fall was rapidly approaching. The equinox would be the turning point for the king. Then, at the winter solstice, he'd lose his crown and be driven away, a beaten, haunted man. She'd seen it happen every year since she could remember.

But this time it was happening to her and Od. She didn't want it to happen to Od. She loved Od. He was strong, and wonderful in bed. He could go on and on for hours and did such incredible things to her with his hands and his tongue and his . . . She shivered in delight just thinking about it. The only time it had ever been better was with— No! She didn't want thoughts like that breaking in! She had to forget Voden! Forget the cattleshit-smelling barbarian. Damn him! Damn him . . . and yet . . . and yet . . . She'd loved him.

She shook her head to clear it of the Aesir. Od, think of Od. She smiled slightly at the thought. But the winter was coming and the Disir would do things to Od, things that would destroy his manhood and make him a stumbling, weeping shell. She'd seen it happen, even to the most virile of her mother's kings.

Fiorgynn had always been willing to accept it because she'd never loved any of them. At least not that Freyja knew of. Maybe in the beginning. But then she must have grown used to it. I don't want to grow used to it, Freyja told herself. I want Od. I want him whole and lusty and . . .

There was more to it than that, she realized with a shiver. The very thought of losing Od opened a dark, empty place in her mind. She'd lost so much, so swiftly. Voden first. Then her mind. Then her mother. Too many losses. She wasn't really well yet, no matter how she appeared to others. My dreams, she moaned inwardly, my horrible dreams. If Fiorgynn were here, she'd be able to explain them. Or at least listen to them and take them seriously. Eir just looked at me like I was mad.

Maybe I was. Maybe I am. There's no one I can really talk to, no one I can trust with my thoughts, my feelings, my fears, my dreadful, dreadful dreams. She shivered. Od at least holds me when I wake up crying. Holds me and makes me forget everything for a while. I don't know if I really love him. But by Audhumla, I *need* him! If he were gone . . .

What to do? Could she defy the Disir? Who would back her if she did? Yngvi might have been willing to. He was a friend of Voden's. He didn't like the old ways. There were others too. Rota, the new head of her personal guard, had indicated as much. She'd rebuilt the whole guard with Valkyrja who had trained with Freyja and were totally loyal to her. She was even sure some of the people in Folkvang were discontent with the extreme return to the old ways that the Distingen had enforced since Fiorgynn's death. Yes, there were those who might back her.

Not enough, though. Without Yngvi, without a force of fighters larger than her personal guard, she couldn't match the power Syr, Vor, and the Distingen commanded. She'd hoped to make a personal alliance with Yngvi no matter what had happened with the larger negotiations with the foresters. But now. . . Why had he attacked without even trying to find out what the mission was about? They'd carried the yellow banner of parley. Was he an implacable enemy? She sighed. It didn't make much difference now. The Distingen was about to vote, and she knew how it would go. And how would it go with her and Od?

Everything went as she had expected, as it had to go. She left quietly, unable to meet the triumphant eyes of Syr.

"My Vanadis?"

Freyja looked up to see the bowed head of Rota. "Ah, yes, Rota," she responded. "I've been sitting here thinking so hard I didn't notice you. What do you want?"

The Valkyrja straightened up. Her expression was that of a person who has something to say that they're not too sure of and they know won't be pleasant to hear in any case. "Well, it's that arrow, the one Syr showed."

"Arrow? Oh, yes, the one Syr said killed Lofyn."

"The same. I looked at it."

Freyja leaned forward, intrigued by Rota's manner. "And?"

"And I swear I've seen it's like before. Not a very well-made arrow. Surely not as good as those made by foresters. More like . . . more like one made by a townsman."

Freyja frowned. "A townsman? Well, townsmen make arrows and hunt in the forest nearby. So?"

"I just wonder what an arrow made by a townsman was doing in Lofyn's heart."

Freyja was silent for a moment as she let this information sink into her consciousness. "Are you suggesting," she asked slowly, "that it wasn't the foresters who attacked the peace mission?"

Rota dropped her gaze. "It is not the place of a mere captain to suggest any such thing, my Vanadis. I merely mention the odd circumstance. That and the fact that at least two of the other arrows that came back in the wounded were of town making, not forest crafted."

Freyja's eyes half closed as she mused. "How convenient it

turned out to be that the peace mission was ambushed. Unusual, but convenient. It made declaring war against Yngvi so much easier."

"Yes," Rota replied. "And the state of emergency gives the Disir so much more control, so much more say in what happens. The city will soon be flooded with Valkyrja that hardly know the new Vanadis. Most have never even seen you. But they have all seen Syr, they are all loyal to the Distingen."

Freyja made a decision. "Rota, can you get to Yngvi?"

The Valkyrja bowed her head. "Yes, my Vanadis. I know him well. Several times during festival we—"

"Good. Go to him. Tell him what's happened. See if . . . if he has any ideas."

"Yes, my Vanadis. I will leave tonight." Rota bowed low and began to leave.

"Thank you, Rota," Freyja said as the warrior reached the door. She bowed again and left. For some time Freyja sat and thought. There was much to think about.

The guards had slung the Valkyrja on a pole like a slain deer in order to carry her more swiftly through the forest. Yngvi grinned when he first saw her. He knew Rota well and realized how angry she must be at this rough treatment. The young woman was trying as hard as she could to swallow her anger. Yngvi decided not to provoke her any further.

"Rota," he smiled broadly, "a captain of the personal guard of the Vanadis? You've done well by yourself since last we saw each other. Here, let me help you get those ropes off. I trust my men were gentle?"

The Valkyrja looked sharply at him, but seeing no smile on his face, she grunted a noncommittal reply. When she'd taken off her bonds and been given back her ax and knife at Yngvi's insistence, she looked around her with open curiosity. They were in a shallow cave, perhaps twenty feet deep by forty wide, with an opening about half as wide. Three fires were burning, and around each were some ten men. It was clearly a temporary camp.

Following her gaze, Yngvi said, "We keep on the move a lot, monitoring what you Valkyrja are doing and giving you a harder target to hit. This is only one of several groups scattered all over the western forests of Vanaheim."

"The Distingen has declared war against you, Yngvi,"

Rota said. "They're bringing Valkyrja from all over Vanaheim to run you down and destroy you."

"Huh," the forester replied, his brow furrowed. "From all over? Sort of changes the odds, doesn't it? Won't just be the garrison at Folkvang anymore. Damn."

Harbard was sitting next to his leader. "Not so good, that. They means to hunt us out, eh?"

Rota nodded grimly. "Syr and Vor are determined. You're not just a nuisance anymore. You're a major threat."

"Ah. How's that?"

"Freyja isn't as easy to control as they expected," Rota said proudly. "The Distingen has tried very hard to take us back to the old days since Fiorgynn died. They've been enforcing the old rules with a vengeance, even some that haven't been followed for generations. Most of the younger people in Folkvang are angry about it, but there was no one to lead us."

"What about Freyja?" Yngvi asked.

"They kept her a virtual captive for a long time, surrounded her with their own people. The only one aside from Syr and Vor that saw her was Od."

Yngvi grinned. "Aye, and I'll wager he saw a lot of her!"

"They used him too. Freyja loves him, or thinks she does. Since Voden left, well . . ."

"Aye, I know. That was horrible. For both of them. The Vettir only know where he is now, but Beyla bless him all the same. Go on. You've more to tell."

Rota nodded. "Freyja began to realize what was going on. I think she's worried about what will happen to Od soon. I wouldn't be a bit surprised if Syr intends to go back to the ancient practice and actually kill the king at the solstice! In any case, I ended up as the captain of Freyja's personal guard. On my own I've been cleaning out her household, staffing it with people loyal to her and not the Distingen.

"This peace mission was her idea. She realizes you may be the best ally she has . . . maybe the only one with enough force to offset the Distingen's control of the majority of the Valkyrja."

"Got there too late, we did," Harbard said glumly. "Managed to catch us one of them fake foresters. He sang a pretty tale when we stuck his feet in the fire. Died, he did, not very tough, but he told us all he knew. Syr sent the lot a 'em."

The Valkyrja nodded. "I realized that when I saw some of

the arrows. Town made, not the kind of thing a forester would use at all. I told Freyja. She asked me to come see you. She hopes you have some ideas."

Yngvi nodded grimly. "I'd best have some, Rota. I'd best have some damn good ones. We're fighting for our lives now!"

SVARTALFHEIM

VI

To Voden's surprise the Svartalfar not only accepted their surrender but treated both Kao-Shir and himself with marked respect, and even a tinge of awe. Perhaps they knew something of the horror that dwelt in the mound and were impressed that the two of them had survived it.

The leader of the forest men was a short, slender, but powerful man of indeterminate age named Anhur. He moved with fluid grace and had remarkably large, intensely black eyes that sparkled with humor and intelligence. As soon as they had surrendered, Anhur sent off a runner with the news of their capture.

Surrounded by some twenty of the Svartalfar, they traveled southeastward, back toward the spur of the Smoking Lands that thrust northwestward from the main range. After several days of rapid marches, the ground began to rise and become rocky. At the same time the trees thinned out and openings appeared in the forest. Crossing one of them, Voden looked up and saw towering mountains in the distance.

When Voden asked where they were being taken, Anhur answered readily enough. "You go to see Khamuas, the Kheri Heb, the Chief Priest-Magician of our people. He is the Uert-

Hekeu, the Great in Magic, and so he leads the Ennead, the Council of Nine, that rules our people. He dwells in Ro-Setau, the Gate of the Ways, the mighty city that is the birthplace and tomb of all Svartalfar. The Kheri-Heb alone has the authority to deal with a case as complex as yours."

Voden looked over at Kao-Shir and got a smile and a shrug by way of reply. Obviously it made as little sense to the old man from the far-off Sunrise Empire as it did to the young man from Asaheim.

Another day brought them to a vast opening in the forest. As they came from beneath the trees, the whole party stopped and stood gazing at the sight before them. "Ro-Setau," Anhur pronounced with a sweeping gesture of his arms. A mile or so to the south a great hill rose at least a hundred feet into the bright sunlight. It was shapaed like an H with a tail sticking out from its left side. At the point where the tail met the H, a gigantic building loomed. Even from where they stood, Voden could make out the almost endless number of huge columns that held up a vast roof. The edge of the roof was covered with gilt and glinted brightly in the sunlight. To the left of the massive structure were many smaller ones, runnning, one after the other, all the way to the end of the tail.

To the right of the building was a large open area covered with a multitude of shapes too small to make out from where they stood. Farther to the right, on the crossbar of the H, was another large building. It appeared to be square, made of some dark material, almost fortresslike. Other buildings were visible but lacked any interesting or distinguishing characteristics. A series of three earthen ramparts faced with timber surrounded the entire hill, beginning almost at the point where the hill met the flatter ground and rising to just below the buildings. The Aesir thought he could make out figures patrolling the ramparts.

Voden had never seen anything like Ro-Setau. The largest city he had ever experienced had been Folkvang in Vanaheim. Without even measuring, he knew ten Folkvangs would fit into Ro-Setau without filling it up.

They were about to start for the city when a sudden shift in the wind brought an overpowering odor of death and decay sweeping toward them from the hill. Unable to control his surprise, Voden blurted, "What . . . what is that stench?"

Anhur looked at him coldly before answering. "You speak

of the Field of Auf, the Field of Corpses. That 'stench' is the Ba ridding itself of the flesh that keeps it from the Paradise of Aalu. When the dross is gone and only the bones remain, then the Ba makes its long and perilous journey past the Manu Mountains in the west, down the Valley of Amentet and into Tuat. If it manages to find its way through the dangers there, it heads across the deserts, past the demons and monsters that dwell in those dry and deadly wastes until it reaches Aalu. If it can overcome the final barrier, the hideous serpent Ankh-Neteru, it may enter paradise and wait in a land of plenty for the day when it will rise again. But enough. We must go now. The Kheri Heb awaits."

The smell of rotting corpses became so strong, it was all Voden could do to keep from gagging. Kao-Shir gave him a stern look and acted as if the air was as fresh and balmy as that of a spring day. The Aesir gritted his teeth and tried to follow the older man's example.

When they entered through the great gate in the rampart that guarded the left leg of the H, Voden noticed several guards armed with spears, standing on top of the rampart and staring down at them with mild curiosity. On the other side of the gate the Aesir discovered the origin of the death stench that hung so heavily in the air. He found himself walking down a broad avenue paved with tight-fitting stones. The avenue ran, straight as an arrow, through the middle of the open area he had seen from the edge of the forest. This, then, was the Field of Auf. He was close enough now to see the things that had been too small to make out at a distance. Everywhere were raised platforms on which lay corpses in various stages of decay and decomposition. Some were fresh and just beginning to swell. Others were mere shreds of flesh and hair covering startlingly white bones. Voden held down his gorge, tried to breathe through his mouth, and kept his eyes on the paved avenue they walked.

Once through the Field of Auf they turned right into the crossbar of the H and approached the large building there. The area they transversed seemed to be some sort of marketplace, and for the first time Voden saw women and children. Aside from the children, who peered with open wonder, the Svartalfar stood in silence, their soft, dark eyes slightly averted, and watched them pass. They didn't seem so much curious as respectful.

As he had discerned from a distance, the building they were approaching was built of dark stone. It seemed to be square, perhaps two hundred feet on a side, but no more than twenty feet high, he estimated.

When they got to the entrance, their escort halted. Anhur walked up to what appeared to be guards and conversed quietly with them for several moments. Eventually one of the guards came over to Voden and Kao-Shir.

The man's appearance made Voden shiver. His face was slack and lifeless, the skin a grayish black rather than the rich, shiny ebony of the other Svartalfar. The eyes were even more disturbing. They were flat and lusterless, devoid of all emotion. They seemed somehow sightless.

The guard took two strips of black cloth from a pouch that hung from his belt. Anhur said, "You must be blindfolded before you can enter Mesektet, the palace of Khamuas. If you could see, the demons and spirits that guard the way to its center would blast your soul through your eyes and drag you to Tuat, the Realm of the Dead."

"Ahhh," said Kao-Shir, obviously pleased. "I was right. Tuat is the same Niflheim and Ti-yu! Tuat, hmm," he mused. "Tuat. What an interesting language. Notice, Voden, they speak the Common Tongue but sprinkle it with strange words that seem to be from another language."

"This 'other' language, outlander, is the True Tongue of the Svartalfar," Anhur informed them as the guard tied their blindfolds in place. "It is far more ancient than the Common Tongue, or even the Elder Tongue. We brought it with us from the southern part of Muspellheim. It was our language long before the cursed Dark Empire enslaved us. We have never forgotten it."

"A good policy," Kao-Shir nodded. "Is it possible for mere outlanders to learn more of this True Tongue?"

"None have ever been found to be smart enough," Anhur snorted derisively.

"Hmm," the old man responded thoughtfully.

Voden felt two cold, clammy hands take hold of his arms and begin to move him toward the entranceway of the Mesektet palace of the Kheri Heb Khamuas. A hollow, emotionless voice came from his right. "Do not pay attention to sounds you hear. Do not answer if your name is called. And do not try to look. It would be your doom. There are many demons here, serpent-monsters like Seba."

"Or creatures like Serqit, with her claws and deadly tail," added another dull, lifeless voice on his left.

Voden could tell when they entered the building. The warmth of the sun was suddenly cut off and a damp cold slammed down around them. He shivered. For a few moments he tried to keep track of the way they were walking. As the twists and turns mounted, however, he became confused and gave up.

Finally they came to a place where the guards stopped and stood motionless. Voden could feel a strange tension in the air, and thought he detected the slightly metallic smell of snake. Straining his ears, he managed to catch a slight, distant slithering sound. Gradually it grew louder and louder until it filled the air. The hair on the back of his neck rose, and despite himself, he began to quake with fear. He knew the thing was approaching and that from the sheer volume of the noise it made as it moved, it had to be monstrous.

The guard on Voden's right began to chant softly. "Eder edesen edergeh edesen, unites merem edesen, unites emey edesen." He repeated it four times, his voice singsong and gentle. Then the guard on the left began to chant, "Protection behind, Protection that comes, Protection!" Three more times he spoke the words as the slithering grew and then began to move in front of them. Voden realized they must be standing near the crossing of two corridors and that the creature making the noise was passing before them along the intersecting corridor. Softly, beneath his breath, he begged Fornjot for aid.

After what seemed like an eternity, the slithering sound receded and Voden realized the creature had gone by without seeing or sensing them. He heaved a sigh of relief and moved forward quite readily when the guards tugged at his arms.

The twisting and turning became more complex than ever. Voden lost all sense of direction and of time. The trip to the center of Mesektet seemed eternal. He began to feel drowsy.

With a start, he jerked awake. Must have dozed for a second, he thought, feeling the hands of the guards still on his arms. Must have dropped off as I was walking. Strange dream, he remembered blearily. Thought I heard . . .

He heard it again. A soft, low, throaty voice whispering his name close to his ear. "Voden," it said, "Voden, come to me. I want you. I need you."

Voden almost stopped dead in his tracks. He knew that voice, knew the lust and desire that filled it. It was Freyja! Freyja as she had been when the two of them had been drugged on the mandragora so long ago! She wanted him, needed him!

"Yes, oh yes, Voden! I'm wet and aching for you! My body needs your thrusting love! Ahhh, I burn for you! Put out my fire, lover! Come to me! Come! Take off your blindfold and see my body! My naked breasts need your lips on them! Come, lover! Come, Voden! Take me!"

The Aesir began to struggle with the guards. Freyja was there! Freyja wanted him! And, oh gods, how he wanted her! But the guards were incredibly strong. Tug and pull as he might, Voden was unable to break their hold on his arms, unable even to lift his hands to rip off the blindfold so he could feast his eyes on Freyja's body. He wailed and cursed, twisted and jerked. The guards' grip never loosened. And their voices never stopped chanting.

Exhausted, panting and shaking, Voden heard Freyja's voice fade into the distance. He wept bitterly, damning the guards, the Svartalfar, Khamuas, Fornjot, and anyone else he could think of.

Gradually his mind began to clear. The words the guards had whispered to him as they had entered the palace came back to him. "Do not pay attention to sounds you hear. Do not answer if your name is called. And do not try to look. It would be your doom." Then he remembered what Anhur had said about the way to the center of Mesektet being guarded by demons and spirits that could blast the soul through the eyes.

Was that what had happened to him? Had it been a demon pretending to be Freyja? Had it twisted his mind in some way to make him love her once more? Freyja had never loved him! It had merely been the mandragora! Damn! he cursed, I've put all that behind me! I broke the power of Eir's drug and of Freyja! I'm free of them now! The Vanir, the Disir, Fiorgynn, Freyja, none of them control me any longer. I am Voden Vafudar, the Wanderer!

It sounded hollow even in his own ears. He wept again, this time for himself.

• • •

Eventually he felt the sudden return of warmth and realized he once again stood in the light of the sun. The guard on his right reached up and removed the blindfold. For a few moments the bright light dazzled his eyes. Then, slowly, his vision cleared and he gazed around.

He found himself in a square courtyard perhaps a hundred feet on a side. The walls that surrounded the yard were decorated with a profusion of colorful pictures. As he gazed at them in wonder, he began to realize they formed some sort of sequence, that they seemed to tell a story. He saw armies in the clash of battle, led by huge striding warriors. He saw long chains of captives, lashed and driven into slavery. Here and there what could only be gods and demons tortured or aided dark-skinned men and women. Off to one side he saw a scene of fire and devastation. Following it was another of a multitude of people wandering across burning deserts and towering mountains. He looked at Kao-Shir, who had joined him on the left, and saw that the old man from the Sunrise Empire was as impressed and fascinated as he was.

Their eyes turned toward center of the courtyard. There stood a small building, no more than twenty-five feet on a side. It had a flat roof held aloft by numerous columns. Just inside the first row of columns a wall rose to cut off any view of the interior.

Then a door opened in the wall and a short figure dressed in a plain white robe came out of it and approached them across the open courtyard. As the man drew nearer, Voden was startled to see he seemed to be not much more than a young boy with smooth skin and large, soft, shining black eyes. He had simple, straight features, and surprisingly full lips.

The boy appeared more a little man when he stopped in front of them, and with a gesture dismissed the guards. Then he turned a dazzling smile at them, spread his arms in welcome, and said, "I am Khamuas, at your service."

Voden was too stunned to say anything. Kao-Shir nodded pleasantly and replied, "Ah, yes. I'm Kao-Shir and this is Voden. We are both at your disposal."

"I know," Khamuas said with a boyish grin. Turning to Voden, he nodded. "So this is Voden, the desecrator of holy places. And obviously a Hekau, a magician of no small merit, since he survived the demon that lurks in the mound." He tilted his head to one side the way a bird does when it is looking at something. "Not a likely looking Hekau, and an even less likely looking desecrator."

"I . . . I didn't realize it was holy ground, Kheri Heb. I—"

"Nonsense. You clearly have the Galdar-power. You reek of magic. There is no way you couldn't have felt the character of that place. Why, all I have to do is look at you with my second sight and—" Suddenly Khamuas stopped speaking. His hand flew to his mouth and his eyes started in astonishment. His face became ashen and he stepped back a pace. "You . . . you . . . wolves walk with you. And ravens lead the way. You . . . you . . . no! It cannot be!"

He took another step back, then sank to his knees. Taking a handful of dust from the floor of the courtyard, he poured it over his head and wailed. "No! Nooo! It cannot be, it cannot!"

Finally he stood and looked beseechingly at Voden and Kao-Shir. "Can't you just disappear? Evaporate? Aren't you nothing but bad dreams come to trouble an old man? Please just go poof! and vanish." When they simply stood there gawking at him, he sighed and muttered, "I knew it was terrible luck when I saw that damn mouse on the twelfth day of the first winter month. Damn! It always is!" He stepped up to Voden and ordered, "Hold out your hands, young man! And keep those wolves at bay. I especially don't trust that big gray one!"

As Khamuas looked at his outstretched hands, Voden asked, "You see wolves following me?" The Kheri Heb nodded and muttered, "Of course. Anyone with second sight can. A big gray and a black."

"Yes," the Aesir nodded in confusion. "Geri and Freki. And the ravens are Hugin and Munin. But I didn't know anybody else could see them. I mean, no one ever has and—"

"What happened to this finger?" Khamuas demanded, holding up Voden's left hand. "'Where is it?" he asked, his voice cracking slightly, as if he were afraid of the answer.

Kao-Shir reached into his pouch and pulled out the silk-wrapped bundle. "Here it is. A demon's trapped in it."

"Oh, by the balls of black Hap, that caps it!" the distraught Kheri Heb cried. "By the beak of Nekhbet, by the tooth-filled snout of Sebek, the fate that has hounded us ever since we left the land of Hepr is upon us!" He threw himself to the ground and heaped more dust over his head as he wailed and thrashed his feet about.

Stunned, not knowing what to say or do, Kao-Shir and Voden stood with open mouths and watched the antics of Khamuas, the Chief Priest-Magician of the Svartalfar.

Suddenly the little man stopped and stood up. His face was calm again as he dusted off his robe. It was no longer white. "Damn," he muttered as he looked down at it. "Have to get it washed again." He looked up. "I only have two white ones to greet guests with. Don't wear them often because we get very few guests in Ro-Setau.

"I imagine," he sighed, "you wonder what has upset me so. Yes, I can see you wonder. It would be a wonder if you didn't wonder. Damn that stupid mouse! Never, never, never will I see a mouse on the twelfth day of the first winter month again! Dreadfully bad luck!

"Ah, well. What upsets me so, to continue, is that you, young man," he pointed to Voden, "are in all likelihood the Upuatu, the Opener of the Ways. Don't bother to deny it. You wouldn't know if you were. At least not on any level one as inexperienced in magic as you obviously are could reach. That rotten little mouse! I should have known something like this would happen!

"For eons beyond counting, ever since we had to leave the land of Hepr, the mighty river that rises at Silsilah from the lakes known as Uadj-ura and Maat, we have been expecting, indeed eagerly awaiting the prophesied arrival of the Upuatu. His coming means that those whose Ba has survived the journey to the Paradise of Aalu will once again take possession of their bones, that flesh will cover them, and that they will walk among us.

"At least, that's one way of interpreting it. The other way is that the coming of the Upuatu means the end of the world and that all the living will join the dead, either in Tuat or in Aalu. Many eons ago I believed the first version, but as time has worn on, I fear the second seems more likely."

He sighed deeply. "Aiiie, aiiieee. Yes, once I believed the first version. That was when we were still captive in Muspellheim, slaves to the Seven Sons. When the First Dark Empire fell, I was sure it presaged the imminent appearance of the Upuatu. The Ways would be opened, the dead walk again, and the Svartalfar would become a great and powerful people. No one and no thing would be able to stop us. We would simply turn southward and go back to the land of Hepr. Once more we would live on the banks of the sacred river and our lives would be wonderful.

"But it didn't happen that way. No, oh no. The demons came swarming from the Kur. They ravaged Muspellheim. We had to flee across endless deserts and towering, fire-crowned mountains. We had to flee for our very lives. Many died without benefit of the Field of Auf. Their bones lie scattered only the god Neith knows where. They cannot join us. Not ever."

He stopped talking for a moment, overcome by emotion. "Then," he began again, his voice still shaky, "we came here and found this hill. I knew at once it was Tatenen, the Primeval Mound, the first solid thing to form from the waters of Nun during the creation of the Universe.

"I commanded that my people build this mighty city here, a smaller copy of the great Khnum, which is eight times this size, which now probably lies in ruin next to the sacred Hepr. I still had hope then, hope the Upuatu would come and that his coming would mean the return to greatness for the Svartalfar.

"But that hope died centuries ago. I have studied the magic books: the *Hor-Dedef*, that tells how to call up and speak to the dead; the *Shabaka*, that tells of mighty magic and names the gods; the *Ami Tuat*, that reveals the meaning of all the hours of the night; even the *Shat-en-Sbaa*, that tells of the Gates on the Way. All of them, all, have I mastered. I have found much, but never have I found hope.

"For days on end I have prostrated myself before the seventy-seven gods of my people. I have made endless sacrifices to the Shetai, the Hidden Ones, the most powerful among the gods. Countless times, I have beseeched Neith to look on me with favor. And what has his response been? 'I am all that has been, that is, and that will be. No mortal has yet been able to lift the veil which covers me. There are secrets you cannot know.'" His shoulders slumped. "Yes, yes, Neith is right. I am eons old. Yet I am merely a mortal man. And there is no answer, no hope.

"And now you come, you with the wolves following you! You who enter the mouth of Tuat and contest with demons and win! You who enter and sleep in our holy place and leave unscathed! You, who without knowing it, without even caring, are the Upuatu and are destined to open the Ways and bring death and destruction upon the world and the Svartalfar! Oh, damn that mouse!"

Khamuas stopped and looked at both of them, his eyes bright with tears. "But, then," he said, "I suppose you're both hungry and tired after your long journey. I don't get too many guests here, you know. In the old days in the land of Hepr, my palace was always filled with guests. Ah. Come. It's hot out here in the sun. Let's go inside and have something to eat and drink. If the end of the world is coming, there's no sense in meeting it with a dry mouth and an empty belly!"

VII

Two servants brought trays of fruits, nuts, and dried meat. They were also given goblets filled with a clear, sparkling beverage that tasted somewhat bitter and astringent to the mouth but warmed the belly nicely and utterly banished thirst.

Once they had taken the edge off their hunger, Voden and Kao-Shir gazed about themselves in wonder. They were in the central room of the small building in the center of the courtyard. The room was unusual in that it had seven walls. On each wall were eleven painted figures. Some were bizarre monsters with human bodies and animal heads. Others were mixtures of several animals at once. A few were completely human. Every now and then a figure appeared draped in opaque robes which hid its shape and features from view.

Noticing their curiosity, Khamuas said, "Those are the seventy-seven gods of the Svartalfar. That first panel contains pictures of Nun, Khepera-Ra-Tum, Shu, Tefnut, Seb, Nut, Usire, Eset, Suti, Zehuti, and the veiled Neith. In the beginning there was nothing but Nun, just an endless watery waste, a primordial ocean that filled the entire universe. Everything was all mixed up in Nun. Nothing was separate.

"But then Seb, the solid earth, formed in the midst of Nun.

74

It happened right here at this hill, Tatenen, on which we built Ro-Setau. When Seb had separated out from Nun, Nut—the sky—likewise was born. And, to keep them apart, Shu, the wind, was formed. With Shu came Tefnut, the rain. Most glorious of all, though, was the creation of Khepera-Ra-Tum, the sun as it rises, at high noon, and as it falls into the west at night. From these as parents, the others were born, even the dread serpent of Tuat, Apep, and the master of the dark world, Seker, who dwells in his castle Ament and is guarded by nine powerful serpents."

He sighed deeply. "All that happened long ago. Or maybe it never happened at all. Things were simpler then, and the line between what was true and what you wanted to be true was much vaguer than it is in these degenerate times.

"I remember in the days when the Svartalfar were free and dwelt next to the sacred Hepr—"

"Just how old *are* you, Kheri Heb?" Kao-Shir interrupted.

"How old? It's been eons since I calculated. Let me see. . . . The First Dark Empire lasted, oh, about a hundred sars. That's, umm, thirty-six thousand years. It's been about five sars since it fell, which makes eighteen hundred more. We didn't fall slaves to the Dark Empire until about halfway through its history, say about, umm, twenty thousand years ago. Hmm. That makes me about twenty-five thousand years old, give or take a couple thousand.

"You look surprised? Well, I guess that is older than most. Though not older than some. I met a creature named Heimdall when I was a mere lad who claimed to be well over one hundred fifty thousand at that time. Said he'd seen the rise and fall of three previous worlds and was doomed to watch as six more were destroyed. Some sort of curse or something."

"How fascinating!" Kao-Shir responded. "This Heimdall must have been around when the San Miao became so wicked that Chu Jung was forced to destroy them! That must have been one of the worlds he saw fall."

Khamuas nodded. "Possibly. He claimed to have been there when Khepera-Ra-Tum became angry with the Svartalfar and sent out his Eye in the form of Hathor, that goddess right over there"—he pointed to one of the drawings—"to destroy us. The Eye threw down the city of Henshu, and all within it died, drowned in their own blood. Abu, built on an island in the Hepr, was washed away. Annu, mighty Annu, was leveled, all seven thousand of its temples blasted. Even Amit was devastated by the wrath of the Eye.

"Luckily Khepera-Ra-Tum relented and decided not to exterminate the entire race. He let the cowering remnants survive. For many sars we dwelt like wildmen, living amid the tumbled ruins of a greater world. Then slowly we rebuilt. Sadly enough, we didn't do so rapidly enough. The Sons of Muspell swept down on us while we were still too weak to resist. They marched us off north, away from the Hepr, to become their slaves."

"Why didn't you just return after the First Dark Empire fell?" Voden asked.

"Ah, we tried. Amid the flames and devastation we headed south, past Sippar, even to Larsa, which still stood, ruled by the wise Ziusudra who honored the Igigi. Full of compassion for our plight, he gave us aid and succor, provided us a place to rest a while, helped heal our wounds, then provisioned us and sent us on our way.

"But the whole continent of Muspellheim had been ravaged by the wrath of the demons from Kur. Mountains had risen where before plains had stretched to the horizons. Seas had come crashing across the land. And in the south, between where we stood and the sacred Hepr, stretched a vast, dense jungle filled with bottomless pools of quicksand and the deadliest beasts any man has ever beheld. Many of us died there, poisoned, rended, drowned, eaten alive. We failed. We had to turn back and make the trek northward once more.

"The short of it is that we ended up here. Now we wait for the fall of another world, for it is written in the *Shat-en-Sbaa*, the Book of Gates, that the Upuatu shall come to open the Ways and that the demons will come from Tuat once more and destroy the world." His voice rose in excitement. "Yes! Horrid Seker will march at the head of his monsters! Apep will writhe beside him, the mighty serpent that would crush the world! All the Uamentiu serpents will slither forth to spew their deadly poison! Arat, Aqebi, Septhra, Abth, Sethu, Bata, Saititemuit, Rerek, Nehaher, Bata, all, all will come!" In his excitement he stood and waved his arms, his eyes wild with fear. Spittle flew from his lips and his whole body trembled. "See! Here comes Seba of the twelve heads! Serqit with her deadly tail! Sebja, both serpent and leopard! Nau, Kanut, Nehebkau, those shadows that devour! Ah, ah, and Sekher-Remu that feeds on those too weak to struggle!

"But amid the horror there is a promise! The Svartalfar shall be united! The living and the dead shall be one!"

He plopped down next to them once more, as calm as if nothing had happened. "That's what it says. I'd show it to you, but you couldn't read it.

"By the way, that's what the Field of Auf is all about. We take our dead and expose them there. When the flesh rots off and the Ba is free to find its way to Aalu, we take the bones and put them in jars in that building you saw over to the far side of the field. The Ka stays with the bones. It's a kind of spiritual essence that never dies. It stays with the bones, and then when the Ba returns, it can find the right bones by finding the Ka, which is its mirror image. Yes, yes, that whole big building is filled with nothing but bones. Floor on floor of bones. Millions of them! Billions! The bones of every Svartalfar that has died since we left the Hepr and became slaves!"

He paused and mused silently for a moment. "At least that's one way to read the *Shat-en-Sbaa*. As I think I mentioned earlier, in the last few thousand years I've been wondering if things are as simple as I used to think. Could it be, I wonder, that what is really meant is that the living will join the dead? I mean that the living will all die instead of the dead coming back to life? Maybe once the Ba is gone, it's gone for good. Maybe the *Shat-en-Sbaa* simply points to the eventual extinction of the Svartalfar. Seems to me that's every bit as likely an interpretation."

He sighed deeply once more. "Now you can fully appreciate why I was so upset to see you, young man. You're the Upuatu, and no doubt about it. Brrr. Those two wolves that follow you everywhere give me the creeps! Are you positive you have them under control? They don't look very friendly."

Suddenly he brightened up. "Of course, at least soon I'll know which interpretation of the *Shat-en-Sbaa* is right. We've had quite a controversy over it in the Ennead. All nine of us disagree! Can you imagine that! Nine different interpretations! Teta, the old fool, thinks the Upuatu will open the way for us to go back to the Hepr and there join our dead ancestors! Ha! And that nitwit Djadjamankh thinks it means we will all become free-floating Ba and just drift around the world in one happy family! Such silliness! Hertataf is a bit more sensible. But Imhetep, Sa-Asar, Hor, Nekht-Neb-E, and Ubaner... well, the less said about their nonsense the better! I got so disgusted with the whole lot of them that I haven't met with the Ennead for about six hundred years now! But soon I'll have to. Must tell them all about this. Ha! Soon they'll see I've been right all along. That's one good thing about this. Yes, indeed.

"Now as to your fate, young man, well, that's in the hands of the gods. But Pethe—that's the god of revenge, you know, right over there—wants justice because of the sacrilege done to our holy spot. It's especially holy to Zehuti, the god of magic, there on that first wall, since it's a burial place for the Hekau, our magicians. Inferior ones, I'll grant you. None lived more than a couple hundred years. But still, something must be done.

"Your Sa-Ankh must be very powerful. That's what we call your magical life essence. That thing in the mound was after it, you know. Yes, your Sa-Ankh must be very powerful for you to beat it."

He cocked his head to one side and peered at Kao-Shir. "You say you have the demon captive? Let me see it again, eh?"

Carefully, Kao-Shir took the finger from the pouch and unwrapped it. It moved slightly as he set it on the floor between Khamuas and himself. The Kheri Heb carefully poked it with his own finger. "Demon all right. And caught in your finger by its own ring! Ha! That's a pretty trick if I've ever seen one."

Khamuas fixed his bright eyes on Voden. "So, your penalty is to give me that finger. I'll have use for that particular demon, oh yes. That will satisfy Zehuti at least. As for Pethe ... Ah, I have it! Pethe is good friends with Sekhmet, that one over there with the lion's head. Sekhmet, as you can probably tell by the way she's armed, is our goddess of war and battle. So, a simple combat to the death will make her happy and thereby pacify Pethe!"

Voden stared. "*Simple* combat to the death?"

"Yes, yes," Khamuas nodded eagerly. "That will clear things up nicely."

"Uh, whose death?" Voden asked.

"Whomever's," the Kheri Heb shrugged. "Doesn't much matter to Sekhmet or Pethe."

"It matters to *me*! Besides, if I die, then what happens to the prophecy? What happens to the Upuatu and the opening of the Ways?"

Khamuas shrugged again. "I've been wrong before. If you're the Opener of the Ways, you won't die. If you aren't, well, then that damn mouse meant bad luck for you instead of me. At least there's that to be thankful for!"

Kao-Shir, who had been silently taking the whole thing in, decided to speak. "Excuse me, Uert-Hekeu, but isn't there a problem here you haven't considered?"

"What? A problem? Could be, could be. What do you think?"

"Well," the old man from the Sunrise Empire began, "should Voden die in combat, who would be left to control his wolves?"

The Kheri Heb paled and looked nervously behind the Aesir. "Umm. Yes. Dear me, I hadn't thought of that. Umm. Don't like the look of the gray one at all. Has a nasty sneer. And that black looks hungry all the time. Mean, both of them. Yes, you're right, of course. Uh, do you have any suggestions? I mean, we can't let Pethe remain angry. Oh, no."

Kao-Shir appeared to think deeply for a moment. "Hmm," he began, "I have a half-formed idea that perhaps the Uert-Hekeu can help me work out.

"Now let's see. Zehuti is satisfied with Voden's finger. And Pethe will be avenged if Sekhmet, his friend, is pleased. Is that correct? Good. Well, wouldn't Sekhmet, as a friend of Pethe, be even more satisfied if a friend of Voden's fought the duel to the death? Sort of a friend-for-a-friend deal?"

The Kheri Heb had brightened visibly. "Why . . . why, yes! Why that is a wonderful solution! Let one of Voden's friends fight the duel for him! Then if that friend dies, Voden can still control the wolves! Wonderful! The only problem is, which one of Voden's friends will fight for him? Did he bring some with him? Why wasn't I informed of this? Are there guests I haven't seen? This is most upsetting!"

Kao-Shir smiled and raised his hand. "I refer to my most unworthy self, Oh mighty Kheri Heb."

Khamuas gawked at him. "You? You will fight a duel to

the death on behalf of Voden? But . . . you're an old man!"

"Old? Why I'm a mere two hundred eighty-seven! A youngster when compared to one of such august years as yourself!"

"True," Khamuas said smugly. "But then, I'm a great magician and you're not. Two hundred eighty-seven is quite respectable for an ordinary mortal. Well, if you're up for it, I imagine I can find someone to fight you. Yes." He rose. "Stay right here. I'll only be a minute arranging it."

When the leader of the Svartalfar had left the room, Voden turned to Kao-Shir and burst out, "Are you crazy? Why—"

The old man held up his hand to halt the Aesir. "Voden, I know what I'm doing. You forget that I trained for many years with the Warrior Monks of Kara Khitai."

"But—"

"But nothing. I owe it to Vestla. And to you. If I hadn't dallied in getting here, none of this might have happened. It's somewhat my fault, so the solution is somewhat mine too. Besides, think of all I'll learn about their fighting style!"

Khamuas reentered the room with a huge grin on his face. "It's set! Anhur, the very captain who captured you and brought you here, will be honored to fight with you! Oh, this will be such fun! I haven't seen a duel to the death in over two thousand years! I can hardly wait! Come, let's go to the entrance to the maze and await the arrival of the guards."

They left the building and crossed the courtyard to the opening in the outside wall where they had entered. While they waited, Kao-Shir asked, "Why must we use the guards? Surely you know the way yourself."

"Oh, I did, once a long time ago. I built this whole thing, you know. The maze is a miniature replica of the twelve divisions of Tuat. Monsters and all! Charming. But it's been a long time since I built it, and I fear I've probably forgotten a few of the turnings. And there are the seventy-five chants that must be given in exactly the right place at the right time, or before you know it, a demon's got you. Nasty things, demons. Lots of teeth and claws and fangs.

"Besides, even *I* have to go blindfolded so the demons won't steal my soul through my eyes."

"But how can the guards do it?" Voden asked.

"Oh, they have no souls. They're the soul-dead, those without a Ba. They have no Ran, no True Name. No Khaybet, no Khu. Only the Ka inhabits their bodies and animates them. Demons would still destroy them, of course, for the fun of it. But with the seventy-five chants and no souls, they are nearly invisible. Now and again one is taken, but in general they do well."

"Are they born that way?" Voden wondered.

"Oh, my, no," Khamuas answered. "No, I make them that way. That is how I stay so young, you see, by eating the Ba of others."

Voden and Kao-Shir exchanged a look and dropped the subject. The guards arrived after a while and blindfolded all three of them. Once more they plunged into the cold depths of the maze.

A great number of people awaited them on the other side. Anhur stood in their midst, ribbons in his dark hair, white paint smeared in stripes around his body and left arm. His legs were colored with red. His only piece of clothing was a black loincloth held in place by a golden cord.

"Ah," the Kheri Heb said when he saw the man, "you must be our champion, Anhur, beloved of Sekhmet." The man bowed low and murmured that he was honored. "True," Khamuas replied haughtily, "so true. Well, let's get on with it. Let's have the battle in the Great Square. Lead on."

With Anhur at their head, followed by the Kheri Heb, Voden, and Kao-Shir, the crowd passed behind the Mesektet palace of Khamuas, down a broad avenue, until they reached a large square surrounded by low stone buildings. There even more Svartalfar were waiting, crowded on the rooftops to gain a good view.

Anhur went to the center of the square, where several men were marking lines on the pavement. He came up to Kao-Shir and asked what weapon the old man wished to use. Kao-Shir gripped his staff at both ends and twisted. The staff came apart in the middle to form two short sticks, bound in iron, each about thirty inches long. He swirled them about in intricate circles and replied with a smile, "I choose the sticks."

Anhur looked quizzically at him. "I have never seen this weapon. Think carefully old man. I will fight with the short spear of my people. It is razor sharp and can cut you from head to toe in one slice. Would you fight it with mere sticks?"

Kao-Shir nodded. "I'll go easy on you, Anhur, old boy. Don't worry. I'll let you look good." The Svartalfar gave him a baffled stare, then shrugged and walked to the opposite end of the seven-sided figure that had been marked on the pavement of the Great Square. It was perhaps twenty-five feet across.

Khamuas stood in the center and watched the preparations. The Kheri Heb was obviously enjoying himself immensely, waving to people in the crowd, shouting out the names of those he recognized. Voden hovered next to Kao-Shir as the old man stretched his muscles slowly and carefully. "Are you sure of this, Kao-Shir? I mean, isn't there any other way out?"

"Not that I can think of," the old man said. "Any suggestions? No, I thought not. Not worried about me are you? Hmm. Well, not very flattering, but quite nice." He straightened up and looked at the Aesir youth, his face serious. "Voden, in all honesty you wouldn't last two minutes with Anhur. That short spear fighting is something I've seen before. Nothing in your training has prepared you for it.

"I, on the other hand, know it and have fought against what is probably a very similar style. Now have patience and a little faith and we'll soon be on our way again."

Seeing that both contestants were ready, the Kheri Heb motioned for silence. He spoke into the quiet. "Kao-Shir fights Anhur to please Sekhmet to satisfy Pethe. The blood of one must flow. Let the one that holds or retreats or shows any cowardice be judged harshly by Djadjau, the weigher of hearts in the great fire-roofed hall in Tuat. Let Am-mit and the six-times-seven judges tear apart the one who yields and cries halt. Begin!"

Anhur and Kao-Shir moved toward the center of the seven-sided area and warily circled each other. The Svartalfar gave a few test thrusts and a slash, trying to feel his opponent out. The yellow-robed old man met and blocked them easily, knocking them aside.

"You are swift as a serpent, graybeard," Anhur said softly.

"And you," Kao-Shir grinned back. "But beware Anhur, this serpent has two heads."

Anhur leapt in lightly, aiming a thrust at Kao-Shir's face, then changing it into a slash for his hands as the old man raised his stick to block. Kao-Shir's second stick knocked the slash aside, and the one that had blocked gave Anhur a sharp rap on the knuckles. The Svartalfar stepped back, surprise on his face. "It will take more than that to defeat me, old one," he said.

"Come to me then dark one, for I have much, much more to give." Anhur stepped in again, thrusting toward Kao-Shir's stomach. The old man pivoted to the right and struck the short spear downward with one of his sticks while the other lashed out and struck the Svartalfar on the side of his head. Kao-Shir sprang back before Anhur could reply.

The dark man moved more cautiously now, and the crowd, which had been loud at the beginning, became utterly silent. Even Khamuas had ceased looking about and was intently watching the battle. Several more times Anhur jabbed or slashed, only to be met by Kao-Shir's swirling sticks. Every time, the old man smashed him in the head or slammed his knuckles. The Svartalfar felt dizzy and his hands were hurting badly.

Anhur decided it was time to do something drastic to bring this fight to a close before the old man managed to hurt his hands so badly he could no longer hold his spear. Without the weapon the man from the Sunrise Empire could simply beat him to death with his sticks. It was not a fate a Svartalfar warrior would relish.

The dark man circled warily, looking for an opening. Wherever he probed, though, the whirling sticks met and blocked him. He decided on a desperate move. Stepping swiftly to one side, he slashed at Kao-Shir's hands, cutting the left one across the knuckles. He whirled the butt of his spear around and knocked the left stick flying. With a grin of victory, he stepped in again and slashed from left to right, aiming at Kao-Shir's right hand.

The old man was smiling gently as he met the blow, his stick pointing toward the sky, slamming with bone-crushing force on the knuckles of Anhur's left hand. Moving in like a flash, he snaked his left arm around the inside of the Svartalfar's right arm, then around the outside, and twisted quickly. The man's spear described a downward arc and went flying off to the right, narrowly missing several people in the crowd. Kao-Shir gave the Svartalfar's arm a quick jerk and the man grunted with sudden pain. The stick in Kao-Shir's right hand came down twice on the back of Anhur's head, and with a flip Kao-Shir sent him flying to the left. He was unconscious when his body slammed into the crowd. "Two heads," the old man said calmly, looking at the blood ooze slowly from his slashed fingers. "You nicked one head and forgot the other, Anhur."

A dead silence held the crowd as Khamuas walked slowly over to Anhur. He drew a knife from his robe and grabbed the unconscious man by the hair, pulling his head back and exposing his neck. As the blade rose to slash, Kao-Shir threw his remaining stick, hitting the Kheri Heb's wrist and sending the knife spinning into the crowd.

"Enough," Kao-Shir called in a powerful, commanding voice that caused everyone in the square to hold their breath and stand stock still. "Sekhmet is satisfied. She has my blood. There is no need to shed any other. Pethe is revenged."

"But," Khamuas whined, rubbing his aching wrist, "Anhur has been dishonored. He must die. It's all that's left for him. Besides, I could use his Ba."

Anhur groaned and stirred. His eyes opened and looked up into those of the Kheri Heb, who still held him by the hair. Then the Svartalfar warrior looked over at Kao-Shir. The old man smiled at him. "Well, if Anhur wants to, he can come with us. He's a damn fine fighter. No one has nicked me in a good hundred years. I'd like to learn more about this Svartalfar way of fighting. What do you say, Voden?"

The Aesir nodded. "If he'll join us, we'll have him."

"Oh, damn," Khamuas said with disgust, "that's part of the stupid prophecy too! Oh, how I hate that mouse! Take him then," he muttered as he let go of Anhur's hair. "Take him and good riddance to the lot of you!"

With that the Kheri Heb of the Svartalfar stormed out of the Great Square in a towering huff.

VIII

THE three travelers were silent as they headed northwest. Anhur, slightly favoring his badly wrenched right arm, led the way with the sure swiftness of one born and bred in the forest. He knew every path by heart, no matter how faint and narrow the trace might be. Voden felt confident the man was even familiar with the runs the little black mice made across the forest floor. He didn't have much time to think about it though, for Anhur moved swiftly, as if glad to get away for Ro-Setau and the Kheri Heb. It was all the young Aesir could do to keep up.

As the fading light announced the coming of night, Anhur stopped near a rock outcropping and indicated with a gesture that Voden and Kao-Shir were to go around to the left. They moved in the direction he'd indicated, and the dark man faded into the dusk, going back along the trail they'd just traveled to see if they were being followed. About five hundred feet along the rock face they discovered a small opening. Kao-Shir crept in, lit one of his strange fires, and after checking out the cave, motioned for Voden to follow.

The cave was much larger than Voden expected. It was a good fifteen feet to the domelike ceiling, and the chamber was perhaps twenty-five feet in diameter. Along the back wall was a collection of sealed jars, chests, and various other items, including a bundle of spears, all neatly arranged. Kao-Shir had started a fire in the middle of the chamber at a spot where scorch marks and charred wood indicated other fires had been built in the past.

It was a half hour before Anhur suddenly appeared at the entrance to the cave. He came in, surveyed the scene, and immediately went to one of the sealed jars. He opened it, reached inside, and came back with a packet. Squatting down next to the fire, he opened the packet. Inside were dried vegetables, some grainlike substance, and what appeared to be strips of dried meat. Kao-Shir produced his tripod and pot. Going to another jar, the Svartalfar returned with a gourd of water. The water and all the other ingredients went into the pot and soon a delicious-smelling stew was merrily simmering away. Voden realized how hungry he was. By Fornjot, he thought, I haven't eaten a thing all day!

For a while the three of them sat in silence, gazing into the fire and watching the stew bubble. Without any preamble Anhur began to speak, his voice soft at first, but gradually growing in strength as he told his tale.

"Long, long ago, many, many sars in the past, before the First Dark Empire had fallen on the land of Hepr and carried the Svartalfar off into slavery, there was a wise and kind Kheri Heb who ruled the entire length of the sacred river Hepr, from its origin in the two lakes Uadj-Ura and Maat at Silsilah, to its vast delta. His name was Osiris and he was loved by all the Svartalfar. He kept the magicians of the Ennead under control and only allowed them to conjur in ways that helped the people. All our people were happy then, and every Ba found its way to Aalu.

"But, of course, as good men will, Osiris had enemies. One of the most powerful and dangerous was his own brother, Sutekh. Ah, Sutekh, born prematurely on the third day between the time when the old year has died and the new is not yet come to be! It was a terrible, stormy day, and he was brought into the world too soon, with unfinished white skin and half-baked red hair! Only evil men loved Sutekh, but, alas, there are always plenty of those about!

"Well, as Osiris grew older and older, Sutekh began to press him and plead with him to turn over the reins of rule.

'You are aged,' he said, 'incapable of vigorous leadership. It is time for a younger man to take over and bring our people back to their former glory. You have no heir. The double crown of the Kheri Heb should fall to me!'

"Osiris knew the character of his brother, and yet he loved him well and true. He realized that a good deal of what Sutekh said was true. Enemies that had long been mere primitive tribes dwelling tentatively along our borders were becoming stronger and more aggressive. There was much a younger leader could accomplish.

"Osiris also had a sister, the lovely lady Anqet. She was as popular with the people as the Kheri Heb, and had always been at odds with her brother Sutekh. When she heard what Sutekh was saying, she went at night to Osiris and pleaded with him not to yield to their brother. 'He is the very spirit of evil,' she said. 'Do not allow him to rule, for he will enslave the people and allow the magicians of the Ennead to do what they wish!'

"Osiris heard her, a frown on his noble brow. 'But Sutekh is right, sister,' he said. 'I am growing old, and I have no son to succeed me. He is the next in line. Perhaps it would be best to abdicate now and let him wear the double crown of the Kheri Heb. Then at least I would be around to watch him.'

"Anqet sat and thought deeply for a while. Then a gleam came to her eye and she stood and began to dance for her brother. Ah, how the lady Anqet could dance! Her swaying hips heated the blood of her aging brother. Her waving arms aroused him. Her dainty feet moved so sweetly he was carried away with desire. And her hands, weaving, stroking, oh, they brought him to a boil! In a passion he took her, and as often a candle burns brightest just before it gutters out, his seed spurted hot and fertile into her womb and she conceived a child.

"Knowing the danger she had placed herself and the unborn one in, she fled and hid from Sutekh. Her evil brother was enraged when he heard what she had done, and sent men to find her. But she was well and truly hidden in a distant city called Khemmis, for she was mighty in magic.

"Sutekh frothed at the mouth. His white skin turned as red as his hair. In a fury he fell on his brother Osiris while he was resting in his palace in Nedyt and treacherously slew him. Then he cut the Kheri Heb's body into fourteen pieces and threw them out into the desert to be eaten by jackals.

"Even those nasty animals loved Osiris, however, and rather than eating him, they took the pieces of the dead man in their mouths and carried them to Anqet in Khemmis. When she saw what had happened to her brother, she wept and wept.

"The people wept with her. And groaned. For the yoke of cruelty that Sutekh fastened on their neck was heavy. He ruled from the very palace in Nedyt where he had slain Osiris. And as Anqet had foreseen, the red-haired monster allowed the magicians of the Ennead to do as they wished. Horror walked the land and no man nor woman was safe. Fear ruled along the banks of the sacred Hepr.

"Sutekh was Kheri Heb. His rule, though, would not be secure until he had found and killed the child that Anqet bore. He redoubled his efforts, but to no avail. All nature rose up against him to hide Anqet and her unborn child.

"In seven months the child was born. He was a beautiful, strong boy, with a sweet and loving smile on his face. Anqet called him Horus, the lofty one. A true son of Osiris, he was quiet and sparing of words, but kind and generous in all his actions. He grew swiftly, and within a year had gathered many followers. Among them were four mighty chieftains: Amset, Hapi, Tuamatef, and Kebhsnauf.

"With his followers and his mother, Horus left Khemmis and marched to Nedyt, to depose the monster Sutekh. With him, mounted on his forehead, he carried the eye of Osiris, for Anqet had magically kept the parts of her brother's body from rotting.

"A bitter and bloody battle followed. Many men died in agony, for magic as well as spears sped through the air and fell on all alike. Ah, the way to Tuat was crowded! The sacred Hepr was red with blood and filled with corpses.

"Horus and Sutekh met in personal combat. For hours they battled, flinging countless spears and spells against each other. Anqet rode next to her son in his chariot and used her magic to shield him. Sutekh had his closest supporters, the members of the Ennead, evil magicians like Atir-Atisau, Smauimatemu, Bathetet, and the vile Haari, ranged beside him to meet and repel the attacks of Horus. Yes, and Smuat-Tekaiu and Tauarhasa-Quina-Hama. Even Sennfet-Ta, so steeped in evil he cast no shadow, fought by Sutekh's side against Horus and Anqet. A mighty force against but two!

"Oh, how the battle raged and swirled around them! Finally, though, Horus and his allies began to gain the upper hand. Sutekh realized he was losing and fled in wild disarray. Many of his followers were slain, gashes in their cowardly backs! Ah, the evil Sutekh, his red hair flying out behind him, his white skin paler than ever—for fear he would be caught —fled northward. And finally escaped when Horus and Anqet turned aside to help the wounded and comfort the dying.

"Then a new age came to the Svartalfar! It was the time of the young Osiris returned! What joy there was along the Hepr!

"Like all happiness, it was short-lived. Sutekh went north and plotted with the Sons of Muspell. He told them that the Svartalfar were weak and badly wounded from the recent war. Sadly, he told the truth.

"The Sons of Muspell swept south. Alalgar of Nunki, Enmeenlu of Badtabira, Ensibzi of Larak, Enmeendur of Sippar, all of them, all, came marching down upon us. And behind them came thousands and thousands of warriors.

"Horus rallied the Svartalfar and met the Sons of Muspell in a battle that shook the heavens. Ah, the howling and screaming! The clash and roar! The sulfurous smell of magic and the dry dust rising high in to the air, so high as to darken the sun at noontime! For days it raged, to and fro.

"But Sutekh was right. We had been badly weakened by our battle to free ourselves from his rule. We fought hard and well, for we knew we were fighting for everything. We killed ten of them for every one of us that fell. But for every one we slew, a hundred more leapt to fill their place. One by one we fell, but we had no reserves. Yet we were determined to die to a man, defending our Kheri Heb and his mother.

"Then came the blow none of us expected. A great serpent-dragon appeared. It was the mighty Musirkeshda, and it grabbed Horus before any could defend him. His own magic was too strong for the hideous creature to defeat. It could only carry him away, and it did.

"With Horus went the heart of our army. We collapsed and were quickly defeated. The Sons of Muspell rounded us up, every man, woman, and child, and marched us north to serve as their slaves.

"They rewarded Sutekh by placing him over us as Kheri Heb of the slaves. So hated was he that he did not live long. He was slain, most gruesomely, by his own servants. Little good it did us, for we remained in chains.

"But there was one who was free! The lady Anqet had not been taken! Once again she had fled and hidden, no one knows where. To this day she is free. And to this day she searches the world over and under for her son and our rightful ruler, Horus. For know that he yet lives! He is chained and bound in some evil place by the magic of the First Dark Empire, but he lives! Some day Anqet will find him and set him free. Or he will free himself. Or some hero will come along and free him. Then the Svartalfar will—"

Anhur stopped and looked at both of his listeners. He smiled sheepishly. "It actually happened, you know. I was there, a leader of the Kheri Heb's own guard. I fought beside Horus and saw Musirkeshda swoop down and grab him. I helped the lady Anqet escape. That is why Khamuas hates me so. And also why until now he was never able to lift his hand against me."

"Who is Khamuas?" Kao-Shir asked.

"He is the son of Sutekh."

Kao-Shir nodded understanding. "Ah. And why was he so willing, even anxious, to get rid of us?"

Anhur nodded toward Voden. "Because he is afraid the young man here is the Upuatu."

"But why not just kill us?" Voden asked.

The Svartalfar smiled slowly. "He has not the power. He tried several times, though you were not even aware of it. He failed in the maze, he failed in his house in the courtyard, he failed in the combat. You are well protected, at least from *his* magic, young man. And your wolves frightened him badly. They have an evil look about them. He was very worried about what they would do if he harmed you."

"Anhur, how long were we in Khamuas's house?" Kao-Shir asked casually. Voden gave him a strange look.

"Ah," Anhur grinned at the old man, "you sensed it! You were there for about a year."

Voden looked from one to the other in astonishment. "A year? We were in the Kheri Heb's house in the courtyard for a year? Why . . . why it couldn't have been more than a few hours!"

Kao-Shir smiled at him gently. "Voden, look at Anhur's forearm. Do you see that scar there, on the left one? It wasn't there when he brought us to Ro-Setau. I'd wager he got it not long after we entered the maze. It looks about a year old. I saw it when we began our combat."

"Very good," Anhur nodded in approval. "I got it in a skirmish with some of Khamuas's men about a month after I delivered you to him. They tried to ambush me."

He turned to the young Aesir. "You see, Voden, if you are the Upuatu, Khamuas's time is limited. The prophecy says that you will find and free Horus and that he and Anqet will return and wrest the double crown of the Kheri Heb from the spawn of Sutekh. He knows that I, and many others, would aid Horus should he return. With me out of the way, Horus and Anqet would be that much weaker, and he might be able to upset the prophecy.

"At least that was his reasoning. There are times when I think his age and evilness have corroded his mind and he is not completely sane."

Kao-Shir chuckled. "So I noticed! He kept yelling about that damn mouse he saw."

"A very bad omen, that one," Anhur nodded. "Yes, seeing that mouse frightened him a great deal. A sensible, sane man would never react so strongly. But then Khamuas—"

"Am I . . . am I *really* the Upuatu?" Voden asked.

Anhur shrugged. "Who knows? Khamuas seemed to think so. But to be perfectly honest, I haven't the slightest idea. It would be a bit strange for the Upuatu to be someone who wasn't a Svartalfar, but I suppose that's no stranger than a lot of the things I've witnessed in the last several thousand years."

"Are you really that old?" Voden asked wonderingly.

The Svartalfar nodded. "Yes. And Khamuas is even older. He retains his youth by sucking dry the Ba of others. That's because he's evil, and it's the only way he can survive. I live on because the lady Anqet gave me that gift for the service I did Horus. And because both she and her son want me to march beside them when they return to battle the son of Sutekh."

Kao-Shir swept his arm to indicate the cave and its contents. "And this hideout?"

"Just that," the Svartalfar answered. "A hideout. Every now and then the Kheri Heb decides to kill me and I have to disappear for a while. This is where I come. Sooner or later it passes and I can go back to Ro-Setau."

"Will you do that this time?" the old man queried.

Anhur looked at him thoughtfully, then switched his gaze to Voden. He was silent for several minutes, as if carefully considering his answer.

"Well," he began, "perhaps not. I am intrigued by the idea that this Aesir might be the Upuatu. And equally intrigued by you, Yellow Robe. You fight damnably well for such an old man. I could learn much from you." He paused and looked at Voden again. "And perhaps even you have something to teach me, young man. You survived the thing in that mound and walked away free from Khamuas and Ro-Setau. Neither of those accomplishments is to be taken lightly. Yes, it might be far more interesting to tag along with the two of you. Certainly it would be more interesting than spending the next year or so in this cave!"

He paused for a moment, a dreamy look coming over his dark face. "And," he said slowly, "there is always the possibility that you *will* find and free lord Horus. I would give much to be there for that event!"

"We're flattered by your assessment of our abilities." Kao-Shir said with a mock bow of his head. "And though I can't speak for my young friend, I would be happy for your company."

They both turned to look at Voden. The young Aesir shrugged. "Oh, well, it's fine by me, I guess. I originally intended to travel alone, but, well, it doesn't seem to have worked out that way. There've been a couple of times when having someone to cover my back would have been helpful. Uh, do you think the stew is ready? It smells very good, and I'm a bit hungry."

"Spoken like a true philosopher!" Kao-Shir laughed. "Yes, it's ready! And I wager I'm as hungry as you are! We'll eat and then be on our way."

Anhur shook his head as Kao-Shir began to serve out the stew. "No, I don't think so. I checked back along our trail and there is a force of about thirty men following us. I rather imagine they hope to ambush us sometime tonight or tomorrow morning. There's a good spot a few hours from here. No, I think it would be wisest to lie low here for a couple of days. I covered our tracks when I came in. They won't find us."

"Good," Voden nodded. "I mean, the idea is good. The stew is, too, Kao-Shir."

After they had finished their meal, Anhur looked curiously at Kao-Shir and asked, "You look like a man from the Sunrise Empire, yet dress like one of the warrior monks from Kara Khitai. So far as I know, no man of either of those lands has ever walked these forests. Why are you here?"

Kao-Shir sat back and arranged his yellow robe comfortably around him. "Many years ago I lived in the Sunrise Empire and owned a fine palace. I was high in the government and had a beautiful wife, handsome children, servants, horses, chariots, robes, jewels—everything. Everything that makes the walls of a prison, that is. Ah, I was happy in my ignorance!

"Then one day a plague struck the province where I was governor. My wife and children died. The servants ran away. The neighboring governor took advantage of my distraction and spread lies about me at court. The Emperor gave him permission to invade my lands and make me prisoner. I was captured, tried, found guilty, and cast out penniless into the street to be jeered and laughed at by those who formerly sought my favors.

"Only one man, an old carpenter named Hung-Chun Tao-Jen, who had worked about my palace doing odd jobs, remained a friend. 'Li Erh,' he said, for he alone called me by the name I had chosen for myself, 'Li Erh, you are a lucky man! The Emperor has done you great good!'

"'How can this be?' I cried in dismay. 'Look at me, you old fool! I am ruined!'

"He laughed and smiled and nodded his head. He took me by the hand and bade me follow him. Having nothing else to do, and intrigued by what he had said, I followed. We walked out into the country until we came to a gnarled and twisted tree. He motioned to me and we sat side by side in its shade, for it was a hot day.

"'Observe this tree, Li Erh. It is the kind carpenters call a Stink Tree. Useless! The trunk and branches are so twisted and distorted and full of knots one can't cut a single straight board from them! And the wood doesn't even burn well! Useless!

"'Yet here it stands. And all around are the stumps of trees cut down in their prime to build palaces like your old one. Yes, twisted, gnarled, useless, here it stands and we sit in its shade on a hot summer day! No carpenter has its end in mind.

No ax is being sharpened to cut it. No charcoal burner casts an envious eye toward it. Useless! Someday it will die of old age.'

"I pondered his meaning. 'You mean I was too useful and was bound to be cut down?'

"Hung-Chun Tao-Jen nodded delightedly. 'Yes! Yes! You understand! I knew you would! Now hear this story and un-Jerstand even more. Once a prince went into the jungle to hunt. As he approached a huge old tree, all the monkeys but one fled. The prince, thinking to take sport with the stupid monkey took out his bow and shot an arrow at the creature. The monkey deftly dodged the arrow. Frustrated, the prince shot again. This time the monkey caught the arrow. Amazed at the cleverness of the monkey, the prince shot several more times, and every time the monkey baffled him. Enraged, the prince signaled to several of his hunters and they all shot at the creature at once, hitting it again and again and killing it.' He looked expectantly at me once more.

"I thought carefully. 'You're trying to tell me, old man, that I was too clever, too successful, and drew the aim of many archers to my own undoing.'

"'Exactly,' the old carpenter nodded. 'Your mind is sharper and your understanding greater than I had expected. It must be your long ears! Now one more tale. Once a tiger caught a fox and was about to eat him when the fox cried out that it would be unwise of the tiger to devour him. The tiger paused and asked how that could be. The fox told him that the gods had made the fox the leader of all the animals, and would be angered if the tiger would treat him so rudely as to eat him. The tiger scoffed and said that such a thing could not be true. Then, the fox told him, why not let me prove it to you? Let me go, and follow right behind to observe. And you will see how all the animals give way before me in respect. The tiger agreed, and followed right on the fox's heels. To his astonishment, the fox was correct! As soon as any animal saw the fox, it stepped aside and slunk away. Happy he had so narrowly missed angering the gods, the tiger let the fox go.

"'The fox was so proud of himself that he went boldly on his way. The other animals, remembering how the tiger had been right behind him, continued to give way for a while. But it wasn't long before the fox overplayed his trick, and in try-ing to bluff an elephant, was stepped on and squashed.'

"I nodded. 'The power I had was not my own, did not come from me, but was merely the borrowed trapping of the Emperor. But how can I get power for myself? How can I avoid being shot at by archers or stepped on by elephants in the future, old man?'

"'Be like the tree we sit beneath. Be useless rather than clever. Follow the Tao. Live quietly through non-action. Remember that the five colors blind a man's eye, the five notes make him deaf, the five tastes dull his palate. Yes, and if he gains goods hard to come by, he loses those still harder to gain. Be for the belly, not the eye.'

"'How can I learn to be like this?' I cried. 'It sounds very difficult!'

"'Ah,' he chortled with glee, 'what I say is easy to understand, yet no one understands it! It is easy to do, yet no one does it! It is easy to learn, yet no one learns it! If you seek learning, Li Erh, you must know more every day. More and more, always more! And always more to know! There is no end to it! But in the pursuit of what I teach, you must do less and less each day. Less and less, until you do nothing at all. And then when you do nothing at all, nothing is left undone!'"

Kao-Shir smiled at their mystified looks. "So he spoke, and at first it made as little sense to me as it does to you. But I did as he suggested. I spent several years with him at his home in Tzu-Hsiao Kung. He taught me carpentry and a great deal more. Finally he sent me away to live as a hermit in a cave on a nearby mountain. I lived there peacefully for many years, trying to apply what I had learned from Hung-Chun Tao-Jen. I tried to enter the Tao and do nothing but follow its flow. That way I accomplished everything."

Anhur shook his head. "Sounds like gibberish. How can doing nothing do something?"

"We build a wheel of thirty spokes around a hub," Kao-Shir said, "but it is because of the nothing at the center of the hub that the wheel can move the chariot. We make a vessel out of clay. It is the nothing inside the clay that makes the vessel useful. We cut doors and windows into the walls of a house. It is because of the nothing in those spaces that the house can be lived in. Nothing, then, is what makes something capable of acting and being useful. We must take advantage of the usefulness of nothing."

Anhur shook his head again in mild disgust, but Voden looked intently at the old man. "This Tao you speak of, Kao-Shir, my mother spoke of it often. Did you teach her about it?"

Kao-Shir smiled and nodded. "Indeed! And many others in the Floating World! Though she was by far my best student."

"Will you teach me?" Voden asked, a plea in his voice.

The old man hesitated. "Umm. Well, I don't know. There really isn't much to teach. Hmm. I could give it a try. But with your Galdar-power, Voden, I'm not too sure you can really . . . Hmm. Then again, learning the Way of Non-Action might be an aid to you in developing your power. Yes, yes, it might indeed. I'll have to think about it."

"In the meantime," Anhur said with a yawn as he rubbed his right arm and shoulder, "I for one would like to sleep. That's the kind of doing nothing I'm personally very good at!"

IX

THEY remained hiding in the cave for two weeks. Every morning Anhur went out and checked the surrounding area. Every afternoon he returned with the same news: there were still many search parties looking for them. "Khamuas must have had second thoughts about letting us go," Anhur said with a grim smile. "He'll give up soon enough, though. Don't worry. He can't keep his mind on anything for very long."

Voden found he badly needed the enforced rest. His struggle with the demon in the mound and his subsequent experiences in Ro-Setau had weakened him more than he'd realized. Once he began to eat and sleep sensibly, it seemed as if his body couldn't get enough. The truth of the matter was that he never noticed the powders Kao-Shir was putting in his portion of the stews the old man constantly prepared. The yellow-robed traveler was well aware how much the young Aesir needed rest to repair the strain on his mind and body. Kao-Shir understood that Voden's recent experiences had stirred up the Galdar-power within him and he needed time to allow it to settle once more. The old man knew that Voden was not mentally and spiritually strong enough yet to handle the full power he possessed. If it should break loose, it might well burn him out and destroy him.

During Voden's waking hours, Kao-Shir began to teach him the art of fighting with the staff. "Don't ask about the two sticks technique, Voden," he said, his voice gruff but his eyes sparkling with humor. "That's one I keep to myself. It's never a good idea to teach everything you know. Then you'd have nothing left to defend yourself with against your students."

Anhur often watched the training sessions and added some of his own fighting techniques with the short spear. By the end of the second week Voden was beginning to wonder if he had ever truly known how to fight. Either man could defeat him easily. Yet both praised his quick learning and rapidly improving skill.

"Perhaps in a year of so, you'll get it," Kao-Shir estimated with a slight smile.

Anhur shook his head and said, "Two years. Maybe three. Then you'll be formidable, lad. You'll know the weapons of your own people, the Vanir, the Svartalfar, and some of the techniques of the warrior-monks of Kara Khitai. Whew! A one-man army!"

Voden just groaned, felt the many aches and bruises on his body, and began to go through his drills once more.

One day Anhur didn't return from his morning's scouting trip until late in the afternoon. "I've been extra thorough today," he reported. "Cast a much wider search pattern. It's as I suspected. Khamuas has given up or forgotten about us."

"Neither," Kao-Shir replied gently. "He's just shifted his method of looking. I've been sensing probings from another realm. He has given up finding us by locating our bodies, but now he's sending spirits out to seek us. Things, I think, from the realm you Svartalfar call Tuat. I sense a serpent's nature in many of them."

Anhur turned ashen. "Those must be the four and seven serpents known as the Uamemtiu. They do indeed come from Tuat. Khamuas controls them with the spells he learned in the book of magic known as the *Ami Tuat*." He shuddered. "Unclean work for a Kheri Heb to engage in! Horus spent his time fighting such monsters, not making allies of them!" He looked at Kao-Shir. "Are we doomed, old man?"

Kao-Shir smiled and replied, "Doomed? No, hardly

doomed. In a bit of a bind, yes. But I've taken precautions. I've spit in the four directions. Ghosts and spirits hate human saliva, you know. And I've done a few other things I've picked up here and there in my wanderings." He pulled a small stone from his pouch and held it out. The head of a tiger was carved on it. "This is a Shih Kan-Tang. I have several. They're ward stones and offer protection against all sorts of evil influences. In addition, as further guard measures I've cast the Shen Tu and Yu Lei spells on both the cave entrance and the main approaches. Nevertheless, I don't think we should stay here much longer. Despite my efforts, if we remain in the same place for too long, the things that hunt us may be able to sniff us out. Best we get moving."

The Svartalfar sighed with relief. "Moving again. Yes. An excellent idea. The search parties are gone. We can leave at once. Let's just gather a few supplies and go! The farther we get from monsters like Rerek and Satitemuit, the better!"

Within the hour, despite the fact that it was already late afternoon, they were on their way. Anhur claimed to know a perfect spot to spend the night. It was beneath an overhanging rock and was easily defensible, being enclosed on two sides. He'd stocked it with firewood and water several months ago. Voden realized that the Svartalfar had many secret places set aside in case of emergency. The dark man had not lived so long by luck alone.

They arrived at their refuge about an hour after dark. There was a decided chill in the air. With surprise, Voden realized that fall must be approaching. Kao-Shir started a fire and fixed a stew for them, adding several powders from his pouch and accompanying his cooking with much muttering of strange phrases and a good deal of waving his hands in odd patterns. Both the old man and Anhur seemed nervous. Voden felt on edge himself.

He slept fitfully, noting, every time he awoke, that Kao-Shir sat near the fire, wide awake, staring out into the night. On one occasion he woke to smell the metallic odor he associated with snakes. It was extremely strong. He looked about. Both Kao-Shir and Anhur were standing just beyond the fire and peering into the darkness. The old man heard him move and turned with a slight smile. "Sleep, Aesir," he whispered. "We'll wake you if there's need." Reassured, Voden fell back into a fitful slumber.

He wasn't sure what hour of the night it was when he suddenly sat bolt upright, his mind ringing with the call that had woken him. As though he'd asked the time aloud, Anhur answered him. "It's the eighth hour of the twelve that comprise each night and mirror the divisions of Tuat, young Aesir. It is a dread hour, filled with serpents. We've already managed to get through the seventh hour, that in which Apep, the Great Serpent himself, holds sway. But this is the hour of the Uamemtiu, the four and seven who hunt us. We may have need of your help."

Kao-Shir's voice came from the other side of the fire. It sounded hollow and strained. "They come," he muttered. "Four and seven. Remember, Voden, you've already fought one demon and won. Your iron knife is of great potency. And your sword can slash demon flesh. Be ready. Join us here at the edge of the night. I can see their burning eyes. The four and seven come."

Feeling the hairs on the back of his neck rise, the young Aesir stood and went to join the other two. He unsheathed his sword and held it in his right hand. Then he drew the ancient iron knife his grandfather Buri had given him so many years ago. He hefted its weight, admiring once again its perfect balance. The blade held an edge well, and he kept it razor sharp. Sure of his weapon, he began to softly chant his Power Song.

The smell of serpent was even stronger, and Voden was certain he could detect a slithering sound coming from beyond the firelight. "Have they found us?" he asked Kao-Shir in a whisper.

"It would appear that they know we're in the area. They don't seem to have pinpointed our precise location," the old man answered. "I'm trying to shield us, but I'm not sure it will be enough. There are many of them."

"Four and seven," Anhur muttered, his voice strained. "One would be enough to make a brave man shake with dread. We must face the whole lot!"

"Shouldn't we douse the fire?" Voden asked.

"They aren't looking with their eyes, Aesir," Kao-Shir answered. "The light they seek comes from within. Once they find us, then they'll use their eyes. And we'll need the light to fight them by. I wouldn't want to meet four and seven serpent demons in the dark."

"I wouldn't want to meet them in the middle of the day," Voden admitted with a shudder. "I guess we'd best keep the fire then."

Anhur's sudden hiss of indrawn breath directed Voden's attention. "There," the Svartalfar said, pointing out into the night. Voden's eyes followed his outstretched arm. A pair of red eyes were glowing in the dark. Suddenly they were joined by another and another. A tension filled the air. It drew tighter and tighter, until Voden felt like screaming.

Without warning the tension broke and Kao-Shir let out a long sigh that was half a moan. "They're through," he said simply. "They've breached the shield. They come." He gave a wave toward the fire and it sprang up, pushing back the night to give view to what lay in the blackness.

A growl came from Anhur's throat as the first sinuous form came into view. "Ah, the hooded one, Arat! And there, Sethu. Ah, and now Rerek and Nehaker! That one that looks half leopard and half snake, that one is Sebja. Now Aqebi and Abth and Satitemuit slither up to join the others. Where are the other three? Where are Bata, Sethra, and Khepri?"

"Perhaps they had a previous engagement," Kao-Shir muttered. "Are you disappointed they didn't show up? We could always ask the other eight to wait for them."

"Are they going to attack?" Voden asked in a voice tight with fear.

"Oh, no," Kao-Shir replied. "They're just here to watch over us for the night. Bad things walk in the dark, you know, and—"

Before he could continue, Arat, the hooded one, struck out at Anhur. The Svartalfar, for all his fear, was ready and leapt to one side, slashing out with his spear. The serpent missed, but Anhur did not. The blade of his spear ripped a long gash in Arat's side. With a hiss of fury, the snake slid back behind the others.

Voden could still barely believe his eyes. Not one of the hideous serpents was less than twenty feet long. All had vicious fangs and glowing red eyes that held an evil intelligence. One in particular drew his attention, the one Anhur had named Sebja. The creature was half leopard, half serpent, and the halves kept shifting and blending into each other. It was repulsive and fascinating at the same time. See how smoothly it moved, flowing gently, softly toward him. See how it slid, now on speckled paws, now on speckled scales. See how it slithered—

Voden snapped his attention away from the thing's motion. It was too close! He jumped awkwardly back as it struck, narrowly missing his face. He went down and rolled, coming up, his sword ready, his mind focused on the demon as it struck again. He dodged to the left, then jabbed out with his sword as he rolled again. Bouncing to his feet, he faced the thing once more, noting with pleasure that his sword had gashed it on one flank. It leapt at him now, a roar on its cat face, fangs bared. Voden dropped beneath and stabbed upward with his sword, which struck deep in Sebja's gut. The monster gave a hideous bellow which was a combination of a cat's scream and a snake's hiss.

The monster twisted suddenly, all snake now except for its hind legs. Voden felt the sword jerked from his grasp. With a curse he sprang back, just in time to avoid the striking snake head, mouth agape, poison fangs reaching. He slashed down with his knife. The strike went true and the blade cut through the serpent's coils as though through butter. Sebja roared and hissed again, writhing and squirming in agony. The knife hurts the creature more than the sword, Voden realized suddenly. He struck out again and gashed the monster deeply.

Sebja became mostly leopard and spun about. Leaping away in great bounds, the demon retreated into the night. Voden looked around to see how his companions were doing. Anhur had just thrust a spear deep into the gaping maw of the hideous Rerek. Kao-Shir was smashing the skull of Satitemuit with a whirling blow from his staff. Arat lay on the ground, slashed and mangled. Bata was crawling weakly away. Abth was trying to open a mouth nailed shut by one of Anhur's spears. Voden could see several other of the four and seven retreating into the night beyond the fire.

Suddenly weak and sick, he retched and retched. Then his knees gave way and he sat down in a heap. Kao-Shir came to his side and looked down at him. "What?" the old man asked, his white eyebrows rising in wonder. "Are you quitting just when the party is getting interesting? Ah, well, it matters little. It seems our guests have had enough and are going home. But it was fun while it lasted, right Anhur?"

The Svartalfar was leaning wearily on one of his spears.

"You have a strange sense of humor, man of the Sunrise Empire. But you fight like Sekhmet herself, so I suppose it doesn't much matter."

"Will they be back?" Voden asked weakly.

"Not tonight," Kao-Shir responded. "And perhaps not for several more. They've wounds to lick, and even demons take time to recover from a beating the likes of which we gave them. But they'll be back, never fear that. Each of us has been marked by at least one of them. They've tasted our blood. They know us now and can find us much more easily than before."

"Marked," Voden muttered. "What do you mean, marked?"

The old man pointed, and Voden followed his gesture. His left pantleg was slashed into ribbons and red was seeping through. Gingerly he pulled the doeskin back and viewed his leg. Four gashes ran across it, oozing blood. It was the mark of a leopard's claws. Sebja had hit home at least once. Quickly he checked himself for other wounds. His right forearm had been lightly clawed.

"We all have something like that, Voden. We'll have to clean our wounds carefully. Demon's bites always fester. A bit of magic will help, too, of course, but a good cleaning is critical." Kao-Shir began to heat some water in his pot. While waiting for it to boil, he checked himself, Anhur, and Voden for any further injuries. "All in all," he said in cheerful summation, "we gave a lot worse than we took!"

"This time," Anhur commented gloomily. "Now they know us and how we fight. Next time we won't come off as well."

"That's why we must move as soon as our wounds are cleaned and bound. We must go this very night. From now on we travel at a much faster rate, Anhur. We need to put as much distance between ourselves and this place as possible. This is the spot they'll return to when they're healed. Let's make their search as long and as hard as we can!"

By dawn they'd covered a good deal of ground and all three were exhausted. Their wounds were beginning to ache, and strained muscles were beginning to stiffen. Kao-Shir only let them rest long enough to take some nourishment, then he drove them on again. The rest of the day passed in a dull blur for Voden. He barely realized it when they stopped for the night. In a daze he ate his stew and crumpled to the ground right where he sat, sleeping deeply until Kao-Shir shook him awake in the predawn darkness.

For two weeks Kao-Shir drove himself and his companions onward at a merciless pace. They traveled northwest, then north. At first, the trip was like a bad dream. Voden was so exhausted each night that he fell asleep before he could even talk to the other two. He rose in the morning in such a daze of weariness that the days were nothing more than an endless motion of putting one foot in front of the other and trying not to stumble too often.

After the first week, though, his tough young body began to adapt to the pace. He was still tired every evening, but he awoke refreshed and began to take notice of his surroundings. The forest seemed to be changing in some subtle way. He couldn't quite put a name to it, but they were leaving one area and coming to another.

Then one afternoon, about two and a half weeks after the attack by the Uamemtiu serpents, they suddenly came out of the forest and looked over a vast expanse of water. To the right and left it stretched on as far as the eye could see. Voden knew he was gazing at the Amsvartnir Sea.

Anhur gave a long sigh of gladness. "We are no longer in the lands of the Svartalfar. I have been feeling things change for some time. But this is proof. We are north of Svartalfheim, somewhere on the western shore of the Amsvartnir Sea. I have never seen it before. It is . . . incredible."

In companionable silence the three stood and feasted their eyes. Kao-Shir sniffed great lungfuls of air. "Sweet water. Incredible. I have seen and smelled the Sunrise Sea. And the Eastern Sea. But they are salt and smell of it. This is sweet, fresh water, drinkable, delightful. There is so much of it! Never have I seen anything like it! My trip to the West is justified by this sight alone!"

Voden gazed northward. "Somewhere up there," he said, his voice dreamy, "the shore bends back east and then southeast. On a point of land thrusting southward lies Mimir's Well. Groa went there and traded her eye for wisdom. My mother told me to go there as well. They were almost her last words. 'Look deep in Groa's other eye! Go to . . . go to . . .' Then she died. I knew what she meant. Groa's other eye is with Mimir at the well. She wanted me to go there to find . . ." He shook himself out of his dream and looked at Kao-Shir. "I'm not certain what she wanted me to find. But I decided I had to go."

"Yes, I know, Voden. Vestla was a deep woman, deeper than anyone knew. She was blessed, or some would say cursed, with the power Vidolf gives to a few so that they may look into the future. The price paid is great. The gods only know what it cost Vestla. You're right to heed her advice. It wasn't lightly given."

The old man looked at both his companions. "We have indeed left the land of the Svartalfar. The power of Tuat and its demons is weaker in this land. The four and seven of the Uamemtiu will find it a much more difficult task to locate us now. We no longer have to travel at such a pace."

Anhur nodded and grumbled, "Good thing too. Look about you. The leaves are already beginning to turn. We'd best prepare for the winter, for it comes, Uamemtiu or not. We need a secure cave, dried meat, nuts, berries, fruit . . . oh, many things. It really wouldn't do to escape the serpents and then die in the snow."

Kao-Shir laughed at the Svartalfar's dour expression. "Ah, Anhur, the winter is an easy enemy compared to the Uamemtiu!" .

"You won't be so quick to say that when you're up to your ass in snow, Yellow Robe," Anhur growled. "These western winters are something to behold. And I for one would rather behold it from within a nice warm, dry cave! Let's find one." He peered northward. "It looks to me like the land rises in that direction, and I almost think I can see some bluffs in the distance. Let's go there and look for a place. We don't have as much time as you might think! It could easily snow in another month!"

Anhur's estimate was off by two weeks. The first snow came a mere two weeks after they'd located a large and well-protected cave and begun to stock it. The snow didn't last for long, but the cold weather stayed and made them hurry their preparations for the coming season all the more. They laid away all the provisions they could, including a plentiful supply of firewood. Anhur was an expert at this business of stocking caves, so the other two followed his instructions.

They had another two weeks of cold but clear weather, and then winter struck with a vengeance. For two days the snow howled across the land, until it stood four feet deep in some places and drifted to seven or eight in others. A few more days of clear weather followed, and then the snow returned once more. When it left the second time, it was almost impossible to travel.

Voden was reminded of the winter so long ago when he'd been in Vanaheim. He was also reminded of an even more unpleasant winter. His dreams were haunted by images of men on plunging horses fleeing and pursuing each other through deep drifts. He had visions of faces exploding in gore as axes slammed into them. Once more he struggled through the snow, his right shoulder a bloody agony, held up by Geri and Freki. He woke from his dreams more tired than when he had lain down.

Kao-Shir watched him with care. He knew it was the natural reaction to the recent stress the young Aesir had gone through. The battle with the demon in the mound, the struggle with Kahmuas, the fight with the serpents from Tuat, all had drained Voden's Galdar-power. He'd been forced to call on powers far beyond his understanding and control. Now he was suffering the backlash of such use. The old man from the Sunrise Empire felt sure he'd recuperate swiftly.

He also knew that there was much to be accomplished this winter. In the spring Voden would head north again, toward his fate. Kao-Shir knew he'd have to go alone. The most the old man could do was help train him and be sure that he went stronger than ever. Voden's fate was a heavy one, and the young man would need great strength to carry it out. You haven't given me an easy task, Vestla, he said to himself. Ah, but then following the Tao was no easier for you than it is for me. He shrugged and smiled. I'll give the lad two more weeks to rest, and then it's back to work again. There's so much to learn and so little time!

DARK EMPIRE

X

THE slender, dark man knotted the cords together carefully, his brow furrowed in concentration. As his hands moved with slow precision, he muttered strange words under his breath. Finishing the joining of one, he picked up another and began to add it to the others.

From across the small room Jormungand watched with undisguised curiosity. What in the name of Namtaru was Surt up to now? For months the Black One had pored over the huge, musty tome of ancient magic, the *Utukki Limnuti*, which they'd rescued from the Ruins of Badtabira. One morning, without warning, he'd slammed it shut with a curse. For the next three days the slender man had sat unmoving, a terrible frown darkening his face. Then, equally without warning, he'd risen late one evening, and without so much as a word or glance, stalked from the room.

When Surt had returned the next morning he was carrying a large sack over his shoulder. He seemed pale and drawn, as if he'd been through some great ordeal. The Black One had thrown himself into bed without a word and had slept until that evening. Waking and taking a simple meal, the slender man had opened his sack and taken out yards and yards of a dull gray cord. For the last two days he'd been carefully and slowly knotting the cord together to make . . . Jormungand wasn't sure.

The huge warrior tore his eyes from Surt, laid back on his bed and stared at the ceiling. I won't ask him, he told himself. Even if it kills me, I won't ask him. He knows I want to know. He's dying to have me ask. He's being silent on purpose, playing with me the way a cat plays with a mouse. But I won't ask . . . I won't . . . I—

Jormungand sat up suddenly, slamming his feet onto the floor with a resounding thump. "All right, damn you, you win! What in Nergal's cursed name are you doing!?"

A hint of a smile passed quickly over Surt's dark features. When he raised his head to look at the warrior, however, his expression was blank and neutral. "Doing? I'm knotting cords together. What else?"

The warrior slapped his knee in irritation. "I know you're knotting cords together. I have eyes. I want to know *why* you're knotting cords together."

Surt held up the tangle of knotted cords. "I'm making a net. Surely you've seen nets before."

"A net? A net! What does a wizard want with a net? Are you going to become a fisherman?"

The slender man nodded solemnly. "In a sense, loyal Serpent, yes, I'm going to become a fisherman." Surt began to tie another knot, mumbling his strange words.

Jormungand glowered at his master. "I never get a straight answer from you. 'Making a net. Going to become a fisherman, loyal Serpent. But only in a sense.'" He paused. "I don't like that 'loyal Serpent' business, either. Whenever you're about to ask me to do something that no sensible person would even consider, you start calling me 'loyal Serpent' or 'brave Serpent'."

Surt looked up. "Do I really? Must watch that."

"Well, what is it this time? Must I slay Mushrussu with a fork? Attack Marduk's legions with a sharpened stick? Return to Badtabira to fetch a button that fell from your robe? Eh? What? Tell me. I'm dying to know. No, I take that back. *Dying* is a bad choice of words."

The Black One gazed intently at the huge warrior who sat across the room. After several moments he sighed and set down the tangle of cords. "Can't concentrate with all this racket anyway. Yes, faithful Serpent, I owe you an explanation, for indeed I *am* about to ask you for your aid once again."

He stood and began to pace energetically back and forth. "I gained a great deal of power when we rescued the *Utukki Limnuti* from its tomb beneath the Ruins of Badtabira. Seven sevens of demonic names it contains, along with the spells necessary to summon and command each demon." He looked triumphantly at Jormungand. "I've been able to send night demons to haunt the dreams of my old enemy Borr, to shatter his peace of mind and haunt his soul with dread and horror!" He shrugged. "An easy task, really. The man's not even properly warded. Easy, but worthwhile, for it prepares him for the true weight of my vengeance.

"Yes, faithful Serpent, I've gained great power! I'm almost the equal of Adad, the fool who reigns as Patesi of Maqam Nifl and Borsippa, and whom I intend to attack and defeat. Just one more trial, one more task to be completed, the most dangerous and glorious of all, and I'll be ready to challenge him!"

Jormungand held up his hand to halt the torrent of Surt's words. "One moment, faithless Black One," he said sarcastically. "Seems to me I've heard this lecture before. I remember a certain magical message that would give you the power you needed . . . *if* I would help you open it. And then there was a certain book of magic you had to have to get the power you needed . . . *if* I would go with you to Badtabira and find it. Now you talk of a new trial and a task, 'the most dangerous and glorious of all' is what I believe you said. Somehow I have the feeling I'm going to have to go along on this one too. I think you'd better tell me about it, Surt."

The slender man sighed and sat down. "All right. The power I gained from the *Utukki Limnute* is limited, rather badly, because I didn't do something else first. I can send night demons to befoul the dreams of an unwarded barbarian, but I can't begin to have the kind of control necessary to send them against someone like Adad."

In spite of himself, Jormungand was interested. "And what is this something you didn't do first?"

Surt gave him a long, measuring look and then sighed even more deeply. "It's not something that can be answered simply. It takes background. There's a great deal you'd have to know—" Jormungand's look stopped him short. "All right, all right. I'll start at the beginning."

He paused, collecting his thoughts. "Existence consists of three planes. The first, the one we live on, is the plane of gross materiality. Most of the things that inhabit this plane are simply and only material, like rocks and trees and animals. Man is the exception, for man has a spiritual dimension to his makeup. Man can transcend this lower plane and pierce the next higher one, the spiritual one.

"As this lower plane of existence consists of material things, so the next higher consists of immaterial things. Gods, demons, things of that sort."

"Huh?" Jormungund interrupted. "I thought the gods were above our world and the demons below it. You mean they're all on the same level?"

Surt frowned. "Above and below are common ways of explaining it, but they really don't have any meaning. The planes interpenetrate. Best just to realize that the spiritual plane is above ours in the sense that it is not material, but ethereal.

"Above the spiritual plane is a yet higher one. We have no name for it because it can't be limited by a name. Some call it the sacred, but that doesn't seem adequate to me, for sacred implies good, and that idea is too limiting. There are places where it's named the Utterly Other. Now and then a writer will simply leave a blank space on the page when he refers to it.

"In any case, whatever it's called, it transcends and comprehends the other two planes. Everything in them is a reflection of that higher plane. *It* is the only true reality.

"As I mentioned, Man, although of the lowest plane, has a spiritual element in his makeup which allows him to penetrate the next higher plane. Gods and demons have, as part of their makeup, the ability to penetrate the highest plane. Some men, those specially gifted and those of great skill, learning, and daring, are also able to penetrate that highest plane. In doing so, they partake directly in what is most real, that is, the sacred, the Utterly Other, or whatever you choose to call it.

"But I wander from my point. A magician seeks to comprehend all of existence within himself. By experiencing it all, by absorbing it into himself, by subjecting it to his will, he's able to command it and shape it to his desire.

"How is such a thing possible, you wonder? Existence is so vast, so varied. How could any individual being hope to encompass it all?"

Surt rose and began to pace again, his voice fast and excited, his movements quick and energetic. "Ah, but that diversity is illusory! Yes! As one of the greatest of wizards once wrote, 'That which is below is like that which is above, and that which is above is like that which is below.' For, you see, existence is all of a piece, all cut from the same cloth. The complexity of it is simply the failure to see that underneath the variety there is a unity, a unity which transcends and joins the diversity in oneness! Existence is one! Everything is simply a shadow of that highest level. *It* is the only reality and *it* is undifferentiated and singular. Neither this nor that, it is all.

"Everything in existence is a mirror of that highest level. Each of us is a microcosm that duplicates the macrocosm. Every aspect, every factor in a man corresponds directly to an aspect or a factor of the universe. We are a mirror to totality. The ordinary human being isn't aware of this. The magician is, and seeks to bring the microcosm within himself under control. Since the microcosm and the macrocosm are mirror images of each other, by learning to control the one, he gains the power necessary to control the other. He gains access to the higher levels of existence and hence more command over the things of the lower level.

"To gain access to the higher levels, the magician must first open a doorway to the spiritual level. Once he has done this, he can come in contact with the gods and demons of that level and learn to control them. A doorway to demonkind is known as a Bab-Apsi. One to godkind is called a Dur-An-Ki. The spells in the *Utukki Limnuti* have allowed me to open a Bab-Apsi of great power."

"But," Jormungand interrupted with a smile. "Now comes the important part, the qualifying *but*. This is where things always get more interesting."

Surt gave the giant warrior a sour look. "Yes. But. To truly achieve power over the forces of any level of existence, the magician must return to the origin of power, the point when and where existence began and power was first organized and used. Once he repeats this act of origination himself, taking it into himself, then, and only then, can he truly wield power."

"Fascinating. So what has all this to do with me? I don't

use my brain or my spirit to rule the world. I depend on this," he said, drawing his huge sword from its scabbard.

"I'll get to that. I told you it was complex. In fact, to return to the when and where of the origin of power, the magician has to leave this plane of existence and travel to another."

"Fine. A trip will do you good. You've been spending too much time slouched over that *Utukki Limnuti*," Jormungand said lightly. Then he stopped and gave Surt a hard look. "Unless, of course, you have to go back someplace like Badtabira."

"I only wish it was that easy. You see, to penetrate to another plane, we must die on this one. We must cross the man-devouring river Hubur. We must approach the first gate of Aralu and call to Neti. Then we must follow him through the seven gates, meet the gaze of Ereshkigal, and be hung on a stake."

Jormungand stared at Surt with wide, unbelieving eyes. "Did I hear you say something about 'we' going to Aralu?" The slender man nodded unhappily. "Have you taken total leave of your senses? By Namtaru, Surt, go to Aralu of your own free will? That's the most insane thing I've ever heard you say. And you've said some incredible things! Let Neti take us from gate to gate? Let Ereshkigal fix us with her eye and hang us from stakes? Mad! You're utterly mad!"

Surt held up his hand in protest. "Hardly mad. The only way you can go safely to Aralu is if you go voluntarily. And only then if you go on a certain kind of mission and are properly warded and prepared. You have to know, for example, that Nergal and Ereshkigal have secret names, and that if you speak those names you can command them once. You have to know—"

"Fine," the giant warrior said, "but why take me with you? You're perfectly capable of hanging on a stake all by yourself. I have no desire to return to Aralu any sooner than necessary. I've already crossed the Hubur once and stood in the dust before the first gate. You yourself pulled me back, Surt. There on the Vigrid Plain you dragged me from Aralu. Why return?"

"Or is there something more here, something you've forgotten to mention? You wouldn't need me unless there's something more."

The slender man looked down at the floor of the tiny room for a few moments, then looked up again. "Well, yes, there is something else. The trip to Aralu is only the first part of the journey. The easy part."

"The easy part? I can hardly wait to hear the rest," Jormungand replied sarcastically.

"Umm, yes, well. Just beyond Aralu is the Kur."

Jormungand stared at Surt in utter amazement. "The Kur? You intend to go to the Kur? To the realm of demons?"

"Not exactly. Umm, you see, we're going to the edge of the Kur, right up to Apsu, the Dreadful Abyss. To where Tiamat dwells."

The giant warrior was speechless. His mouth worked, trying to find and form words. For several moments nothing came out but a faint hissing. Then he stopped, swallowed, and said weakly, "To . . . to where Ti—Tiamat dwells? Tiamat and Mushrussu and Musirkeshda and . . . the rest of the eleven?"

Surt nodded, his own face looking drawn and pale.

"What . . . what do you intend to do there?"

"Battle and kill Tiamat èven as Marutukku did at the beginning of time. Thus will I reenact the origin of power and the ordering of existence."

Jormungand shook his head in awe. "You are totally mad! How in Nergal's rotten name will you defeat Tiamat? Mere magic won't work against the mightiest dragon of them all."

The slender man reached down and grabbed the net that lay on the floor. "Here! We'll use this net to snare the beast. Look at it closely, faithful Serpent. It's made of fourteen cords bound together with seven sevens of knots, each tied with great care and dire spells. See this cord? At first I thought to make the net from loeding, for it's incredibly strong. Luckily I realized Tiamat is far stronger. Then I decided to use dromi, which is twice as strong as loeding. But Tiamat would burst that too. So I settled on this. It's called gleipnir and is woven from the noise a cat makes when it moves, the beard of a maid, the roots of a mountain, the sinews of a bear, the breath of a fish, the spittle of a bird, and . . . ah, but I dare not even utter that last ingredient. It's mighty, Serpent, so strong, even Tiamat will struggle within it in vain."

The giant warrior took the net in his hands and tested its strength. He pulled and tugged, his muscles bulging from his exertions. Finally satisfied that it was perhaps possibly as strong as Surt claimed, he looked at the slender man and asked, "And once you have Tiamat enmeshed in your net, what will you do to kill her? You're not strong enough to send a sword through her scaly hide, Black One."

Surt smiled confidently. "I've made a bow and decreed it our weapon. I've fixed the arrowhead to the shaft. We'll hang the bow and quiver at our side. We'll grasp the club in our right hand. We'll set the lightning before us and fill our body with flame.

"But most important of all," he continued, his voice dropping to a confidential whisper, "I've summoned the storm demon, the evil wind, Imhulla, to give us aid. And Abubu, the mighty rain flood. More than this I cannot say, Serpent, for words have a way of reaching Tiamat's ears."

"What . . . what's my role in all this, Surt?"

The slender man's eyes were gleaming with an eerie light. His voice was deep, and almost seemed to be coming from somewhere beneath the earth. "You're a mighty warrior, Serpent. I'm a wizard. Apart, we are no match for Tiamat. But together . . ."

"Together?" It had become very dark in the room, and Jormungand had to strain to see Surt.

"Aye, together. We go to face Tiamat as one being. A single creature with your might and my magic! We'll blend, leaving our mortal bodies here behind, blend into a new being of such power even Tiamat will be unable to withstand us!"

"When . . . when are we going?" Jormungand mumbled, fear and dread clutching his heart with greedy fingers. The blackness that gathered in the room was palpable now, and the giant warrior could feel it pressing against him.

Surt laughed wildly. "We're already on our way, loyal Serpent! That last knot I tied was the final one! The net is complete, the bow and arrows are ready, the club is to hand, Imhulla and Abubu are summoned, the lightning is set before us, and we are filled with fire! We stand in the very center of the Bab-Apsi I've created, the doorway to the nether world! We go now!"

The darkness roared and crashed down over Jormungand's head, obliterating him and sweeping him away.

He stood facing an endless wall. There was a door directly in front of him. Behind, he heard the vicious snarl of a mighty river. He didn't need to be told that it was the Hubur, or that *its* rushing waters were the red-black color of clotted blood.

He also knew what the wall meant. He held his hand up to rub his eyes, hoping it would all fade away. It wasn't his hand! He stepped back staring at the strange hand, and cursed out loud in a voice he'd never heard.

Easy, brave Serpent, said a voice he recognized. He looked quickly around and he realized it had come from within his own head!

Surt? he asked wordlessly. *Is that you?*

Yes. This body we are in is the one I told you about. We share it. May I suggest that you let me do the talking while we are here in Aralu? You can do the moving and the fighting. Now let's see, we need to name this body. Ah, I have it! We'll call ourselves Kudram.

How does the body seem to you, Jormungand? I tried to pick one that would suit you, one that would fight well for you.

Jormungand moved the body's arms and legs, stretched and twisted, took the club that hung from the right side of the body's belt and gave a few practice swings. *Not bad,* he grudgingly admitted. *Strong, quick, obviously a trained warrior. So we're Kudram, eh? All right, then, let's go. I take it that's Aralu over there and that that's the first gate.*

Correct, Surt acknowledged. *The wall is made of lapis lazuli. The gate is called Ganzir and is the face of Aralu. Neti waits behind it. We must knock to gain admittance.*

Done, Jormungand said, and strode forward across the dusty waste until he stood before the gate. Raising a fist, he slammed it into the gate again and again, the thunder of his pounding shaking the very air around them.

The gate opened a crack and a hideous face peered through the opening. Jormungand caught sight of a small creature with a lion's head, human hands, and the feet of a bird. Its body was covered with darkly gleaming scales. "Eh? What's this?" it asked grumpily. "Who're you? What do you want? Eh? Speak up?"

"I am Kudram and I seek admittance to Aralu," the huge warrior roared. "Open Ganzir, the face of Aralu, and let me in."

Neti, the gatekeeper looked nonplussed. "Eh, eh? You *want* to come in?" He opened the gate wider and looked the warrior up and down. "You're not weeping and wailing, not gnashing your teeth or rending your flesh. Eh? What is this?"

Kudram roared with laughter. "Of course not, fool Neti! I want to come in! Now open wide and take me to Ereshkigal!"

Shaking his head and muttering beneath his breath, Neti opened the gate Ganzir wide. As Kudram stepped inside, Neti closed the gate with a resounding thud. "Now," the little gate-keeper said officiously, "whether you come in of your own free will or not, the rules are still the rules. Take off your warrior's helm. You must leave it here."

"What, pray, is this?" Kudram said in anger.

Neti instantly grew in size until he towered over the warrior. His hideous visage was filled with power and malice. His lips curled back and his fangs were bared in a snarl. "The decrees of the nether world have been perfected. Do not question the rites of the nether world!"

Do as he says, Surt urged. *He has great power. And don't worry. I've accounted for all of this.*

Jormungand mumbled as Kudram took off his helm and handed it to Neti. The gatekeeper, once again his normal size, hummed tunelessly and placed the helm on a shelf filled with a multitude of other headgear. Jormungand saw crowns of the type called shugarra; merchant's caps; the strange, conical headgear worn by the urigalla priests; and many others.

Neti led the way to the second gate, opened it, let them through and then closed it firmly behind them. Again he turned to Kudram and held out his hand. "You must leave your club here." Jormungand grudgingly forced Kudram to hand it over. Surt chuckled and said, *The decrees of the nether world have been perfected. Do not question the rites of the nether word. You're learning, brave Serpent, you're learning.*

I just hope I'm not going to regret listening to you later, Surt, Jormungand replied as they approached the third gate. *By the time we get through all seven gates, there's not going to be much left.*

There'll be nothing left, to be precise, Surt declared. *We'll stand before Ereshkigal as naked as the day we were born.*

Oh, splendid! And how are we going to fight her and Nergal, then?

With our wits, loyal Serpent! With our wits!

Of course, Jormungand grumbled in reply. *I wish I was as confident as you are.*

Neti led them through the seven gates of Aralu, one after

the other. At every gate he took something else from them. At the seventh and final gate he stripped them of their clothes. Kudram stood naked. "In there," Neti said, pointing the way. "Ereshkigal and Nergal wait. You're lucky. Lord Nergal is here this time of the year."

Kudram entered a vast area. In the middle were two gigantic thrones of bloodred rock. On the right-hand one sat Ereshkigal, the queen of Aralu. Jormungand found that he was unable to keep her figure in focus. One moment she seemed beautiful, with dark skin, huge liquid eyes, flowing midnight hair. The next she melted into a hideous corpse, half rotten, with bone showing through where flesh hung loose in great, fetid strips.

The presence on the left-hand throne was altogether impossible to look at directly. It seemed an area of intense blackness, a void that sucked up and swallowed all light and life. It gave off an aura of evil so strong that even looking at it from the corners of one's eyes made the mind reel and the stomach heave. Jormungand knew it was Nergal, lord of hosts, king of Aralu.

Around the thrones, stretching off as far as the eye could see, were stakes, each with a corpse hanging from it. Some were fresh. Others were in the last stages of decomposition.

Kudram strode forward to place himself in front of the thrones. *Remember*, Surt said, *let me do the talking*.

No problem, Jormungand replied. *I don't have a thing I want to say to either of those two*.

Ereshkigal turned her baleful eyes on them and spoke, her voice like a scream echoing in an endless cavern. "Who is this that comes before the king and queen of Aralu? Who is this that comes through the seven gates to stand in our presence?"

"I am Kudram," Surt replied. "I have come here willingly."

"Yet you came," Ereshkigal said. "Now I will fix you with my eye of death and you will become a corpse and be hung on a stake."

Kudram held up a massive hand. "Hold thy eye, Allatu." He turned to face the darkness on the other throne. "Hold thy glare, Meslamtaea. By the knowing of thy True Names, I command thee to obey me and do my will."

Ereshkigal hissed in anger and drew back. Nergal laughed, the sound so evil it made Jormungand's mind turn cold with fear. "Thou knowest my secret name, my True Name, the name Ninlil gave unto me when he created me. I am bound to do thy bidding once.

"But know, Kudram, or whatever your True Name might be, that you are in Aralu. You must pay the price of being here. Before I can follow your command, you must die. You must hang on the stake for three days and three nights. Then the kurgarru and the kalaturru will come and direct the fear of the rays of fire on you. Sixty times the kurgarru will sprinkle the food of life on you. Sixty times the kalaturru will sprinkle the water of life on you. Then you will rise and we will do your bidding."

The darkness reached forth and took Kudram in its icy grip. There was no chance for struggle. A searing pain crashed through the giant body, and Jormungand and Surt cried out together as the stake skewered them.

Three days and three nights later they stood once again before the thrones of Ereshkigal and Nergal. The queen of Aralu looked at them sternly and asked what Kudram wished. "I beg leave to pass in safety through the Kur, to the very edge where it adjoins Apsu, the Dreadful Abyss. There I will seek combat with the mighty dragon, Tiamat."

There was a long silence as the king and queen of Aralu digested this request. "So," Nergal said at last, "as I thought. Kudram is not your True Name. You have our leave to go. You may pass back through the seven gates. As you go, you may take back those things Neti took from you as you entered. You may pass in safety through the Kur, even to its very edge where it borders Apsu, the Dreadful Abyss. What passes there between Tiamat and you is your own affair. But should you fail to defeat her, you will once more enter Aralu. And this time you will not leave."

Kudram bowed low to Ereshkigal and Nergal, then turned on his heel and strode off. At the first gate he regained his clothes, and at each succeeding gate the thing he had left there, until at last he stood once more before Ganzir. "You'll be back," Neti said as he closed the gate. "Sooner or later, you'll be back." Jormungand turned the giant body around and made an obscene gesture at the gatekeeper. The little creature slammed Ganzir shut in reply.

• • •

The less said about their journey through the Kur, the better. Demons of all sorts approached and taunted them. They saw sights that were beyond description, that the mere mention of would blast a man's soul for all eternity.

Eventually they approached the edge of the Kur where it met Apsu, the Dreadful Abyss. On one side was a dusty land of pain and horror, on the other an emptiness so utter, it chilled the mind and shriveled the soul.

There, between the two, in a vast cave, dwelt Tiamat and her brood of eleven monsters. Kudram unfolded the net and held it in his left hand. He took the club from his belt and held it in his right hand. Thus prepared, he strode to the mouth of the cave and cried out in a great voice, "Tiamat, old dragon, toothless one, slime lizard, fangless serpent, salty fish, come out and fight! Come, creature of chaos! Come fight Kudram!"

I hope you know what you're doing, Jormungand mumbled as they heard an answering roar come from the cavern's mouth. Before Surt could reply, Taimat slithered and crawled her bulk from the cavern.

Both of them were appalled at the vastness of the primeval chaos dragon. It spread from horizon to horizon. There was no way to focus on it, no way to keep it all in view. In any case, it was impossible to look on for long. It changed constantly, shifting shape, each succeeding one more hideous and frightening than the last. Kudram lowered his eyes in dismay.

Surt began to chant softly, his words alien and frightening. "Enuma elish la nabu shamdmu shaplish ammatum shuma la zakrat," he began. Immediately a huge wind arose behind him and began to trouble Tiamat. The dragon reared back and roared at it. Then Jormungand heard the word Abubu repeated again and again in the chant, and suddenly a raging torrent crashed down from the sky and slammed into the dragon, driving it back and making it bellow in even greater rage.

Kudram advanced on Tiamat now, his club raised, his net ready. The monster struck out at him, but the warrior was quicker, and slammed his club into the beast's head, crushing it to pulp. Immediately another head grew and struck again. Once more the warrior countered, and the club destroyed the second head. Again and again the dragon attacked. Again and again Kudram met the attack and triumphed.

Taimat went into a frenzy and became like one who had lost all reason. The dragon cried out loudly and violently, shaking the whole nether world with her rage. She shook and quivered to her very roots, and the universe shook with her. It was all Kudram could do to keep his footing on the heaving ground.

Once more the winds and Abubu, the storm flood, struck at Tiamat. The beast lurched to the attack again. But this time the club was knocked from Kudram's grip by the force of the monster's attack.

For an instant the giant warrior stood defenseless and dismayed before the awesome might of the dragon. *The net!* Surt screamed. *Use the net!*

Jormungand came out of his daze and raised Kudram's left arm, casting the net at the monster. The net spread out and enmeshed Tiamat. Bellowing, the dragon thrashed mightily about, but true to Surt's prediction, was unable to tear the mighty cords of gleipnir.

In a sudden rush, Tiamat charged at them, her vast mouth open to devour them. Surt cried out one word in a mighty voice, "Imhulla!" A great wind arose, one that made all the earlier ones seem mere breezes. It raged and roared and drove straight into Taimat's maw, so that the dragon could not close its mouth. The raging wind filled her belly, distending it, forcing her mouth open even wider.

Now, Surt cried, *use the bow, brave Serpent! Shoot arrows into her mouth!*

Jormungand snatched the bow from his side and pulled an arrow from the quiver. He set the arrow to the string and used every ounce of strength in Kudram's mighty muscles to draw it back behind his ear. He let the shaft fly straight for the dragon's gaping mouth. No sooner had the first arrow left the bow than he was nocking a second. A third and a fourth followed in rapid succession. One after the other they sped through the air and into Tiamat's maw.

The shafts struck true, tearing at her interior, cutting through her inner parts, splitting her heart in two. With a bellow of anguish that shattered the stars in heaven, Tiamat thrashed about in wild death throes. Kudram grasped the net with all his might, keeping it closed so as to contain the dying but still deadly dragon.

Kudram hung on for what seemed like an eternity, his muscles straining, his frame nearly pulled apart by the twisting of the great dragon as she died. Slowly, though, the monster became calm as death settled over all her limbs.

Groaning, Kudram stood slowly upright. His whole frame ached. Great gouges covered his body where the monster's claws had raked him during her death struggles. He tottered weakly, barely able to keep his feet. Exhaustion swept over him in towering waves, threatening to overwhelm him at any moment.

It is done. Tiamat has been met and defeated. Surt's voice was weak and without energy. It echoed hollowly with a fatigue as great as that Jormungand felt. *We can return now. We can take Kudram back to Aralu and return to our own bodies. I am ready now to face Adad.*

Jormungand groaned. *I suppose I'm going to have to go along on that one, too, Surt?*

The Black One failed to answer. But it really wasn't necessary, for the giant warrior already knew what his master would say.

YU-LAN HUI

XI

HE circled carefully, placing each foot precisely before trusting his weight to it. His eyes never once left the spot just below his opponent's throat. Looking there, he could see any shift of weight, any body or arm movement, as soon as it began. Even if it was just a feint, he would know it was coming and see when it changed.

His opponent was shorter than he was and very swift. Voden knew the man could attack as swiftly as a snake could strike, the razor-sharp head of his spear flicking in to stab and slash almost faster than the eye could follow. The only way he could avoid being slowly cut to ribbons was by attacking and forcing the other man to defend. Even then, his opponent's quick slashes were crippling and deadly.

Voden feinted to the left with his spear, then dropped the tip and thrust. The other man blocked and countered, stepping to the right. Using the momentum of the block, Voden swept his spear point up and slashed at the man's head.

Rather than backing up, the opponent stepped in, his body swaying low over his leg, weaving in toward the young Aesir. Before Voden could retreat, the butt of the man's spear struck him at the point where his leg joined his hip. The man pushed,

127

and Voden felt himself buckle slightly. He tried to bring the butt of his own spear down on the back of his opponent's neck but found himself slightly off balance.

Before he could regain his balance, his opponent slipped the butt of his spear behind Voden's leg and hooked it behind his knee. Then he wove his body back out and up, pulling up on the spear at the same time. The young Aesir's leg flew out from under him and he sprawled backward. As he hit the ground he tried to roll, but the other man's spear slammed into the floor of the cave, right next to his head.

"Dead, Voden," Anhur said with a chuckle in his voice. "That technique is called 'weave in, weave out.' Very effective, don't you think?"

Voden grunted agreement as he stood, brushing himself off and catching his breath. He turned to Kao-Shir. "Anything else?"

"Well, yes, there is," the old man replied, a twinkle in his eye. "You did two wrong things. First, you accepted Anhur's rhythm rather than either imposing yours on him or following the flow of the Tao. Second, you were too brave in your strategy."

"Too brave? What do you mean, too brave?"

Kao-Shir scratched his head and looked down at the ground. "My first teacher, Hung-Chun Tao-Jen, was a master of the bamboo staff. From him I learned the art of Huo-Pu Chang, Shortening Your Opponent's Life. The key to this art is contained in the saying, 'One who is fearless in being brave will shorten his life, but one who is fearless in being timid will shorten his opponent's life.' This 'fearlessness in being timid' consists in following the Tao. The Tao excels in overcoming, though it does not strive; in responding, though it utters no word; in attracting, though it does not beckon; in laying plans, though it appears thoughtless."

Anhur snorted derisively. "Old man, how can anyone follow instructions like those? They make no sense! Best to teach him something he can use, like 'weave in, weave out'!"

Kao-Shir laughed. "Once a farmer saw a rabbit dash into a tree trunk that stood all alone in the middle of one of his fields. The poor creature hit the stump so hard it broke its neck and died. Joyously, the farmer picked it up and carried it home. His wife made a wonderful stew of it. The next day the farmer went back into the field and sat waiting for another rabbit to bash into the stump. He did the same the following day and the next. Every day he sat and waited for another rabbit, neglecting his chores. Eventually his farm failed and his family was forced into poverty."

The Svartalfar laughed. "Ah, old Yellow Robe, you've got a tale for every purpose! I suppose the point of that one is that what works once may not work again? Ha! I thought as much! Then why not just teach Voden several techniques? Why not a hundred? One is bound to work!"

"Would the farmer have been a wise man if there had been a hundred stumps in the field?" Kao-Shir asked slyly.

Anhur threw his hands up in defeat. "I give up! You riddle around so much you make my head hurt! And yet you yourself teach the lad to fight with the staff as you were taught by that Hung-Chun fellow. If techniques are no good, why do you teach them to him?"

"So that he can forget them. The mastery of techniques is only for the purpose of teaching the body and the mind how to move properly. Once that is learned, one must unlearn it."

The Svartalfar rolled his eyes and muttered, "'Learn so you can unlearn.' And what is that supposed to mean?"

"Once the great king Tai Hao had a butcher who was a master at cutting up an ox. Every move of his body, every slice and cut, was like a dance. The ox literally fell apart at his feet. The king was so impressed by his technique, that he asked him how he did it.

"The butcher thought for a second, scratched his head, and said, 'Sire, I have no technique. Oh, I admit that I have studied the art of butchery. When I began, all I could see was a huge ox lying there before me. I had to get a new chopper every month back then! But as I learned the techniques of cutting and slicing, I began to see the whole ox as a collection of parts. I learned to use this cut to cut here, that slice to slice there. Since I could picture the parts in my mind, I could hack and slash until I had them in fact. At that time I needed a new chopper once a year.

"'Now I see neither whole oxen nor parts. I don't see with my eyes at all. Rather, I sense with my whole being. As I cut, I follow what is there, switching from this cut to that slice without thought, as the situation demands. What good is a technique that doesn't fit the situation? Change, flow, move with what is there, not with what you have studied. There are spaces between the joints. Those spaces are wider than my thin blade. When the thinness finds the space, there is all the room needed. The chopper moves like the breeze. When a hard place is reached, I do not struggle with it, hacking and straining. I slow down, hold back, barely moving the blade. I watch, I sense, and thump! suddenly I am through and the pieces fall apart. Since I have begun cutting this way, I have had the same chopper for nineteen years and it is as sharp as new!'

"That," Kao-Shir continued, "is what I mean by forgetting technique. You learn it, then forget it and simply let it flow without thinking. As I said before, in pursuit of learning, even in the learning of the staff or spear, one tries to know more and more each day. But eventually one must reach the point where he learns less and does less every day. When one knows and does nothing at all, then anything can be accomplished."

Anhur groaned in exasperation. "All this talk about doing something by doing nothing is giving me a headache!"

"Well, it isn't exactly doing nothing, Anhur. What I mean is, not doing anything unnecessary or contrary to the Tao. Most importantly, I mean not doing anything aggressive or hostile. Tai Hao's butcher, for example, never tried to force his cutting. He simply acted with whatever circumstance he found himself in. The use of unnecessary force simply creates a countervailing force, a reaction. If no force is applied, no reaction takes place, no opposition is created. I call that kind of doing nothing Wu Wei, Inaction. As Hung-Chun Tao-Jen used to say, 'Nothing in the world is softer or more yielding than water. Yet when it attacks hard and strong things, they cannot stand against it.'"

"Old man, it's true that water can wear away the hardest stone. But, by Sekhmet's mane, it takes eons! If someone's coming at you with a sword, you don't have eons!"

"No, but you want to meet his attack as *if* you were water. Absorb it, yield to it, blunt it by being soft. If you meet it like a rock, then it will be like two rocks smashing together. The harder will simply break the softer."

The Svartalfar warrior considered. "Well, there's something to be said for that, though it's not an easy thing to do. Human nature is to react and strike back with force matching force. How do you change that nature, eh?"

"You must give up all desire, even that of wishing to win

or to lose. You must return to the original simplicity of your nature before the five colors blinded your eyes, the five sounds deafened your ears, the five tastes spoiled your palate. You must be like the Uncarved Block."

Anhur shook his head. "There you go again! Now you want Voden to act like a block!"

Kao-Shir chuckled. "Not quite. All I mean is that if he strives to learn thousands of techniques, he might not learn the exact one needed to parry a particular attack. He may know millions, but the lack of that one defeats him. By having so many, they simply get in his way. If instead he learns a few and then forgets them and follows the flow of the Tao, he will adapt like water to any attack and defeat it. By being unformed, like water or the Uncarved Block, there is no place to attack him. That is why the weak can overcome the strong. That is how the yielding overcomes the hard."

"You keep on mentioning the Tao," Voden said. "My mother talked of it too. What is it, Kao-Shir?"

"You would have to ask that," Anhur muttered. "I was afraid you were going to ask that! We are in this cave, snowed in, no way to even get out for a walk, and you have to ask a question like that! By the veil of Neith, this old Yellow Robe will talk riddles for the next two days if you encourage him like that, lad. Ask him something sensible, like how to disarm a swordsman with a wildflower! But by the teeth of Am-mit don't ask him questions like that one!"

Kao-Shir bowed his head to hide his smile. His face was sober when he lifted it again. "I wish I could give that kind of answer, Anhur, one that lasted two days and told what the Tao is. I fear I can't."

"Ah, all praise to the Shetai! How long will it be? Only a day? Only the rest of the afternoon?"

"Alas, much shorter. I can't tell you what the Tao is, Voden. It's beyond words, for words differentiate things and the Tao is utter undifferentiation. I could tell you what the Tao isn't. . . ."

"For example—not that I'm interested, mind you, but just for example—what isn't it?" Anhur queried sarcastically.

The old man shrugged. "It's not this, not that. Point to anything, and it's not that thing. Don't point, and it's not that either."

Anhur groaned. "I knew I shouldn't have asked, even in

jest. Please stop, old man. Beat me with your staff. But
please, please stop beating my poor sore mind! Let's change
the subject. Quick, Voden," he appealed to the young man,
"think of a question that requires a simple answer."

Voden smiled. "All right. Umm. Let's see. Kao-Shir, you
told us why you left the Sunrise Empire, but you never told us
why you came to the West."

The old man looked down at the ground for several minutes before replying. "Well, to be honest, it's really a bit em-
barrassing. I mean, the reason is."

"Aha!" Anhur crowed delightedly. "We've found a topic he
doesn't want to talk about! Press him, Voden! Force him to
answer!" He turned to Kao-Shir. "And make it brief, old
man."

"Umm. Well, the fact is, I decided I wanted to become
immortal."

"Immortal?" Anhur asked, startled. "You mean you wanted
to live forever?"

"That's what the word means," Kao-Shir replied dryly. "I
would think one as old as you would know the meaning."

"Well, I'm hardly immortal. I just live a long time. When
the Upuatu comes, well . . . who knows. If I just find Horus
and help to take back the double crown, I'll be happy to die."

"I wanted real immortality. So I turned all my learning, all
my knowledge to the problem, and made up a potion. I combined powdered jade and rhino horn, ground, dried cicada and
frog, ash of white tiger fur, some Li Chih fungus, and a couple of other things I hesitate to mention. I mixed it all in an
iron vessel and let it sit and strengthen until autumn was at its
height. Then I offered fervent prayers to both Shou-Hsing and
Tun-Fan Shuo and drank it down."

"And . . ." Anhur prompted. "Did it work?"

"Well, I admit that the next day or two *seemed* like living
an eternity. You see, I got violently ill. I was coming out of
both ends so fast, I was sure everything in between was going
to disappear! Ugh! I can still taste that nasty stuff!"

The Svartalfar laughed loudly and slapped his thigh. "Ha!
Serves you right! Dried frogs, indeed! So you felt so foolish,
you had to leave and come west, right?"

"No. I was more determined than ever to achieve immortality after that experience. After all, coming that close to
dying just increased my desire to live!

"I came west to find Hsu-Mi Lou, the mountain where Hsi Wang Mu lives. Legend has it that it lies somewhere west of the Kunlun Mountains. You haven't seen it by any chance?"

"I don't know. What's it look like?"

"Well, four rivers flow from it to the four quarters of the world. It's surrounded by a vermilion river that flows around its base three times. It's so tall that it reaches the sky, and its roots reach as deep into the earth. On its summit there's a door where the winds come from."

Anhur considered. "No, can't say as I have seen one quite like that. Vermilion river, eh? No, no vermilion rivers in Svartalfheim that I've ever seen. What's so special about this, what's her name. . . . ?"

"Hsi Wang Mu. She's Queen of the West. She has tiger's teeth and a leopard's tail. Three green birds feed her. And she grows the peaches of immortality. They take three thousand years to ripen."

"Uh, what happens if you get there just a few days after the last of the crop's been eaten?" Anhur asked innocently.

Kao-Shir shrugged. "I guess you wait. I never really thought of that."

Anhur shook his head. "Do you really believe that, Kao-Shir?"

The old man looked at the ground for a few heartbeats, then cocked his head slightly and peered at Anhur. "Well . . . not exactly. But it makes a good story."

The Svartalfar guffawed and clapped Kao-Shir on the back. "Ha! I'll bet you've got a tale for every occasion! Somehow, Voden, I don't think we're going to get a straight answer from our yellow-robed friend here. But we do get amusing ones, I admit!"

Voden smiled at the two of them. "You were in Kara Khitai and studied with the warrior-monks. Tell us of that."

Kao-Shir nodded. "Little enough to tell. Hard work in the practice yards for years and years. They taught me the long and short sword, the dagger, the ax, the pike, the bow, short and long spear, the staff, and the sticks. I learned the techniques of the Tsao-Kai-Ssu, Quick Death, and Huo-Pu-Chang. And then, when the body and spirit were mastered, I apprenticed to Sheng mu, a great sorceress. With her I studied Shen-Pien magic and became a Men Kuei, capable of using Sha, the power of killing with a touch. I learned the seventy-two names of the Ti-Sha—the stars of evil influence, and the thirty-six names of the Tien-Kang—the stars of good influence. Eventually I attained the level of Hsien Sen. Had I stayed, I might have achieved Chen Sen or even Sheng Sen, but I was restless and moved on to Prin."

"Still searching for immortality, old man?" Anhur asked gently, impressed in spite of himself.

"In a way."

"Have you found it?"

"Again, in a way. What I've found is the Tao. Now I am part of it and my individual life means very little."

"You mean you're no longer afraid of dying?" Voden asked.

"What is there to fear?" The old man responded. "If and when I die, I'll decompose. My left shoulder will become a cock and I'll welcome the morning sun every day. My right shoulder will become a falcon and ride the summer's breezes. One leg will be a tree, another a flower. Rather than being a small, differentiated part of the Universe, I'll dissolve and spread out through the entire Universe.

"I entered life because it was my time. I'll leave it in accordance with the same law of the Tao. What man worries over where and what he was before he was born? Why then should we worry over where and what we are after we die? We come from the Tao, we return to it. Nothing is gained or lost in the flow."

The three of them stood in silence, Voden and Anhur watching Kao-Shir in wonder, the old man watching something far beyond the walls of the cave.

It was a hard winter. Kao-Shir said that Tung Lu, the god of snow, must be angry with them. He lit seven lamps and sacrificed while facing west to try and appease the Black Ruler, Shui-Hsing, the god of winter. Apparently the god wasn't listening, because the weather continued to alternate between bitter cold and furious blizzard.

Both Voden and Anhur noticed that Kao-Shir was becoming more silent and introspective. When they quizzed him as to the reason for this, the old man was reluctant to answer at first. They pressed him, and finally he yielded.

"I didn't want to upset you." He sighed. "A time known as Yu-Lan Hui is approaching. It's a dreadful time. During it, for some fifteen days, the gates of Ti-Yu are open and the demons come pouring out. The Kuei shamble forth, their hideous faces leering, their bones rattling and clanking. They lurk in every shadow to catch the unwary. The Lung, the Mang Shen, and the Na-Chia slither out as well. There are a thousand of the Na-Chia. She Wang, the king of the serpents, comes with them. Wu Kung Ching, the giant centipede, creeps forth. And the Pi-Li-To take the bodies of the dead and walk once more." He shuddered. "It's a horrible time, very dangerous. It lasts until the birthday of Ti-Tsang, the king of Ti-Yu. Then they all go back, taking many hapless victims with them. Gruesome.

"Ordinarily I'm well protected from such as those I mentioned. But this year is somehow special. I feel a change in the air." He turned to look at Anhur. "I fear that in some manner Khamuas has leagued himself with Yen-Lo, the king of the demons. Perhaps through his control over the four and seven serpents of the Uamemtiu. Perhaps they are somehow related to the Mang Shen or the Na-Chia. I don't know. But I don't like the way things feel. Something is very wrong."

Anhur looked worried. "Is there anything we can do?"

Kao-Shir shook his head. "No. I'm doing what I can. I've placed all the Shih Kan-Tang ward stones I have around the area to help protect us. I've also called on Chin-Kang and Chung Kuei, two gods who are experts at slaying demons. They'll help. But . . ." He shrugged. "I fear we'll just have to wait and see."

"When is this Yu-Lan Hui?" Voden asked.

"It begins in about ten days," came the quiet reply.

The days fled all too swiftly, and the tension in the cave mounted rapidly. Kao-shir was constantly wandering about, muttering strange things and waving his hands in the air. Here and there on the walls of the cave he drew bizarre symbols with bits of charcoal from the fire. His pot was boiling day and night and a heavy, sweet-smelling haze filled the air.

Then came the day when he announced in dire tones, "Tonight at midnight Yu-Lan Hui begins. We should be safe for the first day or two. After that . . . it's anybody's guess."

XII

YU-LAN Hui was ushered in with an incredible blizzard. Even deep in their cave, the three could hear the howling of the wind. Outside, it was almost impossible to stand against its strength, and the snow slashed with such power that it hurt.

"This storm comes from one of the cold hells," Kao-Shir told them. "It's driven by the fury of Ao Shun, the Lung, or dragon, of the North Seas. He's searching for us."

Aside from the storm nothing much happened for the first five days of Yu-Lan Hui. Voden began to relax, but Kao-Shir was grimmer than ever. "They're searching," he told them, his voice filled with menace. "Searching and searching. I can feel them. Their net is closing in on us, I fear. More horrible, though, is the number of them coming to attack us. Four and seven serpents from Tuat we might be able to battle again. Alas, what comes against us now is far greater than that!"

"We'll fight them nonetheless," Anhur proclaimed solemnly. "Let them feel the bite of a Svartalfar spear head! We'll send many back where they came from to lick their wounds!"

"Sadly, my friend, while they lick their wounds, they'll

136

like as not munch on our bones. No, standing and fighting isn't the answer in this case."

"We can't run," Voden said. "We wouldn't get twenty feet in that storm before we froze to death. Besides, they'd track us down outside just as easily, and with the snow that thick, we'd never even see their attack until it was too late."

"I wasn't thinking of leaving the cave to go outside, Voden," the old man said softly. "I was thinking of going somewhere else."

"Somewhere else? What do you mean by somewhere else?" Anhur asked, his look intent, his attention focused sharply on Kao-Shir's face.

Kao-Shir half closed his eyes. "It's hard to explain exactly. Somewhere else is about as precise as I can be. Perhaps it's also somewhen else."

"This is no time for riddles, Yellow Robe!"

"I'm sorry, Anhur, but I really can't be much more specific than that. Once, long ago, I studied with a great wizard named Fu Hsi. He showed me many wonders, but the greatest by far were the Pa Kua, the Eight Forms of the Universe.

"The Pa Kua are used primarily to study and understand the flow of the Tao through the Universe. The Universe is ever changing and ever changeable. It's always in transition, always in the process of being something else.

"At the same time, though, this process of constant change is cyclical. It turns back on itself, a whole endlessly becoming itself again and again. There's no ending, no beginning, only a constant movement out and back. Everything contains its opposite, and nothing is surer than that once an extreme has been reached, it will recede and move to the other extreme.

"The Pa Kua forms reflect this endless process of change in its simplest form. Each of the eight reflects a phase in the eternal cycle. By studying these relationships, one can learn to understand the flow of the Tao and how to act in consonance with it. One learns when and how to act, when and how not to act."

"Fortune telling!" Anhur snorted.

Kao-Shir smiled. "In the hands of the uninitiated, yes. But in the hands of one who understands the Tao, it's a different matter. To study the Pa Kua is to enter into direct contact with the Universe."

Anhur shook his head. "I don't understand what that has to do with our problem."

"Right now, nothing. Earlier I consulted the Pa Kua—fortune telling as you would call it, Anhur. It told me this was a time to follow the principle of Hsu—Calculated Inaction. Soon, though, will come the time of Ming I, the Darkening of the Light, and we must be ready for it. Great courage will be required. You will have to do exactly as I tell you. The danger is extreme for this is a time when the power of the light has been wounded and darkness walks the face of the earth. With able helpers I can make progress against that darkness. Without . . ." He shrugged.

Voden looked at Anhur. They both looked at Kao-Shir and nodded. "You can count on us," Voden said.

Two more days went by. The storm still raged. The character of the wind had changed, however. It was no longer so forthrightly brutal. Now it seemed more subtle, more probing. Rather than howling insanely, it hissed and moaned as if sniffing something out. The air in the cave became charged with the presence of unseen things. Power was building as the net made by the things from Ti-yu drew tighter and tighter.

The next morning came without a dawn. Kao-Shir, his face drawn and haggard with the strain, called the two of them to his pot, which bubbled in the center of the cave, pouring forth a foul-smelling, yellowish-green smoke. His voice was a harsh whisper. "They are all around us," he began, his eyes darting this way and that. "The Na-Chia, the Mang Shen, the Pi-Li-To, even She Wang slithers around, just outside the cave. My ward stones have held thus far, but not much longer. They are gathering forces. Wu Kung Ching comes. And Yen-Lo. More of the Lung are on their way. Our defenses will not last out the day."

Anhur looked about in worried perplexity. "I can't see a thing, Yellow Robe, but I can feel them. Yes. They have that cold feeling of Tuat about them. Damn! What will we do when the wards crumble and they're through? There are so many of them!"

"Don't be swept away by the seeming unfavorableness of circumstances," Kao-Shir responded. "Don't let your steadfastness be shaken. Be strong inside, maintain your spirit. If there's to be any appearance of yielding, let it be an outside thing only. Keep the center firm. This is a time of darkness. Be cautious and reserved. Try not to do or even think anything that might awaken the overwhelming enmity of those that come to find us. Keep your mind and spirit neutral and invisible. They seek hate and fear. Give them nothing to find."

"They'll find us anyway," Anhur mumbled.

"Yes, but not as soon. I need as much time as I can gain to prepare. I've fasted now for three days. I've somewhere to go, but my wings are lowered. I wait for the right moment. I—"

A crash of thunder almost knocked them off their feet. Kao-Shir and Anhur were so stunned that they failed to act as the snakelike form appeared and charged them. Voden, though, was ready. His sword flew from its scabbard and his knife appeared almost magically in his hand. With a cry of "Sigfod!" he threw himself at the monster, stopping its charge short of the two older men. He slashed at its head, cleaving the scaly skin in a great rip. The thing struck at him, foot-long fangs barely missing his arm. He stabbed out with his knife, and as the serpent moved to avoid it, changed the thrust to a slash and raked its side.

With a hiss that shook the walls of the cave, the monster struck again. This time its aim was better and its fangs drew two red lines across the young Aesir's left thigh, ripping the deerskin breeches as if they were thin parchment.

The shock of the thing's strike nearly bowled Voden over. He staggered back and almost went down. With a roar of anger he regained his balance and threw himself at the monster, his sword a blurred arc of razor-sharp metal, his knife whistling through the air faster than eye could follow. Both weapons struck home, and with the strength of a mighty war horse, the Aesir gave a heave and flung the serpent down to the floor of the cave. Sword and knife rose and fell several times in rapid succession, and the monster writhed and twisted, hissing horribly. Voden stood back, raising his weapons and crossing the blades. "For you, Sigfod!" he cried in a bellow.

Anhur rushed to his side. "Good work, lad! Let's get that wound tied up, though. It looks nasty. Are these things poisonous, old man?"

"Not that one. Others are. They'll be here soon. Are you all right, Voden?"

Too winded to speak, the young Aesir nodded.

"Bring him here, near the pot, Anhur. And bring all your weapons, and anything else you want to save. Some food and water too. We may need it. Hurry, there isn't much time now! The rest will break through any minute!"

While Anhur scurried around doing Kao-Shir's bidding, bringing things from all parts of the cave, Voden, trembling and pale in reaction to his wound, helped organize and stack things near the fire. Kao-Shir went to the serpent with a small bowl and collected some of the black blood slowly oozing from its gaping wounds. Once he had as much as he wanted, he paced off a circle about fifteen feet in diameter around the fire. At the northern end of the circle he drew a figure on the floor of the cave in the serpent's blood. Voden craned his neck to watch. The symbol was three broken lines, one atop the other. The old man mumbled as he carefully drew the lines. "Docile, I draw Kun, the belly, the ox, protect me, Mother Earth." He then went to the southern end of the circle and drew a figure consisting of three solid lines. "Here is strength, here is Chien, the horse, the head, protect me, Father Heaven." Swiftly, he moved to the east side of the circle, casting nervous glances over his shoulder as he did so. "Enough, Anhur," he called softly. "Get within the circle and stay there. No matter what, stay there!"

Kao-Shir reached the east and drew a new figure in blood. It was a broken line between two solid ones. "Ah, bright Li," he chanted, "the pheasant, the eye, fire and sun protect me." He moved to the west and drew a solid line between two broken ones. "Here is danger," he intoned solemnly, "here is Kan, the pig, the ear. With water and the light of the moon, protect me."

The air was becoming charged with power. Voden felt his hair rising of its own accord. His skin tingled strangely and his mouth felt dry. The pain in his leg ached dully when he sat still, but even the slightest movement sent sharp needles of agony shooting through his body. He watched as Kao-Shir, his face pale and sweating, walked to the southeast part of the circle and drew a new figure. This one was a broken line atop two solid ones. The old man chanted as he drew, his voice harsh and strained, his breathing heavy. "What pleasure is Tui, the sheep, the mouth, the endless marsh. Protect me." The old man crossed quickly to the southwest and drew two solid lines over a broken line. "Deep goes Sun, penetrating to the core of the matter. It is the fowl, the thigh, wood and wind. Protect me." Now he moved directly up to the northwest and marked the floor with a solid line above two broken ones. "I mark down Ken, the form that makes all halt, the dog, the hand, the towering mountain. Protect me."

The old man stopped and mopped his face with the sleeve of his robe. He looked at Voden. "Is my staff in the circle?" The young Aesir nodded. "Good," Kao-Shir replied. "Now comes the tricky part. Anhur and Voden, much will depend on you now. Whatever happens, don't leave the circle. Something will come soon and I'll battle it with magic, trying to use my Sha—my power of killing with a touch. But I won't be able to kill it, only stun it. I must lure it through the hole in the circle. When I do, fall on it, kill it. Its dying will give us the power we need to complete the spell. You *must* kill it. Otherwise, once I close the circle, we'll be trapped there with it alive! Do you both understand? Good, I don't—"

A roar deafened them all as two gigantic hellhounds with four eyes and wide flaring nostrils came bounding through the walls of the cave. With a howl they flung themselves at Kao-Shir, who stood outside the circle at its northeastern side.

The old man leapt to meet the dogs, dodging to one side at the last moment. His open hand reached out lightly and slapped one of the hounds. It shrieked in agony and disappeared in a burst of flame. The second rounded on Kao-Shir and leapt for his throat. He thrust his hand out to meet it in midair. With a scream and an explosion, it disappeared.

The explosion knocked Kao-Shir over and he bounded quickly back to his feet. Voden could see that his beard and eyebrows were badly singed. His face looked burned as well. The old man looked tensely about him, as if expecting something to appear at any moment.

"Damn you, Yen-Lo," he called out, "show yourself! I know you're here somewhere! Those were your dogs I killed, the ones that guard the road to your palace in Ti-yu. Get off your damn buffalo and come fight me! Or are you too much of a coward? Is your leg still aching from the sores and worms?"

A bellow sounded from behind him, and Kao-Shir whirled just in time to see a huge water buffalo charging out of one of the cave walls. He threw himself to one side and the beast barely missed trampling him into the floor.

Voden stared in horror and wonder. Riding on the back of

the black buffalo was a green monster dressed in red. In one hand he held a gigantic mace, in the other a noose. His face was too hideous to look on. One of his feet was shriveled.

"Are you such a coward you cannot meet me man to man on foot?" Kao-Shir cried. "Has Chaya so unmanned you that you kick no more? Come fight me. I fear neither you nor your damned birds!"

With an angry roar the monster leapt from the back of the buffalo and charged Kao-Shir. Yen-Lo was at least twelve feet tall, and his mace a good five feet in length. He swung its ponderous weight as if it were a feather. Kao-Shir jumped lightly back and laughed at the monster. "You swing like a chambermaid! Swallowing molten copper has made you weak!"

Yen-Lo shrieked in fury and attacked again, his huge mace whistling through the air. The old man ducked and spun to the left. Yen-Lo followed, his noose snaking out and nearly catching Kao-Shir. Again the monster attacked, and again the old man barely escaped. His motions were slowing down as his fatigue grew. Yen-Lo gave a bellow of anticipation and attacked again.

Anhur grabbed one of his spears and leapt to the northeast breach in the circle. "I'm coming, Kao-Shir!" he cried. Voden lunged and grabbed him around the waist, pulling him down and back. "No!" the Aesir screamed. "He said to stay in the circle!"

"But he needs help!" Anhur shouted, struggling to break free. "Dammit! Let me go! That thing'll kill him!" Voden hung on for dear life, pinning the Svartalfar beneath him. The dark man cursed and fought back, but Voden refused to let go.

Yen-Lo leapt forward again, swinging his mace first, following with his noose. Kao-Shir ducked both. The mace came back and barely clipped him on the shoulder, knocking him head over heels across the cave. With a roar of victory Yen-Lo sprang to the attack. His mace rose high for a crushing blow, but when it descended, shattering rock, the old man was no longer there. He'd twisted to the side and regained his feet. In panic he began to run around the circle from the north toward the south. Yen-Lo followed close on his heels, screaming out with victory, his long legs covering two steps for every one of the old man's.

Around the southern side of the circle they sped, then up

the eastern curve. As they reached the northeastern point, Kao-Shir suddenly stumbled and fell. Yen-Lo raised his mace on high and struck with all his might. At the last moment the old man rolled to one side and sprang unexpectedly to his feet. He struck out with both hands and hit Yen-Lo solidly in the side. The monster shrieked in agony and stumbled. Kao-Shir hit him again and the creature twisted to his left, stumbling through the northeastern point of the circle.

Kao-Shir leapt in after him, crying out in a commanding voice, "Kill him!" Voden and Anhur threw themselves on Yen-Lo, stabbing and ripping his body in a frenzy. The monster fought back, his claws ripping Voden's back and arms, almost tearing Anhur's shoulder off. But the two thrust again and again, grimly sticking to their task.

While they fought, Kao-Shir took some of Yen-Lo's flowing blood and marked the final symbol at the northeast point of the circle. It was two broken lines over a solid line. "Chen," he cried, his voice powerful and commanding, "movement to close the circle! You who are dragon and foot, the eldest son of Heaven, let thy thunder roar and protect me!"

An incredible clap of thunder threw all three of them down to the floor of the cave, making their heads ring and their sight fail. Stunned, Voden lay atop the still body of Yen-Lo.

For long moments none of the three could even raise their heads to look and see what had happened. Then Anhur groaned and sat up. "By the gods!" he gasped, and threw himself facedown on the floor of the cave again.

Voden opened one eye to look and instantly shut it again. "By Fornjot!" he cursed, his voice shaking with fear, "where have you taken us, old man?" He opened his eye again, then both of them, and stared about in wonder.

The cave walls had disappeared, and in their place was a vast blackness studded with the cold light of an infinite number of stars. They were moving in the emptiness at an incredible speed, the stars flashing past so fast the eye could barely follow them.

Suddenly the scene changed and they were on the surface of a planet, watching a huge red sun slowly rise over the horizon. Voden looked at Kao-Shir, wonder on his face. "Where . . . where are we, Kao-Shir?"

The old man turned his head and looked at him calmly. "The Pa Kua are a mirror of the Universe. They reflect all its movement and becoming. We are in the center of the Pa Kua. We move through the Universe. We are that somewhere else I spoke of, somewhere the monsters of Ti-yu cannot follow. The killing of Yen-Lo provided the power we needed. As long as we stay within the Pa Kua, we are safe." He sighed and muttered, "It worked."

"Can we . . . can we get back?" Anhur asked, his voice weak and shaking. "Are we here forever? Can we return?"

Kao-Shir nodded. "Yes. When the power supplied by Yen-Lo runs out, we will return. Until then, enjoy the show. It's not often one gets a tour of the Universe, you know."

They plunged into the center of a star, then spiraled around a gigantic planet that glowed and hissed at them. They dove into a cluster of comets, and circled a double star. Skimming the surface of unknown worlds, they watched armies of monstrous crystals battle to the death, and saw giant lizards living in harmony. Wonder piled on wonder until they were dizzy and aching.

At times nothing was visible but endless blackness. Then the entire world was suddenly alight with a million colors that throbbed and danced to an unheard rhythm.

Exhausted, the three of them fell asleep as a gigantic star exploded right next to them, spewing out its very stuff to spread across the infinite darkness. Voden lay atop the body of Yen-Lo.

They awoke to find themselves spinning wildly through a purple sky, pursued by violet clouds that shot lightning at each other. Silently they ate and drank while one star was born and another died a red death.

On and on they swept. They ate when they were hungry, drank when they were thirsty. Other than that, time no longer had any meaning. There was nothing to judge it by.

Then they saw an incredible thing. A vast, amorphous creature spread across their view, stretching as far in every direction as they could see. They were plunging toward it, toward what Kao-Shir declared was the left side of its belly. Down and down they fell, until they actually penetrated it. Darkness enveloped them, a darkness so absolute they couldn't even think thoughts. To the very heart of that ultimate darkness they plunged, then out again through a gate and courtyard.

Leaving the darkness, they found themselves high above a

world. With alarming speed they drove downward toward its surface. Their speed became so terrific that Voden was forced to close his eyes. Without a sound they struck the surface and went deep within. Then, again without a sound, they burst forth into the very cavern they had originally left.

Shakily Kao-Shir got to his feet and walked to the edge of the circle he had created. The symbols were dull and dead-looking. The body of Yen-Lo had shriveled up until there was virtually nothing left of it. Cautiously the old man stepped across the northeast symbol. He stood and looked around the cave. Everything seemed normal.

He turned to the other two and beckoned to them. "Come," he said softly, wonderingly, "they're all gone. Yu-Lan Hui is over. The gates of Ti-yu are closed. The demons are back in their places."

Voden, still aching from the wounds inflicted by the serpent's fangs and Yen-Lo's claws, limped from the circle. He sniffed the air. It smelled different. Slowly he moved toward the entrance of the cave. Reaching it, he looked out.

"Kao-Shir, Anhur," he called excitedly, "come here! The snow's melting! It smells like spring is coming!"

The other two joined him at the entrance and stared out at the landscape. It was still covered with snow, but there was no mistaking the softness of the air. Spring was approaching.

Anhur turned to Kao-Shir. "How long were we gone, old man? It only seemed like a few days, but . . ."

Kao-Shir smiled gently. "But it had to be several months," he finished for the Svartalfar. "Yes, I believe you're right. We've been gone about two months. Winter is over and spring is here. For one, I'm glad!"

"For another, I am too!" Anhur shouted with glee. "Now when you start spouting your nonsense, I can go out for a walk!"

MIMIR'S WELL

XIII

VODEN sat on the north side of a short spur of land that thrust eastward into the Amsvartnir Sea. To his right the blue water stretched off as far as the eye could see. To the left lay the green depths of the Western Forest. No one knew how far west it spread for no one had ever penetrated its fastness and returned to tell the tale.

Northward, the forest and the sea ran side by side until they disappeared in the hazy distance. That way lay Mimir's Well. That way lay his journey.

He sighed deeply and faced the issue that had been bothering him ever since the snow had begun to melt. *His* journey lay to the north. Not Kao-Shir's, not Anhur's. He loved the two men dearly. They'd taught him a great deal, even if most of what Kao-Shir said didn't make much sense. His lessons on staff fighting had been wonderful, though, as had Anhur's instructions on combat with the spear. He knew that the time he'd spent with the strange man from the Sunrise Empire and the little Svartalfar would be something he would look back on with great fondness and gratitude. Without Kao-Shir, he realized, he never would have escaped from the demon in the mound or from Ro-Setau. Without Anhur, they would have been ambushed by Khamuas's searchers or destroyed by the four and seven serpents from Tuat. And without Kao-Shir's strange magic, the demons from Ti-yu would have meant the end for all of them. Yes, they'd been a good team.

He sighed again. The time for teamwork was over. The rest of his journey had to be made alone. He'd planned to do the whole thing that way, even rejecting the offers of Yngvi and Honir to accompany him and share the danger. It hadn't worked out that way, luckily! But now. . .

Mimir's Well was his to find. No one could share in the task. He had to go, ask to drink at the well, and pay whatever price it took. He shuddered at the thought. It had cost old Groa her eye! Would he be willing to pay such a high price? Yes, he thought grimly, and more. Vestla had told him to go to the well. Deep inside he'd wanted to go ever since Groa had told him she'd drunk from the well to gain knowledge.

Knowledge! He'd always had a burning desire to know everything there was to know. He wanted to understand why the sun rose and the moon shone and the stars were so cold and the clouds looked like rabbits and the rain fell and the trees grew and the Galdar-power was within him and what his visions and dreams meant and . . . Ah! It went on and on. He burned with the need to take it all in and digest it and *know* it! Even as a small child his favorite word had been *why*. He chuckled, remembering the annoyed looks of the adults in Asgard when he'd incessantly questioned them. What a nuisance I must have been, he thought with a sense of pride.

In Vanaheim, too, he'd questioned and tried to learn as much as possible. The Thiodnuma, wrestling, the Elder Tongue—it had gone on and on. He felt sure the Disir had finally found his curiosity as annoying as the Aesir had.

Then the Galdar-power had come. And Jalk had taken him to the cloud realm where the animals had rebuilt him and Raesvelg had given him his Power Song. Later, after the mandragora had nearly driven him mad, he'd gone to the Great Tree itself, to Yggdrasil, the great ash that was the world. There he'd been taught by the Mother of the Animals, Father Bear, and the twisted thing. Much of what they'd told him was gone from his conscious mind, sunk deep somewhere inside him, down where the Galdar-power lay coiled around the very center of his being.

So much to know! He knew he'd barely scratched the surface of his Galdar-power. And what were these strange things in the leather bag around his neck? He touched the bump beneath his shirt gingerly. There was great power in those oddly marked pieces of bone. He could feel it reach out and stir the power that lay latent deep within his own body and mind. If he could discover how to use them, who knew what power he might unlock?

The key to the whole thing was Mimir's Well. His mother had told him to go there. She'd said he had a dire fate. To face such a fate, he had to know as much as possible . . . *had* to!

But knowledge such as Mimir had to give could not be shared by others, no matter how close or well-meaning. He had to go to the well alone, ask alone, make his sacrifice alone, receive his knowledge alone. There was no other way.

He looked back toward the forest with a gentle smile. He'd left Kao-Shir and Anhur there, arguing over one of Yellow Robe's little stories. It had been about the training of a fighting cock, and the Svartalfar had declared it to be utter nonsense. Voden's smile turned to a chuckle as he imagined the scene with Anhur waving his arms in mock exasperation while Kao-Shir sat still, his face solemn but his eyes twinkling with repressed merriment.

His expression turned sorrowful as he thought of what he had to do. How will I tell them I must go alone now? he wondered. No matter what I say, I'm bound to hurt their feelings.

"No matter what you say, you're bound to hurt his feelings, old man," Anhur said, shaking his head in disapproval. "We've been traveling together so long, we're almost like a family. To desert him now . . . well . . ."

Kao-Shir looked skyward, as if imploring the gods to help him. "Let me explain one more time then—"

Anhur raised his hand to forestall the old man from the Sunrise Empire. "Oh, I understand. You think he must make this last leg of the journey to Mimir's Well on his own. It must be his own accomplishment, nothing must be owed to anyone, he must come before this Mimir person completely alone. What makes you so sure you're right? You admit you know nothing of Mimir, have never met him or her or it, don't even know if there is any such thing as a well. And yet you think Voden has to go wandering all over the Western Forest to find this—"

"All right, all right, I admit everything you say. I didn't want to use this last argument because I didn't want anyone to know, but . . ." He paused and looked over his shoulder, then slowly around at the forest. Satisfied no one was close, he motioned Anhur to bend closer. "I fear something much greater. I fear Khamuas, the serpents from Tuat, and the demons from Ti-yu."

Kao-Shir nodded solemnly as the Svartalfar's eyes widened and he cast looks over his own shoulder at the dark places beneath the trees. "Explain," he said in a whispery voice.

"Those from Tuat can find us more easily because of you. Those from Ti-yu can home in on me. Khamuas is hardly likely to have given up finding Voden and destroying him. Now, the lad has been marked both by a serpent from Tuat and one from Ti-yu. I've done my utmost to undo that and have been fairly successful. The monsters will have a hard time tracing our young friend.

"But they won't have a hard time tracing us. And if we're with Voden, then . . ."

"Ah," Anhur nodded, understanding, "yes, they can follow him only because they can follow us. We lead them to him. By Sekhmet's fangs and claws! I should have thought of that!"

Kao-Shir shrugged. "You aren't of as suspicious a nature as I am, old friend. That's because you've never served in the court of the Emperor of the Sunrise Empire. I remember one time when that owl-faced Hui Tzu decided that I coveted his post as prime minister of the province of Liang and—"

"This is no time for stories, you old fool! Voden is in danger! What are we going to do?"

"Do? Why, nothing. What else is there to do?"

"Nothing? *Nothing?* Well . . . well . . . there's got to be something we can do!"

"Hmm," Kao-Shir said innocently. "I guess there is *one* thing we could do."

Anhur eyed him with sudden suspicion. "What is it?"

"We could let him go his own way north toward Mimir's Well while we went south and east. . . ."

"Yes!" Anhur cried, "yes, and lead the monsters and Khamuas a merry chase! They'll think Voden is still with us and—" The Svartalfar stopped and glared at Kao-Shir. "Damn you, you tricked me! You've gotten your way! We're going to abandon the boy and let him go wandering all over the forest looking for this damned imaginary well and this Mimir person and—"

"And," Kao-Shir interrupted, "keep Khamuas, the four and seven from Tuat, and a whole host of nasty things from Ti-yu, off his trail. Our journey won't be any easier than his, my forest friend. But ours will make his a lot safer."

Anhur growled and muttered under his breath. "All right, you win, you damned yellow-robed twisted-tongued tale-telling old—"

"Now, now," Kao-Shir scolded with a scowl, "be a grace-ful loser. As my master Hung-Chun used to say—"

"Damn your master Hung-Chun to Tuat! Dammit, Kao-Shir, how in the holy name of the Hepr are we going to tell Voden that we're abandoning him?"

Voden stood watching until the two old men had completely disappeared in the depths of the forest. Then, with a slight lump in his throat, he turned and headed northward.

The leaves were yellow and golden. Many had already fallen to add a fresh layer to the forest floor. The wind came from the north and held a slight scent of ice. It undoubtedly blew directly from the Icerealm. Winter would come earlier this year than ever before. He'd never been this far north in his life.

He looked over his shoulder. There it was again, that strange sense of being watched, of being followed. Nothing definite he could see or hear, just a feeling. Everytime he turned around, there was nothing. Several times he'd doubled back on his trail to see if he could surprise someone or some-thing, but nothing had ever shown up. Could it be that one of the demons hadn't been fooled by Kao-Shir's and Anhur's ruse? He shrugged. If so, there wasn't much he could do about it until the monster attacked.

But it didn't feel like a demon. There wasn't that sense of evil threat that he'd learned to associate with things that came from the dark realms of Tuat and Ti-yu. No, this was differ-ent, curious, interested, almost friendly. Still, he didn't like the idea of anyone or anything following him.

In the last few months he'd gotten quite used to his solitude. At first he'd talked to the animals he'd seen, gossiped with the birds and salamanders, asked after the health of the squirrels. Gradually, though, the vast silence of the forest had imposed itself on him. The sighing of the wind through the trees, the rustle of the leaf against leaf, the creaking of the branches, had gently invaded his mind and lulled it into a peace it had not known for many years. With a calmness like that of the forest itself he'd traveled beneath the shadows of the towering trees. The solitary journey became a badly needed time of mental and spiritual rest.

Now he paused, looking about him. Where to now? he wondered. I've rounded the top of the Amsvartnir Sea and come south and east again, following its shore. Now the water is coming back north once more, so this must be the point of land Mimir's Well is supposed to be on. But where?

How should he go about finding it? Walk a careful search pattern? Or simply trust to luck? He looked at the sky again. Not much more time before winter set in. Maybe a month at most. He'd have to try the search pattern. Be as thorough as possible. He began to plan it in his mind.

Two weeks later he knew it was a failure. He'd quartered and requartered the entire area and found nothing. No Mimir, no well, no trace of any living being . . . other than the animals of the forest and whatever it was that followed him. He watched as the squirrels gathered nuts and scampered up trees. The message in their action was grim. Perhaps he'd best just get ready for winter and try looking for the well again next spring?

He shrugged and nodded to himself. Might as well give it one more try. Where to go? Did it make any difference?

He decided it didn't and set off at random, not looking around for familiar landmarks. For most of the day he wandered about, following birds and chipmunks, then tracked a column of ants hurrying somewhere. He felt remarkably at peace, and when he looked up from the ant train, he didn't at first recognize what he saw.

There, in the middle of a small clearing, was a tiny log house with smoke rising from the chimney. In front of it was a well built of dark gray stones and capped with a roof of wooden shingles. It seemed so ordinary and unexpected at the same time that he simply stared at it for many minutes.

Slowly he approached, his heart beating wildly. As he entered the clearing, an old woman came to the door of the cabin and stared back at him across the open space. He stopped, suddenly unsure of what to do or say.

"Eh," the old woman croaked in a voice seldom used, "eh, what's this as comes out of the woods, then? Seems to be a lad, yes, seems to be. But what's a lad doing way out here in the woods? No folks around here, there isn't, no, no, none at all."

She limped across the clearing, her hand shading her eyes. "Eh, not seen one like this before. No, we've not seen his like before. Must be one of the new races, the new men. Yes, yes, must be. Long way from home he is, isn't he? Yes, yes. All alone too. Dangerous to walk the forest alone.

"But, eh, eh, he's come to see us, he has. Come to see Mimir, he has. Even the wolves won't eat them as come to see us, no sir. Feared of eating something that crazy, they are." She wheezed a cackling laugh.

Voden stood transfixed by her stare. She was hideous, her nose long and pendulous, her lips flabby and drooping, both eyes squinty and bloodshot. Her brown skin was incredibly wrinkled and every crease was filled with ground-in dirt. Something resembling a cross between hair and dead, gray straw hung from her head. A wispy beard scraggled from her long, narrow chin. Perhaps three rotten teeth remained in her mouth.

"Come to visit with us. Yes, yes. What are you called, young one? Speak up. You can't visit us if you're silent as a stone now, can you?"

"I'm . . . I'm Voden. Voden Vafudar, the Wanderer."

"Eh, eh! Wanderer indeed! Yes, yes, you've wandered far enough to find us, you have! But finding us is not enough, no, no, it surely isn't! Why have you come, young one?"

"To . . . to drink from the well. I—"

The old hag exploded with wheezing, sputtering merriment. "Eh! Eh! Eh! To drink from the well, he says. Did us hear him right? Yes, yes, to drink from the well he said, he did indeed!" She stopped laughing and fixed him with a sharp, hostile eye. "And does he think a drink from Mimir's Well is given freely, just for the asking, is that what he thinks?"

"N-No . . . I . . ."

"No, no he says. Eh, what then did he bring us? Eh? What precious things did he bring?"

Voden looked stunned. "Precious things? Why, I don't have any precious things. I mean . . ." He snatched his sword from its scabbard. "Kao-Shir said this was precious. Made by wizards in a faraway land. Almost magical. Here, will that do?"

The old hag scoffed at the blade. "Bah! Junk! What need have we for an old piece of metal?" She waved her hand carelessly. "Look what you hold, young one."

With a sudden squawk Voden dropped the serpent that writhed in his grip. Shaking, he looked from his hand to the old woman to the snake that wiggled off between the trees. "Came from the forest," she grumbled. "Let it go back, we say. What else have you got?"

Carefully the young Aesir pulled the iron knife Buri had gifted him with so long ago. The old woman scowled darkly as she saw it. Shaking her head, she gestured for him to put it back. "Not that, not that. We don't like that. It is what it is and can't be changed to anything else. Not from this world did it come, not from here. No, no, from the sky it came. Put it away, we don't like it at all."

Trembling, Voden reached beneath his shirt and pulled out the pouch. He handed it to Mimir. "I . . . I don't really know what these are. But if they're precious, you're welcome to them."

Mimir opened the bag and looked within, muttering the whole time. As she saw the contents, she suddenly fell silent and looked up sharply at Voden. "Where did you find these?" she asked, her voice hard and commanding.

"I . . . in a mound, far to the south in Svartalfheim. They—"

She closed the bag and handed it back to Voden. "These are indeed precious, more so than you realize, young fool. They are the Bones of Audna. But you cannot give them away because you do not own them. They own you."

In dismay Voden tried to find something to say. The old woman scowled. "Nothing more? Nothing to give us for a drink of water from our well? You must not be very thirsty then!" She turned away and began to limp back to her cabin.

"Nothing for us," she mumbled beneath her breath. "Eh, eh, nothing of value for us!"

"Wait!" Voden cried, trying to gather his wits. "Wait! What do you want? I'll give you anything I have! Name it!"

The crone turned slowly back and fixed him with her red eyes. "Eh, eh! Now he pleads with us he does! Anything, he says, anything!" Her voice became hard and ruthless. "Do you know what *anything* covers, stripling? It covers your mother's soul, your sister's life, your brother's breath, your father's damnation. Yes, yes, old Groa told you she gave us an eye for a drink. Was it only an eye, though? Why did her husband never come back, eh? If it was only an eye, the bargain was too easy. Think young one, think long and hard before you use the word anything again." She turned and went into the cabin, slamming the door behind her.

Voden stood rooted to the spot, unable to think or move. Gradually he came to himself. Mimir had refused everything he'd offered. That was something that had never occurred to him, that Mimir might not be willing to trade a drink for anything he had. With a groan of despair, he sank to his knees. What would he do now? To come all this way . . . his mother had begged him . . . Kao-Shir and Anhur had led the demons . . .

He looked up and it was morning. The sun's rays slid sideways into the clearing, gently pattering across the side of the log hut. The door opened and a young maiden came out. She was lovely, with long dark hair, a sparkle deep in clear black eyes. Her skin was a rich brown, firm and faultless. Her lips were bowed to show brilliant white teeth.

Slowly, gracefully, she floated up to Voden. "Still here? Have you brought us anything better than what you had before? No? Well, well, what can be done?" She sat down next to him and regarded him with somber eyes. "You've come a long way, through much danger, to reach us. You must be very brave. And very thirsty for a drink from our well."

Voden nodded in confusion. "The . . . the old woman . . . where . . . ?"

The maiden laughed heartily. "Oh, don't let her frighten you. She said dire and ominous things. But then, she had lived for so long and seen so much evil in the world."

"Is she . . . I mean has she . . ."

"She's gone for now. Don't worry about her. I'm here and I'll try to find a way to help you. But remember, *anything* is much too big a word. The thing we want for a drink must be precious to *you*."

"But I didn't bring anything. I—"

"It doesn't have to be something you own in the usual sense. Groa gave her eye. Now you're obviously a warrior. Would you give your right hand for a drink?"

"Yes!" Voden blurted. "Oh, yes!"

The young woman shook her head. "No, no that won't do. You obviously don't value your right hand all that much to agree so readily. It has to be something you really value. Knowledge never comes cheaply, no matter how you acquire it. Sometimes you can spend your entire life searching for it. Even then it often eludes you. Many people think they've gained it only to discover at the last moment that they've been fooled and that what they thought was gold is but brass. Others find it, only to realize it isn't what they'd hoped it would be, that where they sought beauty is ugliness instead." She paused and smiled slightly. "Knowledge may not be as satisfying as you dream, Voden. It doesn't necessarily make you free or happy. Only wisdom can do that."

"But aren't they the same?"

Her laugh filled the clearing. "No! No, indeed they are not!" Her expression shifted instantly, becoming serious and considering. "There is one kind of knowledge, though, that can lead to wisdom. But it is the hardest of all to gain. And the most dangerous to seek."

Silent for a moment, she regarded him with veiled eyes. "There is one other thing to remember about the well, Voden. It gives you the knowledge you most need, not necessarily that which you most want. The decision is not yours but the well's."

Voden looked around the clearing with something like despair in his glance. "What can I do?" he asked plaintively. He gestured toward the well. "I know where knowledge is to be gained. All I need is to be allowed to give something so that I may drink. What do you want? Tell me and I swear I'll give it!"

The woman returned his gaze steadily. "Swear not so

lightly young man. This is not an ordinary place."

Voden looked at her more closely and his eyes widened. "You . . . a few moments ago you were young . . . now you're . . . well . . . you're older. I mean . . . you . . ."

The woman nodded, a mysterious smile curving her lips. "We are Mimir—maid, matron, hag, three in one, one in three. Urd, Verdandi, and Skuld some call us. Others name us the Nornir. We call ourself Mimir.

"You would drink from this well and gain knowledge, Voden. Then know the price you must pay!

"We shall pluck the living eyes from your head and do with them as we please! Raw and bloody shall we pluck them!

"Think on that for a while, young Aesir! For there is more to the bargain than appears at first sight!"

XIV

My eyes? Both of my eyes? Ripped from my face by Mimir's long-nailed fingers, gouged out, blood spurting, pain searing, shattering my mind and body...my eyes? Never to see again? To be trapped entirely inside my head? No glistening snows in the moonlight, no red-washed sky in the evening, no intense green of deep summer forest, no faces of those I know and love? Both my eyes? How could I find my way through the woods? How would I fight the demons that still pursue me?

Is this the grim destiny my mother foretold? To wander about the world, a wise but blind man? Or am I to live in an even smaller and filthier hovel than Groa does, mixing love potions and curing sick cows?

No! By the ax of Sigfod, no! I'll walk away from here! I'll leave and go back to Asgard! I'll become an Aesir warrior, marry and raise children! I'll ride with my father to fight the Jotun and smash the Vanir! I'll...

What of the Galdar-power that coils within me? Will it allow me a life like that? And Jalk's training? And Kao-Shir's? And the things the Mother of Animals, Grandfather Bear, and the twisted thing taught me? What of the changing

160

of my body in the cloud realm by the animals? What of Raes-velg and the Power Song and the things the mighty eagle spoke? What will happen to Geri and Freki, to Hugin and Munin? Think of the Rite of Oski and the mandragora, the changes living among the Vanir made in me. Remember the pain of learning things not meant to be known by a boy, a young barbarian, a filthy Aesir smelling of cattle dung.

And think of what mother said as she lay dying.

By the gods, what am I going to do? Fornjot is as cold and disinterested as always. There are no others for me to call on, none to listen and heed. Oh, if only Kao-Shir or Anhur were here! They'd know what to do! Or Jalk! Yes, Jalk would know. He'd tell me what was necessary. I . . . I . . .

Mimir won't wait forever for an answer. My eyes! Both of my eyes! To come this far and be asked so much!

Why? Why have I gone through all this? All the pain and horror among the Vanir, being tied to a dead goat, my mind blasted with Eir's drugs then made mindless by the mandra-gora. Oh, Freyja, they used us both so miserably! The mad-ness when they took us apart, the agony of not having you or the root, ah, ah!

This journey, this constant battle against things that lurk in the nether world, the demon in the mound, the serpents from Tuat, the monsters that poured from Ti-yu, why, why the struggle to arrive at this point when I'm asked for my eyes? Is this the price I must pay because I've killed to get here? Killed a Jotun, killed Svartalfar, killed . . . killed the boy named Voden?

By the teats of Audhumla! There're tears running down my cheeks. Tears! From my eyes. Oh, damn, my eyes!

So much to get here, so much, so many lives, so much agony, so much . . . Why? Is there a reason? Is there ever a reason? Is this the dire fate my mother spoke of? To have to make this decision? How much is knowledge worth? My eyes! To be blind!

But will I be blind if I have knowledge? There are so many things I can't see now. So many things that are hidden from me. These are things that can't be seen by the eyes, but only by the mind, and only through knowing. Is that why I must give up my eyes? So that I can finally see the things I'm meant to see?

"Well, young one," the old crone wheezed, "have you

made up your mind? Haven't got all day, we haven't. Sun'll be down soon, shadows growing long, darkness coming. Yes, darkness coming, especially for those with no eyes. Endless darkness filled only with the fantasies of vision. Have you decided, young Voden? Or will you creep away, beaten, whipped, to live a fool and a coward the rest of your miserable life?" She gave a coughing laugh and began to turn away, muttering curses beneath her breath.

Voden swallowed hard and called to her, his voice husky and cracking. "Wait. Both my eyes? Both at the same time?"

The hag whirled back to him, her clawlike hands extended at the ends of her scrawny arms. "Both!" she hissed malevolently. "Both torn out with these claws, Aesir!"

The young man shuddered, staring in horror at the outstretched fingers. "And . . . and what will you do with them?" he mumbled.

"Do? We'll do as we please! Perhaps make a stew of them and pop them between our teeth! Perhaps leave them out on the ground, staring at the sky, for the birds to peck and tear! Perhaps we'll throw them in the well! Ah, hah, hah! We'll do as the well tells us, young fool! Young coward, you cringe! You have no need for knowledge! Be gone, you waste Mimir's time!"

"No, damn you, no! I won't go! I've come so far, gone through so much! My mother said I should come here! She wouldn't . . . she couldn't . . ."

"Vestla is dead, fool. She's returned to merge with the Tao. Neither she nor the Tao give a damn about you and your pain. You're alone. You must decide. No one, no one in the entire Universe can help you this time, Voden. Yngvi and Honir cannot rescue you from this as they saved you from the mandragora. Jalk cannot bring you back from the edge of this void. Geri and Freki cannot carry you across the river. Even Raesvelg cannot give you a song powerful enough to fight this battle. We are Mimir. Nothing is more powerful than us. Except the well. And it's from the well you wish to drink. The well demands your eyes. Even Fornjot couldn't bargain with the well. Even Audhumla would have to do as bid.

"Will you drink or no? Decide now!"

"I'll drink!" Voden shrieked.

The old woman moved faster than Voden had thought possible for anyone. She darted forward, her fingers poised to strike, her mouth twisted in a leer, and plunged her nails into his face. A searing pain shattered him. He screamed in agony as fire exploded in his eye sockets. The nails of the crone's fingers jabbed deep and encircled his eyes, then with a sudden twist and wrench, pulled out and away, each one bearing an eyeball.

Voden collapsed, gasping, unable to think in the midst of an ocean of towering waves of anguish and the most incredible pain he'd ever experienced. It shot deep within him, uprooting the very center of his being, twisting and turning it in every direction.

Yet he didn't lose awareness. He could hear Mimir shouting in triumph and knew that she was holding the eyeballs aloft. Then she spoke to him in a thunderous voice that filled the world and almost exploded his head. "Rise, worm of a man-child! Rise and come to the well of Mimir!"

He struggled upright, the surges of pain almost knocking him over. Somewhere he found the strength to stand. An iron hand gripped his wrist and guided him. After a few steps he bumped against the stone wall that surrounded the well.

"To the well I offer the eyes of Voden," Mimir's voice roared. "The well takes what it wants and gives what it wants." There was a moment's pause, as if Mimir were listening to something. Then she spoke again, her voice deep and strong, but softer now. "The knowledge you receive is what you most need, not what you most want! The well has spoken!"

With rough strength she pushed him down so that his head was near the surface. "Drink!" she hissed. "Drink!"

Voden took a mighty gulp and gasped. The water wasn't cool at all! It was burning, searing, flaming down his throat and into his stomach! The heat of it filled him, overwhelmed him. He felt himself being consumed by living flame.

Mimir pulled him up and propped him against the side of the well. He almost fell, but she braced him. "Now for what the well has decreed shall be done with your eyes, Voden. One, the right, shall go back as before to look out at the world and know the glory and the horror of it all." He felt her hand before his eye socket, a slight pressure, and then the eye was back. His vision was bleary, but he could see the old crone's hideous visage next to his face.

"Now the other eye, the left eye. It, too, shall go back into your head. But it shall face inwards so that you may see yourself and know what you and all men truly are. This is the knowledge you need most, for without it the rest makes no sense and has no purpose. This will be the greatest test of your life, Voden. To plunge within the dark void of yourself and find a place to stand. Without inner knowledge, outward understanding is but a shabby robe to cloak foolishness." He felt pressure against his left eye socket as the eyeball slid into place.

"Now your journey truly begins, Aesir! Now you must be a real warrior! Not with mere axes, knives, or swords, but with your mind and spirit! Now you must hone and learn to wield the only weapon that will never fail you! Go!" With a scream of mad laughter she pushed him away from the well.

Voden, the vision in his right eye still blurry, stumbled and nearly fell. At the last moment he caught himself and stood upright. He turned to look at Mimir and found himself alone in the midst of the forest.

Then he opened the eye that turned inward and screamed. With a moan of horror and despair he collapsed in a heap.

Hours later he regained consciousness and cautiously opened his right eye. It was dark. Overhead, through the thin leaves of fall, he could see the occasional twinkle of a cold star. He sat up and stared around at the dark forest.

The motion made him queasy, but he decided to stand anyway. Bracing himself on a small tree, he swayed up. Nausea hit him in a wave and he nearly tumbled back to the forest floor. Grimly he clung to the tree and retched with long, sobbing heaves. Still gagging, though dry, he slowly regained his balance and began to feel stable.

Only one eye, he thought. Things don't look right with only one eye. The other eye must stay closed. It *must*. He gritted his teeth at the sudden return of nausea at the thought of what he'd already seen with his left eye, the one Mimir had put in backward so he could look within himself. I won't look again, he told himself.

Yet I must, he realized. I must look. If I don't, then all my suffering, all my pain will be for nothing. The knowledge I came here to gain will never be mine unless I look.

I must know what I am! I must see myself as clearly as I see the rest of the world! I must look . . . now!

He opened his left eye wide . . . and plunged into chaos. He rode his horse through the deep snow and suddenly whirled it around. The face of the pursuing Jotun loomed out of the swirling whiteness, a look of surprise flashing across it. The horses crashed together and Voden slashed at the man's face with his ax. The blow slammed home and the Jotun was flung back with a shriek, his face blossoming red with a fountain of blood and shattered bone. Voden screamed with a fearful joy and laughed with mad glee. Yes! Yes! This was good!

He turned and grabbed Freyja, throwing her to the ground, ripping the clothes from her body with a wrench. He kicked her in the ribs. The Vanir girl moaned, and he laughed. He kicked her again and again, until she stopped moaning and her side was soft. Then he threw himself on her and raped her. She came to as he was brutalizing her. She cried out, and he smashed her nose. Then he pulled out his knife, placed it at the point where her throat met her chest, and slowly leaned his weight against it. She writhed and cried out in pain. He roared with laughter as she died, choking on her own blood.

He picked the baby girl, Vili, up by her heels and smashed her against one of the pillars that held up the house. He swung her repeatedly until there was nothing left but a bloody pulp. The whole time he was doing it he cursed his dying mother and laughed hysterically.

His fist smashed into his father's mouth, turning the gaping, pleading, whining hole into a bloody pulp. He struck wildly, over and over, until the pleading stopped. Then he turned and pulled his iron knife from its sheath. He slashed downward twice, swiftly, surely, then reached and wrenched his father's manhood from between his legs. He stuffed it into the moaning ruin of a mouth and choked him to death with it.

There in the slime of his deepest mind he committed every hideous crime imaginable. He wallowed in violence and gore, killing, maiming, raping, destroying, an endless orgy of mindless brutality.

This, he realized, is what is beneath all the rest, beneath the layers that hide what I really am from the world. This is me at my simplest, most elemental, truest level. I am this beast, this destroyer, this bloody monster that wades through the agony and pain of others with a triumphant leer of insane happiness on my lips. Everything else is false, a masquerade, a play of shadow.

Then he discovered that this was not the bottom after all. There was a level below that, one so primitive it was nothing but the dull joy of eating and evacuating, eating and evacuating. Deeper yet he plunged to mere mindless existence.

Suddenly there was nothing, a void so deep and endless it filled the entire Universe. It was death, the final and utter dissolution of self, an emptiness that swallowed all in its vastness. He gazed into it, for it was within him. His spirit quailed and he shrank back, trying to close his inner eye, trying to block out this final and ultimate horror. Too late, too late, his mind cried. You've looked too long and too deep.

With a cry of anguish and hopelessness, he stumbled off into the forest, laughing and sobbing.

He had no way of knowing how long it was before he became conscious again. It could have been days, or even weeks. He remembered brief visions of running through the trees, his clothes in tatters, his bare feet bloody and raw. At other times he'd half woken when the vermin or carrion he was hungrily stuffing into his famished mouth was so vile, it reached the humanity buried deep within his insanity and so revolted it that he was shocked aware for an instant. But such moments were rare and quickly slammed back beneath the weight of his madness. He hadn't the strength to close his left eye.

Yet now he was awake, aware, his inner eye firmly shut, his outer eye open, looking sanely at the world. It was night, and a fire was burning brightly near where he lay. He himself was wrapped in some kind of animal pelt. He stirred slightly. There were fur mittens on his hands, fur boots on his feet. Beyond the fire there was snow and then darkness guarded by the gray forms of barren trees.

"You were naked when I found you. Naked but for that leather sack around your neck and that knife strapped around your waist. Your mind was naked too. You were raving, insane, bellowing all sorts of obscene things." The voice came from behind and to the left. Voden sat up slowly and turned to see who owned it.

The man who stared back at him was odd. His face was long and very narrow, with a pointed chin covered by a neat white beard. The nose was also long and narrow, aquiline in shape. A thin line of a mouth, almost lipless, lay unsmilingly beneath the nose. The eyes were large and almond shaped, their color the white of newfallen snow. The skin that covered the face was equally white, as was the few wisps of hair that escaped from beneath the man's fur hood.

He stood slowly, towering over Voden. The young Aesir could see now that the man had only one ear, the left one. It was large, and pointed at top and bottom. He was very tall and very slender. Voden estimated he was the tallest man he'd ever seen.

"I am Heimdall," he said finally.

Memory stirred. "Heimdall? Somewhere I . . ."

The tall white man squatted next to him and peered into his eyes with curiosity. "Hmm. Back partway. Not all the way, but sane again. You need more time to orient yourself." He stood, took several steps, and sat down, his back leaning against a log. "So, I'll tell you who Heimdall is while your mind gets used to being sane again.

"I was born at the beginning of time at the edge of the world. My father was Hallinskidi and I am sometimes called by that name. My mothers were nine maidens, the daughters of Aegir. They were Gjalp, Greip, Eistla, Eyrgjafa, Ulfrun, Angeyja, Imdr, Atla, and Jarnsaxa. I was made strong with the force of the earth, with the power of the cold sea, and with a deep magic made with the blood of a sacrificial boar.

"In those first days men were like wild animals and lived as do the beasts of the forest. Very much as you were living when I found you. They had no clothes, no tools, no homes. They ate vermin and slept in piles of leaves.

"One spring I came across the Western Sea from the edge of the world and landed on their shore. They came creeping from the forest. I taught them many things. I showed them how to make clothes to cover their nakedness. How to build shelters to keep the rain and the cold out. How to trap small animals and plant grain. I gave them names, called them Ai and Edda, Afi and Amma, Karl and Snor, Dreng, Thegn, Breid, Bundinskeggi, Segg, Fljod, Jarl and Kon. I named them all and taught them their tasks."

The white man's pale eyes held a faraway look that made them seem to glow from within. He sighed. "Then I made a mistake. A terrible mistake." His voice dropped to a mere whisper, and Voden had to lean forward to catch his words. "I taught Jarl, one of my favorites, to make weapons—the curved bow, the smooth-shafted spear, the flaring ax, the

double-edged sword, the swift knife. Worse yet, I taught him
how to use them. I even . . . even . . . when Kon came to me
complaining of what I had given to Jarl, I even taught him
something never meant for men. I gave him the secrets of the
runes, their age-old meanings. When he mastered them, he
had the strength of eight men, could blunt a sword or ax so
that it would not bite, could lay the sea to rest, and so much
more. Too much more."

Heimdall shook his head in sad remembrance. "Too much
more. The others of my kind, those who had been born at the
beginning of time at the edge of the world, became angry with
what I had done. They called me to account. They sat in
judgment of me. Dyauh, Bhisma, Aditi, Daksa, Savitr, and
the other Primordials sat in judgment and found me guilty.
They gave me mortal form and placed a curse upon me.

"Now I must walk the world and view the fruits of my
teachings. Nine times must I watch worlds being born and
grow. Nine times will I see races born to rise and reach for the
skies. Nine times will I watch them plunge to ashen death and
grim destruction. I live for all time and must participate in it
all. All the pain, all the horror, all the—"

"Heimdall?" Voden interrupted. Memory came like a bubble from deep within a dark pond, rising suddenly to the light.
"Heimdall. Yes. I remember now. Khamuas, the Kheri Heb of
the Svartalfar, spoke of you."

The white man nodded vaguely, considering. "Khamuas?
Possibly. The name sounds familiar. I was in the land of Hepr
when Khepera-Ra-Tum became angry and sent out his Eye in
the form of Hathor to destroy the Svartalfar." He sighed
deeply. "Yes, that was the second of the nine. The first was
the fall of the San Miao. The third was when the First Dark
Empire came crashing down in smoking, demon-filled ruins."
He fixed Voden with an intense look and said softly, grimly,
"Now I await the fourth. It will come soon enough. I am sure
of that now.

"But you awake once more. You are conscious, your mind
is working, the insanity driven back down where it belongs. I
can see it in your eye."

Voden nodded slowly, taking stock to make sure that what
Heimdall said was true. "Yes. I . . . I feel very tired. But I can
see you and understand what you say. I . . . you . . . you say
you found me in the woods, naked?"

"Quite naked. Except for a layer of dirt and leaves. And as I mentioned, your knife and that bag around your neck. You were running about, groveling in the dirt, eating vermin and carrion, howling and screaming, waving your arms in the air and bellowing nonsense. Some of it was words, most just grunts and moans. I followed you around, and slowly you became calmer. When it seemed safe to approach, I brought you to my camp and got some clothes on you. Not a moment too soon, either. It's been snowing for several days now. You would have frozen to death."

"How . . . how did you happen to be way out here?"

Heimdall gazed at him silently for a few minutes, considering him with his pale eyes. "You have been to see Mimir," he said finally. "Once I went to the well and traded an ear for a drink. As a result I can hear grass growing in the fields and the wool growing on a sheep's back. I need less sleep than a bird and can see a hundred leagues, day or night. I wished to go and drink again. For a year I have been searching for the well. I have found nothing. Then I came across your trace and realized you were looking for the same thing. Since I was having no luck, I followed you. I lost you. You just disappeared one day. Then, a month later, I found you wandering the forest."

Voden was silent for a long time, trying to digest it all. "I . . . I don't feel crazed any longer."

"No," Heimdall nodded, "you began to come out of it about a week ago. You kept muttering something about getting your eye closed. When I found you they were both wide open all the time, both the blank one on the left and the normal one on the right. Now the left is closed. The one on the right is always open, even when you sleep. It is strange. But then, you have been to see Mimir and drunk from the well. Those who drink from the well are always strange."

Voden turned his head and stared into the fire with his right eye. "I drank from the well," he muttered. "Groa gave an eye and never got it back. You sacrificed an ear. I was asked for both eyes. Both! I gave them. And got them back in a way I never expected. Now one is always open and the other must be kept closed. The one that's closed has seen more than it should, the open one hungers to see yet more."

"You speak in riddles."

Voden laughed, the sound of it hollow and bitter in his own

ears. "I live in riddles. My whole existence is nothing but riddles. Or perhaps the whole thing is but a dream? Is life only a bad dream, Heimdall? And is the dream itself but a dream? I don't know. I know too much to know the answers any longer. All I have now are endless questions."

Voden's eye began to glow with a strange light. "My right eye sees the world, Heimdall. Sees it more clearly than the eyes of most, but sees it as it is, nonetheless. The other eye looks within. With it, I've seen to the depths of my own soul. I've plunged to the bottom of evil and despair. That's how I became mad."

Heimdall looked deep into Voden's open eye. "I have seen worlds fall. Worlds made rotten by the evil of the men that built them. I have seen dreams grow, age, turn sour, and curl back on the dreamers to corrupt and destroy them. I have seen death in many guises and forms, some lovely, soft, delightful, others hard and bloody. Do not tell me of evil, Voden. Do not tell me of the horror that lurks within you. It lurks within all."

"But is there any hope, then, Heimdall? Is there any reason to be sane, to live, to go on? I was better off before I drank from the well. Then I still had hope!"

The cool gaze of the white man was steady. "You closed that inner eye, Voden. You are no longer insane. How did you manage it if there is no hope, no reason to live? Think!

"I have watched the destruction of worlds, true, and am doomed to see yet more fall. It is a fate I cannot escape until nine have come and gone. Nine! Imagine the evil that can be packed into nine worlds!

"And then imagine the glory, the love, the tenderness, the beauty that also lives in those worlds. Is it less than the evil? Does it weigh nothing in the scale? Think! You know the answer! You closed that eye yourself!"

Voden groaned and held his head in his hands. "I . . . I can't . . . it's too soon, Heimdall. My mind's a chaos. There's only a thin layer of control. It's too fragile, too new. I . . . I need time to rest and absorb what I've seen. Maybe then . . ." He looked up at the white man, a plea written across his features. "Will you stay with me, Heimdall? Will you help me?"

Heimdall gave him a long, serious look. Then the white man shrugged and a slight smile lifted the corners of his mouth. "I have washed and clothed your naked body. I have cared for you for weeks now. Yes, I will continue to help you,

Aesir. Why?" He closed his eyes slightly and stared off into the night beyond the fire. When it came again, his voice was soft and musing. "We are bound together, you and I. I am the Ram, you the Wolf and Raven. I can see into the future, sometimes. Brief glimpses. Soon I will blow my Gjallarhorn for a fourth time, to sigr l the fall of a world. We will fight side by side in a great battle to make way for a new and better time. Yes, we are bound together. It will not always be a comfortable pairing, but it must be, regardless. I will do a thing that must be done, yet receive no thanks for it."

He looked up suddenly, his eyes back in focus. "But that is enough talk of such things! We must eat now. You are conscious for the first time in many weeks. For once you can feed yourself! I am tired of being your nursemaid!"

VANAHEIM

XV

THE fall and winter had been a time of growing danger for Yngvi and his men. The Disir had called in the Valkyrja from as far away as the River Geirvimul and set them on his trail. Time after time he and his chief lieutenants had barely escaped with their lives. The foresters struck back again and again, but for every one of the woman warriors they killed, two more showed up to take their place. When one of Yngvi's died, there was no one to fill the empty spot.

As spring approached, the gathering in of the Valkyrja was almost complete. Small garrisons had been left at key points to the west of the Gunnthro and Slid, but the vast majority of the fighting force of Vanaheim was now camped in and around Folkvang.

In the city itself things appeared calm on the surface. One simple fact, however, gave the lie to appearances: Od was still king. When the time had come to strip him of his title and his manhood, when the weeping women had gathered in the courtyard of the royal compound, Freyja had refused to bring Od out to them. Many had been aghast at this blasphemy. Others secretly smiled.

The Disir had been furious. Yet when the Distingen met, it

had been impossible to reach a decision on what action to take. This was largely the result of the fact that Syofyn had returned earlier than Syr had planned. The youngest of the Disir, now that Lofyn was dead, Syofyn had immediately taken Freyja's side and had managed to win Hlin and Syn to her cause as well. When Vor and Syr had tried to have Freyja declared dead so that they could name a new Vanadis, even Eir and Gna had refused to go along with such drastic measures and temporarily joined forces with Syofyn. The result was that nothing had been done about Od. Sides, however, had clearly been drawn.

The division of the Distingen became even clearer when an attempt was made to pick a new Disir to replace Lofyn. Vor proposed Gomul, an ancient like herself, deeply steeped in the Seidar-magic. Syofyn, on the other hand, advanced the name of Gefjon, a young woman known for her beauty and purity. After numerous attempts to break the resulting tie vote, the matter was tabled and the Distingen, for the first time in memory, had only eight members.

Inevitably Folkvang itself began to reflect the division among its rulers. The party of Syr, demanding a return to the old ways and practices, took to wearing a black band around their left arm. In response the party backing Freyja wore a white band around their right arm.

The arrival of the Valkyrja only complicated matters. Some of the older warriors sided with the partisans of Syr. Others, generally the youngest, supported the Vanadis. The great majority, however, were more confused than anything and tried to avoid entanglement with either side. The major problem they faced, of course, was the question of whose orders to follow. Technically the Vanadis commanded the Valkyrja. In fact the older Disir, especially Syr, had been giving most of the orders for many years. Fiorgynn had never taken a great deal of interest in military matters and had left them primarily to her oldest advisers. A further complication was the fact that Freyja had been trained with many of the younger warriors and had known many of the older ones as teachers.

Although Freyja did everything she could to delay and divert the hunting down of Yngvi and his men, she didn't have enough power to halt it completely. As spring came closer, she began to realize she would be unable to stop the massive drive

Syr planned against the foresters. Yngvi and his men had killed Valkyrja, and the women warriors, even when they supported Freyja, were angry about the death of their fellows and determined to avenge them.

In early spring Freyja sent Rota to Yngvi with word that the offensive sweep would begin in about a month's time. Yngvi counted his resources and came to the grim conclusion that he and his men had no option but to flee into the barren mountains known as the Smoking Lands. "We can't cross the Gopul and go into Nidavellir," he told Rota. "The Dverg have a treaty with the Distingen and would help hunt us down. We can't break through to the west, there're too many Valkyrja between us and the Gunnthro. All that's left is the south and the Smoking Lands."

Rota shook her head. "You'll never survive there. It's too barren. No game, no fruit, no roots, nothing. You'll starve."

Harbard scratched his shaggy head and mumbled, "Lass is right, she is. Best go north."

"North?" Yngvi asked. "Out onto the Himinborg Plain? How long do you think we'd last against the Aesir? We don't even have horses."

"Huh," Harbard grunted, "didn't know we was at war with Borr and his lot. Fought beside 'em several times. Liked 'em well enough, I did. Know quite a few of us, they do. No, didn't know they was at war with us. Maybe not too friendly to the Distingen after what happened to Voden, but us?"

Yngvi looked appraisingly at Harbard. "You may have something there. Why didn't I think of that?"

"Never been north to fight is why. Always here in the woods with Jalk, you was. No offense, mind, but us as has been north see the Aesir a bit different."

"Sounds worth a try to me," Rota said. "Harbard's the likely one to go and talk to Borr. Do you know him, Harbard?"

Harbard grinned slyly. "Oh, well, we've emptied a jug of mead or two, we have. Aye, I know Borr. Know Gagnrad even better, and that's the same thing nearly. I'd be willin' to give it a go. You should come too, Yngvi. Borr owes you for the favor you did young Voden. Weren't for you, the lad would still be doped with that damned mandragora and a slave in Folkvang."

Yngvi paused thoughtfully. "I guess Byggvir and the others could manage to stay a step ahead of the Valkyrja for a week or so. Yes, by Beyla, it's worth a try!"

The Warrior's Hall was packed when Yngvi and Harbard were brought in by Gagnrad. Word had quickly spread that two of the foresters from Vanaheim were in Asgard, and every man for miles around watched to hear what they had to say. The way the treaty between the Vanir and the Aesir had been broken was common knowledge, but since the death of Fiorgynn, very little news had come out of the forests to the south. Everyone was curious to know what was going on. Once before the Vanir had been dangerous enemies. Would that time return again?

Seated in the High Seat, Borr watched the two Vanir stalk self-consciously between rows of jeering, laughing warriors to reach the open space where guests who wished to address the assembly stood. The older, shaggy one he knew. Harbard. Good man. Sturdy. Deadly with a bow or throwing ax. Handy to have around in a fight. Not bad as a partner in a drinking bout, either.

The other he also recognized, though he'd only seen him once, on the edge of the Idavoll Plain where the River Gunnthro pours out from under the dark forest into the bright sunshine of the open, rolling lands of the Aesir. Only once, but he would never forget that time.

At first, when Fiorgynn had told him Voden was dead, he hadn't known what to do. Then his anger had risen and he'd been ready to attack the Vanir, even though he and his band were badly outnumbered. Suddenly a new group had appeared. In their middle was his son Voden, looking older and stronger than ever. There had been an air of calm and firmness about him that had made Borr proud.

His pride, however, soon turned to dismay. Voden had changed. He refused to come back to Asgard, refused to return home to Asaheim. Instead he'd wandered off to find Mimir's Well. Damn, he thought, angry even now, what a crazy thing to do! I go to find Groa's other eye, he'd said, or something like that. By Sigfod, everyone knew the old witch-woman only had one eye! She'd lost the other one ages ago, before Borr had even been born. How could anybody find an eye lost that long ago? What nonsense! Yet when he'd told

Groa about it, the old woman had nodded and muttered what sounded like a prayer for the lad.

Bah! Foolishness! Voden belongs here, next to his father, fighting the Jotun, and perhaps now the Vanir as well. Damn!

Borr nodded to Harbard and Yngvi, then with a slight smile said, "So the Vanir again send us warriors to fight the Jotun. Rather small war party."

Harbard grinned. "Aye, small it is, Skullcracker, but big enough to double your strength in a raid and triple it in a drinking bout!"

A shout of approval greeted the Vanir's words and several warriors shoved drinking cups into the two men's hands. "Not mead any longer, now that the Vanir have stopped coming," Gagnrad said. "But honest Aesir ale."

Harbard took a long swallow and smacked his lips. "Whew," he grunted. "Not Beyla's brew, but plenty of sting nonetheless. Just have to drink a bit more to get the same results."

"Not as good while you're drinking," Borr added, "but a lot better the next morning! I like your mead, Vanir, but it likes me not! Or how else to explain the attack it makes on my head the next day?"

"Just all those Vanir bees tryin' to find a way out of a thick Aesir skull is all!" Harbard bellowed with glee. The warriors roared, and even Borr laughed heartily.

"There's more than angry bees in Vanaheim these days, though," Harbard began, getting down to business. "This here's Yngvi. You know him, Borr. Friend of young Voden's. He's the leader of us foresters and he's the one been stinging the Disir lately."

"Only now we've stirred up a hornet's nest ourselves," Yngvi said, "and the stinging's as much on their side as ours."

"So," Borr rumbled. "Give us the tale. It sounds worth the hearing. Bring more ale, Gagnrad, and stools. Telling is dry work and I'd not have this cut short by thirst."

As Yngvi's story unfolded, the Aesir became progressively quieter and more attentive. When he reached the part about the gathering of the Valkyrja, a murmur of concern spread among the benches. Every Aesir knew that an army that size could be used against more than one enemy. Once the foresters were crushed, would the Disir disband it or turn it northward to settle old scores?

"And so," he finished, "we come to ask help from those we've fought beside in the past. We'll fight to the last man, whatever you decide. But then the Disir will be totally in control, and only Beyla knows what those whores of Aud-humla will do."

A thoughtful silence settled over the gathering. Eventually Asgrim, a chieftain from the southern Himinborg Plain, rose to address the hall. "I know Harbard," he began. "Fought next to him twice. He's a good fighter."

"In the old days, before the treaty with the Vanir, I tangled with the Valkyrja now and again. They'd raid our farmsteads when they thought we'd gone too deep into their forests. Always killed everyone and everything but the girl children." He scratched his grizzled beard. "Did unpleasant things to the men and boy children, they did.

"We've got farmsteads and Aesir families in places they were never in before the treaty. Places south even of where they used to raid. Lot of them are going to die if it comes to war. I can't help but remember the bodies of those boys." He sat down amid total silence.

Another warrior stood. He was from the Idavoll. "I've not the years of Asgrim, but I'm as good at reckoning as any here. We're hard pressed by the Jotun to the north. Since the treaty was broken off with those to the south, we've all felt the cold to our backs. Best we be careful on how we act. Things are unsettled, for sure, but that's better than open warfare, say I."

Hrolf, an axeman of renown, rumbled to his feet. "The Vanir are dangerous. Even as allies they were dangerous. Not these lads as stand before us, mind you. I've stood back to back with many a one and never asked for a better. I mean those black-robed bitches and their damned Valkyrja.

"Now Harbard and Yngvi, they're fighting our battle, in a way. The longer they keep the Valkyrja occupied, the longer those bitches stay off our backs. They can do a lot better job of it than we can. They know the forest, know every ambush spot in it. Keeping them going as long as possible can only be to the good. Remember, the spring is soon over and the River Iving will be crossable once more. That means Jotun. I'd rather not be facing two ways at the same time."

From warrior to warrior the debate moved slowly and surely. Most seemed to favor some sort of help for Yngvi and his foresters, but no one seemed to be too sure what form it should take. Gagnrad, one of the last to speak, thought it was time to reverse the flow of warriors and send some Aesir south to help Yngvi and the foresters who'd come north to battle the Jotun. "Remember," he said with a sly wink, "those that go would learn something few of us know, something that could be handy in the future. They'd learn the Vanir art of forest fighting."

When the last man had spoken, all eyes turned to Borr. The Aesir chieftain was silent for a long time, then looked down at Harbard. "Once, when we'd drunk a great deal of mead and pledged eternal friendship, you told me a tale. It was a strange tale of a time long ago. I'd have you tell it again."

Harbard looked startled. "The story of Non? Aye, it's an old one to be sure. I had it of my uncle, who had it of his, who had it of his, and so on to the beginning of time. Only trustworthy men know it, and they only tell it to others of their like. The Disir know nothing of it, nor does any woman." He looked around uneasily. "To tell it to so many..." He sighed and cast a glance at Borr, who nodded to him encouragingly. "Well, if it helps, I guess it can do no harm. But you all must swear never to repeat it in woman's hearing. Do you swear on your uncle's heart?" A rumble of agreement greeted his request. "Well, then, more ale, for it's a thirsty tale, to be sure."

Harbard settled himself more comfortably on his stool, took a long swallow of ale, and sat for several moments staring into the distance. "Long, long ago," he began, "in a time so distant that even the echo of it is gone from most men's memories, the world was a vastly different place. Cold of winter never came to scour the land, nor heat of summer to parch it. Then the only people that walked the face of Yggdrasil were those made by Audhumla, licked from the smoking ice of Gunningunga Gap. They were few in number and lived on the milk that flowed from Audhumla's tits. Norfi was one. Another was Naglfari. Then there was Aud and Annar, Delling and Mundilfari, Bil and Hjuki, and Vidfinn. They lived beside the spring called Byrgir and never went hungry or thirsty, never suffered from cold or heat. They went about naked, for clothes weren't needed.

"They were fair to look at and seemed much like you and I. In fact, they were very different. For, know you, there were no men or women in those ancient times. Every being was both or neither. All things were created by Audhumla and had no need to breed. They had no cocks or tits or vaginas. Such things didn't exist.

"How long that age lasted, no man can tell. Since creatures were never born and never died, there was no way to mark time. Nor was there a sun or a moon in the sky to measure out the years and months. Life flowed like a great, smooth river.

"Eventually Audhumla tired of the monotony. Every new creature she licked from the ice was much like the last. She became bored. She called all her creatures to her. Grasping each one, she tore it in half to make two beings. In every case, though, her tearing was badly done and one of the new creatures was different from the other. Some had cocks. Others had breasts and vaginas. Audhumla looked at her handiwork and found it faulty. She picked all the creatures up and threw them far away.

"Suddenly the creatures were on their own. They could no longer live on Audhumla's milk, nor drink from the waters of Byrgir. In fear, they huddled together, each half trying to find the other half of the original being. They tried to fit themselves back together again, but it was impossible. For a short time they could form a single beast, but never for very long.

"Soon, they began to realize how different they were. They covered their bodies and hid themselves from each other's eyes. One group called themselves men, the other took the name of women. The women looked at their bodies and saw they had breasts but lacked cocks. Instead, they had holes and vaginas. This made them jealous. They captured one of the men and cut his cock off, keeping it for themselves. This made the men angry and frightened, so they ran off into the forests. The women stayed behind and built a village where they lived.

"It soon became evident, however, that neither men nor women could live alone. The men desired the women and the women desired the men. So from time to time the men would creep up and grab a woman and take her back to their camp in the woods. There they would all join with her. When they'd all satisfied their need, they'd let her go again.

"This kind of treatment angered the women. So one of their greatest witches devised a way of putting teeth in every woman's vagina. That way, whenever a man would join with them, they could eat him up.

"Such a thing couldn't be allowed to continue. One of the

strongest men, known to all as Non, decided something had to be done. He crept close to the women's village and waited for night to fall. Then, in the darkest hour, he slipped into the hut of a woman named Ginnar. She felt him and knew what he wanted. Smiling evilly in the dark, she gnashed her teeth and spread her legs to receive Non. But Non was ready. Instead of thrusting with his cock, he thrust a long, hard stone into her vagina. Ginnar bit down on it and shattered all her teeth. Then Non joined with her and gave her great pleasure. Before he pulled out, though, he left a little part of himself behind. 'You'll have to be satisfied with that,' he said, 'because now your teeth are gone.'

"The next night Non did the same thing with another woman, and then again and again, until he'd broken the teeth of every woman. But because he left a little of himself behind every time, the women were satisfied. They became even more satisfied when new things began to grow in their bellies. Now they had something the men didn't have! As long as the men left a little part of themselves behind, the women could take that part and make it into a new being!

"Most of the women were satisfied with the arrangement. There were still some evil women, though, who wanted to have teeth in their vaginas. Non had known such a thing would happen, so he had destroyed the secret of the witch-woman. The way of putting teeth in the vagina was lost. The evil women raged and frothed at the mouth. They declared they would rediscover the method and began to study the magic that became known as the Seidar. They took the name of Disir. They haven't discovered the secret of how to do it yet, but they're still trying. That's why the men of Vanaheim live mostly in the forest and the women live in the cities."

Harbard paused for a moment and took a deep drink from his cup. With a gratified sigh he wiped his lip. "And that," he said, finishing up his tale, "is what this war between us is truly about. The Disir wish to chew us up. If they win, they will. And once they've chewed us up, they'll be after you."

"We'd be a hard lot to chew," Gagnrad said, attempting humor. A nervous laugh ran about the benches.

"Not," Harbard replied, "if they ground you between two stones to soften you."

Borr nodded. "Aye. That's the crux of it. The Disir hate us because in Asaheim the men rule. They'll grind us between the Jotun and the Valkyrja and then try to chew us up.

"The only question is, What kind of help can we afford to give you? Spring will pass and the Jotun will begin to raid again. We'll raid in return. Their power grows once more. That damned young Hrodvitnir is uniting more and more of them behind his leadership. He's a fighter, by Sigfod, and loves to make war on us. We'll be having our hands full."

"We're asking two things of the Aesir," Yngvi said. "First, if we must leave our forests, the right to pass through the plains. Second, whatever help you and your warriors can give to fight the Valkyrja. We fought by your side against the Jotun. Now fight by ours against our enemy."

Borr let his eyes drift around the hall as the buzz of conversation rose to a dull roar in response to Yngvi's requests. Some of the men would clearly be happy for a chance to fight the Valkyrja. Mostly they were warriors from the southern part of Asaheim, men from the lower parts of the Himinborg, Idavoll, and Aesir plains. All their lives they'd tangled with the women warriors, and saw them as hereditary enemies.

Others, though, weren't as eager to direct any forces southward. They were men from the north, from the areas close to the River Iving, where the Jotun swarmed to raid and murder. For them the most immediate danger was from the Sons of Ymir. Any forces diverted toward the south would simply be strength taken away from the danger in the north.

Borr sighed. It was the same problem as always. For a while, when the treaty with the Vanir had been in force, things had been easier. They'd been able to concentrate on the enemy to the north. Many Aesir farmsteads had been spared the scourge of Jotun raids and many innocent lives had been saved.

Then everything had changed. The Vanir had broken the treaty by their treacherous treatment of his son. Voden had gone wandering. Now Vanir fought Vanir. He shook his head. Things were happening in Yggdrasil, things he didn't like or understand.

His dreams, for example. He shuddered inwardly as he thought of them. They'd become more frequent, more vivid of late. In them he sometimes found himself on the Vigrid Plain again, pillaging caravans. Surt, the slender little robber and cutthroat from Muspelheim, was there too. Those were the good dreams. The bad ones were filled with Surt's curse that night of the battle where Borr had won Vestla, his wife. He saw the slender man lying in the dark, raised on one elbow, his other hand stretching out accusingly, the fingers weaving strange patterns in the air. Once again he heard the dying man's curse ringing in his ears: "Take me or take my curse. Take me, or I'll take you and all your spawn and all your people! Take me or die, Aesir!"

The rest of the dreams were better left unremembered. Surt's face, huge, twisted, demonic, laughing. Other demons, hideous, threatening. He shuddered and turned his attention back to the real world of the hall.

Discussion has gone on long enough, Borr decided. He held up his hand to ask for silence. Gradually the noise died down. He looked over his warriors and then down at Harbard and Yngvi. The two Vanir were attempting to appear calm, but Borr could see their tension in the way they sat their stools and gripped their drinking cups. I'll be passing sentence on them, he realized. So be it.

"Harbard and Yngvi bring us grim news of a danger risen behind our backs once more. It's a grave danger, one we can't ignore.

"Yet neither can we ignore the fact that it's not an immediate danger. Right now the Vanir kill each other. Aesir don't die in Vanaheim. They do die in Asaheim, slain by Jotun.

"We owe the foresters a debt of gratitude. They've fought beside us. But we owe a greater debt to our own, to our wives and children, who without our swords and axes would perish miserably beneath the blades of the Sons of Ymir, the foul, night-raiding Jotun. There's a conflict of honor and practicality here.

"We can't mount a major expedition to fight with the foresters. That much is plain. Nor do our Vanir friends ask for such. They ask the right to sanctuary if forced from their leafy haunts by the Valkyrja. I say give it to them." Cheers of agreement met these words. Yngvi and Harbard both smiled with evident relief.

"They ask for more, though. They ask for arms to help them make the raven's feast, to spread the wolf's work through the forests of Vanaheim. Not for a vast host do they ask, but for whatever help we can provide.

"Now I see some shake their heads in concern. Those are they who live closest to the Jotun. They worry rightly. Others

I see who clench their fists and grit their teeth in their eagerness to pick up ax and fly to pile the brown-clad bodies high. They are those whose families and friends have been killed or driven from their farmsteads by the Valkyrja. They, too, are right.

"How to balance one right against the other? This is no easy thing for a man to do. So let each man look into his own heart. Does he hate Jotun or Vanir more? Which would he fight? Where will his sword or ax do the Aesir most good? Those who choose to head into the forests with Yngvi and Harbard, provided they don't number more than one in three, have leave to go and fight. They also have leave to stay here in Asaheim with us, for there will be warfare aplenty in the north this summer.

"Decide by the morning. The foresters have little time to tarry. Whichever you choose, you'll be striking a blow at the enemies of Asaheim. And, by Sigfod, be sure you strike hard!"

A roar of approval greeted his decision. Yngvi and Harbard rose and went to the High Seat to clasp his hands in thanks. He looked at them both and smiled grimly. "It's not enough. But it's the best we can do."

"It's generous and will suffice," Harbard said gruffly.

"I hope so," Yngvi muttered. "For all our sakes, I hope so."

XVI

"YOU'RE positive they're Aesir and not just foresters pretending to be Aesir?" Syr asked.

Hild drew herself up even straighter than usual. Her black eyes glittered with offended pride. The slight streaks of gray in her hair gave her a dignified air that was matched by the severity of her uniform. The only indication that she ranked high within the Valkyrja was a small insignia on her left shoulder. "The Disir forgets that I have fought the Aesir on many occasions," Hild said coldly. "I know them well. Further, I do not make idle suggestions. I check my facts thoroughly before I speak. There are Aesir fighting alongside the foresters."

Vor gave Syr a warning look and said mildly to the Valkyrja, "Syr is overwrought. Forgive her foolish doubt, Hild. If one with your years of experience and service say it is so, then it must be so." Hild looked slightly mollified. "The next questions," Vor continued, "are how many Aesir are with the foresters, and why are they there?"

The Valkyrja nodded. "My estimate is that there are no more than a hundred of the barbarians with Yngvi."

"A hundred?" Syr growled angrily. "Is Borr with them?"

187

Hild shook her head. "No. There do not appear to be any chieftains with them. I would hazard the guess that they have come on their own to fight with Yngvi for 'glory.' That would fit with their rather primitive notions of warfare. When they grow tired of the fight, they will doubtless head north again to sit in their smelly halls and sing foolish songs praising their own courage and reciting their exploits."

"Well," Vor mused thoughtfully. "All you say is doubtless true. But still, I think there is more than glory seeking behind this. That could account for a few, say twenty or thirty. It doesn't make sense for nearly a hundred. No, there's more to this than glory. I smell Borr."

"The man can't be a big enough fool to make war on us," Syr snarled. "He can't fight on two fronts at the same time and he knows it. There simply aren't enough—"

"Ah," Vor interrupted, "but he isn't fighting on two fronts. He has Yngvi doing most of the fighting for him on this front. The few warriors he sends south don't materially weaken him against the Jotun, but they do help to shore up the foresters and give them heart. He embroils us in a war without embroiling himself. Yes. It becomes clearer now. Yngvi and Voden were friends. Voden is Borr's son. This whole thing with the foresters is very likely one of Borr's plots. I'd not be surprised to discover the Aesir behind all this."

"By Audhumla, sister, I think you're right!" Syr said excitedly. "And if that's true, then there's only one way to end it all. We must attack the Aesir! Defeat Borr and Yngvi falls too!"

Vor gave Syr a considering look. "You hate the Aesir badly, eh, sister? And Voden too. You've a personal score to settle with them all?"

"Yes!" Syr answered without thinking. "Yes, I would—" Something in Vor's glance made the Disir stop uneasily.

"Fool," Vor said coldly. "You've been letting personal hatred blind you. No wonder you've made so many mistakes. You carp on the hot-bloodedness of young Syofyn while your own runs just as feverishly with the fires of revenge. Fool. This situation was and is very complicated, and grows more so every day. There are forces at work here that are beyond your meager ken. This is the time for a serpent's cunning and coldness.

"Attack Borr, you say? Aye, and while we walk to Asgard he rides his horses around our flanks and cuts us to ribbons. And here in Folkvang, how long do you think it would be until Freyja pulled open the gates and invited Yngvi in? You would find your hot blood quenched then, Syr, with cold metal.

"No, we do not attack Borr. We do everything we can to avoid attacking any Aesir on our borders, even those whose farmsteads encroach on our forest. We will not give Borr any pretext to declare war on us to defend himself. Why do you suppose there are so few Aesir with Yngvi, and none of them chieftains? Because Borr has no legitimate reason to send them. As long as we're not officially at war with the Aesir, he has no power to send anyone except those willing to go on their own. But if we attack him, ah, then he could do much, much more."

"But Borr and his dare not invade Vanaheim," Syr protested. "They're warriors of the plains. They know nothing of fighting from tree to tree. We've nothing to fear."

"Disir," Hild said, "remember that those Aesir fighting with Yngvi are learning the very art you speak of. Further, many of Yngvi's men have fought side by side with the northerners and would be more than willing to aid them in an invasion."

The look of surprised realization that flooded Syr's face made Vor chuckle maliciously. "Aye, sister, now you see it! Borr is no brainless barbarian to be hated and easily destroyed. He is a wily, crafty enemy who has laid his plans well. The treaty, our men going north, Voden and Honir here, now Aesir learning our style of fighting in our own forests— this is not the work of a fool, sister. You've allowed your thirst for revenge to blind you to the truth. And think on one thing more, sister. What will happen when young Voden returns from Mimir's Well? For mark my words, return he will. What then? Borr has woven his web well. Very, very well, by Audhumla."

Vor turned to Hild. "Tell all Valkyrja that we're giving a bounty for every Aesir killed. I'd rather kill one of them than ten foresters. Once they're all dead, we'll have only Yngvi to deal with. Borr will not step into the middle of that. No. Once we've put the Aesir here in Vanaheim out of the picture, we'll have destroyed a critical piece of Borr's scheme. Kill them, Hild, kill them all.

"But bring one to us alive." Her voice dropped to a vicious purr. "Yes, one alive. We will do things to him and then send him back to Borr—a messenger and a warning."

The Valkyrja nodded curtly and left the room. Vor sat and for some time watched the door through which the warrior left. Eventually she allowed her eyes to find those of Syr. "There is one more thing we must do, sister."

"Freyja?" Syr asked, her tone full of malicious eagerness.

Vor nodded. "Aye, Freyja. But not Freyja."

Syr looked at her in confusion. "What do you mean?"

"Only that we must strike at Freyja by not striking at Freyja. The cursed girl is too strong. She's surrounded herself with supporters. The damned royal hall is a virtual fortress, complete with its own army ready to die for the stupid little bitch. No, we can't strike directly at Freyja. We must aim our blow at her weak spot. We must aim at that fool Od."

"But he almost never leaves the royal hall unless it's with Freyja or a guard of Valkyrja. There's no way to get him alone and stick a knife in his ribs."

"A knife?" Vor grinned and shook her finger at Syr. "Shame on you, sister. Such a crude method isn't what I have in mind at all. There are ways to reach Od that no one as young and unschooled as Freyja will even see."

"You mean the Seidar-magic?" Syr asked, her voice dropping to a mere whisper. The older woman nodded gravely. "But to use Seidar against a Vanadis . . ." Syr left the words hanging.

Vor laughed out loud. "Against a *true* Vanadis, yes, using the Seidar would be dangerous, even deadly. Curses have a nasty way of rebounding from those steeped in magic. But Freyja is hardly wise in the arts of Svarthofdi. Fiorgynn was never much a one for magic and never saw to it her daughter received more than the bare rudiments of an education in such things. The girl spent all her time in the practice yards with the Valkyrja.

"Even then we're not going to attack her directly, but indirectly through Od. The plan is simple. I've suborned one of Freyja's maids. The silly girl will bring us a few hairs from Od's head. Something no one will even miss."

Syr rubbed her hands together with pleasure. "Yes, yes!

With a hair or two we can weave a spell and kill the fool! Then—"

"Kill?" Vor interrupted. "Who said anything about kill? If we were to kill Od with magic, even one as untutored as Freyja would smell it out. No, nothing so drastic as killing. That would give Freyja and her friends a martyr, a rallying point against us. We must be far more subtle than killing, sister."

"Are you suggesting a disease, like Fiorgynn's?"

"Never repeat yourself, Syr. No, even more subtle. Od will simply go wandering off. He'll disappear." She leaned forward and fixed Syr with her dark, burning eyes. "We'll use the hair to create a calling spell, one to bring him to us. Then we'll have time to weave a stronger spell, one of forgetting."

"You'll wipe his mind?" Syr said with a gasp.

"Aye, partially. Everything from the last few years will go. Then we'll fix a wandering spell on him, send him off and never see him again."

"He'll spend the rest of his life wandering the world," Syr said softly, "a beggar without enough wit to find his way home. Lost until the day he dies, alone, unknown, in an unknown land."

"Yes," Vor smiled cruelly, "and without her beloved Od, Freyja will be just as lost."

Eir looked at the body that lay on the bed, restlessly turning this way and that, muttering and crying out from time to time. She turned to face Vor and Syr, her mouth a harsh line, her eyes filled with bitterness. "Are you happy?" she said in a low voice. "Ever since Od disappeared she's been like this. I've never seen anything like it. Nothing brings her out of it. She's somewhere frightening and she can't get back, in an endless nightmare that won't stop." Syr started to interrupt, but Eir cut her short. "Don't even bother to deny it. I know you did nothing to her directly. I also know you're responsible for the disappearance of Od. The little maid talked. When she realized what she'd done, she went immediately to Rota and confessed the whole thing. Poor child, I've had to give her something to calm her too."

The old healer gave Vor and Syr a hard look. "I wonder if you were aware that Freyja's pregnant? There's no telling what this will do to the baby. If she doesn't come out of it soon, she could lose the only part of Od she has left."

She gestured to Freyja. "She knows what you did. It was the maid's confession that made her realize what had happened. Audhumla help you both if she recovers." The healer looked back down at Freyja and her voice became husky with emotion. "Why couldn't you have left her alone? She's suffered so much. Voden, her mother, now Od, maybe even her child. Why couldn't you simply leave her alone?"

"Is there anything we can do to help?" Vor asked, her voice heavy with sincerity.

Eir laughed bitterly. "Help? You, help? Get out of here, both of you. I'm leaving specific instructions with Rota that under no conditions are either of you or any of your minions ever to be admitted to the royal hall again. Now, get out, damn you, get out!"

She stood in a dark place where grotesque things moved stealthily around her. The stench of rotting flesh almost stopped her breath. A cold so deep it burned wrapped around her body and squeezed her flesh. This was the place where the mind and soul came face to face with their greatest terrors and most dreadful dreams. She looked around, trying to find a way out. There was none. One could only move forward toward whatever doom awaited.

A figure rose in front of her, the flesh long gone from its face, eyes mere emptiness. But deep within the darkness, she could see a growing light of hellish red. The jaw opened and a cavernous voice filled with anguish and desire echoed out. "Dive in, dive in, dive into my eyes. Here lies the way you must go. Here lies madness and wisdom. So close are they, so mixed and mingled in my mind. Come share them, for know that I am Mardoll."

An ancient time rolled through her mind, a life lived in caves and deep forest groves. Blood ran on altars. Ideas so hidden that no mind had thought them for eons stalked her sanity down dark and noisome corridors far beneath the earth. A foulness overwhelmed and buried her, driving her far from her youth and humanity.

Then she was through and Mardoll was behind, not left, not forgotten, but a part of her, a hidden corner of evil power and grim knowledge. Another reared up to block her path.

She recoiled as the figure rose high above her, skeletal, leer-ing, knowing.

"Horn am I. Dreaded while I lived. More dreaded yet in the grave. Come, your path lies with me for a while. I will whisper in your ear of powers not dreamed of. Come, walk with me."

A hard skeletal hand grasped her arm and forced her close. A fleshless mouth began to hiss obscenities into her mind. She fought to keep them out, but it was no use. Her sanity teetered and fell crashing and roaring over an endless cliff. She laughed and shrieked hysterically, fear tearing her to pieces. She screamed and screamed. But the whispering never stopped, and every word sank deep in her memory.

Suddenly a new horror rose before her. She closed her eyes as tightly as possible, yet it made no difference. The thing was in her mind and couldn't be shut out. "Gefn I was called. Most dire and fearful giver. Free were my gifts when given, but heavy the price paid later. I am here within you. You must know me now." She moaned and sank to the cold, dank ground, as Gefn opened herself within an already shattered mind. Knowledge so dark, so utterly evil that the very thinking of it made her mind turn cold and hard, flowed over her in a clinging slime.

Then Gefn was gone and a vast shadow took her place. "Hel be I, of ancient times, before humans walked the earth. I have no shape of womankind, no armed and legged form. My mind and thoughts are twisted and strange, not made for human mind. My power is raw and primitive and vast as dark of night. You will fall long within it until you reach that unnameable thing that lies at its center and creates it all."

With a cry, she felt herself being torn and twisted in a hundred different directions. Parts of her mind drifted off into the void. In terror she tried to hold them, but it was no use. The power of Hel's inhuman mind was greater than any force she possessed. Disintegrating, dissolving, she fell, fighting all the way. At last, exhausted, knowing there was no hope, she closed herself into a tiny ball around the most essential ground of her being and let the rest go. Stripped to a point of self, she fell swiftly and freely.

And stopped.

For a while she just lay there, relishing the peace and

absence of pain and fear. Then, slowly, carefully, she uncurled and looked out of her pure essence at what surrounded her.

She was in the middle of an infinite, empty space, lit by a dark light. Empty? No! Full of a presence! She curled back up, tighter than ever.

Time passed. She uncurled again. The presence didn't seem hostile or evil. It was . . . beyond that. She looked out.

"I am Svarthofdi," the very space itself breathed. "Welcome. You have reached me. In doing so you have passed through great evil and your character and spirit have been tested in its cold, destroying fire. It is an initiation that shatters and withers many more souls than it spares. To survive its harsh demands you have had to shed everything but the very seed of your being. Now I will fertilize that seed and make it grow. You are no longer to be what you were but what you can be, so that you may become what you must be. Yggdrasil trembles at its very roots and you must be ready. Learn now the Seidar!"

"Eir! Eir, she's waking up! She's coming back!" Rota cried, tears of joy pouring down her face, "Oh, come quickly! Freyja's coming back to life!"

I only pray it's so, Eir thought as she ran to Freyja's room. I only hope she comes back sane and— She stopped dead in her tracks as she saw the young woman sitting up in the bed. The dark eyes looked up to catch her own. For a moment her heart stopped. Oh, Audhumla, what's happened to her? What is this thing in her flesh?

Then Freyja spoke, softly, sweetly. "I'm back, Eir."

The old healer tried to speak, but her throat was so tight her voice wouldn't work. She swallowed twice quickly and tried again. "Freyja. Where have you been?"

"Wandering," the young woman replied, dropping her eyes to the floor. "Looking for Od, my husband, my king. I've wandered the whole world over, among strange people in far-off lands. I took many names while I wandered—Mardoll and Horn, Gefn and Hel." She looked up again, tears in her eyes. "I didn't find him, Eir. Though I wept tears of red gold, I didn't find him."

Eir's mind was reeling, the names Freyja had mentioned so casually spinning around crazily. Oh, Audhumla, what have we done, what have we done? she wailed silently. Involuntarily, under her breath, she uttered a forbidden word, "Svarthofdi."

Freyja looked at her, tears gone, eyes glittering and dangerous. "Yes," she whispered in a way that made Eir shake inwardly. "Yes. Svarthofdi. Tell them, Eir. Tell them."

The healer had never seen the oldest member of the Distingen shaken before, but now Vor's hand was clearly trembling as she raised it to stroke her chin. Syr was sitting, her mouth agape, her eyes wide with shock, unable to move or speak.

"So," Vor said in an unsteady voice. "Svarthofdi? You're sure she mentioned Svarthofdi?" Eir nodded without comment. "Yes, well then. It seems something has happened here."

Eir laughed harshly. "Indeed! I've known Freyja for longer than either of you. I midwifed her birth, started her breathing, nursed her through childhood, the mandragora, and now this. I know her as well as her own mother did. Maybe better." She fixed them both with a knowing glare. "And I tell you the thing that came back from that wandering both is and isn't Freyja."

"You . . . you speak in riddles," Syr muttered weakly.

"Riddles?" Eir responded sarcastically. "Then let me make it painfully clear to you. Freyja, little Freyja, the daughter of Fiorgynn, a child who has never studied more than the rudiments of the Seidar-magic, is now more powerful than either or both of you combined. She may not realize it herself yet, but it's true. The dark power of Svarthofdi shines from her eyes!"

Eir turned to leave the two of them, then stopped and turned back. "You should know that the baby survived. She still carries it. I wonder what kind of child it will be, for it went through what Freyja went through." She shook her head. "You have many things to answer for. The results of your meddling will reverberate through Yggdrasil for a long time." With a parting glower, she turned again and left.

"What . . . what are we to do?" Syr pleaded, turning to Vor.

The ancient wise woman had regained her equilibrium. "Do? Precious little. Our plans against the Aesir are already afoot. Nothing Freyja can do will stop them. With the Aesir in Vanaheim out of the way, it will be a simple matter to crush Yngvi and his foresters. With them destroyed, her major source of support is gone. Then we can work on those here in Folkvang who so foolishly back her in defiance of the old ways.

"Do? We'll do nothing. Nothing, that is, except weave some strong warding spells. If Eir's right, we're playing a new game and we'd best be on our guard from now on!"

Hrolf sat with the other five Aesir and spoke softly. "I tell you, it's not imagination. I saw it with my own eyes. Bjarni was mobbed by them. They totally ignored the foresters and tried to take him alive."

"Did they make it?" Sigurd growled through clenched teeth.

"Take Bjarni alive? Hah! He started stamping and biting his shield. 'Berserk! Berserk!' he shouted. Then he began frothing at the mouth and went mad. Must've killed ten of them before his heart burst and he dropped dead. I counted twenty-three arrows, five spears, and three of those damn throwing axes in him. No, they didn't take Bjarni alive."

"But they might take the next one they try for," Viga-Glum said darkly.

"Aye," Hrolf responded, "they might." He shivered. "I'd not like to be that one. I don't mind a clean death, my sword in my hand, the way Bjarni died. If it's rune-writ, why, let it come, says I. But to be taken alive by the Disir's minions—"

"No need to say it," Viga-Glum interrupted. "We all are knowing what you're thinkin'."

"Why not say it?" snarled Hinar. "It's the damned Seidar-magic you're feared of. Nothing unmanly in that. By Sigfod, I fear it myself, and there's none as can say I'm not a man!"

Hrolf looked around at them all. "That's not all. Sure you've noticed the rest."

Viga-Glum nodded. "Aye. The way they come for us. Even pass the foresters by to get to us. All their arrows, all their spears, all their cursed axes and knives are aimed at us first."

"So?" Hinar challenged. "Does it make you tremble? Are Aesir afraid of all the arrows and spears and axes in Vana-heim? I fear them not."

"Then you're a damned fool," Viga-Glum replied. "They're coming after us special, trying to kill us off first. Damn me if it ain't so. I come here to fight, not be a target."

"Aye, and that's the truth of it," Hrolf agreed.

"I'm leavin'," Viga-Glum said. "I like the way the Jotun fight better than this creepin' around in the woods, hiding behind trees and leaping out at people. I've done my part like I promised. Now I'm goin' back to Asgard, hoist a few ales, and raid the Jotun. Who's with me?" Hrolf raised his hand. After a moment Sigurd's went up. The silent one of the five, Bolli, scratched his chest, grunted, and nodded.

Hinar looked at the other four, his expression sour. "Well, I'm stayin'. Least I am till I kill a few for Bjarni. He was my cousin and we came down here together. Needs a good end for his song, he does."

"Berserk is good enough end," Hrolf said. "I saw him go down. I'll help with the song. Come along with us, then. We'd not want to leave you all alone among strangers. Then if you died, who'd there be to make *your* song?"

Hinar grumbled a while longer, but finally agreed.

The next morning only foresters were left in the camp.

XVII

"Not a one of the Aesir are still here, Yngvi. I've sent runners to other groups to see if there are any there. Even if there still are, I've got my doubts they'll be stayin' long, now as some have left," Harbard said.

Yngvi nodded. "Aye. They finally noticed what we saw. The Valkyrja were singling them out, passing us right by to attack them. It's exactly the kind of thing Vor or Syr would think up. And damn me if it hasn't worked."

Harbard shrugged. "I'd not stay around if that happened to me, I wouldn't. Fightin' for glory's one thing. Bein' target for slaughter's another. Can't say as I blames 'em all that much."

The leader of the foresters looked down at the ground and nudged a rock with his foot. "Question is," he muttered, "where's that leave us? We've been holding our own lately, thanks to the help the Aesir gave. Now I wonder."

"Oh," Harbard said heartily, clapping Yngvi on the shoulder, "we can do all right ourselves, we can. Aesir were a help, got us over the worst of the summer season, they did. Fall'll be here soon, then winter, and campaignin'll have to stop. We can hold out till then for sure!"

Yngvi looked up, his face serious. "Aye. We can hold out

till then. But what about next spring? How long can we keep it up, Harbard? They're slowly bleeding us to death. How long can we keep it up?"

Rota's grim expression matched Freyja's. "Yngvi and Harbard are being optimistic, if you want my opinion. They'll make it to winter, but they'll lose a lot of men doing it. Worst thing is, I've got a feeling that Hild has no intention of stopping the hunting because there's snow in the forest. She comes from beyond the Svol, and her troopers say she's had them fighting in the snow before."

The Vanadis nodded. "Vor made a good choice when she picked Hild. I wish I'd been wise enough to win her loyalty. Ah, well, no sense in sighing over dropped porridge. Yngvi may have to retreat north."

"And spend the winter on the open Himinborg? He and his men would never survive it. They'd have to take shelter with the Aesir. I'm not sure the farmers of the south would take kindly to putting up a bunch of Vanir all winter. Their own crops weren't too good this year. There'll be hunger in many halls."

"I fear you're right. Rumor has it there's been a noticeable cooling between Vanaheim and Asaheim now that the northerns are gone. Tension is running fairly high along the border." Freyja frowned. "We need Yngvi. Without him we'll be forced to compromise with Vor and Syr. I don't honestly know what that would mean, but you can be sure it wouldn't be pleasant!"

"There's got to be a way out of this, Vanadis! Magic or some clever plan for a surprise attack or some such."

Freyja stroked her slightly bulging stomach and smiled sadly. "No, Rota, there doesn't have to be a way out of this."

Hild pointed with her finger to a dot marked on the map. "This shows the center around which Yngvi's own group operates. There are dots for the other five groups. Each works more or less independently. We used to think there was centralized control, and indeed there may have been, but if so, our constant attacks have disrupted that and it no longer exists. Runners go between the groups on a fairly regular basis, but the leaders almost never meet anymore. Too busy trying to stay out of our reach."

Vor nodded. "Yes, yes, I see. Each group defends its own area. If you enter, they either attack or retreat. That way they cover more territory and can meet you at any point. But it also means they're thinly spread."

"Right," the leader of the Valkyrja responded. "The trick is to concentrate on one area, one group, with all our forces. Up to this point, we've been scattering our efforts too much, trying to track down all the groups at once. But if we attack them one at a time—"

"They won't be able to support each other!" Syr interjected excitedly. "Yes, strike quickly and unexpectedly enough and the other groups won't even know about it until it's all over and done with!"

"That is our intention," Hild replied with a sour look at the Disir. "We are going to strike at this group," her finger stabbed the dot farthest north on the map, "commanded by Byggvir."

"Why not strike directly at Yngvi, in the middle?" Vor asked.

The Valkyrja gave a superior smile. "That would seem logical at first glance. Strike at the leader and defeat him. Then the rest will crumple. Logical. At first glance.

"Yet if one thinks a minute, things are not quite that straightforward. Yngvi is their leader, true. However, this is not a tightly knit operation. Byggvir, Vak, Herteit, Skilving, even that skinny Thud, are totally capable of continuing without him. They have had plenty of practice lately, and are all holding their own quite convincingly. Any one of them could take over Yngvi's place at once, if such a thing were even necessary. I would wager it would not be. They would simply fight on the way they've been fighting.

"So there are no advantages to such an attack. What are the disadvantages? Yngvi's group is the biggest and possibly the toughest. Harbard is with him, and that is something to take into consideration. That man is probably the best fighter among the foresters. Also, if you attack in the middle, it is very easy to be outflanked by the groups on either side.

"I think we could still win, but the victory might be very costly and not yield as much as we would get from attacking Byggvir. First, we destroy a large number of foresters. Second, we cannot be outflanked on the right. Third, we cut off

Yngvi's access to the Aesir. That last reason is possibly the most important of all."

"Why?" Vor asked, knowing it was expected.

"For one thing, it stops the possible reappearance of the Aesir warriors. They would have to pass our lines before they could get to Yngvi. And for another, it cuts Yngvi's line of retreat to the Himinborg Plain."

Vor nodded. "Very well thought out, Hild. We did well to place our trust in you. This final fall campaign against the foresters will end the—"

The Valkyrja shook her head firmly. "No. This will end nothing. This winter we continue to fight."

"Fight? In the winter?" Syr asked. "Why, we've never fought in the winter before."

"I have," Hild said proudly. "And I will this winter too. The foresters won't be expecting it. By spring they will be so battered, it should not take much of the summer to finish them off completely!"

Should have known things were too quiet, Byggvir thought as he fitted another arrow to his bow. He drew and shot at a brown-clad form that dodged quickly between trees. The scream told him he'd hit. Damn, he cursed silently, there's so many of 'em! Maybe twice as many as usual. He signaled to the men nearby to fall back on the hill. Better chance to hold 'em off there. Runner should reach Vak in a while. Vak was always alert and ready. He'd send reinforcements faster than you could curse Audhumla. Damn, there are a lot of 'em!

Lettfeti ran lightly and swiftly through the forest. He'd almost run into a party of Valkyrja just after starting out. There were so many more than usual! Byggvir was right to send him out to Vak for help. Speed was very important. Time to turn it on and not worry so much about being quiet. Couldn't be any more Valkyrja around this far away. He put on a spurt of speed.

The ax caught him in the side of the head. Another hit his chest. A spear entered his stomach and came out his left side. Two arrows struck within about four inches of his heart. The group of women warriors he had run into were on their way to surround Byggvir by outflanking him on his right.

• • •

They swept up the hill in a brown tide, their axes and knives out for close fighting. Byggvir pulled out his own knife and jumped to meet them. He dodged a slash of an ax and went under the arm, stabbing deep in his opponent's side. Grabbing and throwing the Valkyrja's body, he managed to trip up another warrior. A third thrust and gashed his side badly. He slashed her across the arm and then turned the slash into a stab to the stomach. Blood poured out her mouth and she fell back. Another came at him from the right. She threw her ax with deadly intent. Byggvir tried to dodge but was too slow. It struck him in the right shoulder and bit deep. Before he could recover, the woman was on him, her long knife stabbing twice, so swiftly he was unable to block her. He grabbed for the blade and caught it, slicing his hands to the bone. Trying to regain his balance, he coughed and was startled to see blood spurt out. Suddenly he could taste it in his mouth and feel it in his nose.

Damn, he thought, damn. So many of them. Another ax hit him from behind, but he was already falling.

"Slaughtered," the man sobbed for breath. "Every one of them slaughtered."

"Byggvir too?" Yngvi asked.

"Aye. Byggvir too."

Yngvi lowered his head. Good-bye, old friend, he thought. Then he took hold of his emotions and turned to Harbard. "Has Vak sent any news?"

"Aye, just a moment ago. About seven men made it out before the ring closed. Two're so badly wounded they won't be fightin' till next spring, if they live. Vak was alert, as always. Some of his scouts found that runner, Lettfeti, dead in the woods. Figured what had happened and let Vak know. Vak sent a strong party to hit the Valkyrja from the south, take 'em on their left flank. Too late. Already over when they got there. Woods are full of Valkyrja up north. Vak's got scouts out all over the place. A mouse couldn't creep up on that lad without his knowin' it! He'll not be caught napping."

"Tell him to fall back on us at the first sign of any massing of the Valkyrja. Damn Audhumla's eyes! They're going to try and hit each group separately! Send runners to Thud, Herteit, and Skilving. Tell them to be as alert as Vak. Especially

Skilving. They've cut off our retreat to the north, Harbard. Next they'll try to hit Skilving and cut it off toward the south and the Smoking Lands. Send the survivors of Byggvir's group to join Skilving. They've got good experience and Skilving could use the help. Damn!"

Yngvi stood deep in thought while Harbard arranged everything. When the older man had finished, he came back to stand next to his leader. For a few moments the two of them were silent, then Yngvi sighed and turned to Harbard. "It's got to be Hild. That damn woman is one hell of a warrior and leader. This must be her idea. Pick us off one by one."

"How do we stop her?" Harbard asked.

"The only way is to be twice as alert. Double patrols, triple, if necessary. We can't let a train of ants escape our notice. We've also got to be ready to come to each other's assistance at a moment's notice. And we need a series of relay runners so we can get messages between groups at top speed. Harbard, I've got a sinking feeling this is only the beginning of Hild's plan."

"What do you mean?" Harbard asked, a worried expression on his face.

"Hild thinks things out. She doesn't just attack, she has a plan, a goal beyond the attack. I wouldn't be at all surprised if she continues to attack all winter long."

Harbard's worried look turned to one of dismay. "But . . . but if she does that, how're we to hunt? We need the winter, we do, to make more arrows and mend things and put up food and . . . The winter? You think she'd fight all winter?"

"Aye, I do. She knows we need the winter. The Valkyrja don't. It's that simple."

"Damn," Harbard muttered. "Damn. And now we can't retreat to the north. It looks like the Smoking Lands after all."

Yngvi nodded. "That's why we can't let her do to Skilving what she did to Byggvir. Barren as they are, the Smoking Lands may be our only hope for survival."

The fall was a time of blood in Vanaheim. Forester and Valkyrja alike died in greater numbers than ever before. Hild pressed hard, but Yngvi's men fought back with a wily, stubborn determination and a desperate bravery that awed even the Disir. Despite Hild's best efforts, she was unable to repeat her victory against Byggvir. An attack against Skilving was repulsed with such a great loss that she hesitated to try again. Slowly, stubbornly, the foresters retreated south toward the Smoking Lands.

Winter fell on the land like a raging animal. The first storm was a month early and incredibly fierce, lasting for five days and smothering the forest beneath several feet of snow. Within a week another storm raged out of the northwest and added another foot. The temperature plunged, freezing all the rivers except the defiant Gunnthro near Folkvang. Despite Hild's intentions, campaigning came to a halt.

It was a winter much like the one when Voden had been a hostage in Folkvang. The snow was so deep that all travel came to a halt. Weather imposed a peacefulness in Yggdrasil that men could not accomplish on their own.

At the height of the winter Freyja's child was born. It was a little girl, and her mother named her Hnoss. The baby seemed unnaturally calm and quiet, with large eyes that looked out at the world with an intelligence far beyond the ordinary. Eir again wondered what Syr and Vor had brought into the world.

Within Folkvang tension was higher than ever. Many of the younger Valkyrja were tired of the war against their own people. It was one thing to fight Aesir or bandits, but these were Vanir. Rota worked hard to introduce the younger leaders to Freyja. Most were impressed by the Vanadis, by her grace, charm, intelligence, and knowledge of their ways. Here, after all, was a Vanadis that had studied the Thiodnuma with Geirahod. They became aware that Freyja did not support this war, that it was the work of the Disir. The things Freyja said made sense to them, far more sense than the rabid desire to return to the old ways preached by Syr. Sympathy for the Vanadis and her cause began to grow.

"I tell you it was a viper!" Syr was shaking as she spoke. "A forest viper a good five feet long!"

Vor looked skeptically at the Disir. "A forest viper? This time of year? How did it get into the city? Burrowed through the snow? And how did it get past all the guards? Surely it was a dream, Syr."

"By Audhumla, I say it was a viper! Right here in my room! I . . . I opened the door and it was there. It reared up and hissed at me. I barely jumped back in time and slammed the door before it could strike." She shuddered. "I'll prove it to you. Come look and see for yourself!"

Shrugging, Vor followed her sister Disir to her room. Cautiously she opened the door. An angry hiss came from the room before the door had moved more than a few inches. "You see," Syr whispered, fear heavy in her voice. "A viper! I told you!"

Vor flung the door open. There in the middle of the room was a mottled brown snake, its triangular head poised above its curled body, mouth open, fangs showing. Vor studied it carefully, then made a sign with the fingers of her left hand and muttered strange words beneath her breath. The snake disappeared.

Syr, who had been looking over her shoulder, squawked with surprise. "Where . . . where did it go?"

Vor turned and scowled at her. "If you had kept your wits about you, you would have noticed that your viper wasn't real. Look, there where it was." She pointed to the floor of Syr's room. Several long hairs lay on the spot where the snake had been.

Syr went forward and gingerly picked them up. "They're mine," she muttered. Then a look of comprehension dawned on her face and she turned to Vor. "Freyja," she whispered in shock.

Taking the hairs from her, Vor nodded. "Yes. Little Freyja trying out her powers. We're too well warded to be hurt by minor spells, and she doesn't know enought to weave major ones yet." She held the hairs up in front of Syr's nose. "But if we are careless, like this, then she can work small magicks to unnerve and bother us. If she'd been stronger, sister, the viper might have been real. Don't make foolish mistakes. The girl is dangerous."

Grimly, Syr took the hairs back. "Yes, sister, you're right. I've been sloppy and overconfident."

Vor snorted. "It's a nice touch, really, to use your hairs to get back at you. After all, we used Od's hair to strike at him. Yes, a nice touch." She turned and left.

Syr stood for several moments at the open door of her room. She glowered at the retreating back of Vor, then down at the hairs she held in her fingers. She remembered the viper. A chill went up her spine. Freyja was dangerous. Yngvi was still at large. Hnoss, though only a baby, was strange and disturbing. Things were becoming too complicated. She felt her control slipping.

Yngvi looked sourly at the flowers peeking through the last of the snow. "Ordinarily spring is my favorite season," he said to Rota. "Somehow this year I fail to see the beauty in it." She nodded and waited for him to continue. "Winter was hard on us. Hunting was poor because of the snow. We made plenty of arrows and fixed our bows, but we were hungry most of the time. The men are tired. They'll fight. They don't have much choice. But they're weary to the bone." He sighed and kicked at a pile of snow. "Rota," he said, looking up and catching her eye, "we won't make it through the summer. It'll take a miracle to save us."

Rota smiled as best as she could. "Freyja's working on it, Yngvi. Hold on as long as you can. Something's bound to happen."

"Aye," he replied dully, "aye, something's bound to happen. And I tell you, I fear what it will be."

Rota sat in shock as Freyja outlined her plan. "You're not to tell Yngvi or any of his men about this," the Vanadis said sharply. "Tell me now if you can go through with it. If you can't, I'll find someone else."

The Valkyrja dropped her head and stared at the floor. By Audhumla, it was horrible! How could...But it just might work. If they could involve the...Yet it was a terrible thing Freyja was suggesting. A terrible thing!

She looked up at the Vanadis. Freyja was wearing Brisingamen, the necklace Borr had given her mother many years before, when Voden and Honir had been exchanged for Frey and Niord. The Vanadis was gently stroking the figure of Nidhogg, who curled about the root of the great tree. The baleful creature's ruby eyes seemed to gleam with an evil light all their own. Rota shivered and let her eyes meet Freyja's. She tried to speak, but couldn't find her voice at first. After swallowing two or three times, she nodded and said, "Even... even the little ones?"

Freyja nodded, her face hard and cold. "It must be exactly as I've said. I've thought this out carefully and understand all the ramifications of what I'm asking you to do. Everyone must be included. There's no time to lose. You must decide. Now."

The Valkyrja moaned inwardly, swallowed again, and said, "Yes, my Vanadis. I will do this terrible thing. May Audhumla forgive us all!"

Asgeir didn't like the feel of things. He turned to Karl, his eldest son, and motioned him near. When the young man had arrived by his side, Asgeir spoke softly. "Something in the woods this evening. Do ye feel it?"

Karl was silent a moment, searching the shadows that were fast falling around them. "Aye, Father, aye. Could it be a forest cat? Or forest wolves?"

His father shook his head. "No. That'd be more likely in winter or early spring. Most nearly summer now. Wolves be off to the east. Cats, maybe, but it don't feel like no cat." He stopped and sniffed the air. Suddenly tense, he gripped Karl's arm and said in a low growl, "Lad, back to the hall as fast as your legs can carry ye! Then run to Njal's and warn 'em!"

Karl was about to run off when he heard his father mutter one word. "Valkyrja." He ran faster than he'd ever run before.

Rota stood amidst the smoke and blood and wept. Three halls, seventeen children, eleven adults. They'd all been killed cleanly, quickly. No torture for the men or the boys. Swift, clean, honorable death. Yet she wept bitterly for the innocents she herself had slain. Even the little girls, she moaned. Even the sweet babies. Audhumla forgive us. We have no choice.

The Warrior's Hall was struck silent at the news. Borr leaned forward from the High Seat and motioned Gagnrad to bring a stool and a pitcher of ale for the exhausted messenger. "Three farmsteads raided?" The young man slumped onto the stool and nodded. He took a deep drink. "Everyone killed? Even the children?"

"Even . . . even my baby sister," the messenger shuddered with remembered horror. "My father stayed behind and tried to stall them. He . . . he . . ."

Borr nodded with compassion. "Asgeir was a good man, a strong warrior, a true Aesir. The skalds will make a great song to sing him to the hall of Fornjot. But they killed everyone?" The young man nodded again. "And you're positive it was Valkyrja?" Another nod. "Damn," Borr muttered. "Damn, damn, damn, damn."

Gagnrad stood and looked over the silent hall. "We have no choice," he said. "Where the Vanir attack once, they will attack again. Yngvi and his men must have been beaten. Now they turn north in the height of their bloodlust to strike at our people. We must strike back! We must avenge the blood of slaughtered Aesir!"

The men roared in agreement.

Borr sat back and watched wearily as warrior after warrior arose to echo Gagnrad. Cheers rang out again and again until the very rafters of the hall shook with them.

Why? Borr kept asking himself. Why have the Vanir done this thing? Is Yngvi finished? Then Freyja must have given in to the Disir as well. This smelled of Vor and Syr.

Yet it was foolish. The fight with Yngvi must have hurt the Valkyrja. To launch a new war this soon was foolish. The Disir weren't foolish. It didn't make sense. Valkyrja attacking three farmsteads and slaughtering everyone, even the women and girl children. There was something wrong here. Something very wrong. The world was becoming as eerie and frightening a place as his dreams. His dreams! He shuddered to think of them. They'd gotten darker and more horrible than ever. Every time he so much as closed his eyes to nap, demons and monsters leapt out at him!

I'm growing old and tired, he thought sadly. The world is becoming too much for me. Things are changing and I can't change with them. I can't sleep. I walk around in a haze of exhaustion. This is the time for careful thought, deliberate counsel, planning and wisdom, and I'm not sure I'm capable of it.

Nor is anyone else, he realized as he looked over the hall. Our blood is up. We're going to strike the Vanir as hard as we can. And while we do, the Jotun will be behind us, watching and waiting.

DARK EMPIRE

XVIII

THE small room was electric with tension. Jormungand stood in the center of a protective pentagram that Surt had drawn on the floor. The giant warrior was grim-faced and totally armed for battle, his sword and dagger at his sides, his harness polished, his mail shirt on and his helmet in place.

He turned and looked as the slender, dark man came walking backward through the door. "Is everything ready, Black One?" he asked, his voice a vibrant hiss.

Surt nodded. "I've prepared the room, drawn the magic circle, the protective pentagram, the invoking hexagrams. In the north I've set the yellow square with the sigil of the bull painted in black. In the south I've placed the red triangle with the mark of the lion. In the east I've put the blue circle with the sign of the vulture in yellow. In the west I've drawn the silver crescent with the sigil of the scorpion. The windows are sealed, and Ningishzida, the serpent, stands relentless guard over the door.

"My magical implements are consecrated and ready. I went to the east and at sunrise cut a hazel wand with a bloodstained knife. I went to the west and at sunset formed a cup from silver taken from a tomb. I went to the south and at noon

211

forged a dagger from a piece of sky iron. I went to the north and at midnight fashioned a shield of copper and marked it on one side with a hexagram, on the other with a pentagram. I went to the center at a time between all others and from virgin iron I beat out a sword, quenched in the blood of murdered maidens, a bloodred ruby set in its hilt.

"For seven days I've fasted and purified myself. On the third day of the new moon I went to the shore of the Niflsea and built a fire of hemlock, hellebore, and henbane. There, as the sun rose, I cut the head from a virgin black cock. I threw the head into the misty waters, drained the cock's blood into my left hand, and lapped it up. I burned the carcass on the fire, its sweet odor rising to please Nergal, and jumped into the water. Stripping off my old clothing, I left the sea, climbing backward onto land. I donned these black robes. They have no buttons, buckles, hooks, or knots to slow the flow of power from me.

"For a full year now I've been readying my demonic allies, casting stronger and stronger bonds over them. Now Humbaba, the dread giant whose beard is made from human entrails, answers my beck and call. He is armed with sevenfold terrors and is horrible to all flesh. When he roars, it is like the raging of a storm. His breath is a blast of flame and his jaws are death itself. He will be a match for Adad's ally, Pazuzu.

"Lahamu, one of Tiamat's eleven, does my bidding. I will use her against her sister, Mushrussu, Adad's helper and your enemy, loyal Serpent. Abubu and Imhullu you know well. I will cast them against Resheph, one of Adad's storm demons. Ishum, with his burning eyes, I will set on Ishkur. They will be well matched. Sibbi, with its seven poisonous bodies of death, will come to my aid in my struggle with Adad. Sibbi will do battle with Rimmon, Adad's favorite. And Zu, ghastly Zu, the giant, lion-headed storm bird, the mightiest demon in the skies, will be sent to attack Teshub, master storm demon of them all.

"Everything is ready, Serpent. My long years of poring over ancient tomes, of harsh discipline, of deep concentration, of careful scheming, have reached their climax. I'm about to attack Adad! I'm about to realize the first fruits of my revenge. I'm about to become Patesi of Maqam Nifl and Borsippa!" Surt's hands had turned into claws, his face twisted with malice, his body writhing with anticipated joy over his coming revenge. "Soon I'll smash them all! Marduk, An, Enlil, Enki, Nannar . . . even Utu, if necessary! And then I'll sweep north to bring the bane of forests to Borr and all his filthy, barbarian brood! All! I'll destroy them all!"

Jormungand watched Surt's performance with skeptical eyes. "Very nice, Black One. Well thought out, well planned. Except for one little thing."

Surt looked at him in surprise, his jubilation cut short. "What thing?"

"Oh," the giant warrior said casually, "just a little thing. A little thing called Ninurta, the demon of the south wind. You've got six of Adad's allies covered, Surt. You forgot the seventh."

The slender man gave Jormungand an uncomfortable look. "You misjudge me, brave Serpent. I haven't forgotten Ninurta. I'm ready to summon Imdugud, the wind demon, if Ninurta should show up. Imdugud is a mighty—"

Jormungand snorted derisively. "Huh. Imdugud. Mighty, yes. As mighty as Ninurta, no. There's a hole in your plan, Black One. You haven't prepared adequately against the seventh demon."

Surt became angry. "I have, I tell you! I've knotted cords! I've made figures of clay! Besides, Ninurta's far to the south. If I strike quickly, Adad will never have time to summon it." His face became earnest, his eyes almost pleading. "Now is the time to strike, loyal Serpent. I . . . I can't wait any longer. My power has grown to the point where it's getting more and more difficult to hide from Adad. If he should discover me and attack when I'm not ready . . . I must act now, Serpent. Trust me. Support me. I may well have need of your mighty arm."

"Against Adad? What can I do against a wizard like him? Oh, I can battle his demons. I've already done that when I fought Mushrussu. But . . . no, Surt, this is your fight. Wizard to wizard. Black magic to the death." He stopped for a moment, peering about anxiously. "I'm . . . uh . . . well enough warded, aren't I? I mean, none of these demons can get to me, can they?"

Surt's expression was grim. "They shouldn't be able to, no. But once the forces start to build, there's no telling what will happen." He hesitated for a moment, as if trying to decide whether to tell Jormungand something or not. Finally he sighed and said, "You must realize, brave Serpent, that if I fail, the power that holds your wards in place will slowly drain away. You'll have to fight your own way clear of this."

Jormungand nodded. "Uh-huh. I figured that much out on my own. That's why I've been sharpening my sword and dagger for the last week." His sigh matched his master's. "Well, I guess there's nothing for it but to do it, eh, Black One?" Surt nodded. "Let's get on with it then. And," his face became serious, "good luck."

Surt walked to the center of the magic circle he'd drawn in the middle of the floor. Lying there, legs bound tightly, was a black bull. "The bull," he said, "is sacred to Adad. This one is perfect: black as pitch, without even seven white hairs. It's never been struck with a rod or touched with a whip. I've tied it with a cord of goat's hair and placed it upon a reed mat within the magic circle. Now I'll use it to entrap Adad!"

Surt went to the brazier that sat atop a golden tripod next to the bull. There was a pure flame burning brightly in it. He reached into his robes and pulled out several chips of wood. "Aloes wood, ash, and cedar I cast upon the flames to draw the mind of Adad," he intoned. He reached in his robe again and came out with a blue powder and some feathers. "Powdered lapis lazuli and feathers of the peacock do I burn for the wind-riding master of the storms." The smoke rose from the brazier and began to fill the room, making the walls disappear and the space seem almost infinite. Jormungand looked around. It was as if they had been transported to some misty limbo without boundaries. Surt poured two more things on the fire. "Blood of stork, brain of young stag, be sweet in the nostrils of Adad."

The magician walked up to the bull. The animal watched him with wide, frightened eyes. From beneath his flowing black robes Surt pulled a dagger and a wand. In the bull's right ear he whispered, "Great bull, exalted bull, loved of Adad, treading the holy herbage!" In the creature's left ear he whispered, "Oh, bull, spawn of Adad, storm lord's child!" With a quick motion of his wand he struck the bull on the forehead between the eyes. It slumped down. The slender man leaned forward and slowly drew the dagger across its throat. As the bright blood began to spurt from the gash, he pulled a cup from beneath his robe and caught the blood. He drank

deeply, then threw the rest on the flames. They leapt high in
response. Turning the bull on its side, he cut deep with the
dagger, reached through the wound and ripped out the animal's heart. It was still beating spasmodically as he held it
aloft. "Oh, Adad, sky strider, storm walker, come for this
offering!" He threw the bull's heart onto the brazier and added
pieces of cypress wood, cedar, and pease-meal. "Come,
Adad, come," he chanted.

The giant warrior noticed a darkening in the air over one of
the invoking hexagrams. It became deeper as Surt continued
his chant. Suddenly there was a roar as if great storm winds
were raging. Lightning flashed, thunder bellowed like a vast
bull, and a giant being stood in the center of the hexagram.
Jormungand couldn't make out its features, because he found
he couldn't bear to look directly at it. Nevertheless, he knew
who it was. The being grasped lightning in its right hand, a
mighty ax in its left. A magnificent drum hung around its
middle. It was Adad.

"Who dares to summon Adad, Patesi of Maqam Nifl and
Borsippa?" a voice as wild as a hurricane demanded. Jormungand shrank back from it, nervously checking his pentagram
again to make sure all the lines were well-drawn.

Surt drew himself up to his full height and responded in a
voice that seemed to come from caverns beneath the earth. "I,
Surt the Black One, servant of Nergal, Lord of Hosts, King of
Aralu, Mighty Magician, summon you to do battle."

Adad shouted with laughter. The whole world shook with
his hilarity. "Surt the Black One? What foolish Kishpu sorcerer have we here who dares challenge Adad? Adad, who
walks through the heavens with his brothers Sin and Shamash!
Quake and quail, worm, for Adad will smite you!" The figure
muttered a quick chant. With a flash and a smell of sulfur, a
monstrous form appeared. "Pazuzu," Adad commanded,
"smash this upstart!"

With a howl of mindless fury, the great storm demon,
lightning shooting from its eyes, pounced on Surt. The Black
One didn't flinch, however. Instead he laughed wildly and
waved his hand. "Come, Humbaba," he cried in a dark voice
that echoed eerily, "come rend Pazuzu!"

Between Surt and the pouncing storm demon a huge figure
suddenly appeared. From its hideous face hung a beard of

human entrails. A cedar club as large as a tree trunk was in its hands. Fire shot from its eyes and its roar made the heavens shake.

Pazuzu and Humbaba met in a crash that threw Jormungand to his knees. The two demons grappled, howling and roaring, twisting about, striking and biting at each other. Pazuzu knew that if Humbaba once got a grip with his jaws it was all over, for the giant's jaws were death itself.

For a moment Adad watched the conflict in surprise. Then he turned a considering look on Surt. "We have no mere Kishpu sorcerer here it appears. You can counter Pazuzu. Can you handle Ishkur, I wonder?" Adad pointed his scrawny fingers at the air and gave a mindless howl of an incantation. Fire flared, unbearably bright, frighteningly hot. A monster of flame stood at its center.

Surt responded immediately. "Ishmu, Ishmu," he cried, summoning and demanding in a voice that would not be denied. There was a roar of flame, a brightness equal to that of Ishkur, and a second fire demon appeared and threw itself at the first.

The Patesi of Maqam Nifl and Borsippa was clearly shaken. "Rimmon!" he commanded. "Rimmon, come and blow this foulness from the face of Muspellheim!" The storm demon barely had time to form when Surt invoked Sibbi, the seven-bodied monster with its seven deadly weapons. The two met with a deafening clash.

Adad was beginning to frown. In quick succession he summoned two more of his allies—Resheph and Mushrussu. Surt countered with Abubu and Imhulla for Resheph and Lahamu for Mushrussu. The battle raged all about the two magicians, demon striving with demon, swirling in snarling, vicious combat. The noise was mind destroying. The earth shook and heaved with the force of the monsters' tread.

Seeing that Surt's allies were holding their own against his, Adad decided it was time to play his last few pieces in this wizard's game. Six was his secret number, and he was about to call his sixth demon. If it wasn't enough, he'd be forced to take a dire action, the calling of a seventh and final ally. He didn't like the idea of so extending his strength, but he realized he had no choice. This Black One was far mightier than he'd so foolishly assumed at the beginning. He started to wonder if he'd made a mistake coming right into the man's own territory. It had been a trap, he now knew. The bull, the scents of aloes, ash, stork blood and the rest had been used to lure and snare him. Can I get out? he wondered.

The ancient wizard lifted his hands and began to chant. He was calling Teshub, one of his mightiest demons, a storm monster of almost frightening violence. The very air became so heavily charged with the power of his calling that the other demons momentarily paused in their struggles to see what was happening. The air became dense and darker than ever. An oppression that sent the mind gibbering settled over the area. A dull roaring began to sound in the distance. Something vast and elemental was rushing toward them.

Surt felt the coming presence with a tinge of fear and awe. Teshub, he told himself. Teshub comes. It is time to summon Zu. He shivered. It was a fearful thing he was about to do, for Zu was a difficult demon to control. If his strength should falter for even an instant . . .He shivered again.

The Black One began to chant a dreadful series of sounds, which twisted and distorted the mouth that spoke them and the ear that heard them. The gathering dark created by the coming of Teshub was made blacker yet. An air of foreboding made everyone—wizard, warrior, demon, and dragon—pause and shudder.

Surt felt the sweat standing out on his forehead. Even from where he stood, he could see the patches of perspiration that stained Adad's robe. The slender man's hands shook slightly with growing fatigue. This is harder than I'd ever imagined, he admitted. I only hope I can beat Adad before the strain exhausts me and I lose control of my allies.

With a roar and a scream that knocked every creature in the area to its knees, Teshub and Zu appeared overhead, already locked in mortal combat. Teshub was a darkness that boiled with violent power, formless, chaotic, constantly changing. Zu was a vast bird with razor-sharp claws and a lion's fanged head. Zu snapped and tore at Teshub while Teshub tried to overwhelm the storm bird.

His mouth open in astonishment, too awed to even be afraid. Jormungand stood and watched the titanic combat. For a few moments the other fighters also watched. Then with snarls and bellows they fell on each other once more, and the world dissolved into a boil of noise and lashing power.

The battle raged on. Adad felt his weariness growing. I

must call Ninurta, he admitted. The south wind is my last hope. His face haggard with fatigue, he glared with hate at Surt. The man's tired to the bone, even as I am, he realized. Ninurta might be the thing that finally breaks him.

Adad pulled himself upright and tried to draw power for the calling of Ninurta. For several moments he worked at it, until he discovered there simply wasn't enough energy available there in this hexagram drawn by his enemy. I must escape, he decided, escape back to my own rooms and carry on the fight from there. Surt was clever enough to draw me here. Now I wonder if he was clever enough to make my escape impossible?

His first try didn't work. The invoking hexagram was perfectly drawn, the power names correct. Surt had done his job well. Adad began to panic. If I can't get back— Then he noticed something and smiled. A bit of dust. Just a bit. Just enough. Casually, so that Surt wouldn't see what he was doing, Adad began to push the dust toward the lines of the hexagram. When it was close enough, he called out to the Black One. "You're stronger than I thought, wizard! But neither strong nor clever enough! Farewell! I go to call Ninurta! Weep and wail, foolish worm, for soon the south wind will drag you to the Kur!" With that he kicked the dust over the line of the hexagram, and in a flash of sulfurous smoke, escaped across the disrupted line.

Surt was so taken aback by his rival's disappearance that he stood staring for several moments. Then he raised his hands to heaven as if to claw the stars from their places, and howled his anger. "He's escaped!" he raged. "He goes to call Ninurta! Serpent, we're undone!"

Jormungand looked at his master, his heart sinking lower than it had ever sunk before. "What . . . what of Imdugud?"

The Black One beat his head with tight fists. "You yourself told the truth of Imdugud. He's no match for Ninurta. He'll hold Adad's minion for a while, but the south wind will triumph. Our time is limited, faithful Serpent. We've failed!"

Surt slumped hopelessly down next to the body of the black bull. Jormungand looked at him in dismay. Surt defeated? Surt whimpering like a whipped child? He roared with anger and frustration. "No! By Nergal's damned balls, no! Think, Black One! There must be something we can do!"

His master looked up at him with dull eyes. "I must call

Imdugud," he mumbled. "We'll live a little longer that way." The slender man paused, then sat upright, a light growing in his eyes. "Last longer," he muttered. "Perhaps long enough to—" Surt jumped to his feet. "Serpent," he called to the huge warrior, "do you think you could leave your pentagram and make it to my magical circle? It would be a very hazardous ten feet, but a mighty warrior like you might be able to do it."

Jormungand gave his master a piercing glance. "Leave the pentagram? Leave my protection? Walk ten feet through the middle of twelve demons locked in final combat? Why?"

"I cannot send you from there. You must be here for me to send you."

"Send me? Send me where? Somewhere far from all this, I hope. Even Badtabira would be a pleasure right about now."

Surt looked anxiously over his shoulder. "We haven't much time for explanations. And Adad might hear in any case. I'll send you to his palace. There you'll find and kill him. His demons will all be here, struggling with my allies. He'll be defenseless. Find him and kill him, brave Serpent. It's our only hope!"

It took the warrior only a moment to make his decision. With a shrug he threw himself across the line of his protective pentagram. Instantly he was battered by the power of the battling demons that swirled around him. Winds tore at him, fire lashed out and scorched him, shrieks and howls deafened him and turned his mind to jelly. He staggered, more falling than walking, toward Surt and the magical circle.

Almost there, he told himself. A few more steps. He felt himself suddenly whirled about. Two vast eyes met his. An endless mouth filled with teeth leered at him. Unthinkingly he ripped his sword from its sheath and slashed wildly at the hideous face, not knowing or caring which demon it was. It retreated a step in surprise, and he threw himself back toward Surt and safety.

With a thump he hit the floor. The Black One was instantly at the edge of the circle, repairing the damage of Jormungand's entrance had caused before any of the demons could enter and attack them.

Triumphantly Surt stood over the stunned warrior. He pulled off the talisman he wore always, the one he had taken from the dead wizard on the Vigrid so many years ago, and put it around Jormungand's neck, tucking it carefully under the warrior's mail shirt. "When you've completed your task, hold the talisman in your left hand and call on me. It'll bring you back here." Then, with a few mystic gestures and some muttered words, he sent his servant reeling through dark emptiness.

Jormungand landed on his feet, his sword ready. The noise of his arrival alerted the four men who stood guard at the door of the hall. For an instant they stared at the intruder. Then one ran for reinforcements while the other three rushed forward to attack. The giant warrior grinned with pleasure as the three guards ran toward him. Real men! Warriors like himself! Not demons or dragons or wizards, but real human beings! With a hiss of joy he leapt to the attack.

His opponents were charging in a tight group, almost shoulder to shoulder. It was their undoing. Jormungand dodged to his right, stepping outside the end guard, switching his sword to his left hand as he moved. He dropped to the ground and swept his weapon out to the left in a great, flat arc about chest high. The blade caught the man in the ribs and sliced through his side, cutting his heart in two. He fell like a rock.

Jormungand jumped across the dead guard and smashed his weapon down on the middle guard's head, splitting his helmet and spattering his brains out in a gray shower. The third man died as the Serpent struck out and skewered him through the chest.

With a laugh of brutal pleasure the huge man ran to the door and carefully peered out into the hall. To the left he could hear the sound of many hurrying feet. The guard who had escaped was coming with reinforcements. Jormungand ran to the right. After a few yards the corridor turned sharply left, then right again where it came to an end at a cross corridor. He looked cautiously around the edge and saw a wide hallway. Far down the hall in either direction he could see groups of guards hurrying toward him. Behind he could hear the cries of the men who had discovered their slaughtered companions. Damn, he cursed, they know the layout. They're going to come at me from all sides.

Directly across from the corridor where he stood, he noticed a door. Deciding quickly, he stepped into the wide corridor and reached for the door. He heard the guards raise a shout as they saw him. With a gesture of defiance to the group to his left, he opened the door and stepped through.

Jormungand found himself in a small, square room with a door on the left-hand wall and one on the right. He went to the one on the right and opened it. There he entered another room, identical to the first, except that it had a door on the opposite wall as well as on the right. He took the right-hand door again.

As he stepped through it, he began to curse beneath his breath. The room was the same as the other two, but with doors in all three walls. He went quickly to one of the doors, opened it, and peeked through. Identical.

He felt his heart sink. A maze, he told himself. It's a damned wizard's maze. I could wander in here for days, maybe until I die. His breath hissed out in a series of rolling curses. He racked his brain, trying to remember if Surt had ever said anything about mazes and how wizards constructed them. In frustration he slammed his fist against the wall. Damn the Left Hand Path and every wizard that walked it! Damn Surt! Damn Adad! Damn . . .

He stopped. The Left Hand Path. That's what the wizards call black magic. Left hand. He turned and traced his way back to the first room. Yes! In every one there were at least two doors. Perhaps if he always took the left-hand door . . . He shrugged. Might as well give it a try, he told himself. I certainly don't have anything to lose, and it just might work.

He went through room after room as swiftly as possible, constantly feeling the pressure of time. How long will it take, he worried, to get out of this damn thing? If I ever get out.

He pulled open another door and almost tumbled into a huge room. It stretched off so far he almost couldn't see the other end. Dark shadows hung from the ceiling, collected in the corners, and shrouded the far side of the hall. He closed the door behind him and began to walk warily across the room. His footsteps echoed oddly, even though he did his best to walk quietly.

When he was less than a third of the way across the vast empty floor, he sensed a stirring in the shadows at the far end. Two great eyes suddenly blinked open, bottomless eyes full of swirling color, eyes that drew the mind, eyes that—

"No!" he shouted out loud. His voice came back to him a thousand times, hollow and ghostly. Those eyes, he didn't dare look into those eyes! With a shudder he realized who, or rather what, they belonged to. He'd almost been lost in them once before.

Mushrussu! The dragon's bulk slid sinuously forward. This was the very same monster he'd fought that night so long ago in the dark and deserted streets of Maqam Nifl. But how could that be? He checked to make sure, avoiding the creature's eyes as he did so. Yes. It was the same long, snakelike body, covered with armored scales that shimmered with an oily light. Six stubby legs held the body up, legs that ended in feet that bore razor-sharp claws. The tail ended in a poisonous sting very like a scorpion's, but much larger and more deadly. The head was that of a hellhound, red-furred and filled with daggerlike teeth dripping with a slimy substance Jormungand knew was poisonous.

There was no mistaking that this was Mushrussu. Yet how could Mushrussu be here? He'd seen the creature in Surt's room not more than half an hour ago, locked in mortal combat with Lahamu. Did this mean the Surt was defeated, dead, dragged off to Aralu? If so, I don't have a hope, he told himself. I've got to find out.

The dragon stopped its slinking approach and regarded him. "Man," it hissed in a voice that resembled the screaming of lost souls, "I know you. I marked you. You are mine. Come, I will take you to my cave in the Kur and crunch your bones forever. Quake, mortal worm, for I am Mushrussu."

"You can't be Mushrussu," Jormungand replied, making his voice as loud as possible. "I've just seen Mushrussu someplace else, battling for her life against her sister dragon, Lahamu. If you're there battling her, how can you be here too?"

Mushrussu laughed mightily. "I am a creature of the spirit realm, worm! When I come to this gross material realm you dwell in, I take a physical embodiment that matches my spiritual one. My true essence remains behind in my own realm. I am a powerful spirit and hence can take several physical embodiments at the same time."

Jormungand smiled secretly. The dragon had told him what he wanted to know! Surt was probably still alive, still battling Adad. There was time left to complete his task!

He walked toward the monster, trying to decide how to attack it. Was there a way to gain the upper hand quickly? he wondered. He remembered his last combat with the beast. It struck with its fangs, then with its tail. Have to watch that tail, he reminded himself. It was more dangerous than the head. As he approached, he tried to delay Mushrussu's attack by asking more questions. Perhaps he could even gather some useful information.

"Why are you here, Mushrussu, rather than in your cave at the edge of Kur, crunching bones with your mother, Tiamat?"

"I am Adad's greatest ally! He always has me here on guard!"

Jormungand sensed he had touched the monster's pride. He decided to push a little harder. "Greatest ally? Greater than Pazuzu? Greater than Resheph?"

Mushrussu pulled herself up to her full height, her first pair of legs rearing off the floor and pawing the air. "Greater than either or both combined!" the dragon bragged.

"Surely not greater than Ishkur or Rimmon?" Jormungand moved slightly to the left, looking for a possible opening. Hiding his action by turning his body, he loosened his knife in its scabbard.

The dragon roared with offended pride. "Greater than Ishkur! Much greater than Rimmon!"

Jormungand stopped. This was a good place. He tensed his muscles. "Greater than Teshub, mighty Teshub?"

"Greater! Greater! Teshub is a worm compared to my majesty! I and I alone guard my mater's door. Does Teshub do such a thing?"

The giant warrior laughed silently. This dragon is a mine of valuable information! I'm only a few yards from my goal! He decided to prod the monster one last time to see if he could learn anything else. "Ah, but are you greater than Ninurta?"

The monster stopped dead and gave him a searching look. "Ninurta isn't one of the six. He's the seventh."

"But are you greater? Are you?"

In a fury the dragon lifted its red furred muzzle and howled at the dark shadows that hid the ceiling, "Yes! Greater! Greater! Mushrussu is—"

As the beast raised its muzzle, Jormungand threw himself forward, his sword cleaving a whistling arc through the air. He struck the dragon on its upper chest, just below the neck, and opened a deep gash almost a foot long. Mushrussu shrieked in fury and struck at him with her tail. Knowing it was coming, he leapt back in the nick of time. He struck it, even though he knew from the last time he'd fought the monster that the area around the sting was too well covered with thick plates of scale armor to be vulnerable to a mere sword.

Mushrussu lunged at him, fangs bared. She missed by a hair's breadth, but a drop of the vile slime that slobbered from her jaws struck the back of his hand and nearly made him drop his sword. It felt like someone had placed a live coal on his skin! He staggered, feeling faint and weak for an instant. The dragon struck with its tail sting again and Jormungand barely managed to leap aside. He was too close to the beast's legs, however, and one shot out to rake his thigh with deadly claws. He felt the flesh tear and the blood begin to flow.

He stumbled back, pretending to be more badly wounded than he actually was. He'd seen something, something he wasn't quite sure of. It looked as if the scales on the underside of the sting were a bit smaller and thinner than those of the upper side! Perhaps the tail was vulnerable from that angle! If he could knock out one of the monster's weapons, he felt sure he could defeat it quickly.

There was something else too. As it attacked once more, he waited as long as possible before dodging. Yes! He was certain of it! Mushrussu wasn't as swift or as strong as the last time he'd fought her! He wondered briefly if trying to keep two physical manifestations going and fighting at the same time was strain on the dragon's capacity. It seemed possible. He hoped so.

He had to get in close, inside the normal attack arc of the sting, so he could slash at it from its weak angle. He pulled the dagger from his belt and flung it at the dragon as it attacked. The blade flew true and pierced one of the monster's great eyes. In agony it reared up and clawed at the dagger. Jormungand jumped forward, just as the tail slammed downward into the floor where he'd been standing. He was inside! Holding his sword with both hands, he spun about and hewed with all his might at the tail directly below the sting. The blade bit and went deep. Poison spewed out, hissing as it hit the floor. He struck again. The sting was severed! He jumped away.

In a paroxysm of fury Mushrussu charged. Waiting until the monster was almost on him, its maw gaping wide to bite him in two, he threw himself to the left while he jabbed his sword at the beast's chest with the power of both arms. The dragon charged on by, wrenching the sword from his grip as it went. One of the creature's feet lashed out in passing and struck him in the chest, knocking him spinning across the floor.

Struggling to rise, he felt his right side. It was sticky with blood and throbbing with pain. If he hadn't been wearing his mail shirt, he realized, the blow would have ripped him wide open. As it was—

He heard a coughing howl and spun to face Mushrussu. His sword had been driven into the monster's chest right up to its hilt. Blood and air bubbles frothed out around it. The dragon regarded him blearily with its one good eye. It coughed and tried to roar again. Dark blood flowed from its mouth, mixing with the poisonous slime and dribbling to the floor. Mushrussu gave him a last look, then turned and started for the opposite end of the room. Jormungand limped in pursuit.

The dragon left a trail of slime and blood. It moved slower and slower until, at the base of a wide set of stairs that led upward into the dark, it collapsed in a heap. Several violent shudders shook the massive creature. Then with a moaning sigh it ceased moving and lay still as a rock.

Jormungand waited several moments. Fearing a possible trap, he crept carefully forward until he stood within reach of the hilt of his sword. Moving with sudden swiftness, he grasped the weapon and pulled it free. Raising it high, prepared to strike at the slightest sign of life, he stood like a statue. Nothing happened. He prodded the gigantic carcass. Nothing. He leaned over and pulled his knife from the thing's eye. It was dead.

Limping slowly, he went to the stairs and looked up. Strange, he thought, I've just killed Mushrussu and I don't feel any elation. Perhaps it's because I know she wasn't the real challenge.

He returned his knife to its sheath and checked over his injuries. The wound on his thigh was still bleeding, though not as badly as he'd feared. His side, however, was worse than it had seemed in the heat of the battle. Every movement, every breath, was painful. Several ribs are broken, he judged. None seem to have pierced my lung, because I'm not coughing blood. But I'm still losing a lot. He felt the torn places in his mail shirt where Mushrussu's claws had slashed the tough metal as though it were mere cloth. Two inches closer, he estimated, and I'd be dead.

Slowly he began to move up the stairs. If what the dragon had said was true, Adad's chambers lay at their top. He tried to move as noiselessly as possible. Perhaps if I catch him unaware, he hoped, I'll be able to strike before he has time to react.

Ahead, glowing slightly in the gloom, he made out two huge doors. He approached them carefully, his senses stretched to their utmost. They were made of some sort of metal, he estimated, possibly tin. Sapphires, amethysts, and carnelians were set into the metal to form strange designs that vaguely reminded him of writing. He looked for a way to open them.

Before he could complete his search, the doors suddenly flew open as a mighty wind roared through them. A great voice, booming like thunder called out to him, "Come in, human, come in. Any man who can penetrate this far into my palace is a mighty warrior indeed and worthy of looking on Adad before he dies."

Jormungand bit his lip in frustration. So much for surprise, he thought. He stepped forward and found himself in a large room furnished with a luxury beyond his wildest imaginings. Rare fabrics and exquisite tapestries hung from the walls. The floor was piled deep in soft, thick carpets. Gigantic pillows were thrown about in wild profusion. Here and there, glittering and shining so brightly they almost hurt his eyes, were chests filled with jewels.

His eyes finally came to rest on a huge figure that stood motionless at the far end of the room. It was Adad. As before, he found he couldn't look at the Patesi's face. But he knew the ruler of Maqam Nifl and Borsippa by the drum tied around his waist, the lightning bolts held in his right hand, and the great ax gripped in his left.

"Ah," Adad said, "I might have known. I have seen you before, in the squalid room of that foolish Kishpu sorcerer . . . oh, what was his insignificant name . . . ah, yes, Sort, or Sart. Yes. You were there in a protective pentagram. You should have stayed. You would have lived longer."

So, Jormungand thought, Surt's still alive! There's still

hope! If only I can get close enough to attack. . . . He began to move slowly forward. Got to keep him talking, he calculated. Maybe he's as egotistical as that fool dragon. "Mushrussu is dead, noble Adad. I killed her."

The Patesi shrugged. "No matter. It will be a minor nuisance to force her to take a material manifestation again. You were lucky, warrior."

"Lucky? Partly." Trying to appear unconcerned, Jormungand took a few steps forward. "I've tangled with her before, years ago, and nearly beat her then. This time she was weaker because she was trying to maintain two manifestations at the same time. I imagine the one fighting Lahamu was defeated as well."

Adad regarded him silently for a few moments. "You know a great deal for a warrior. Too much, in fact."

"I know that if Mushrussu was beaten, then Lahamu could join Imdugud in attacking Ninurta. Things might be even right now, Adad." He took another two steps.

The wizard laughed darkly. "Imdugud and a wounded Lahamu are still no match for a demon of Ninurta's power! You are correct in assuming that Surt tenaciously continues the battle, warrior. But he is steadily losing ground. Resheph has mangled Imhulla and even now is destroying Abubu. Rimmon has slain five of Sibbi's seven bodies. The end is near for both your master and you!"

Jormungand was almost close enough now. Just a few more steps and he would be within range for—

Adad growled like distant thunder and held up his right hand. The lightning hissed and flared. "Do not think to trick me as you tricked my foolish dragon, warrior. You have talked long enough and come close enough. It is time for you to die." With that, the Patesi hurled the lightning at Jormungand. Jormungand held up his sword in a vain attempt to ward off the crackling bolts. They struck his weapon with a flash of light and heat, stunning him and knocking the red-hot blade from his badly burnt hands. The hair on his head was smouldering, and he had to struggle to stay conscious.

The wizard chuckled grimly. He reached for his drum and began to beat on it. "After the lightning comes the thunder," he said. The noise of the drum became louder and louder until it filled the world with its roar. Jormungand covered his ears with his hands, but found he couldn't keep the boom out. His mind reeled anew, his head felt as though it were about to split open. He stumbled beneath the weight of the drumming and went to his knees.

Adad laughed with evil pleasure. "A mighty warrior you may be, mightier than Mushrussu. But you are no match for the power of the storm!" The wizard pulled back his left arm and hurled the ax at Jormungand. "Kill, ax," he commanded as the weapon flew at the giant warrior.

Jormungand saw it coming and staggered out of the way. The ax stopped in the air and turned, making a quick swing at his head. The warrior barely escaped by hitting the floor and rolling. The ax followed, chopping and flinging bits of rich carpeting into the air. Adad watched and shook with laughter. "Ah, ah, what dexterity, warrior! This is true sport to watch a doomed man struggle hopelessly! But sadly, I have no time for such frivolity. I must go now and finish off your master. Good-bye, warrior, may your rest in the Kur be painful!"

From the corner of his eye Jormungand saw a slight flash of lightning as Adad disappeared. There goes our last chance, he thought hopelessly as he leapt to the side to avoid the ax's swing. No way I can fight a magical ax. Damn thing doesn't even give me enough time to pick up my sword. He looked at his blistered hands. Doubt if I could hold it anyway. He ducked and rolled desperately.

Damn, he thought in sudden anger, there must be a way to slow this thing down a little. Maybe then— He jumped to the side. An idea began to form in his mind . . . desperate, he told himself, foolish, last ditch effort. What in the name of Namtaru difference does it make? I'm dead anyway. Might as well try it and see.

He allowed the ax to come a bit closer on the next pass, moving slower, as if tiring. Huh, he thought, no real need to act that one. The wound in his leg had opened again and was bleeding freely. His side was hurting badly now, and he could feel the wetness from his injury there spreading. Don't have much longer, he realized. Blood loss is bound to weaken me pretty quickly now.

The ax made a sudden move, and the warrior failed to dodge in time. The blade sliced into his arm and opened a deep gash from his elbow to his shoulder. Blood flowed anew at an appalling rate. It's now or never, he realized as he staggered back, the shock of the new wound nearly knocking him down.

He stumbled toward one of the walls. The ax swung and missed. He flung himself back. With a crash his back hit the tapestry-covered wall. He stood there, dazed, his arms spread wide above his head. The ax paused for a moment, then drove directly at his head with terrific speed. At the last possible moment Jormungand dropped to the floor. The ax missed his head by the merest fraction of an inch and thudded into the wall, burying its blade a good three inches into the wood. Jormungand pulled at the tapestry and it came cascading down to cover the weapon.

The giant warrior stumbled back toward the center of the room. He was bleeding profusely. Grabbing a piece of cloth that lay across one of the cushions, he quickly tied it around his arm in an attempt to stanch the bleeding. That done, he pulled the talisman Surt had given him from beneath his mail shirt, held it in his left hand, and called to the wizard. "Bring me back, Black One," he cried. He looked over toward the wall where the ax had almost worked its way loose. "And hurry or there won't be anything left to bring back but chopped meat!"

With a sudden flash of light he was gone.

He fell in a heap at Surt's feet. The slender wizard looked at him with hopeless, haggard eyes. His body was drenched with sweat and his shoulders slumped in exhaustion. "You failed," he said dully, his voice hoarse and weak.

Jormungand nodded as he stood shakily. "Killed Mushrussu. Adad was not so simple." He looked out at the battle that surrounded the magic circle protecting them from the demons that raged outside. Humbaba had killed Pazuzu but had been so badly torn in the process that the giant lay on its side, unable to move. Mushrussu, as he already knew, was dead. Lahamu was also dead, torn in half by Ninurta, who now fought with Imdugud and was rapidly approaching victory over the weaker monster. Ishkur lay cold and dead. Resheph had defeated both Abubu and Imhulla and had launched an offensive against Ishum. Surt's fire demon was flickering and fading. Soon Resheph would be free to support Rimmon against the Zu bird. It seemed a certainty that it would only be a few moments until Zu alone of Surt's allies still stood. Stood against Resheph, Rimmon, and Ninurta. The outcome of that battle needed little conjecture. No wonder Surt looked defeated.

The cloth around Jormungand's arm was soaked through. His head felt light and faint. "Do you have anything to stop this flow of blood!" he mumbled to Surt, indicating his arm.

Surt looked blankly at it, then shook all over as if coming awake. A light turned on in his dull eyes. "What is that?" he asked intently, pointing to the cloth that bound the warrior's arm.

"A cloth. I picked it up in Adad's room when the ax cut—"

The Black One pounced forward and grabbed the cloth, ripping it from Jormungand's arm. "From Adad's room?" He held it up. It was a robe. Surt chortled with glee. "A robe! Adad's robe! Loyal Serpent, brave Serpent, we're saved!"

Before Jormungand could respond, the slender wizard was in front of his brazier, throwing powders onto the flame. "Sulfur," he cried, "hated by Adad! Myrrh, dreaded by the storm master! Red sandalwood, despised and deadly to his soul! Wine galls and arsenic, that rot and eat at his body!" The flames leapt high, a violent mix of indescribable colors. Huge billows of smoke poured forth, mounting to the sky, heading like a huge worm in the direction of Adad's palace. Surt stood, the robe over his head, bloodstained and rumpled. He cried out in a mighty voice, his eyes flashing with his hatred. "Adad! Adad! I cast you into the flame! I cast you into the fire with those things that destroy you! I have bound you, I have fettered you, I have handed you over to Gira, who scorches, burns, binds, and seizes the wizards. May the burning Gira undo your knots, annul your incantations, untie your cord. By the command of Barashakushu, son of the Wise One, and of Gira, the burning one, I destroy you, rend you, wipe you from the face of the earth, send you reeling to Aralu! Namtaru carry your name to Ereshkigal! Neti open the gate for you! Nergal ready the stake for you! I give you death!" With a maniacal laugh he flung the robe into the fire.

The explosion knocked them both flat. The flame leapt up into the sky. In its center Jormungand could swear he saw the writhing, tortured figure of the Patesi. A great cry of anguish and horror beat against his ears, deafening him and making his head feel as though it was about to explode.

Suddenly they were back in the tiny room once more. Everything was quiet. No demons struggled, no smoke rose to heaven, no flames leapt high.

Surt looked at him, a slow smile beginning to spread across his features. Then the slender man threw back his head and gave a whoop of joy. He grabbed the wounded warrior and literally lifted him to his feet. In a burst of hilarity Surt danced Jormungand around the room, knocking over tables, chairs, and anything else that got in his way.

"I've done it!" he cried. "I've beaten Adad! I'm the Patesi of Maqam Nifl and Borsippa!"

Surt, dressed in the magnificent robes of the Patesi of Maqam Nifl and Borsippa, approached the towering doors that led into the Hall of Duku, where the Anunnaki met, with more anxiety than he allowed to show. A certain degree of humility and a little awe would not be out of place, he decided, but I can't show the slightest lack of confidence or fear.

Jormungand, resplendent in the shining armor, plumed helmet, and jewel-encrusted sword of a general, followed slightly to his rear. As they mounted the last few steps to the doors, Surt motioned the giant warrior forward.

Jormungand stalked proudly up to a tall, slender man with a dark face, hooked nose, and virtually no chin, who stood before the door, wrapped in a black robe edged in gold. This, Surt had informed him, was Mummu, one of Enki's foremost retainers and Doorkeeper of the Hall of Duku. He looked the man straight in the eye and boomed out, "Hail the approach of Surt, Patesi of Maqam Nifl and Borsippa! Throw wide the doors of Duku, for the Patesi would enter!"

"Patesi, eh?" Mummu muttered beneath his breath. "We'll see about that." Nevertheless, after giving Jormungand and his master a frigid glare, he reached out and touched the doors with the tall staff he held in his right hand. Silently they swung open.

Surt strode boldly forward. The hall was huge, and draped with cloth of gold. On a raised area in the middle stood seven thrones carved from gigantic chunks of precious stone. Surt stopped and took in the magnificence of the scene.

On the center throne sat Enlil Patesi of Nippur, Lagash, and Ashur. He was the Ellilutu, the Sovereign of Heaven, the

Overlord of Muspellheim. The *Tupsimati*, the Tablets of Destiny, were in his control. He lived in a mighty mountain of a castle called Ekur, with his consort Ninlil.

On his left sat the ancient An, the oldest of the Sons of Muspell. He ruled Der and Uruk and controlled the magic of the book known as the *Maqlu*. Next to him sat one of the most beautiful women Surt had ever seen. He knew this was Innina, his consort, and a mighty sorceress in her own right.

To the right of Enlil was Enki, Patesi of Eridu and Kish. He lived in the latter city, which lay on the western edge of Muspellheim on the shore of the vast Western Sea. His castle, called Eengurra, was built on a rock that thrust up out of the sea and was joined to the mainland by a narrow and easily defended causeway. Enki was one of the mightiest wizards in all of Muspellheim, for both the *Nimeqi*, a book of secret magical knowledge, and the *Shipti*, a book of powerful incantations, were in his possession. Seated next to him on a stool of gold studded with emeralds was Damkina, his consort.

Next on the left, beyond An and Innina, was the giant bulk of Marduk. Once a general serving Enlil, Marduk was the youngest of the Patesi and ruled only the city of Muspell. He had been born in Uruk and it was well known that he coveted that city, as well as the lovely Innina. His own consort, Zarpanit, was known far and wide for her beauty, but Marduk lusted after Innina all the same. He held only one book of magic, the *Shurpu*, and it was rumored he was far from having mastered it.

The throne next to Marduk's held an occupant Surt had not expected to see. It was Utu, the ruler of Sippar and Larsa, cities in the far south of Muspellheim. Surt knew Utu was the only member of the Anunnaki who still worshipped and dealt with the Igigi, the original gods of Muspell. He was sure the man had some book of magic, one that he kept very much to himself. Surt was aware that the other members of the Anunnaki owned a total of five books. He held a sixth, the *Utukki Limnuti*. It seemed likely that there was a seventh, and that Utu was the one who had it. Generally Utu refrained from intercourse with the other six Sons of Muspell, and almost never came to meetings of the Anunnaki. His presence made Surt uneasy.

On the right, beyond Enki, was an empty throne. Adad's throne, Surt thought with a thrill. Now my throne!

To the right of his new throne, Surt saw the slender, weak-faced figure of Nannar. Patesi of Ur, Nannar owned none of the books of magic. He was, however, in control of Bubbulu, the Evil Dark, and Sedu, the mighty winged bull. The man's power lay entirely in his magnificent necklace of lapis lazuli. It was rumored the necklace held the soul of one of the great wizard-rulers of the First Dark Empire. Nannar's consort, Ningal, wasn't present.

The Patesi of Maqam Nifl and Borsippa bowed to Enlil and began to walk forward to take his place on his throne. Before he could take two steps, a wall of flame shot up and blocked his way.

"Not so fast, upstart," Enlil boomed. "You've killed Adad, but whether or not you ascend to his throne is yet to be decided."

"Gaudy, Enlil," Innina said in a sweet voice that cut to the quick. "Walls of fire, really!"

"Hold your peace," Enki grumped. "You're not even a member of the Anunnaki, Innina."

The woman laughed deep in her throat and sneered at Enki. "An, my husband wants me to speak. Who am I to deny the wishes of the oldest of the Sons of Muspell? Isn't that right, An?" The old man nodded blearily and coughed a noise that sounded like an affirmative. "You see, Enki, I only follow my husband's wishes." She laughed again at the expression of exasperation that swept over Enki's face.

"The fact remains," Marduk said in his rough soldier's voice, "that this upstart is not able to take the throne until the Anunnaki approves of his ascension."

"True," Enlil said with a nasty smile at his former general. "After all, we can't have just any killer allowed to sit as one of the Sons of Muspell, now can we?"

Marduk stiffened at the insult. Before he could answer, Nannar spoke up in a thin, reedy voice. "Oh, q-q-quite r-r-right, Enlil. W-w-wise decision. The A-a-anunnaki must d-d-decide."

Enlil smiled at him and nodded. "Thank you, Nannar. A voice for moderation and common sense as always."

Enki groaned and scowled. "I think we should give the empty seat to Mummu. He's been the loyal servant of the Anunnaki, standing and guarding the doors of Duku for many sars now. He knows our ways and has some knowledge of magic himself. He would make a good Patesi and an excellent member of this council."

Marduk slammed his hand onto the arm of his throne with a curse. "Aye," he shouted in anger, "and always vote the way his master instructed! Why not ask to put your messenger, Isimud, on the throne? At least he looks two ways at the same time, whereas Mummu would only look your way!"

"And," Innina said gently, "I suppose you would want him to have the armies of Maqam Nifl and Borsippa at his command as well? Really, Enki, there are times when I wonder why anyone ever calls you Lord of Wisdom." She let her eyes drift to Surt. "Personally," she continued, "if the choice is between Mummu and this novice wizard, I'd rather have him on the throne and his handsome general in charge of the armies. So far as I know, neither of them sides with anybody."

"He serves Nergal," Enlil said coldly.

Innina shrugged. "Nergal takes no sides. He rides before all hosts on their way to war. He never favors one army over the other. As long as there's plenty of slaughter, he's satisfied. And no one can say he plays favorites when he judges the dead."

Marduk was becoming angrier by the moment. Before he could explode into words, however, Nannar spoke again. Looking directly at Utu, he said, "M-m-my brother Utu has n-n-not s-s-spoken yet. S-s-seldom is it h-h-he comes all th-th-this way to sit on the A-a-anunnaki. S-s-surely he did not c-c-come just to remain s-s-silent?"

Utu, sitting his throne in a relaxed, almost careless manner, nodded vaguely at Nannar. "No. I came to speak my piece. Perhaps this is as good a time to do it as any." He looked around the group with strangely flat and neutral eyes. "I see you have not improved during my long absence. Not that I expected it, but still, for an idealist like myself it is a bit of a disappointment. Except for Marduk you've all been around a good many sars now and there is, after all, the expectation that with age comes wisdom." He smiled mirthlessly as they all shifted uncomfortably on their thrones.

He sat up straighter. "Let us begin by admitting that there are a few facts in this case. First," he counted it off on one finger, "Adad is dead, killed by Surt. As the official judge in these matters, I was present during the challenge, although, of course, neither of the contestants was aware of it. I can attest to the second fact, therefore—that the fight was a fair one and Surt won by the rules. Adad, it is true, was careless and fought poorly. He allowed himself to be lured to Surt's domain for the beginning of the combat, he forgot to reinforce the guard on his quarters (he had only that nincompoop Mushrussu on guard), he left personal items lying about, and so on. The point is, Surt won. Adad is dead.

"I simply can't imagine that fact will lead to too many tears being shed by this group. Not a well-loved man, that Adad.

"Since he is gone, and since Surt is the cause of his departure, it follows, fact three, that Surt has as legitimate a claim on his throne as anyone in Muspellheim. Certainly greater than Mummu." He gave Surt a small smile that promised neither friendship nor enmity. "Of course, the Anunnaki could always decide that there only need to be six Sons of Muspell to rule, and divide up the property of Adad. Ah, I see some of you lean in that direction. Good. Then pray tell me, who should get Borsippa? And who Maqam Nifl? Marduk? That will give him greater armies than Enlil. Enlil? Oh, that would make him unbeatable. Enki? Again, the problem is the same. With the magical ax and the drum Lilissu at his command, Enki would have more magic available to him than any two other Sons. Give it all to sweet Nannar? Might as well give it to Enlil right off. How about An, the eldest? He might be the best choice, but does anyone here have so low an opinion of the ability and ambition of his delightful consort as to trust her with that much more power?"

Utu leaned back and looked around the thrones again, enjoying the reactions of their occupants. Every one of them was frowning and muttering. It was easy to see his words had had a profound effect. After waiting a few moments, he began again. "So you all see the problem. Consider the alternative: give the title and prerogatives of Patesi to Surt. Despite his obvious talent, he is still a fledgling wizard, hardly a major power to be reckoned with. Yet he is not without his defenses and allies, so no one of us could easily subdue him and make him serve our ends. He would doubtless be a relatively independent force on the Anunnaki."

The Patesi of Sippar and Larsa gave Surt a long, considering look. "Doubtless," he continued at last, "Surt has his own ambitions and schemes, else why risk eternal torture in the Kur? We will discover them with time. Perhaps he will be more of a nuisance than Adad, perhaps not. I move we take a consensus of the Anunnaki on the matter."

Enlil cleared his throat. "Umm. Well, yes, I guess we can do that. Uh, I can't vote, though, can I? I mean, I usually vote only if there's a tie. But now there are only six of us, so—"

"You can only vote if there's a tie," Utu said with a smile. "Those are the rules, Enlil. We must abide the rules."

"Well, I'm damn well against it!" Marduk bellowed. "I think we should send the fellow to Ereshkigal and his master Nergal! We can divide the cities. I'll take Maqam Nifl and An can have Borsippa."

Enki growled. "Take Maqam Nifl, eh? Then you'd have Kish surrounded on two sides! I'm against the upstart, too, but I'll be damned if any city will go to you, Marduk!"

Innina whispered in An's ear and the ancient man spoke out in a reedy voice. "I say give Surt Adad's place. Better that than any of you get it."

All eyes turned to Nannar, who looked down at the floor in embarrassment. Very softly he stammered, "G-g-g-give it to S-s-s-surt. Then we c-c-can s-s-stop all this b-b-bickering."

Attention shifted to Utu, who sat quietly on his throne, a slight smile playing around his lips. "Ah," he said, "Utu carries the decisive vote. Now you all know why he came this long distance, don't you?" He paused and looked each of them in the eyes. "I," he began, drawing the words out, "feel that, considering all aspects of the problem as it appears before us, the best solution is to . . . give the damn thing to Surt."

A dead silence hung in the Duku. Enlil finally broke it by clearing his throat. "Umm. Well, yes. I guess that decides it, doesn't it? Even if I'd be able to vote, I would have joined the majority. So then, Surt," he said addressing the slender man, "you may mount the throne of Patesi of Maqam Nifl and Borsippa."

As Jormungand watched his master proudly mount the steps to the raised area and sit in the throne, he couldn't help but smile to himself. Who would have guessed, he thought, that the shabby survivors of a raid on the Vigrid Plain, two men left for dead, could rise so high? Maybe now Surt would give up his obsession with revenge and learn to enjoy his newfound power and wealth. Yes, Jormungand thought, I'd like that. I'd really like that!

ON THE TREE

XIX

THE winter passed. Voden spent most of his waking hours silently staring at unseen things with his right eye. When he slept, which was seldom and then only for short periods, the same eye stayed open, gazing blankly at the darkness. At all times the left eye remained tightly shut.

Heimdall provided everything for the two of them. He'd built a small lean-to for shelter against the worst of the winter weather, and had filled it with warm, shaggy pelts. An endless supply of firewood surrounded them. And Heimdall's amazing ability to hear a deer walking through the snow several miles away, plus his incredibly keen eyesight, made him an excellent supplier of fresh meat. He was even able to find hibernating animals by listening for their breathing, so they never lacked variety or suffered from an absence of fat meat in the diet.

He treated the young Aesir with calmness and gentle respect. At times, when Voden seemed to be withdrawing too far within himself, the white man would speak to him for hours, describing his journeys and the many things he'd seen and heard, slowly, carefully drawing him back into the world. At other times he was silent for days on end, somehow sens-

239

ing that the young man needed the quiet to work through his recent experiences.

As the winter progressed, Voden gradually became more normal. His facial expression became less fearful and haunted. The look in his right eye changed from one of remembered horror to that of someone who has seen too much but has come to terms with it. He lost his stoop-shouldered way of standing and sitting and walked once more with the upright posture of an Aesir warrior.

Yet though he began to resemble the Voden of the days before he'd drunk from the well, it was plain he was no longer the same person. He was given to long periods of thoughtful, introspective silence. At those times his expression was a combination of wisdom and resignation that made him appear far older than his years. When he spoke, it was carefully, each word weighed and measured to be sure of its worth.

And there was that left eye, always closed, a strange, threatening symbol of what might be, of horrible power that could break loose at any moment. That eye made him seem sinister, even when he was smiling.

One morning Heimdall announced he could hear the spring flowers beginning to grow beneath the snow and could see, about a hundred leagues to the south, the first V of geese winging their way northward. Voden nodded and replied that he, too, could feel life coming back into things. The rest of the day he seemed almost happy.

That night, as the two of them sat and stared into the fire in a companionable silence, Voden sighed and said, "Well, now I've earned my second name." Heimdall looked over at him, his face a question. The young man paused thoughtfully, then continued. "Every Aesir is given his first name, generally by the oldest man in his family. In my case, my grandfather, Buri, Namefastened me Voden. The rest of an Aesir's names are earned. Buri, for example, was called Axehand, because he killed a mighty Jotun warrior with his bare hand. My father was called Skullcracker for similar reasons.

"I earned my first name when I left the plains of Asaheim and the forests of Vanaheim to seek Mimir's Well. Vafudar, the Wanderer, I became. Now I have a new name, one Mimir bestowed on me without knowing it. Now I am Bileyg, the One-eyed."

He paused again, his eye unfocused and his expression

dreamy. "Raesvelg foresaw all this when he gave me my Power Song. Part of it runs, 'Bileyg I'll be and Vafudar till falls the mighty Ash Tree.' The Vafudar part I understood when the time came. Now I see the mighty eagle was right again.

"I wonder, though. Will I become Har and Jafanhar and Thridi? How would one earn names like that? What terrible things must happen to earn the name Ygg? Are they all there within me, only waiting to come out? I wasn't ready for Bileyg, wasn't expecting it. Now I wonder about the others. How will they come, and when?"

The silence stretched out between them until each went soundlessly to sleep.

Morning dawned bright and warmed by a soft wind from the southwest. The smell of new life was heavy about them, and both men drew in long breaths as they ate their morning meal.

When they'd finished, Voden turned to Heimdall and said, "How long have you walked Yggdrasil?"

The white man leaned back, considering the question. "In the form you see before you, since the days of the First Men. But I was born when Yggdrasil first came into existence. Before that there was only the Void, the timeless, evanescent, empty, teeming, fecund, undifferentiated nothing that is nameless and formless yet contains all names and all forms. We call it the Tao, but that is not its name. It is the nothing that gives birth to the One so that the One may give birth to the Two so that the Two may, in their turn, begat the Three which create everything else in the universe." He shrugged. "I came somewhere between the Three and everything else."

Voden nodded and said, "If you've been around that long, perhaps you could tell me how old this knife is and where it came from?" He took the ancient iron knife from the sheath at his side and handed it, hilt foremost, to the white man. "My grandfather, Buri, gave it to me. He said it'd always been in the family, but he didn't know anything more about it than that. Kao-Shir said it's very old."

Heimdall took the knife gingerly, tested its edge, then began to turn it over and over in his hands, examining it with evident interest. "Yes," he finally said, "the knife is very old. From the time of the First Men, I would say. It reminds me of the kind I taught Jarl to make."

"Does it come from the West, then?"

"The West? I honestly do not know. I do not recognize the style and design. That in itself is odd, but there is something even more unusual about this knife. You see, the iron it is made of does not come from anywhere on Yggdrasil. This knife, Voden, was beaten from a piece of Sky Iron, a piece that fell from the heavens eons ago. It is very hard and strong, and filled with a power that cannot derive from earth alone. There is a magic inherent in it." He handed the knife back to the young Aesir.

Voden reached inside his fur robe and pulled out the leather bag that hung around his neck. He lifted it over his head and handed it to Heimdall. "Can you tell me what these are?"

The white man held the bag in his hands for several moments, gazing at it. Then carefully, almost reverently, he untied the knots that bound it and emptied its contents on the fur rug he sat upon. He sighed when he saw the bone pieces, and picked each one up to give it a long, thorough, even loving examination.

When he was finished, he raised his eyes to meet that of Voden. "I cannot imagine where you found these, Aesir, or rather, why these chose you to find them. These are the Bones of Audna. Kon made them with his own hand at my direction. He was their first owner. Another, whose name is too awful to repeat, was their second owner. You are the third."

"What . . . what are they?" Voden stammered, surprised by Heimdall's intensity.

The other man paused a moment, as if listening, then cast a quick glance around to see if anyone was near. When he spoke, it was in a confidential whisper that Voden had to lean far forward to catch. "The symbols inscribed on the Bones of Audna are the runes." He held one up. "This, for example, is the rune of Ur, the Aurochs." Heimdall's gaze became fixed, and his voice took on a singsong quality. "Ur has only one thing in his mind and wide horns, sweeping high above it. He is a fierce horn-fighter who stamps the plain, a striking beast. No creature dares invade that which he bestrides. He stands firmly in this world but penetrates all others.

"And this," he intoned, holding another up for Voden to see, "is the rune of Thurs, fearfully sharp, an evil thing to grasp, even more grim for those who must rest among them!

"Here is Ing, one close to my heart. Eastward over the

waves it came, then went again westward in its wagon. The grain springs tall in its trail. How brightly does it burn!"

He gave himself a mighty shake, as though he were trying to twist himself from the grasp of some powerful thing. For a few moments he sat silently looking down at the bones and their strange markings. His voice came, soft and husky, from somewhere deep within him. "I have not spoken of the runes since I taught their meanings to Kon. It is no light thing to speak of them again, Aesir."

Eagerly Voden leaned forward. "Teach *me* their meanings, Heimdall! When you were talking of them just now it seemed . . . it seemed somehow familiar . . . as if I was regaining knowledge I'd forgotten."

Heimdall raised his white eyes to Voden's and smiled slightly. "It would be that way. You have the Galdar-power in you. The runes and the Galdar-power are closely related."

"Tell me of them, please!"

The white man shook his head slowly. "That I must not do, Voden. I dare not tell you the inner meanings of the runes, nor how to cut and paint them. I may not show you the art of Rune-Risting, nor how to cast spells, nor how to see into the future with them. Once I did that. I taught Kon." He sighed and began to put the bones back in the bag. "I let much evil into the world by that act. And much good. There are many spells. One is called Help because it comforts grief, lessens pain, and even cures sickness. Another must be learned by any man who hopes to become a healer. But there are others . . . dark ones . . . unclean. . . . No. I was judged for my acts and pay the penalty through nine worlds. I must not repeat the crime.

"These are yours now, Voden. The Bones of Audna have chosen you for their third owner. You must learn to use them yourself, learn to unlock their secrets, learn to be worthy of them.

"I cannot even suggest a way. I can only warn you that whatever way you find, it will be painful and unpleasant. Should you master the runes, however, you will truly become Thridi, the Third, even as Raesvelg foretold."

Voden took the bag from his outstretched hand. He looked down at it intently with his right eye. "So much power, so much knowledge. I can feel it, Heimdall. Like a heat pouring from the bones. It lies in my grasp! And yet . . . and yet . . ."

"Do not reach too far, Aesir. Some things are harder to hold than others. The power of the runes is immense. Let it loose before you are ready, and it will burn your mind and your spirit to ashes. Wait patiently. If the Bones of Audna managed to find you, your time will doubtless come. Until then, wait. You have enough to think about after your drink from Mimir's Well."

The young Aesir nodded in thoughtful agreement as he put the bag and its contents back around his neck. "How soon will it be before we can travel, Heimdall?"

"Travel? The snows are melting already. In another month the ground will be clear enough to travel. Where do you want to go?"

"Back to Asaheim, back to my father's hall in Asgard. I . . . I've been thinking a lot and . . . well . . . I looked deep into myself when I had my left eye open. I saw things I didn't like very much. I . . . there are people I have to see . . . words I have to say." He looked down at the ground. "It's hard to explain, but there are some things I've got to work through, and the only way I can do it is to go back there and resolve some . . . things." He laughed quickly, embarrassed. "I can't seem to find any word but 'things'! That's how vague it is, even in my own mind. But I know that's where I have to go right now. Will you come with me?"

Heimdall nodded solemnly. "Yes, of course, I must. You will need me. And, then, I must be there to blow my Gjallarhorn when the time comes."

True to Heimdall's prediction, they were able to start traveling in about a month. The snow, though deep, melted quickly. The only real problems they encountered were the many swollen streams that poured into the Amsvartnir Sea.

They headed south along the western shore of the sea, retracing Voden's steps. The route along the eastern shore would have been shorter, but that would have meant traveling through the lands of the Jotun. The longer way, despite its many dangers, was safer.

By fall they'd reached the southernmost point of the sea, an area of steep hills and heavy woods that lay between Svartalfheim and Nidavellir. The last time Voden had passed this way he had been well south, near the spur of the Smoking Lands that made its last thrust northward at this point. Ro-

Setau lay on the west slope of that spur.

As they traveled, Voden kept a sharp eye out for signs of Kao-Shir and Anhur. He realized the odds were against it, but he often thought how delightful it would be to come across his two friends again. Kao-Shir would have a wonderful time talking with Heimdall. And Anhur would be in positive ecstasy, harrumphing and snorting endlessly about two fools babbling foggy nonsense! Although once or twice he thought he saw some trace of their passing, the farther south he went, the less sure he was. Had they gone by a different route? Could anything have happened to them? They'd indicated they might go to Asgard. Would they be there when he arrived?

The winter was hard, but short. From the southern point of the Amsvartnir Sea they headed due east until they came to the River Gopul. They crossed it on a raft they built, then skirted south of the Himinborg.

As they walked swiftly across the rolling Himinborg Plain, Voden felt a strange tightness growing in his chest. It was a combination of pleasure and pain. How would Borr react to the return of his son . . . minus an eye? Vethur must be a giant by now, a full-fledged Aesir warrior! And Vili! He wondered what his little sister looked like. Even at birth she'd strongly resembled Vestla, her mother.

And then there would be his old friends! Tror, the huge redheaded bull of a son of Volund the Smith. Honir, too, who'd suffered through so much with him in Folkvang. Wonderful, silent, shy, fleet-footed Honir! Of course, he couldn't forget Tyr. Such a fierce boy! Doubtless a warrior of renown by this time. Tyr had never wanted to be anything but a swordsman like his father.

He'd enjoy seeing the older men again too. Gagnrad, Volund . . . He decided he might even go to see Groa, if the old witchwoman was still alive. Somehow he felt certain she would be, but—

Heimdall laid a hand on his arm. Voden looked up and followed the white man's pointing finger. At first he could see nothing but the clear afternoon air to the northeast. Then he saw what Heimdall's sharper eyes had picked up. It was a thin column of smoke, quickly growing larger.

He did some quick figuring. The smoke would be rising from about where Asgard stood. It could be the smoke that

came from the halls of his people. He looked again. No.
There was too much smoke and it was too dark. They were
still a good two hours away, even at a steady jog. At this
distance the fires of the hall wouldn't be visible. Something
else was causing the smoke.

Suddenly pale, he turned and stared at Heimdall. The other
man nodded solemnly. "It is a big fire, Voden. I cannot see
through the rolling hills that lie between Asgard and where we
stand, but I would be willing to wager the smoke—"

"Asgard's burning!" Voden interrupted, his voice hoarse
with emotion. "Asgard's burning! The Jotun must've attacked!" Without waiting to see if Heimdall was following, he
began to run toward the growing column of smoke.

Gagnrad stood, his head down, weary, worn, his body filthy
and covered with blood. "By Sigfod, we fought them! I've
never been in such a furious melee! Borr was like . . . like . . .
he was berserk, a mad, killing thing that wouldn't stop. He
had bodies piled up on either side of the swath he was cutting,
trying to get to that young leader, Hrodvitnir."

He looked up, his eyes dull with fatigue, yet shining at the
memory of the battle. "The Jotun sat on his horse, a wolf cape
on his shoulders, a wolf head for a helmet. He saw Borr coming and laughed for joy. He rallied his men and charged us.
We formed a shield wall around Borr to repel them. Gods! It
rained flashing metal and blood! The air was thick with the
battle cries and screams of dying men! It was a raven's feast to
end them all!

"But we couldn't hold them. They broke through. I went
down, slammed in the head by a stroke that should have killed
me. The fool hit with the side of his sword instead of the
edge. My helmet saved me, but I was still knocked into blackness."

He paused, taking a deep drag on the mug of foaming ale
he held. His hands were shaking badly. He moaned and wiped
the sweat and blood that was dripping into his eyes. "Gods!
Just before I went under I saw it happen! Damn Fornjot!
Damn Sigfod! Damn all the gods to Niflheim! Curse them
all!"

His voice dropped to a harsh, panting whisper. "They
pulled him down by sheer weight of numbers. There must
have been twenty hanging on him, clinging to his arms and

legs, grasping Deathbringer, his great battle-ax. They pulled him down, bound him! And all the while that bastard, that wolf-loving Hrodvitnir sat on his horse, laughing!"

He grimaced in pain as he shifted his weight to find a more comfortable position. "I swear by Sigfod, they took him alive! Those damn Jotun took Borr alive!

"If only we hadn't been so tired, so worn out by the battle with the Vanir and the long march back north, if so many hadn't died in the south by the Gunnthro, we might have been able to save him. . . ." His head dropped forward and he slumped, unconscious.

Tror gently laid him down and looked up at Voden and Heimdall. "The Jotun took him alive. You know what that means."

Voden looked at his old friend. "Yes," he whispered in dread. "It means the Grove of Nerthus."

Tror nodded. There was a silence between them, though it was filled with the groaning of wounded men and the weeping of mourning women. Here and there a child sat next to a dead parent amid the smoking ruins of a hall, wailing its grief to an indifferent sky.

Not able to meet Tror's eye, Voden asked dreadful questions. "Vethur?"

"Dead," came the flat, weary reply. "Killed defending the gate before the main force arrived from the south. There were many wounds on his front, none on his back. He died well."

"But he's dead nonetheless," Voden said bitterly. "And Vili? What of my sister?"

Tror sighed. "Luck there. She wasn't in Asgard. About a week ago Borr sent her out to visit the family of the man he's thinking of pledging her to. They live on the Aesir Plain, just the other side of the River Fimbulthul. She's safe."

Voden nodded. "How is Volund? And Thrud?"

The red-haired giant's face went flat and angry. "Thrud lives, mostly. She was raped by a Jotun when they overran Asgard. Raped and beaten. She'll live. And she'll be avenged.

"My father's dead. He died defending his forge and my sister. I was there." He held up a huge hammer, the one called Mjollnir. Voden recognized it. "That's when I picked up Mjollnir. Picked it right up, light as a feather! And I fought with it! I crushed every Jotun skull I could find! I—"

Tyr laughed grimly. "That's what turned the tide. Tror and

his hammer. Gods, Voden, you should have seen him. He shook the Jotun the way thunder shakes a stormy sky! We rallied behind him. He was our shield! We smashed into the Jotun and hurled them from Asgard!"

Tror picked up the tale again. "Yes. We drove them from the burning city. That was when Borr and the men who'd been fighting in the south showed up. They were winded, but when they saw the Jotun, they gave a roar and slammed into them, driving them north toward Bifrosti's Ford. They swept them . . . a little too far."

"Why were our warriors in the south? Who were they fighting?" But even as he said it, Voden knew. "The Vanir?" he asked. "The Vanir attacked?"

Tyr nodded. "Aye, the damned, treacherous Vanir. They have a new Vanadis, Voden, someone you know."

Voden stared blankly at him for a moment. "Fiorgynn's not Vanadis anymore? Who . . ." Realization dawned in his eye. "You mean . . . Freyja?"

"Aye," Tyr responded. "A worse bitch than her mother. She hates us like poison. They raided our borders and wiped out three farmsteads. Slaughtered everyone—men, women, children. Borr went to avenge our dead. No sooner had the battle started than the Jotun poured over Bifrosti's Ford. The rest you know."

Tror put his hand on Voden's shoulder. "Borr fought the Vanir at the edge of their own forest. He thrashed them soundly. Then he came back north at a dead run and smashed the Jotun. An incredible feat. A glorious last verse for his saga."

Voden shook his head angrily. "No. His last verse will be a painful death on a tree in the Grove of Nerthus! The Trul will sacrifice him to that bitch goddess of theirs!"

Both Tror and Tyr were unable to raise their eyes to meet Voden's single, glaring eye. The red-haired giant mumbled, "Yes. They will. But there's nothing that can be done. We can't mount a rescue party and invade Jotunheim. We're bled dry, Voden. It would take a huge army to cut through to Utgard. We just . . . we—"

"I wasn't thinking of an army, Tror. There's only one way to rescue my father now, and you know it."

Tror hesitated for a moment, as if trying to understand what Voden was talking about. Suddenly it registered. His eyes widened in surprise and he began to protest. "You don't mean . . . but you can't—"

Voden interrupted. "I can and I will. I'm going to get him. Alone."

"But," Tyr said, his eyes shining with excitement, "the only way you can do that is to . . ." His voice faded out as he saw the look on Voden's face. It was hard and terrible to behold, the single eye glowing as if lit by flames from within, the lips pulled back in a wolflike snarl.

"I know," came the reply. "The only way I can do that is to hang on the tree in his place!"

XX

THEY spent the rest of that day and evening trying to dissuade him. Even Gagnrad, wounded and barely able to stay conscious, came to plead with him. "We've lost Borr and Vethur. We don't wish to lose the last of Borr's warrior blood this way. Stay. You can't save him. No man alive can survive nine days and nights on that tree, Voden. We'll lose both of you. We need you here."

Voden looked at him and smiled, his eye hard. "He was your friend. You fought by his side, drank with him, wept with him. Will you abandon him now?"

Gagnrad pulled himself upright. "No, by Sigfod! No! I'll never abandon Borr! By all the gods, I'll go myself! I'll—"

He collapsed back onto the bench. "Ahh, damn damn damn! Who in Fornjot's cursed name do I think I'm fooling? I haven't enough strength to walk across the room without help." He put his head in his hands and moaned in frustration. "Better that sword had done its job. Borr's in trouble and Gagnrad Beargrasp is too weak and sick to share his fate with him. Damn!

"Mark my words, Voden. I said to *share* his fate, not to save him. Damn Fornjot's icy heart, but Borr is doomed. His

250

fate is rune-carved in the Hall of the Gods. He'll die on the tree in Nerthus's grove, a sacrifice to the goddess. I can't save him. You can't save him. All Yggdrasil can't save him. If you go you simply throw away your life."

"It's mine to throw away," Voden answered softly, his eye beginning to shine again. "As to whether or not I can or can't save him, well, that remains to be seen. But look at me closely, Beargrasp. Take the scales from your eyes. Stop seeing the Voden you expect to be there and see the one that really is. Look, old friend of my father, look."

Gagnrad raised his head and stared at Voden. His eyes widened slightly as he noticed things he'd failed to see before. The closed eye, sinister, foreboding. The burning light in the open eye. The face that carried both pain and wisdom, strength and bitterness, determination and resignation. Here was a visage that was both open and hidden, changeable and unchanging, masked and alert. There was a sense of mystery about it, a feeling of tremendous power barely restrained lying just beneath the surface. It made him shudder and lower his eyes. "I . . . I . . ." he stammered, unsure of what to say.

"You have seen," Voden said gently, firmly.

Gagnrad nodded.

"Good," Voden nodded. "Then you understand that I'm going."

"Yes," the older man sighed. "Yes, you're going." He paused and looked up quickly, just as quickly lowering his glance again. "You frighten me, Bileyg. I don't know why, but I fear what you've become. There's a darkness in you . . . an empty place. . . ."

"It's in all men, Beargrasp. The difference is, I've looked deep into it. Now it looks out through my eye."

"And your other eye, Voden?" Gagnrad whispered.

The smile that curved Voden's lips chilled the older man so deeply that he rose without a word and limped away without looking back.

Voden wore a cloak with a deep hood and rode Vethur's horse. Heimdall rode one of Gagnrad's horses. Voden hadn't questioned the white man's determination to accompany him though he'd rejected the fervent offers of his other friends.

They crossed Bifrosti's Ford at dawn and rode northward for an hour before a small group of Jotun saw them. The Jotun stared in disbelief for a moment, then spurred their horses and sped off in the direction of Utgard.

In another two hours they saw a cloud of dust on the horizon. Heimdall shaded his eyes and gazed northward. After a short pause he sat back and muttered, "About a hundred of them. That warrior with the wolf-head helmet and cloak is leading them. He is grinning like a madman."

Voden nodded as if Heimdall had given him news he expected. "Yes. Hrodvitnir. I'd hoped he'd be the one."

They topped a rise and saw the Jotun, drawn up in a long line, waiting for them on the top of the next rise. Without the slightest pause, Voden and Heimdall rode forward.

As they approached the line of Jotun horsemen, the ones in the center fell back to make way for them. The only sound was the blowing of the horses and the creak of saddle leather. When they passed, horsemen fell in behind, forming a large circle around them. Once they were completely surrounded, a new rider entered the circle. He was clad in a flowing wolf-skin cloak. His head was covered with a leather helmet that sported a wolf's head on its crest. The device painted on his shield was that of a rampant wolf, jaws open, claws raking the air in a battle frenzy. He silently regarded the two riders in the center for a moment, then raised his right hand and howled. The other horsemen took up his howl and began to race around the circle, moving forward at exactly the pace Voden and Heimdall kept. After a few moments the warrior clothed like a wolf raised his hand again and they all fell silent, riding quietly once more in their places. Voden turned and gave Heimdall a slight smile of grim amusement.

They rode at a brisk pace for three more hours. Every few moments new riders joined the circle around them. By the time they saw the smoke from the cook fires of Utgard, there were easily four hundred horsemen escorting them.

About half a mile short of the city of wagons drawn up on the eastern shore of the Amsvartnir Sea, they halted as a small group of men on foot approached. The circle opened and the men walked slowly up to Voden and Heimdall.

There were none of them. Each was clad in a long fur cloak made from the complete pelt of an animal. Legs, with claws or hooves, and tails were still attached. On their heads they wore helmets made from the head of the animal they wore over their shoulders. Unlike Hrodvitnir's helmet, theirs hid their faces. They peered at the world through the eye sockets of the animal they were. There was a wolf, a black bear, an elk, a moose, a deer, a long-toothed tiger, a white leopard, a golden lion, and in the middle, towering over the rest and clearly their leader, a gigantic white bear from the Icerealm. Each costume represented the animal that was the Fylgjur, or tutelary spirit, of the man who wore it. Around each neck hung a necklace made from the claws, teeth, skulls, and bones of the other animals that were their Hamingjur, the familiar spirits that attended them.

These, Voden knew, were the leaders of the Trul, the most powerful and dreaded clan of the Jotun. The Jotun Horde was composed of five clans. The largest and most important in matters of war was the Thursar. Most of the war leaders belonged to this clan, and every Warlord of the Horde had come from it since Thrudgelmir had risen and taken that title.

Next in importance was the Rimthursar. Then came two minor clans, the Risar and the Bergettins, composed mainly of those living in the far north and east of Jotunheim.

The fifth clan was different. It was composed of men from the other four who'd been touched by Vilmeid, the dark god of magic, and given the dread Galdar-power. Many died or went hopelessly insane during the long years of testing and trial that had to be endured to develop their skills.

Once past the testing, they were called Shamans and took on important functions within the Horde. When people fell sick, the Shamans went to the Alterjinga, the spirit world, to find the cause, often threatening or bargaining with the spirits until they were able to return the invalid to health. Nothing of significance was ever decided without consulting them. When asked for advice, they would chant for hours and then suddenly fall to the ground, thrashing about, their backs arching, eyes rolling, mouths frothing, teeth gnashing. A thin, whining wail would envelop them, and the air around them would pulse with a strange power. As suddenly as it had started, the fit would pass. They would lie as limp and motionless as if dead, eyes closed, while they muttered strange, incomprehensible words. Other Trul would gather, listening, nodding, and interpreting the speech which they said came directly from the Alterjinga, the realm of spirits that paralleled and interpenetrated our own world. These messages from the Alterjinga held great power for they contained the wishes of both

Nerthus and Gymir, the gods worshipped by the Jotun. These words were treated as commands and followed to the letter by everyone.

There was a darker aspect to the Trul, however. In battle they would find a hill overlooking the scene of the conflict, and dancing and cavorting obscenely, shrieking to their gods, demanding aid from their Hamingjur and Fylgjur, they would hurl curses and magic at the enemy. If the Jotun triumphed, they would scurry from their height to roam the field, slitting the throats of the wounded and picking those to save as sacrifices to Nerthus and Gymir. Some they kept for even darker purposes.

As the priests of Nerthus and Gymir, they cut the throats of sacrificial victims with keen-edged knives made of flint and caught the spurting blood in special bowls of beaten gold, covered with mystical symbols. They themselves drank of the blood as they offered it to Nerthus and Gymir.

This relatively swift death was what awaited the luckiest of those taken alive by the Trul. Far worse was the long, drawn-out death by hanging on a tree in Nerthus's sacred grove, or the exquisite torture of slowly being burnt alive on the pyre of Gymir.

More horrible still was the fate of those chosen by the Trul for a dreadful rite. From time to time they would take a victim, bind him to a large, blood-caked stone that stood in the sacred grove, and then cut the still beating heart or liver from his body. They would carefully examine the quivering organ, hoping to read the future or the will of the gods in it. The reading finished, they would fall on the body, tearing great gobbets of raw flesh from it, gorging themselves in a hideous feast that left nothing behind but a few cracked and gnawed bones.

The Aesir hated and feared the Trul more than all of the rest of the Jotun combined. One of the most potent curses they knew was "May the Trul get you!"

Voden regarded them with open curiosity. The white bear stepped forward and said with a low growl, "What does an Aesir do walking the sacred earth of Nerthus? What does an Aesir do walking beneath the holy sky of Gymir?"

Drawing himself to his full height, Voden glared at the Trul from deep within the hooded cloak he wore. His eye flared with light. "You have my father, Trul. I come for him."

The white bear laughed deeply, humorlessly. "Nerthus has your father. You are too late, Aesir."

"No, I'm not. I claim the right to take his place on the tree. I am his son. That right is mine."

A murmur of surprise ran through the assembled Jotun. Several of the Trul moved forward and whispered to the white bear. The creature shook its head and the necklace around its neck jangled menacingly. "You are Aesir. You have no rights among the Jotun."

Voden's eye blazed furiously. His voice rang out sharply, lashing at the Trul. "I am Voden! I am Vafudar! I am Bileyg! Raesvelg is my Flygjur! Hugin and Munin, the twin ravens fly to my bidding! Geri and Freki run to obey my wishes! Look on my face, Trul, and know who and what I am!" With a gesture of defiance, he threw back the hood and showed himself to the white bear.

With a hiss of anger and fear the creature drew back. "He has the Galdar-power!" it snarled. The other Trul huddled together and growled in agreement. "He has the right to claim as he does!" The bear stalked closer, eyeing the Aesir youth. "Are you indeed what you seem to be? No Aesir has ever had the Galdar-power. Only one eye . . . the other? What does it see? Where did you lose it?" The creature stopped stock still, its breath hissing inward in surprise. "Mimir? You've been to Mimir's Well? You've drunk?"

The Trul moved closer and stared fixedly at him. "Yes," it finally muttered. "Yes, you've been there. You've given to the well and taken what it has to offer. And there is more. I can see through your flesh to your bones! You've been to the Cloud Realm! Your bones have been in the fire!" He stepped back, his gesture showing a grudging respect.

Several other Jotun stepped forward now, men dressed as warriors. They were scowling and appeared angry. One of them addressed the white bear. "This Aesir is the son of Borr. We must kill him and thus wipe out the whole accursed line!"

The shaggy head shook decisively. "No. He has claimed a right which is his to claim."

Another of the warriors spoke up. "Damn his right. He's an enemy. We demand the right to kill him. We demand it now. Wipe this Aesir scum from the face of Nerthus's earth. Remove him from the view of Gymir's eye. Destroy him! Now!" He drew his sword menacingly.

Before he could move, a new figure joined them. It was the warrior dressed as a wolf, Hrodvitnir. Without a word he stepped between the warrior with the raised sword and Voden. He looked the Aesir youth boldly in the eye. The two young men stood less than three feet apart. Each thoughtfully assessed and weighed the other. Voden saw a Jotun shorter than himself, but broader and massively strong. Hrodvitnir moved smoothly and lightly, despite his bulk. More like a forest wolf than anything else, Voden decided. His eyes were black and almond shaped. The hair that showed from beneath his helmet was a shiny bluish black. His nose was hawklike and narrow, his chin firm and cleft. A youthful mustache, thin but long and drooping, hung down on either side of a full mouth. The face seemed open and frank at first glance, but as Voden looked more closely, he realized that beyond that surface appearance it was unreadable.

The Aesir was equally a mystery to the probing eyes of the Jotun. Only one eye, and that one glowing as if lit by flame. The other closed. Not missing. He could see the bulge of it behind the eyelid. Just closed, purposefully, permanently. It made him wonder. Why did it look so sinister?

The rest of the face was strong and typically Aesir, except for the fact that it seemed older and wiser than that of any Aesir he'd ever seen. Older, wiser, sadder, more menacing.

Each liked what he saw in the other. Hrodvitnir turned slowly to face the other warriors. "This Aesir should be allowed to take his father's place." There was a growl of anger from the others, and more than one hand went to sword hilt. Hrodvitnir's lips curled back in a sneer. He looked from one to the other of them, forcing them to meet his eyes, forcing them to waver and look down. He spoke to each in turn, his voice a purring menace. "You'd draw against me, Hrungnir, raper of girls? You'd rape no more. Or you, Hymir, ape-armed fool, do you wish to die? Skrymir, will you draw your sword so I can put some new dents in your forehead?"

Muttering, the warriors dropped their eyes to the ground, and their hands fell to their sides. "But that's Borr's son," the one called Skrymir complained. "How many has Borr slain while they slept in their wagons? Women and children—"

Hrodvitnir interrupted. "Could it be you did not hear what this Aesir asked? Could it be you did not hear what the Trul have said? This one wishes to take his father's place on the tree. Think of that Skrymir." He half turned and pointed to Voden. "He comes to set Borr free by taking his place on the tree!"

His voice dropped lower. "That means he may take his father, himself, and his friend home again, safe and sound, if and only if he can hang on the tree for nine days and nine nights . . . and live!

"Think, all of you, what that means. Nine days and nine nights on that tree. Could any one of you, even the strongest and bravest, last half that long? Could you?" Shifting their weight nervously and looking at each other out of the corners of their eyes, the warriors muttered that they couldn't. "Then how do you think an Aesir will manage it? You fools! The Aesir hasn't come to rescue his father. He's come to die with him! He must hang on the tree for nine days and nights and live. Do you really think he'll succeed? Ha! The fool has delivered himself into the hands of Nerthus. Our goddess will feast on his flesh *and* that of his father!" Hrodvitnir roared out his last words. The crowd thundered back their agreement. "Let him hang!" they cried. "Let the Aesir hang!" Seeing they'd been overruled, the warriors joined in the chant. "Let him hang! Let Nerthus have him!"

Hrodvitnir turned back to Voden with a crooked smile curving his lips. "The fools don't think you have a hope," he said softly, looking Voden in the eye.

"What do you think?" the Aesir replied.

"I think it'll be very interesting. Very interesting indeed."

They took Voden and Heimdall to a wagon at the edge of the sacred grove. The grove stood on a point of land that thrust out in a northwesterly direction into the Amsvartnir Sea. Out beyond the point lay the island of Saevarstod, where Volund had once been kept prisoner as he worked at his forges for Bergelmir. There the master smith had killed the Jotun Warlord's two sons and raped and debased his daughter before fleeing with his children to the Aesir.

Borr lay in the wagon. The Trul had bound his worst wounds, wishing to keep him alive long enough to sacrifice to their goddess, but the Aesir leader had lost a great deal of blood and was only semiconscious. Voden knelt by his side and washed the dried blood and battlefield dirt from his father's face with cool water. He was astonished at how old and careworn that face appeared.

As the coolness of evening crept across the grasslands, Borr opened his eyes and looked up at his son. For a long time he said nothing. Then he smiled and muttered, "So. The Wanderer returns."

The weakness of his father's voice shocked Voden. He was used to hearing the man bellow and shake the heavens with his power. Even over the roar of battle Borr's voice could be clearly made out, urging his men on. Now it could hardly be heard close up. He's more badly injured than I thought, Voden realized.

Borr coughed slightly, a gurgle deep in his chest. "I'm glad you came. How's Asgard?"

"Fine, Father. The damage wasn't as great as it looked when you charged by."

"And Vethur?"

"Fine. He wanted to come in my place but I made him stay. They needed him to help."

Borr nodded. "Good decision." He sighed. "I was worried when he didn't join us in the attack. Glad he's all right." He paused and looked vaguely around. "Where are we? I can't see too well. My eyes are fuzzy. Where are we?"

Voden looked over at Heimdall, a question in his eye. Heimdall returned his look without comment, then leaned over and spoke. "You are in my tent, Borr. I am Heimdall, from beyond the Western Forest. I met Voden in his travels and came back to Asaheim with him to see if what I had been told about the fierceness and bravery of the Aesir was true."

"Uh. Is it?" Borr wheezed and coughed again.

Heimdall looked at Voden. "It is indeed," he replied.

"Gagnrad," Borr muttered. "How's old Beargrasp? I thought I saw him go down."

"He's wounded, as you are. But the sword stroke that felled him was a poor one, with the flat of the blade. His helmet saved his life. You'll see him later."

Borr tried to lift his head. "Better get back. Need me." His strength failed almost instantly, and his head dropped back. "Uh," he moaned, "weak. Why'm I so damn weak?"

"You need a little rest. Father. Then we'll go back to Asgard. Once we're there, we'll compose a song about this double victory. You beat the Vanir and the Jotun! That's a theme worthy of the skalds!" Borr grunted weakly and mumbled agreement. He was having trouble keeping his eyes open. Voden leaned closer and almost whispered. "Now sleep, Father. You need to. You have to get up soon. The Aesir need you."

"Yes," Borr nodded, his voice slurred, his eyes already drooping with exhaustion. "Aesir need me. So tired. Must sleep." His eyes closed for a second, then jerked back open again. Voden saw the dark gleam of fear in them. "Sleep. Can't sleep. Dreams. Horrible dreams." He clutched his son's arm in an iron grip. "Surt. He's after me, Voden. Watch out for him. He's in my dreams. Demons." His eyelids drooped again, the last of his energy spent. In a moment he was asleep.

Voden looked up from his father's pale face to meet Heimdall's stare. "He may not live," the white man said. "I will do what I can for him while you are on the tree, but I cannot guarantee anything. He is badly wounded. I think his lung has been punctured."

The young Aesir nodded wearily. "He will live. He *must* live. I was speaking the truth when I said the Aesir need him. There's no one strong enough to take his place. Now that the Vanir have broken the truce and attacked..." He shook his head worriedly. "One enemy at a time taxed us. But two, one on either side..." He let the words hang in the air between them.

There was a movement at the back flap of the wagon. The head of the white bear peeked in. "Tomorrow you will begin your ordeal on the tree, Aesir," the growling voice said. "We will come for you at dawn." The bear was about to withdraw when it paused as if having a second thought. Voden could have sworn that the expression in the creature's hard eyes softened for but an instant. "The gods be with you."

XXI

VODEN was standing and waiting outside the wagon when the nine Trul, led by the white bear, came for him at dawn. The air was cool and heavy with a mist that rose from the Amsvartnir Sea and spilled out over the land. He was led through the grove to the shore of the sea, where he was instructed to take off his Aesir clothing and bathe in the water.

With quiet dignity he did as he was bid, removing his clothes and placing them in a neat pile. When one of the Trul reached out to remove the leather bag that hung around his neck, however, he seized the man's wrist in an unbreakable grip and softly said, "No." The Trul growled and motioned for the white bear.

The creature approached Voden, his bright eyes sparkling with curiosity. He gazed from the young Aesir's eye down to the bag and back again several times. Then he slowly reached his hand out to touch the pouch. Voden stood utterly still and relaxed as the clawed paw approached. Suddenly the white bear stopped. An odd look of surprise and wonder filled his eyes. He grunted and nodded, withdrawing his hand. "Keep them," he said. "They belong to you and you to them. No other should touch them. Now enter the water and cleanse your body in preparation for your sacrifice."

When Voden climbed dripping from the sea, two of the Trul dried him vigorously with white cloths. When they were finished, the white bear handed him a white loin cloth and white cord to fasten it around his waist. The rest of his clothes had disappeared.

As they returned through the mist to the grove of Nerthus, Voden noticed that groups of Jotun had gathered to silently watch him pass. No one looked at him directly, peering instead from the corners of downcast eyes. When he moved by each group, they would sigh with one breath and begin a low, droning ululation that grew stronger as he went along.

Their progress through the grove was slow and almost stately. Eventually a giant ash tree loomed up out of the mist and the Trul moved directly for it. At its base they stopped and formed a semicircle, Voden in the center, facing the tree. The white bear spoke in a deep and sonorous voice that rose through the mist and penetrated to the farthest reaches of the grove, cutting the ululation suddenly short. "This is the great Ash Tree, the center and pivot of Yggdrasil! This is the tree of Nerthus, its roots thrust deep into her flesh. Her blood flows through it, her tears water it. It is she and she is it."

"It is she and she is it," came the murmur of response from all parts of the grove.

"This is the tree of Nerthus, its roots thrust deep into her flesh. It grows tall and strong because of her bounty. It is she and she is it."

"It is she and she is it," moaned the reply.

"This is the tree of Nerthus, its roots thrust deep into her flesh. Every year she clothes it in new green garments, renewing her promise of plenty to her people. It is she and she is it."

"It is she and she is it."

"This is the tree of Nerthus, its roots thrust deep into her flesh. A gift given to the tree is a gift given to Nerthus, a sign of her children's gratefulness. It is she and she is it."

"It is she and she is it." The refrain held a new note of eagerness and insistence.

"O tree, O Nerthus," the white bear cried suddenly, his voice leaping outward into the mist, "your children bring you a gift! Your children come to show you how grateful we are!

We give him to you gladly, with happy hearts and joyous minds! We give him to hang on you for nine days and nine nights, a sacrifice unto you. Take him to you." From beneath his fur robe the white bear produced a short spear with a leaflike flint point. He held it out until the point touched Voden's naked chest. Slowly, lightly, lovingly, he drew the point across the Aesir's skin, leaving behind a thin line of blood in the shape of a Y with two extra upright prongs. "We mark him for you with the spear, inscribe on him the sign of the tree, your sign, O Nerthus. We mark him for all the world to see he is yours. None will comfort him with bread, nor will they bring him the horn to drink from. His only rest will be with you."

Two of the Trul stepped to Voden's sides and slipped cords around his wrists. Two more took the ends of the cords and threw them up over two limbs that thrust out of the main trunk about fifteen feet from the ground. They moved him forward until he stood at the base of the tree, his back to it. Then two bent and grabbed him by the calves, suddenly lifting him as others pulled at the ropes. He rose up almost to the place where the two branches met. Another rope was passed across his chest, under his armpits, and then around behind the tree. A third and final rope circled his legs just below the knees.

When he was finally in place, the white bear turned to the circle of faces that loomed out of the mist and cried out one tremendous word. "NERTHUS!" Then he turned and looked up at Voden for several silent moments. Without another sound he walked off into the swirling mist. One by one the other Trul came, looked up at him, and disappeared as quietly. When they'd all left, Jotun from the groups gathered in the grove came one by one to gaze wordlessly at him. Eventually Hrodvitnir approached and looked for a long time, his expression unreadable. Next a small warrior arrived to stand and stare, a slight smile curving his lips. He nodded two or three times as if liking what he saw. With a wink and a wave, the slight man walked jauntily off to where Hrodvitnir patiently waited for him.

The last of the Jotun left, disappearing like a ghost into the clinging mist. Voden, hanging from the tree of Nerthus, was alone in the grove.

• • •

From the time he'd woken that morning, he'd been in a strange, lethargic stupor. The mist had contributed to his mood, giving him a languorous sense of detachment from everything that had happened.

Now the sun was high and the mist had burned away. The brightness of the light bounced off the surface of everything he could see, giving the world a harsh, firm solidity. Pain had come, tearing at his shoulder, gnawing at his wrists, stabbing repeatedly through his chest and legs. The sweat ran down his body, turning the mark on his chest into a symbol of fire.

With the hours the pain grew until it was nearly intolerable. Silent, almost indifferent, he endured it. Finally it began to fade, becoming a dull, throbbing background against which he existed in a disinterested aloofness. It was there, much as the sun or the tree was, simply part of a world which he vaguely inhabited.

In the late afternoon, when the sun slanted across his face from the right, two figures came and stood below him. Hazily he recognized that they were Hrodvitnir and the short warrior, who apparently was Hrodvitnir's friend. They looked at him in silence, Hrodvitnir's expression empty and detached, the small man's lit by a mocking smile. Eventually, without Voden realizing it, they turned and left.

When the sun left the sky, the white bear appeared beneath the tree. He stood and gazed wordlessly up at Voden for so long that the Aesir forgot he was there. His words, when they came, were a surprise, a sudden slap of sound that pulled Voden back into the world. "The day is hard on the tree, but the night is worse. By day there is only pain, thirst, and the sun to endure. But at night the grove is a different place. It is sacred to Nerthus, the earth, and the dark allows many things to creep forth that cannot stand the bright glare of Gymir's eye. Some of those that come are solid things, things of this world. They can be dangerous, but they are not greatly to be feared.

"No, there are others much more dangerous. They will not attack the body, for they are not of the body. They will seek out the spirit, the mind, the soul. They will suck away will and bravery as if they never existed. They will gnaw on sanity as if it was a tasty morsel. They will drag you screaming into madness and despair even though you never move an inch.

"You will need great strength and courage to endure the day. Against the night you have no hope unless your magic is very strong. I wish you well, Aesir, though there is no way you can believe it. I see in your eye what once glowed in my own. You walk a thin line between madness and glory. I have walked that line, and I wish you well." He looked up for a few more moments, then turned and shambled off, more bear than man.

Voden discovered that by pulling his legs up and bracing his feet against the bark of the tree, he could take some of the pressure from his shoulders and relieve the dull ache. He couldn't hold the position for long, but even a little bit made him feel better.

He heard a noise below and saw a shadowy figure at the base of the tree. The moon wouldn't rise for several hours yet, so it was too dark to make out who or even what it was. He sensed rather than saw a movement near his face and felt something cold and wet gently touch his cheek. He turned his head and could barely make out what appeared to be a rag on the end of a pole. It carried the slightly sour smell of ale. Cautiously he moved his head until his dry, cracked lips came in contact with it, then sucked greedily as he realized it was saturated with beer. He was able to get a good mouthful before it was lowered out of his sight. In a moment the pole was back, but this time there was a piece of bread attached to its tip. Greedily he snatched it off and carefully chewed it, using his lips and tongue to make sure it didn't fall out of his mouth. Then the rag soaked with beer was back and he drank once more. When the pole was withdrawn a third time he tried to pierce the dark to discover the identity of his benefactor. He couldn't make out anything.

The night wore on and the moon rose. It was waxing and cast a cold light between the trees of the grove. With a start, Voden saw a lean shape glide through the patterns of light and shadow that stripped the ground. It was joined by another and then another.

By the light of the moon Voden looked down into three sets of glowing yellow eyes. They were endlessly deep with hunger and longing. Had he not been tied to the tree, he might have fallen right into their depths.

One of the wolves reared up and put his front paws against the tree trunk. With a critical eye it measured the distance between the tip of its snout and the bottom of Voden's leg. Voden did his own estimate. The wolf could reach it with a good jump. How much could it rip off with one quick bite delivered in the air? the Aesir wondered, a chill of premonition running up his spin. How long would it take him to bleed to death if the wolf bit off his whole foot? If it bit off only a couple of toes? He shivered. The white bear had been right. The terrors of the day were passive ones, working slowly on his body and mind. Those of the night were far more active.

The wolf dropped down among its companions and seemed to be conferring. All three began to pace around the tree as if trying to reach a decision. Voden pulled his feet up as far as he could and waited hopelessly.

He heard a snarl of fear from below and looked down to see all three wolves crouching and backing away from the tree. Two new shapes were flitting through the grove, much larger than the first three that cowered beneath his feet.

With a rush of joy he recognized the black and gray forms. Geri and Freki! His wolves! He hadn't seen them for years, but here they were again, their eyes shining at him, their tongues lolling out in greeting. The other wolves fled in terror, and Voden's two settled themselves at the base of the tree. Geri sighed and said, "We heard you call, little brother, and came to help." Freki nodded and smiled. "These puppies won't bother you while we're here, and we'll stay, every night, until you tire of this foolishness and come down from the tree."

"I . . . I can't come down. I'm tied up here . . . I—"

"You can come down whenever you wish," Geri growled. Freki nodded in agreement. "You know the way. Jalk taught you. Father Bear taught you. You know the way."

"I . . . I've forgotten."

Both wolves sighed hugely. "Then you'll have to suffer until you remember. Now sleep while we stand guard."

Voden woke at dawn as light made things visible in the grove once more. The first thing he noticed was that Geri and Freki were gone. In their place stood the nine Trul. He traded fierce glances with each of them in turn, finishing with the white bear.

There was almost a smile in the bear's voice as he spoke. "You have survived your first day on the tree. Nerthus is pleased. She prefers strong warriors. That way she can drain their energy slowly, savoring every tiny bit. You may live for several days, Aesir. Do so. Nerthus is in no hurry."

Voden croaked a laugh at the Trul. "I will hang on this windy tree nine days and nine nights, spear struck, a sacrifice to myself! Nerthus will never claim me!"

The rest of the Trul grumbled in anger, but the white bear only nodded and said softly, "We shall see, we shall see." They were gone the next time Voden looked down.

For some reason the sun seemed hotter today than yesterday. It burrowed into his eyes and struck at his mind, leaving him dazed and tongue-swollen. He hard the flap of wings and felt a rush of air. Turning his head, he made out the backlit form of a vulture sidling toward him on the left branch. He heard another sound and turned to the right. Two more vultures sat on that branch, hungrily watching him. His eye fastened with fascination on their long, sharp, ripping beaks. Many times he'd seen them tear gobbets of flesh from a carcass. They could do the same thing to a living body that was helplessly tied down.

High above he heard a wild call, and looked up. There, circling down from the clouds, were two black dots that rapidly grew and took on the form of huge ravens. Hugin and Munin! "On our way, little brother!" they croaked. They came in a sudden rush, scattering the squawking vultures in feathery confusion. One sitting on either branch, they whispered in his ears, telling him of the many wonders they'd seen. He laughed and asked them questions, amazed and delighted by their chatter.

The slight form that stood below saw only a tree with a laughing, mumbling man tied to it in the hot sun. The Jotun watched for a while, a sad half smile curving its lips, then turned and walked slowly and thoughtfully away.

By the end of the third day interest and excitement was spreading from wagon to wagon in Utgard. The Aesir was still alive! He appeared to be crazy, talking endlessly to beings no one else could see. Yet neither the wolves nor the vultures, which had always torn at the other sacrifices and killed them in a day or so, bothered this one-eyed Aesir youth.

The white bear stood and looked up at Voden, trying to understand what the young man was saying. Perhaps he was visiting the Alterjinga and was sending back a message of great importance. Perhaps. He sighed. More likely the youth was raving, sliding toward madness and death. One more night. Another day at most. It was a pity really. The Galdar-power was there, raw, unfocused, untrained. Had the Aesir been a Jotun, he would have been taken at a young age and trained. He would have become a Trul. With a backward glance the white bear shambled off into the gathering dusk. The grove was no place to be at night. Things much worse than wolves lurked here. He could feel their presence tonight. The sacrifice was drawing them.

Voden awoke with a start and stared down into the hugest eyes he'd ever seen. They glowed and swirled with a thousand shades of darkness. A voice came with them, a voice from some endless depth that echoed with death and decay. "Tremble, human worm, Nidhogg is here."

Strangely, Voden found there was no fear in him. "Nidhogg," he calmly replied, "what wants the Striker that Destroys with me? I'm not dead yet. Go bedevil one of your corpses."

The serpent hissed in anger and twisted his coils around the base of the tree. "I gnaw at corpses and at the root of the tree, at the very foundation of Yggdrasil. I gnaw and I gnaw and I will bring it all crashing down.

"I am the final death, human worm, the death of a world and all that live within it. I dwell in the lowest regions of Niflheim and no thing escapes me."

Voden looked into those swirling eyes and saw despair. "You are death," he said.

Nidhogg hissed. "I am the ultimate reality. All things end in me, no matter how brave or beautiful. No amount of striving will ever lead to escape. Do what you will, sooner or later it all comes down to the same. I will gnaw at your bones. I will bring the world and everything in it crashing down in ruins.

"I alone am triumphant. I alone am eternal. I am the endless chaos of non-being, the formless abyss that extends to the end of time. Life is but a futile flash in my vast darkness. There is no hope, no escape. Not all your efforts can light up more than a tiny corner of the night.

"Yield, worm, come to me. I claim you as my own. I will gnaw on you myself."

Voden shuddered and moaned. "No hope? Then this pain, this agony, this tree is useless?"

Nidhogg hissed a mighty laugh. "None will even know you came and went. Life is like a sparrow flying suddenly through a lit room in the middle of the night. A moment of light and warmth, of joy and happiness. Then back into the eternal dark and cold. Come to me, soft little worm! I will crush you and end this ordeal."

"But my father—" Voden began to protest.

"He dies anyway. Your suffering is for naught. It is pain for no purpose. Borr is old and broken. He cannot be mended. Soon he, too, will be mine. All the songs in the world cannot change that, worm. Come. I will lift your agony from you. Slip down from the tree and be free of pain forever."

Voden hesitated. The pain he felt was worse than ever. His whole body flamed with it, his mind and spirit a pyre that raged. It was too much to bear. Nidhogg was right. It was for nothing. His father was old and would soon die. Why suffer like this? For the Aesir? For Freyja? For his mother? For Tror or Vethur or Vili or Groa or Gagnrad or . . . Voden? For Voden? Why not yield? Why not lay down the burden? Who would know? Who would care? Who would judge him? Who . . . ?

"NO!" he shrieked. "No! You are like the twisted thing I met on the Great Ash Tree! I will not yield to you!

"It doesn't matter if what I do will pass into the darkness. It must be done anyway. The darkness and the light are one, Nidhogg. You're not the ultimate. The ultimate contains you, contains death as well as life. The abyss you speak of contains chaos, true. But it's from that chaos that order and light are born and burst forth again.

"I could look at the Universe as you do and claim it to be brief periods of light that inevitably flicker out into blackness once more. Or I could say it is a universe of light that every now and then suffers flickers of darkness. Which is right? Neither. Both. Something above and including the two.

"Kao-Shir called it the Tao. Named, it is no longer the ultimate, but I know what he meant now. You're not its master, Nidhogg, any more than I am. We both serve.

"Away, servant! I'll have nothing to do with you!"

With a hiss and roar of frustration and fury, Nidhogg disappeared into the earth.

• • •

The eighth day dawned and Utgard was in uproar. The Aesir lived! The Trul met with the leaders of the other clans. Arguments raged throughout the day while Voden raved and sang upon his tree. Nothing like this had ever happened before. What would they do if the man from south of the Iving fulfilled the nine days and nine nights?

In dismay they all turned to gaze at the white bear. The creature was silent, but there were many who swore that the beast's lips were curved into something resembling a smile.

When the sun rose to mark the beginning of the ninth and last day, Utgard was silent and expectant. The white bear went to stand at the foot of the tree and gaze up in wonder at the figure that hung there, more dead than alive, but still clinging to life with a tenacity that awed him. His head bowed in deep thought, he walked slowly through the grove to a small group of expectant faces. They crowded around him, awaiting the news.

He paused before speaking, gazing out across the grasslands toward Gymir's eye as it peeked over the horizon. The world, he thought, is endless and filled with wonder.

Bringing his eyes back to focus on those pressing around him, he spoke two words. "He lives." Strangely, they all smiled, especially the young warrior dressed in wolf garb, and his slender companion.

XXII

THE Eye of Gymir stood straight overhead and glared down with unusual ferocity. For more than two hours now the white bear had been waiting for something to happen, something final, wonderful, awful, miraculous, ordinary. The figure hanging on the tree had become restless, twisting and moaning as if in great pain or as if about to break through the cocoon of its mortality and achieve transcendence. At times it cried out in a voice that sounded like it came from the depths of the deepest hell, a voice both tortured and demanding.

How much longer can this continue? the white bear wondered. This is the ninth day he's hung on the tree. He looked more closely at the wasted figure of the man. The skin had burnt in the strong sunlight, blistered, begun to peel, and burnt again. As a result the man on the tree was covered with hideous, oozing sores. Who could survive such a thing?

His eyes wandered over the man's face. Both eyes were closed now. The features were drawn and pinched with pain, hunger, the approach of death. The lips were loose and slightly open, showing the man's teeth, giving him a snarling look.

The white bear's gaze drifted to the leather bag that hung

around the figure's neck. There was something of great power in that bag. Perhaps that was what had sustained the man for so long. That and the Galdar-power that dwelt within him.

Suddenly the man on the tree began to tremble violently. In surprise, the white bear stepped back, his eyes riveted on the man's face. Without warning both eyes flew open and the man strained mightily against the bonds that held him. For a moment it almost seemed as if he would break free and soar off into the sky. But then he gave a shriek that shattered the sunlight and made the white bear's ears ache with its force. As though his soul was leaving his body with the cry, the man collapsed and hung loosely, lifelessly on the tree.

For a long time the white bear stood and watched the limp form that hung above him, a sacrifice to Nerthus. Eventually he sighed. Thus it ends, he thought. Without any shaking of the earth or opening of the heavens. The goddess has her offering. Why do I wish there'd been more? Why do I wish Nerthus had been cheated?

With a final glance at the still, lifeless form, he turned and walked wearily away. We'll let you hang on the tree until tomorrow, he decided. You'll fulfill your promise.

Voden stood at the base of a mighty tree and gazed upward. Its branches spread out to cover all the worlds, and reached even up over heaven. Its roots, three in number, thrust down to the very center of existence. One grew from Asaheim, and under it was Urd's Spring, guarded by the three Nornir who runecarved the fate of each man as he was born. Every day the Nornir drew water from their spring, took clay from its banks, and mixing the two together, sprinkled the tree so that its branches and leaves would neither wither nor decay. The water was so sacred that it turned everything it touched as white as an eggshell.

The second root sank into Jotunheim, right to Mimir's Well. The tree was the source of all the wisdom the well provided and the destination of all the sacrifices made to it.

Voden turned to follow the third root but shrank back in horror as he realized it plunged into Niflheim. The Spring of Hvergelmir boiled up from under it, giving birth to eleven steaming rivers that raged into darkness. Half closing his eye in fright, he could make out the writhing mass of dragons and serpents that swarmed around that root, gnawing at it. He knew their names, had heard them from the twisted creature years ago. There were more of them than foolish men realized. The greatest was Nidhogg, but there were others too numerous to name—Goin and Moin, Grafvitnir's sons, Grabak and Grafvollud, Ofnir and Svafnir... He shuddered, wondering if they would destroy the tree. Then, despairing of an answer, he turned his eyes upward once more.

For the first time he noticed the four harts that scrambled around the branches of the tree, ripping and tearing greedily at the leaves and tender young shoots. He couldn't suppress a small cry of dismay. The tree endured more pain than anyone could perceive! The harts devoured it from above, the sides of it decayed, and Nidhogg and his crew gnawed at it from below!

For the first time he gazed about himself. The worlds lay spread out before him. He could count nine of them—three above, three in the middle, three below. Those above were Asaheim, Vanaheim, and Alfheim. Those in the middle were Jotunheim, Nidavellir, and Svartalfheim. Those below, lost to sight in darkness and mist, were Muspellheim, Niflheim, and Nasheim. For a long time he contemplated them, rapt in wonder at their sight.

Eventually he turned his gaze upward again. On a branch not too far above him, he saw a squirrel. The creature was staring down at him with bright, intelligent eyes. He nodded to it and the squirrel nodded back. It came closer, then paused and regarded him solemnly for several moments.

"I am Ratatosk," it said finally. "I know many things, for I run back and forth, up and down the tree, carrying the insults of Nidhogg to Raesvelg and those in reply from the mighty eagle to the Striker that Destroys." The squirrel looked back over its shoulder, then leaned closer to Voden and whispered. "See those four harts? I know their names. Dain, Dvalin, Duneyr, and Durathror." The creature crept even closer, and its whisper sank even lower. "I know something else. The mighty eagle is expecting you. You must climb the tree to meet him. I was sent to guide you. There will be many wonders on the way. Ignore them. You have only one purpose, and that is to see Raesvelg. Follow." With that, the squirrel turned and began to scamper upward from branch to branch.

Moving as swiftly as possible to keep pace with the squirrel, Voden climbed the tree. Up and up he went, higher and higher, always keeping his eye focused on the next branch, ignoring everything around him, It wasn't easy, for this was Yggdrasil, the World Tree, and the entire universe was here in all its wonder. Voden would have loved to linger and see it all. But he realized that Ratatosk was right. He didn't have much time. There was a darkness approaching all too swiftly. He had to hurry.

Suddenly he came into the light at the top of the tree. There, perched on the very topmost branch, was Raesvelg, the mighty eagle. "This is the second time we meet, little one," the eagle spoke, the power of his voice beating Voden to his knees. "The last time I gave you your Power Song. Now I will cause the power that lies asleep within you to awaken and blaze forth."

"You speak of the Galdar-power, mighty one?" Voden asked.

The eagle nodded. "You must learn the secret lore, prosper and wax in wisdom. One word will win you many words, one deed will gain you many deeds. It is time to find the runes and learn to read them rightly, to gain the strong magic, the mighty spells that the great gods made. You must do for the Aesir what Dain has done for the Alfar, Dvalin for the Dverg, and Asvithnir for the Jotun.

"Now you must open both your eyes and look deep within as well as without. Only you can know what lives near your heart, see clearly into yourself. This you must see, must know before you can free the power and grasp the runes. Look now, Voden. Look, see, despair, and triumph!"

There was no choice. The darkness was coming closer every moment. Voden knew he had to act or be swallowed by it, finally and forever. He opened both eyes and shrieked in agony.

Down, down he plunged into an endless abyss, the dark center of his self. Horror on horror welled up and swept over him as he drove ever deeper. Fear and dread numbed his limbs and a weary lethargy stole over his body. How much better to simply let go and float here in the darkness, the eternal, undying black void.

But he struggled on and on. Then suddenly, just as he felt his strength fail, just as the emptiness that gnawed at his mind the way Nidhogg gnawed at the root of Yggdrasil prepared to take its final bites, he broke through to a new realm of light.

In its midst he sensed a vast presence, a total blending of opposites, a unity that transcended everything partial. He sped toward it, picking up speed as he went.

A vague stirring caught his attention. He turned toward it. It smiled at him. "I am Bolthorn. Nine mighty songs will I teach you. Twice nine spells and the runes that control them will you learn. Grasp now the runes. Reach down into the center of yourself and grasp them."

With a second cry, silent yet mightier even than the first, Voden stretched out and grasped the runes. The very symbols that were carved on the bits of bones in the bag around his neck suddenly blazed in hot fire across his view, burning themselves into his mind with a searing agony of unearthly pleasure.

Bolthorn came and whispered in his ear. "This is Feoh, the wealth that is a comfort to one and all, the wealth that goes beyond mere gold and silver, the wealth that runs deep in the soul of men. Feoh is the rune that controls the spell that can comfort grief, lessen pain, cure sickness. No wife of king, no man alive knows it.

"This rune is Ur, the fierce horn-fighter that stands in all the worlds at the same time. It is powerful, and any man who would be a healer must know and master it.

"This third symbol is Thurs. It is an evil thing to grasp, for it is most sharp. Properly cut and cast, it will fetter any foe, blunt the edge of his sword and soften the blow of his staff. No wound can come to him who knows how to use it.

"Here is a fourth, Os, the source of wisdom and of foolishness, both of men and of gods. So powerful is it that if any man bind you hand and foot, simply speak it and all knots will dissolve, all locks spring open, and you will walk free.

"The fifth rune is Rad, demanding action rather than words. It will stop a speeding, well-aimed arrow or spear in flight with but a glance from your eye.

"This rune, Cen, is sixth. It burns bright after strife is done, and lights the way to better things. It is important to know, for if someone would harm you by risting runes on the roots of a tree, the one who wished you ill will come to woe should you but utter it.

"Seventh is Gyfu, giving profound meaning to the acts of every man's life. No sacrifice is too great if given in its spirit.

It is the rune to use if the flames should raise high around a hall. Say its name and the fire will die no matter how far it has already spread."

Bolthorn's voice went on and on, teaching Voden the eighteen spells, naming each of the runes and telling its powers. That completed, nine mighty songs followed, burned into Voden's memory by the gentle power of the voice within the realm of light.

Suddenly it was over. The young Aesir felt himself falling once more. No, not falling, he realized, flying. He would never fall again. Now he knew how to fly!

He soared back to the tree and circled Raesvelg, who called out a mighty greeting. Then he swooped down the tree to its base.

When he opened his eye, all he could see was blackness. He looked up and saw a few stars weakly shining through a high overcast. The moon had risen and set. It was near morning of the tenth day of his ordeal on the tree. He'd fulfilled his time!

The ropes that bound him parted at a word, and he dropped gently to the ground. His knees almost buckled, and he realized what terrible condition his body was in. Concentrating hard, he uttered several spells, healing himself quickly and efficiently. His sores closed and new skin covered the raw places. He laughed delightedly at how easy it was. At the same time he felt the hunger and knew that he needed food and drink or he would perish despite his magic. He reached out with his Galdar-power, found some bread, meat, and ale, and brought them to him. Like a ravenous beast he devoured them.

His senses told him someone of power was approaching. He could discern the aura of the man long before he could see or hear him. He knew it was the white bear, the head Shaman of the Trul. He sensed others of lesser power accompanying the white bear, and stood upright against the tree of Nerthus to await them.

The white bear knew something strange had happened long before he reached the point where he could see the tree. There was a power, a force that hadn't been there earlier. He'd left a dead or dying Aesir on the tree the previous day. What was now awaiting them?

What the Trul saw caused all of them to stop and stare. The

young Aesir stood at the base of the tree, his arms crossed, a slight smile on his lips.

Only the white bear seemed unsurprised. Holding his hands up in the sign of peace, they walked to within a few feet of the Aesir and gazed at him with delight and wonder. "You have survived the nine days and nights on the tree," he said.

Voden nodded. "And I've broken through to my Galdar-power."

The bear smiled. "Yes. Even as Asvithnir, the first of the Trul, did at the beginning of our clan. You are the first of the Aesir to do so.

"You have cheated Nerthus, Aesir, but somehow I don't think she will mind. Power such as yours is not born into the world every day, and for it to happen on her tree is as great a gift as any sacrifice could ever be.

"You must have a new name now to add to your others. Vafudar you are, and Bileyg too. Thridi as well, since you are the third to be owned by the Bones of Audna. I recognize them now, the power that shines from them as they hang in their pouch around your neck is clear and in tune with your own.

"Your new name shall be Jafanhar, for now you are as high as Dain and Dvalin and Asvithnir."

Voden started and hissed in his breath. "It's as Raesvelg said in my Power Song!" He closed his eye and began to chant softly, so that only the white bear could hear.

> "In days gone by I once was Ygg
> Ere Voden they did name me.
>
> And I was Har and Jafanhar
> And also hailed to Thridi.
>
> Bileyg I'll be and Fafudar
> Till falls the mighty Ash Tree.
>
> Then I'll be Ygg as once I was
> Ere Voden they did name me."

The white bear and the young Aesir exchanged long, considering glances. "There's much in this, Jafanhar, much that bears heavy thought," the Trul said quietly. "I know that you will take your father and go now. But I hope you will come back so that we may talk. Things are afoot in Yggdrasil, mighty things, dread things. I sense you are somehow at or near the center of them. Take your father back to your people. But return to Utgard, for you are one of the Trul, even if not one of the Jotun."

Voden bowed his head to the white bear in a show of respect. Then he stood upright and strode off through the grove, toward the wagon where his father and Heimdall waited.

The homecoming in Asgard was joyous and anxious. The Aesir had never expected to see either their chieftain or his son again. Now both had returned. But Borr was virtually on his deathbed, and Voden seemed so strangely changed that he frightened those who knew him best.

Voden sat with his father in their hall. The old man had been placed in the sleeping cupboard where he and his wife Vestla had lain every night of their many years together. There Vestla had breathed her last, and in the same place Borr had once locked himself away, determined to die rather than survive his beloved wife. Now he and Voden worked together on a poem to commemorate the recent double victory of the Aesir over both the Vanir and the Jotun. The work went slowly, for Borr was very weak.

Heimdall came and knocked at the door of the cupboard. He slid the door open and called. "Time for Borr to take his medicine. You will have to wait outside while I examine him, Voden." The young Aesir nodded and left.

The white man was a long time in coming out. When he emerged, Voden stood waiting, a question in his eyes. Heimdall saw it and shrugged. "Your magic and my medicine can only do so much. Borr is old and worn out. He was sorely wounded. Death is very close. I am sorry, my friend, but I see no hope."

Before Voden could reply, there was a thumping from the cupboard. The two of them hurried to the door and slid it open. Borr looked up at them, his face drawn tight with pain. "Take me to the Warrior's Hall. Call the council. It is time." The two men outside the cupboard exchanged glances. Heimdall nodded sadly and Voden dropped his gaze to the floor. "Yes, father," he said softly.

• • •

It was painful for Gagnrad Beargrasp to see the shrunken, twisted figure that slouched on the High Seat. From the looks on the faces of the other warriors that filled the hall, he knew they felt the same. The hall was unnaturally still. All realized that they were witnessing the last council with Borr.

Voden stood next to the High Seat on the right, Heimdall on the left, both ready to render whatever aid was necessary to Borr. Voden held a horn of mead which he lifted to Borr's lips from time to time.

When everyone had assembled, Borr sat up as straight as his weakness and pain allowed. When he spoke, his voice was surprisingly strong. "Aesir," he began, "I'll be leaving you soon to sit with my father and wife in the hall of the gods." He stopped to catch his breath as murmurs of protest filled the hall. "Enough," he continued, cutting them short. "The times are poor for leavetaking. We now have two enemies. The Vanir have turned on us. The Jotun but wait to strike again. I fear to leave my people at such a time."

He stopped again and took a drink from the horn. "The Nornir don't concern themselves with such things, though. My fate is written. I but fulfill it.

"I fear to leave you. Yet my fear is not as great as it once was. For my son has returned. He is a mighty warrior. It is my last wish that he lead you." A murmur of surprise filled the hall. It was most unusual for a chieftain to name his own successor.

Yet the choice made sense. Voden had lived among the Vanir and probably knew them better than any other Aesir except Honir, who was hardly a strong warrior. Voden had also fought against the Jotun, and had even hung on the tree of Nerthus for nine days and nights, cheating the goddess of her sacrifices. The Jotun might well think twice before attacking such a mighty leader!

The men in the hall looked at one another, anxious to discuss the matter in their usual open and rough manner, not knowing how to proceed with a dying leader sitting in the High Seat. Before anyone could speak, though, Voden stepped forward and signaled for silence.

"My father does me great honor. But it's one I do not seek. I'm too young to be leader of the Aesir. Nor am I tried in battle. I've fought many times, but mostly alone, against things rather than men. I don't have any experience in leading warriors.

"But worse than that. I'm not a true Aesir. The blood of Prin runs as strongly in my veins as does that of Asaheim. I've spent many years among the Vanir, learned their ways and even their language. When I should have been here by my father's side, I was wandering far to the west. I have the Galdar-power, I—"

Tror stood and raised his hammer on high. "I'm no Aesir either. No Aesir blood flows in my veins. I was raised among a very different people, far to the west and north of where you wandered. Yet I fight with the Aesir. I'm one with them. None can deny it!"

"No! No!" they cried in unison. "You're ours! You're the shield of the Aesir! You're Tror!"

The red-haired giant turned and stared at Voden. "How much less of the Aesir are you, then, Voden? Your blood matters not. It's only the spirit that counts. The spirit and the will." He made a sweeping gesture, including the hall and everything in Asgard. "This is your home, wherever you may have roamed. Your grandfather is buried here, as is your mother. Borr's body will enter the mound when he's ready. Tyr here was your friend from the time you first walked. As was Honir. And others. How can you say you're not Aesir?"

"I . . . I can't lead you. My destiny lies elsewhere."

Gagnrad rose slowly, his wounds still bothering him. "Your destiny will find you wherever you are. What is rune-carved by the Nornir will be, whether you will or no. Borr is right. We need you to lead us."

Others rose to speak, adding their agreement to that already expressed by Tror and Gagnrad. Voden watched with utter astonishment as warrior after warrior spoke out to confirm Borr's opinion. When all who wished had said their mind, a silence reigned and all eyes fell on the dying man in the High Seat.

"So," Borr managed to gasp out, "it's settled." He barked a harsh laugh. He looked up at Voden's stunned face. "We've a poem to end, you and I. Try these for the last stanzas:

> "Now Borr lays down
> an ax that's dull.
>
> all dented with war's clamor.

> He seeks the peace
> of funeral pyre
>
> and place on God's Hall benches. . . ."

His voice failed and he motioned Voden to him. The young man bent over his father and saw the pain-filled face break into a smile. "We could have been so much more to each other, my son," he whispered in a husky, failing voice. "I've always loved you so, but never known how to say or show it. Forgive me."

With a sigh that filled the room, Borr died.

Voden stood silently for several moments, his head bowed. When he turned to face the hall, every man could see the tears that ran down his face. They heard him murmur "Forgive me, Father. I never knew."

Then Voden straightened up and his eye came back into focus. He gazed at them for a few moments, then his voice rang out, repeating the verses he and his father had composed so long ago at Vestla's death.

> "No purse can pay
> the price of grief
>
> the dismal due of death loss.
>
> But I must face
> my final days
>
> with full man's heart, nor mourning."

GLOSSARY OF NAMES AND PLACES

Aalu—paradise in the religion of the Svartalfar. It lies far to the west, beyond the Manu Mountains. The final approach to it is guarded by the serpent Ankh-Neteru. When a Svartalfar dies, his Ba tries to reach Aalu. First, though, it must go through Tuat, the nether world, and be judged by forty-two judges led by Am-mit.—

Abubu—demon of the rainstorm. Ally of Surt.

Adad—Patesi of Maqam Nifl and Borsippa.

Aesir—a race of farmer-herders living south of the River Iving and north of the forests of Vanaheim.

Alfar—an ancient race, now few in number, who dwell in the forests of Alfheim.

Alfheim—the land of the Alfar. It lies north of Asaheim in the forests south of the Bones of Ymir.

Alterjinga—spirit world of the Trul.

Amsvartnir Sea—a freshwater inland sea to the northwest of Asaheim.

An—the eldest Son of Muspell. He is the Patesi of Uruk and Der. Innina, a sorceress, is his consort.

Anhur—Svartalfar warrior. Friend of Voden and Kao-Shir.

Anunnaki—ruling council of the seven Sons of Muspell

Anqet—sister of Osiris, ancient king of the Svartalfar, and of Sutekh. Mother of Horus.

Apsu—the Dreadful Abyss. The end of everything. Utter, unformed chaos. Tiamat and her brood of serpent-dragons dwell on the edge of it, just within the Kur.

Aralu—the land of the dead in the religion of Muspellheim. It has seven gates, tended by the gatekeeper, Neti, and seven walls. It lies across the River Hubur. It is ruled by Nergal and Ereshkigal. Aralu is located in the Kur.

Asaheim—the land of the Aesir. It is composed of three plains: the Himinborg, the Idavoll, and the Aesir; plus the Valaskialf Plateau. It is bounded on the north by the River Iving and on the south by the forests of Vanaheim.

Asgard—the principal city of the Aesir and home of Voden, Borr, and Buri.

Audhumla—the Nourisher, chief deity of the Vanir, created the world and everything in it.

Auf, Field of—open area of the city of Ro-Setau where corpses are laid out to rot so that the Ba may be freed.

Ba—Svartalfar concept similar to soul. It leaves the body after it has rotted and seeks the paradise of Aalu.

Bab-Apsi—magical opening to the part of the spiritual world inhabited by the demons.

Badtabira—the major city of the First Dark Empire. It was destroyed by demons at the fall of the Empire.

Baru—the book of foretelling, owned by Utu.

Bel—an honorific title similar to "Lord," used in Muspellheim.

Bergettins—one of the five clans the Jotun are divided into.

Beyla—Vettir, or god, of bees; giver of mead.

Bifrosti's Ford—the only good crossing over the River Iving. To the north of Asgard and just east of the Himinborg.

Bones of Ymir—a range of rugged hills to the south of the River Iving.

Borr Skullcracker—chieftain of the Aesir after Buri. Father of Voden, Vethur, and Vili. Husband of Vestla Ravenhair.

Borsippa—city in Muspellheim. To the south of Maqam Nifl. Ruled by Adad.

Buri Axehand—chieftain of the Aesir. Father of Borr Skullcracker. Grandfather of Voden.

Byggvir—forester. One of Yngvi's chief lieutenants.

Der—city in Muspellheim, ruled by the eldest Son, An. It is situated athwart the only opening in the Great Wall, directly on the Great Route to the east.

Disir—a group of eight women who rule Vanaheim with the Vanadis. They are Eir, Gna, Hlin, Lofyn, Syn, Syofyn, Syr, and Vor.

Distingen—ruling council of the Vanir. It is composed of nine members: the Vanadis and the eight Disir.

Duku, Hall of—hall where the Anunnaki meets.

Dur-An-Ki—magical opening to the part of the spiritual world inhabited by the gods.

Dverg—a race of short men who dwell in the mountains and forests of Nidavellir. They are known for their great skill in metalsmithing.

Eengurra—Enki's castle, built on a rock in the sea near the city of Eridu.

Eir—one of the Disir. A healer, deeply versed in Seidar-magic and herb lore.

Ellilutu—title given to the Overlord of Muspellheim, the leader of the Anunnaki. Enlil currently holds this title.

Enki—Patesi of Eridu and Kish.

Enlil—the Ellilutu of Muspellheim. Patesi of Nippur, Lagash, and Ashur. Head of the Anunnaki. Holder of the *Tupsimati*, the Tablets of Destiny.

Enmeenlu—one of the Sons of Muspell from the First Dark Empire. He was Patesi of Badtabira.

Ennead—ruling council of the Svartalfar. Composed of wizards.

Ereshkigal—consort of Nergal and queen of Aralu, the land of the dead.

Fiorgynn—former queen, or Vanadis, of the Vanir. Mother of Niord, Frey, and Freyja.

Folkvang—the principal city of the Vanir. Located where the River Hrid and the River Slid join to form the Gunnthro. Home of Fiorgynn and Freyja.

Fornjot—the Destroyer, chief god of the Aesir.

Freki—one of Voden's Hamingjur, a gray wolf.

Freyja—daughter of Fiorgynn. She becomes Vanadis after her mother's death.

Fylgjur—tutelary spirit of those who practice the Galdar-power.

Gagnrad Beargrasp—Aesir chieftain, friend of Borr Skull-cracker.

Galdar-power—type of magical power granted by Vilmeid. Usually practiced by men.

Ganzir—the first gate of Aralu. Guarded by Neti.

Geirahod—the Valkyrja who was in charge of training in the Thiodnuma. Taught both Freyja and Voden.

Geri—one of Voden's Hamingjur, a black wolf.

Gjallarhorn—Heimdall's horn, which he blows to signal the fall of a world.

Gna—one of the Disir.

Groa—witchwoman of the Aesir. She has one eye, claiming to have given the other to Mimir as the price for drinking from her well.

Gymir—the sky god of the Jotun. The sun is his eye. Sacrifices to him are burned on a pyre. Father of Ymir.

Hamingjur—helping guardian spirits. Animal familiars of those who practice the Galdar-power.

Harbard—forester. One of Yngvi's chief lieutenants.

Heimdall—ancient being. The son of nine sisters. Comes from the west and is doomed to see nine worlds fall. Friend of Voden's.

Hepr—river in the far south of the continent of Muspellheim. It is the homeland of the Svartalfar. Since the fall of the First Dark Empire, it has been unreachable from the north.

Hild—Valkryja warrior in charge of the war against Yngvi.

Himinborg—an area of huge, tumbled boulders to the south and east of the confluence of the River Iving and the River Sid. Also the name of the plain in that general area.

Hlin—one of the Disir.

Honir—Aesir, boyhood friend of Voden.

Horus—son of Anqet and Osiris. King of the Svartalfar after defeating his uncle, Sutekh. Defeated by the Sons of Muspell and carried off by the dragon Musirkeshda.

Hrodvitnir—nephew of Bergelmir. A promising young Jotun warrior.

Hugin—one of Voden's Hamingjur, a raven.

Humbaba—giant demon with a beard of human entrails. Ally of Surt.

Igigi—the original gods of Muspellheim. There are three hundred of them.

Imdugud—storm demon. Ally of Surt.

Imhulla—wind demon. Ally of Surt.

Innina—consort of the Patesi An. A powerful sorceress.

Ishkur—fire demon. Ally of Adad.

Ishum—fire demon. Ally of Surt.

Jalk—practitioner of the Galdar-power. Befriends Voden and helps teach him.

Jormungand—huge warrior who is Surt's ally. Also known as the Serpent because he tends to hiss when he speaks.

Jotun—a race of seminomadic herdsmen who inhabit the grasslands north of the River Iving.

Jotunheim—the land of the Jotun. It is a vast grassland that stretches north from the River Iving all the way to the Ice-realm. On the west it is bounded by the Amsvartinir Sea and the Western Forest, on the east by the Great Eastern Waste.

Ka—permanent spiritual essence that stays with a Svartalfar's bones so that the Ba can find its way back again.

Kao-Shir—man from the Sunrise Empire. Studied with the warrior monks of Kara Khitai. Helped train Vestla, Voden's mother. Friend of Voden. His original name was Li Erh.

Kara Khitai—a country that lies on the eastern side of the Great Eastern Waste, on the western slopes of the Kunlun Mountains. It is known for its fierce warrior-monks.

Khamuas—ruler of the Svartalfar. Son of the evil Sutekh.

Kheri Heb—title of the Priest-king of the Svartalfar.

Kunlun Mountains—range of mountains that lie to the east of the Great Eastern Waste. They run north and south to form the western boundary of the Sunrise Empire. Prin lies high on their eastern slopes. Kara Khitai lies on their western slopes.

Kur—the nether world according to the religion of Muspell-heim. It is the dwelling place of demons and of Tiamat and her serpent brood. It borders on Apsu, the Dreadful Abyss. Aralu is located in the Kur.

Lahamu—dragon, one of Tiamat's eleven. Ally of Surt.

Lamashtu—a she-demon who drinks men's blood and eats their flesh. An ally of Surt.

Lofyn—one of the Disir.

Mandragora—mandrake root, a powerful herb often used as an aphrodisiac..

Maqam Nifl—city of Muspellheim. At the southern end of the Niflsea. Home of Surt. Ruled by Adad.

Marduk—Patesi of Muspell. Originally the general of Enlil's armies.

Mashu Mountains—a range of mountains that stretches across northern Muspellheim from east to west. Just south of the Northern Waste.

Mimir—triple being: maid in the morning, woman in the afternoon, crone in the evening. Guards a well that gives wisdom.

Mimir's Well—magical well that gives wisdom to those who are allowed to drink from it. One of Yggdrasil's roots springs from it.

Mjollnir—hammer made by the master smith Volund.

Munin—one of Voden's hamingjur, a raven.

Mushrussu—a serpent-dragon. One of Tiamat's brood. Ally of Adad and a special enemy of Jormungand.

Musirkeshda—a serpent-dragon. One of Tiamat's brood, allied with Enmeenlu and guardian of the *Utukki Limnuti*.

Muspell—one of the chief cities of Muspellheim. Ruled by Marduk.

Muspellheim—the land where the Sons of Muspell dwell. It is to the south of the Sea of Mists and the Twisted Lands. It was the site of the First Dark Empire.

Namtaru—a demon servant of Nergal. Messenger to the land of the dead, Aralu. He carries the names of those about to die to Ereshkigal, the queen of Aralu.

Nannar—Patesi of Ur.

Nergal—King of Aralu, Lord of the Dead. Also Lord of Hosts, the god of war.

Nerthus—Earth goddess of the Jotun. She "inhabits" a wagon drawn by bulls with golden horns, and goes everywhere with the Jotun. The wagon is kept in a sacred grove. Sacrifices are hung on her sacred tree, an ash. Mother of Ymir.

Nidavellir—the land of the Dverg. It lies in the forests and mountain slopes to the west of the River Gopul, south of the River Sid.

Nidhogg—Striker that Destroys. Worm/serpent/dragon that gnaws at one of the roots of Yggdrasil. It is the symbol of death.

Niflheim—abode of darkness. The nether world in the religion of the Aesir. Nasheim, the realm of the dead, is located in it.

Niflsea—a misty sea about one hundred miles long and thirty-five miles wide. It lies in eastern Muspellheim, just south of the Mashu Mountains.

Ningishzida—serpent demon that guards doors. Ally of Surt.

Ninurta—storm demon of the south wind. Ally of Adad.

Nornir—the three who determine the fate of every Aesir at birth. They are Urd, Verdandi, and Skuld.

Northern Waste—a vast desert that covers the entire northern part of Muspellheim. A fertile plain during the First Dark Empire, it was destroyed by demons during the fall of the Empire. In the far west it is known as the Great Sandy Desert. In the far east it is called the Bitter Quarter.

Od—Vanir boy wrestler, opponent of Voden, who becomes Freyja's first king when she is chosen Vanadis. He is bewitched by Vor and sent endlessly wandering.

Osiris—ancient king of the Svartalfar. Brother of Anqet and Sutekh. Father of Horus.

Pa Kua—set of eight symbols, composed of solid and broken lines. Used by the wizards of the Sunrise Empire to tell the future and to harness the forces of the Universe. Believed to mirror every aspect of the Universe.

Patesi—Priest-king. The title of the seven Sons of Muspell: Adad, An, Enki, Enlil, Marduk, Nannar, Utu.

Pazuzu—storm demon. Ally of Adad.

Prin—a small country that lies high among the valleys on the eastern slopes of the Kunlun Mountains. Famous as the home of the Floating World where courtesans are trained.

Raesvelg—Voden's Fylgjur, a giant eagle.

Ratatosk—squirrel on Yggdrasil that runs messages between Raesvelg on the top and Nidhogg at the bottom.

Resheph—storm demon. Ally of Adad.

Rimmon—storm demon. Ally of Adad.

Rimthursar—one of five clans the Jotun are divided into.

Risar—one of the five clans the Jotun are divided into.

Rivers—the major rivers of Yggdrasil are the Iving, Sid, Gopul, Hrid, Gunnthro, Fimbulthul, Slid, Svol, Thyn, Vegsvin, Non, Geirvimul, Leipt, Vid, Gomul, and Gjoll.

Ro-Setau—city of the Svartalfar, built on the mound Tatenen. It lies on the western slope of the arm of the Smoking Lands that thrusts northward toward the Amsvartnir Sea.

Rota—young Valkyrja warrior. Becomes head of Freyja's personal guard. Friend of Yngvi.

San Miao—first men. Destroyed by the god Chu Jung when the first world fell.

Seidar-magic—type of magical power granted by Svarthofdi. Usually practiced by women.

Shaman—magician/healer of the Jotun. Members of the Trul clan.

Sibbi—seven-bodied demon. Ally of Surt.

Silsilah—the place where the River Hepr rises from the lakes of Uadj-ura and Maat.

Skuld—one of the Nornir. A maid. Identified with the waning moon. Shows the future.

Smoking Lands—range of volcanic mountains to the south of Vanaheim.

Sunrise Empire—a vast empire that lies to the east of the Kunlun Mountains. It stretches all the way to the Sunrise Sea.

Surt—companian of Borr during his raids in the Twisted Lands. After being abandoned on the Vigrid by Borr, he returns to Maqam Nifl and becomes a wizard. Master of Jormungand. Servant of Nergal.

Sutekh—brother of Osiris and Anqet. He overthrows and murders Osiris to become the Kheri Heb of the Svartalfar. Overthrown in turn by Horus.

Svartalfar—a race related to the Alfar, but of mixed blood because of their long servitude to the Sons of Muspell during the First Dark Empire. They dwell to the west of the Dverg, north of the Western Desert, and south of the Amsvartnir Sea.

Svarthofdi—the goddess who gives the Seidar-magic. Common to all races of Yggdrasil.

Syn—one of the Disir.

Syofyn—one of the Disir.

Syr—one of the Disir.

Tatenen—the mount Ro-Setau is built on. Supposedly the first solid land to form from the primeval sea.

Teshub—storm demon. Ally of Adad.

Thiodnuma—the "sweeping people away." A fighting technique of the Valkyrja, akin to jujitsu.

Thursar—one of the five clans the Jotun are divided into.

Tiamat—leader and most powerful of the serpent-dragons that dwell at the edge of the Kur next to Apsu, the Dreadful Abyss. Tiamat is the personification of primeval chaos.

Tiamat's Eleven—the brood of serpent-dragons that dwell in the Kur at the edge of Assu, the Dreadful Abyss. Tiamat is their mother and leader. Mushrussu, Musirkeshda, and Lahamu are three of the others.

Ti-yu—netherworld inhabited by demons in the religion of the Sunrise Empire.

Tror—Son of Volund, the master smith. Boyhood friend and companion of Voden.

Trul—one of the five clans the Jotun are divided into. It consists of magician/healers who are versed in the Galdar-power.

Tuat—the nether world in the religion of the Svartalfar. Inhabited by many serpent-demons.

Tupsimati—the Tablets of Destiny. The most powerful book of magic in Muspellheim. It dates from long before the First Dark Empire. It contains the original names of all being and gives one the power to call up any demon or god. Owned by Enlil.

Tyr—Aesir, boyhood friend of Voden.

Uamemtiu—a group of four and seven serpent-demons that dwell in Tuat.

Upuatu—Opener of the Ways. According to Svartalfar legend, a being whose appearance will lead all the Svartalfar, living and dead, to join together to form a mighty nation once again.

Uruk—city of Muspellheim near the Niflsea. Ruled by An. Home of his consort, the sorceress Innina.

Utgard—the chief city of the Jotun. It lies on the eastern shore of the Amsvartnir Sea, north of the River Sid. It is composed of wagons.

Utu—Patesi of Sippar and Larsa. Worshipper of the Igigi, the original gods of Muspellheim.

Utukki Limnuti—potent book of magic from the First Dark Empire. Originally owned by Enmeenlu. Contains the original names of seven sevens of demons, copies directly from the *Tupsimati*. Thought to have disappeared during the destruction of Badtabira at the fall of the First Dark Empire. Retrieved by Surt from the ruins of Badtabira.

Valkyrja—female warriors of the Vanir. A special group of them form the personal guard of the Vanadis.

Vanadis—title equivalent to queen of the Vanir.

Vanaheim—the land of the Vanir. It consists of a vast tract of forest stretching from the River Gopul in the west to the Valaskialf Plateau in the east; from the plains of Asaheim in the north, to the Smoking Lands in the south.

Vanir—race of forest dwellers who live in the forest south of the Aesir and north of the Smoking Lands.

Vestla Ravenhair—wife of Borr, mother of Voden, Vethur, and Vili. A trained courtesan from the Floating World of Prin. Captured by Borr in a raid on a caravan.

Vethur—Voden's younger brother.

Vettir—gods of the Vanir. They are omnipresent in all things. The Vanir see themselves as siblings of the Vettir.

Vigrid Plain—a salt desert in the Twisted Lands.

Vili—Voden's younger sister.

Vilmeid—the god who gives the Galdar-power. Common to all races of Yggdrasil.

Voden—son of Borr Skullcracker and Vestla Ravenhair.

Volund—a master smith from a people who live far to the north and west of Asaheim. His son is Tror. His daughter is Thrud.

Vor—the oldest of the Disir. Known for her wisdom. Deeply versed in the Seidar-magic.

Yggdrasil—the world. It consists of the Icerealm in the north and Jotunheim, Alfheim, Nidavellir, Svartalfheim, Asaheim, Vanaheim, and Muspellheim, in the south. To the east are Kara Khitai, Prin, and the Sunrise Empire. To the west is the Western Forest, which eventually ends at the Sunset Sea. The image of Yggdrasil is a great ash tree.

Ymir—the first Jotun, conceived by Nerthus and Gymir in a violent storm. One of his legs fathered children on the other, to create the whole race of the Jotun, the Sons of Ymir.

Yngvi—young forester from Vanaheim who befriends Voden. He becomes leader of the foresters upon the death of Jalk.

Yu-Lan Hui—a period of fifteen days, during which the gates of Ti-yu are open and demons come pouring out.

Zu—storm demon with the body of a bird and the head of a lion. Ally of Surt.

interzone

SCIENCE FICTION AND FANTASY

Quarterly   £1.50

- *Interzone* is the only British magazine specializing in SF and new fantastic writing. We have published:

BRIAN ALDISS	M. JOHN HARRISON
J.G. BALLARD	GARRY KILWORTH
BARRINGTON BAYLEY	MICHAEL MOORCOCK
MICHAEL BISHOP	KEITH ROBERTS
ANGELA CARTER	GEOFF RYMAN
RICHARD COWPER	JOSEPHINE SAXTON
JOHN CROWLEY	JOHN SLADEK
PHILIP K. DICK	BRUCE STERLING
THOMAS M. DISCH	IAN WATSON
MARY GENTLE	CHERRY WILDER
WILLIAM GIBSON	GENE WOLFE

- *Interzone* has also published many excellent new writers; graphics by **JIM BURNS, ROGER DEAN, IAN MILLER** and others; book reviews, news, etc.

- *Interzone* is available from specialist SF shops, or by subscription. For four issues, send £6 (outside UK, £7) to: **124 Osborne Road, Brighton BN1 6LU, UK.** Single copies: £1.75 inc p&p.

- American subscribers may send $10 ($13 if you want delivery by air mail) to our British address, above. All cheques should be made payable to *Interzone*.

- "No other magazine in Britain is publishing science fiction at all, let alone fiction of this quality." *Times Literary Supplement*

- -

To: **interzone** 124 Osborne Road, Brighton, BN1 6LU, UK.

Please send me four issues of *Interzone,* beginning with the current issue. I enclose a cheque/p.o. for £6 (outside UK, £7; US subscribers, $10 or $13 air), made payable to *Interzone*.

Name _____

Address _____